Contact!

Drury gasped, realizing the situation.

"What do you want?" He shouted as the figure began to move toward him.

The figure stepped off the curb into the street, cocking its head at him as if it didn't understand.

"What do you want?" he shouted again.

Drury tried to scramble backward, but his shoulders were already pressed flat against the brick of the adult bookstore. The creature leaned down, peering with those wide, soulless black eyes.

Drury screamed. But the scream choked off in his throat.

DO NOT BE AFRAID.

"Why?" Drury managed in a squeak.

I AM HERE TO HELP YOU.

MILLENNIUM

JACK ANDERSON

A TOM DOHERTY ASSOCIATES BOOK
NEW YORK

MILLENNIUM

Copyright © 1994 by Jack Anderson

All rights reserved, including the right to reproduce this book, or portions thereof, in any form.

Cover art by Shelley Eshkar

A Tor Book
Published by Tom Doherty Associates, Inc.
175 Fifth Avenue
New York, NY 10010

Tor Books on the World-Wide Web:
http://www.tor.com

Tor® is a registered trademark of Tom Doherty Associates, Inc.

ISBN: 0-812-52258-3
Library of Congress Catalog Card Number: 94-26027

First edition: November 1994
First mass market edition: October 1995

Printed in the United States of America

0 9 8 7 6 5 4 3 2 1

To: Jamin, Meijken, Brooke, Garrett, Taylor, Emily, Ashleigh, Cori, Sara, Amber, Erin, Rebecca, Christopher, Brady, Curt, Samantha, Kellie, Ryan, Jacob, Carlyn, Schuyler, Stephen, Kevin, Bethany, Conner, Olivia, and Kimberly—my grandchildren—who may see the Millennium.

AUTHOR'S NOTE

It is the nature of government officials to cover up what they cannot explain. Otherwise they may be called upon to explain mysteries that they cannot understand.

In this spirit, the Air Force has eagerly debunked extraterrestrial sightings that could easily be debunked and discredited witnesses who could readily be discredited. But the Air Force has had little, or nothing, to say about Unidentified Flying Objects that were tracked by electronic monitors or observed by reliable witnesses.

The Air Force has also joined in ridiculing people who have claimed they were abducted and subjected to laboratory experiments by aliens not of this world. Yet believable individuals have sworn that this has happened to them, and their accounts are tantalizingly similar.

Add to this mix some recently discovered parchments containing the writings of ancient holy men. They believed God presided over an interplanetary society—worlds without number—with communications and transportation between planets. They thought this earth, because of its wickedness and violence, had been placed under quarantine to prevent the spread of spiritual pollution.

One day scientists may be able to verify whether or not beings from beyond our horizons are actually visiting us—perhaps in violation of a cosmic quarantine. I attempt no such ambitious project here. But this is the stuff that makes fascinating novels. Mine is pure fiction, based though it is on unproven statements and unsanctified scripture.

—Jack Anderson

PROLOGUE

CAMP HOVIND, LANCASTER COUNTY, PA JULY 1983

The nights were so dark, they were frightening.

The cabins were set far back against the line where the woods met the meadow. They were surrounded on three sides by trees, and on nights where there was no moon, the darkness was total and pure.

The nights were good for sleeping, but on this night she was wide awake. She listened to the others. Their noise was a soft chorus of slow breaths. An occasional moan. They were dreaming of boys, no doubt. That was all they thought about, all they talked about.

To be honest, she found boys strangely repellent. Just when one came along that she thought was worth pursuing, the strange dreams would return, and the next day she would wonder what she ever found so attractive.

All she knew for sure was that she wasn't a lesbian. She didn't really know much about lesbians, but she had heard stories. Boys might be repellent, she thought, but to her the members of her own gender often seemed downright strange.

She lay awake in that cool, pure darkness and wondered what was wrong with her. Pushing seventeen and pretty enough to leave a string of broken hearts in her wake. Not the least bit interested in boys.

Maybe she was just moody. Passionate one moment, paranoid the next. Happy, then frightened. Calm, then panic-stricken.

Unfortunately, it never seemed to follow a pattern—at least not one that she could discern. It had nothing to do with the conversation exchanged; not the season of the year or the length of time the relationship had lasted.

The cabin had become quiet now. The snorting and grunts, tossing and turning had all stopped. The breathing was all quiet, slow, and *uniform*. Her teeth clenched together as she listened. Yes, there it was, in a distinctive pattern. Seventeen diaphragms all pulling at the lungs in unison, the air hissing in and out through the nostrils all at the same time, *in, out, in, out* . . .

A tremor went through her, and she tried to force her breathing to conform with that of the others so that, for once, she could be like them. Just once she wanted to talk and laugh about pop stars with hairy chests and ancient English teachers, and periods, and what animals boys were and some of the things they did, and what it was they all really wanted.

Tickets to the World Series. She had seen that as the punch line on a T-shirt she had seen in New York City, and now it returned to her. That was what boys *really* wanted. The truth of that insight suddenly seemed as vivid as the pure blackness surrounding her, and it made her laugh.

Then she froze.

There had been no reaction to her outburst, not even a stirring from the others. Their breathing was still the same, *in, out, in, out*, all in unison.

Her hands knotted around the edge of the sleeping bag and she pulled it close to her face, rubbing the slick softness against her cheek.

Why was she having such trouble sleeping? Or concentrating? One moment she was worried about fitting in; the next she was laughing about the World Series. If she kept it up, she would soon be crying because the World Series had been the one thing Joey had wanted, but the radiation and the chemo had made him too sick to go. Daddy had smiled wistfully and said, "Well, maybe next year, sport," but everyone had known there wouldn't be a next year.

It had hurt Daddy to have to say that. The drinking had come after the funeral, and after the drinking, the divorce.

And there she was, four years later, lying in the dark in a cabin in Camp Hovind for the last time in her life, wondering if she was the only seventeen-year-old in the world who thought she was going crazy.

"You're not crazy, sis. Everyone goes through this. It's adolescence."

She gasped and sat up in bed.

"You'll live through it."

She squinted into the blackness. "Joey?"

"This is something that everyone goes through."

"Joey. You're back!"

She unzipped the sleeping bag and hopped off the bunk, hitting the floor with a thump. She stopped for a moment, looked around, and listened to everyone else breathe.

In, out, in, out . . .

Not again, she thought. Not another one of those dreams where Joey was still alive, the kind that made her wake up crying.

But the voice. She had heard it. He was back. He had been back before, too. She knew it.

"Joey?" she said, louder this time. The others wouldn't be stirring—not anytime soon—and it made her bold. "Don't do this to me."

Suddenly there was light, as pure white and blazing as the darkness had been black. It streamed in from the windows that faced the meadow and filtered in through the cracks in the door. She cried out and fell back, sitting hard on the bottom bunk and rolling off the lumpy form of the sleeper who occupied it.

In, out, in, out . . .

She cried out. Something was horribly, horribly wrong. Nobody was moving, nobody was stirring, nobody was saying, "Shut up and turn off the light." It seemed so obvious to her now. Why hadn't she seen it before? Why hadn't she noticed?

There was a rattling at the door. She looked over at Mrs. Hagerman's bed and waited for a reaction. Mrs. Hagerman, who was in her late forties and bragged about being a survivor type, slept with a loaded .38 just under the head of her bed. On one occasion, when an errant raccoon had come scratching at the door, she had exhibited her willingness to use it.

There was nothing from Mrs. Hagerman. Her breathing couldn't even be discerned from the other sixteen who were all busy breathing, *in, out, in, out.*

Now the door was swinging open, and she raised her hands up to shield her eyes as the light fell on her. There, as a black silhouette, stood a small child in a baseball cap.

"C'mon, sis. They're here."

She shook her head. It was all coming back to her now. No wonder she was crazy.

"No. I'm not going. They promised they'd leave me alone."

"They're not going to hurt you this time, sis."

She squinted at the figure. It didn't seem right to her. Was it a small boy in a baseball cap or something else? Maybe it was something else that was supposed to be a close approximation of a boy.

But the other times when Joey had appeared, he had seemed so real.

"Forget it. I'm not going with you."

"They just want to show you something."

"Absolutely not! They can just leave right now! And you can go with them!"

"Oh, no." The figure moved across the threshold of the door, into the cabin. It turned in the light, so now she could see it in profile. It was a small boy, about seven years old. He wore a New York Mets shirt and cap. "That's no way to talk to me, sis."

"You're not my brother!" she shrieked. "You'd be thirteen now, and you wouldn't look like that! You'd—"

"I'd *what?*"

She was sobbing now. "Never mind. Just leave me alone. You're dead, Joey."

"You don't mean that."

"Shut up."

"You see me here, don't you?"

"Shut up, I said!" She put her hands over her ears.

"And *you* hear *me*. Now I have to go back."

She couldn't hear him, yet when his lips moved, they formed big, burning letters inside her brain.

YOU KNOW WHAT WILL HAPPEN IF I GO BACK ALONE, they said.

"No." She tried to resist.

IF I GO BACK ALONE THEY'LL PUNISH ME.

"You're not . . . You're not . . ."

AND IT'LL BE JUST LIKE THE TIME YOU TOLD ME TO—

"*No!*" she screamed. Suddenly she was on her feet, staggering toward him. Joey saw her coming and retreated out the door, walking backward, eyes scanning her every move. "You're not my brother. You're one of those horrible little—"

"Horrible little what?"

She tried to think, but the words escaped her. They had been there only a second ago and now they were gone. Joey was still moving backward and keeping perfect time with her pursuit. Any other time, she would have thought his movements odd. Now her thoughts were just a confused tangle.

Then the illogic of it all came to her. The slumbering bunkmates. The dead brother alive. The strange pursuit. And stepping outside into light that was whiter and brighter than the most brilliant of days.

By the time the hidden words came to her, it was too late. She had followed Joey into the woods and down a narrow, twisted path into a secluded meadow where her friends would come with the boys. It was impossibly bright there now, and the secluded atmosphere was all but gone. Each blade of grass shimmered like tiny slivers of glass. Joey stopped in the middle of the meadow and stared, his skin translucent in the brightness.

She tried to stop herself, but it was too late. She stumbled squarely into the center of the meadow, stopping next to her brother.

"Glad you could make it," he said.

He looked up. She followed his gaze. Her hands rose to shield her eyes.

The source of the light was right above them, more brilliant than the sun. She felt its heat on her face and arms.

Then Joey was rising up into the air. Her stomach plunged like she was falling down the first hill of a roller coaster, and she whooped as she realized that she was following him up into the light.

Her skin tingled. Her nose and ears and the tips of her fingers and toes felt numb. She looked down. The meadow was a glowing spot below, with two fuzzy blotches that were their shadows.

Through all of this, she didn't panic.

Now, she remembered, she had done all of this before.

She closed her eyes and waited for the breeze. It hit her face and she inhaled. It was hot and smelled of plastic and something sharp and tangy, like surgical antiseptic. Her eyelids were heavy now, and the familiar numb feeling was starting to spread. *This will pass*, she told herself, and it did. Enough feeling returned so she knew when both of her feet were resting once more on a solid surface. There was an urge to look at her surroundings, but she knew her eyes would not yet open.

"Why are you doing this to me?" she said to Joey.

"We're not doing anything to you," Joey said.

"You promised you'd leave me alone."

"We're not doing anything to you."

"I suppose this is all a dream."

"Nothing will happen to you."

"Liar."

"Believe me."

"You always say that. And you always follow it with poking and prodding and sticking things into me." A stray thought intruded—*you're worse than the boys*—but it was gone before it could make her laugh.

"There were complications. Schedules had to be maintained. You were available. You had the genes."

"I was convenient."

"We were fortunate to have you. But things seem to be approaching normality. We are done with you."

"Then what am I doing here, Joey?"

"We wish to show you something."

"I'm not interested."

"It is part of your treatment."

"No. I didn't ask to be treated this way."

"You must be made complete."

She sighed in disgust. "Well, let's get on with it, then."

"Very well." Joey sounded pleased. "We shall."

"Like I have any choice in this," she sniffed.

Slowly her eyes opened. They were standing in a large circular room with polished metal sides and no apparent exit.

"You may proceed."

"After you," she said.

"You know the way."

"Show me," she said.

He led her down a long, curving corridor, and she felt as though she had turned completely around and was going back in the direction from which she had come. She was starting to feel the familiar anxious gnawing in the pit of her stomach as she neared the examination room.

But Joey didn't stop. He kept going, past the white door that looked like all of the others in the corridor. There wasn't even a pause or a glance back. He moved ahead, down the curve of the hall.

She followed him a little farther. He stopped in front of another identical white door, and it opened. He gestured for her to enter.

"What's going on?"

"They want to show you something."

"You," she corrected. "You want to show me something."

Joey cocked his head. "What do you mean by that?"

"You're one of them, right? You're a part of all this."

"I'm a part of you, sister."

She looked at the open door and blinked. "I'm not going in there."

"They only want to show you something."

"Yeah. Right. They want to put cold things into me or shove that needle into my nose. They'll—"

Joey held out his hand, bidding her to go in. She didn't move. She glared at him.

"Trust me. Please."

She moved toward the opening. It was different from before. There was no antiseptic smell that covered up the scent of human fear. There was no feeling of panic spreading in from the others like her in the room. In fact, there were no others like her inside, nor had she seen them in the hallway being led by their keepers. This room was different. So much different that she wanted desperately to go inside.

"Go on," Joey said softly.

"You first," she insisted.

He shook his head. "No. I'm not allowed."

"Why not? You're one of them."

"I am a part of you."

She wanted to say: *Enough with this "part of you" business. Just let me go and get me out of here.* But something was pulling her toward the door and in through the opening.

The room was different. It was not the examination room. There was no row of tables occupied by other people, their blank expressions unable to hide the fear in their eyes.

It was an observation room of some kind, and she was standing on what might have been called the deck, looking through three segmented panes of glass. Beyond the glass were dimly lit rows of what looked like drawers or shelves, each filled with a thick amber liquid. The fluid bubbled slowly, and something dark and spongy hung suspended in the mixture.

Closer to the floor were rows of crystalline baskets, supported by a matching pedestal that seemed to grow up out of the floor. They were filled with shredded white excelsior, and something buried beneath the soft fuzz wriggled and stirred.

Fascinated by the motion, she stepped toward the glass, slowly, almost involuntarily. Her mouth was hanging open in amazement at the sight, and she stopped only after she realized that her breath was spreading fog across the transparent barrier.

The corners of her mouth turned up. "This is—"

GREETINGS.

She turned even though she hadn't heard the words. They burned brightly, like a picture inside her skull. And when she saw the creature in front of her, she gasped. In her fascination, she had forgotten where she was, and now she was being confronted with the end result of a recurring nightmare.

The thing was small, perhaps only a little taller than Joey. It was a white that was translucent under the bright lights. But in the dimness of this room, its complexion seemed chalky. Its head was wide across the top and tapered down to a narrow chin. Set into the top of its skull were two large eyes, solid black and tapering to a blunt point at each end. Its head was mounted on a neck that looked too tiny to support it. The rest of its body matched the neck: skinny, small, and pale.

The creature was too small to be feared on sight, but the memories it evoked made her try to retreat. She bumped against the glass partition, and tried to inch away, shoulders against the cold wall.

The creature raised its arm and a bony finger pointed at her, centered between her eyes.

DO NOT BE AFRAID.

"No," she said. "You're not touching me again."

THAT IS CORRECT.

"I don't believe you."

WE HAVE ALWAYS BEEN COMPLETELY HONEST WITH YOU.

"That's a lie."

WE HAVE NEVER LIED TO YOU.

"But there were things you never told me."

THEY WERE THINGS YOU DID NOT NEED TO KNOW.

"They hurt when I found out."

FOR THAT WE APOLOGIZE. YOU WOULD NOT BE ABLE TO UNDERSTAND. EACH SPECIES IS DIFFERENT. IT IS A LEARNING PROCESS FOR US, TOO.

She was backed into a corner now. Realizing that she was in a thin nightgown, she tried to cover herself with her arms. "What do you want now?"

ALL WE WANT TO DO IS SHOW YOU SOMETHING.

"Why?"

SO YOU WILL BE COMPLETE.

"What does that mean?"

IT IS NOT SOMETHING THAT CAN BE EXPLAINED. IT IS SOMETHING THAT YOU MUST FEEL.

She slowly turned away from the creature to the window. Her eyes fixed on the crystal baskets.

DO YOU ACCEPT THAT?

She gave a tiny shrug. "I guess it depends on what you have to show me."

IT WILL ALL MAKE SENSE. SOON.

Her finger came up and stabbed at the glass. It left a smudge. "What's in there?"

DO YOU KNOW WHERE YOU ARE?

She nodded. "This is a nursery."

YOU ARE VERY INTELLIGENT. WE WERE WISE TO CHOOSE YOU.

"Choose me. For what?"

The creature turned and began to walk away.

"Come back here, dammit!"

DO NOT ANGER. PLEASE WAIT.

At the point where the glass met the wall, the creature paused for a moment, then took another step through and into the chamber. It walked between the baskets and the wall until it was directly in front of her. It stopped and looked at her. It struck her as being a blank look, but memory told her that they looked that way all of the time.

"What are you doing?"

It raised its arm to the topmost level of compartments. THESE ARE FRESH. THEY HAVE JUST BEEN REMOVED. THEY WILL GROW HERE. The arm dropped two levels, to a bigger row of compartments. THESE ARE BIGGER BUT ARE NOT YET COMPLETELY VIABLE. Two more levels down. BIGGER STILL, NEARER VIABILITY. Now both hands spread wide to indicate the baskets. THESE ARE RECENT VIABLES.

"Nine months," she said through the glass.

SIX, it told her.

"What do you give them to make them grow so fast?"

THESE DO NOT REQUIRE THAT MUCH TIME. THEY ARE HYBRIDS.

"Hybrids?" She recalled the word vaguely from a science class. "What do you mean by that?"

The creature said nothing. It stepped up to a basket, reached into the excelsior, and pulled out a large bundle. Then it walked to the wall nearest her and stepped through. She turned to face him.

"This is a hybrid?"

The creature held the bundle up to her. She reached down and scooped it up, holding it close to her, as she had once done with her newborn niece.

LOOK AT IT.

The cloth looked slick but was soft like wool. She moved the flap aside and looked down into the quiet face. It was a baby, at peace, but with a furrowed brow. There was something fundamentally wrong with the way it looked. Its eyes were large and round, and were almost all pupil. There was no color except for a thin ring of violet around the black. Its nose seemed normal enough, but its jaw was long and jutted out from the base of a too-big, too-round head. Its skin was a milky white, but she could see none of the familiar network of veins present in newborns. The child had no neck—*Not yet*, something told her—and its slender body seemed even smaller in proportion to its head than what she considered normal.

For a brief moment, the child made her think of a picture she had seen in a supermarket tabloid, of a baby made up like a wolfling, supposedly born to horrified parents. A laugh welled up inside her, and her lips parted in a hint of a smile, but the bundle stirred. The baby looked up, its eyes fixing on hers. It made a noise—something between a sigh and a coo—and instantly her heart broke. Following an instinct she hadn't known she had, she pulled the tiny creature closer.

"What's wrong?"

NOTHING. IT IS AN INFANT.

"What am I supposed to do with it?"

LOOK AT IT. HOLD IT.

"But why? I mean, why me? Why are you showing—"

The creature cocked its head at her. THIS CHILD IS YOURS.

"Mine?"

THIS CHILD IS MADE UP OF YOUR GENETIC MATERIAL PLUS MATERIALS OF OUR OWN CREATION.

"My genetic material? But that would mean—"

YOU ARE THIS CHILD'S MOTHER.

Revulsion and hatred swallowed up the compassion she had felt. She wanted to drop the child and run, but she could manage only the thought. She was frozen, locked into place with this *thing* cradled in her arms. Her mind raced and her jaw worked, trying to find words.

"This isn't— This is *not* my child. I've never— I'm still a—"

The creature straightened its head, then cocked it the other way. YOU MUST UNDERSTAND THAT WE HAVE METHODS WHICH CIRCUMVENT YOUR PRIMITIVE METHODS OF PROCREATION.

She stared at the infant for a moment as the words faded from her head. They had struck her as wistful, as if their author was almost jealous of the awful animal thing it had tried to dismiss.

"Why are you telling me this?"

SO YOU WILL BE COMPLETE.

"I've never— You've never—"

In a very deliberate gesture, the creature nodded. YOU HAVE MEMORIES?

"Of you?"

Another nod.

"Yes."

WHAT DO YOU REMEMBER?

"About you?"

Nod.

"I remember you. Joey. The hallway. The room— That room downstairs— Down— Wherever it is."

WHAT DO YOU REMEMBER ABOUT THE ROOM?

"I remember—" She closed her eyes and tried to think. The memories were there, she knew, bright and vivid, but they seemed covered with fog, like the last dream of morning an hour after waking. "Bright lights. You. I don't know. I want to remember, but I can't. I feel like I don't want to."

Nod. YOU WILL REMEMBER NOW.

"No—"

CLOSE YOUR EYES.

She tried to fight it, but it was no use. The creature-child tight in her arms, her eyes slowly closed.

ROSABELLE BELIEVE.

It all came flooding back into her mind in a terrible, violent rush. She could feel her heart pounding in her throat, her bare back flat against a cold chromelike table, staring up into harsh white lights. Cool, damp hands were all over her, her arms, her legs, on her thighs and at her temples. A round white face hovered over her, its black almond eyes looking blankly at her, a glistening silver bullet in its milk white hand, and when it touched her midway between her navel and the line of her pubic hair, she began to shriek. Something was in her vagina—something electric that was making her spasm and cramp until tears ran out of her eyes.

She tried to throw herself from one side to the other, trying to get off the table and away and back to Joey, who would surely feel compassion and take her back home, but she couldn't move under the pressure of those cool, damp hands.

"Let me go!" she shrieked. "Let me go let me go let me—"

IT IS ALMOST OVER, MY CHILD.

She remembered seeing the words now, but they had been different. The ones from the creature who had given her the child had been calm and aquamarine; these were scarlet and hurried. She knew they were impatient.

"I'm not your child, you—"

Abruptly the memory stopped. It was summer now. Midday, hot and humid as Maryland was blanketed under moist air from the sea. She was sitting on her back porch, staring at her arm. A mosquito rested on it, its needle down under her skin. Its abdomen flexed, and it gorged itself on her blood.

She mashed it with her thumb and left a maroon blotch behind, mixed with crushed bits of wing and leg.

"What's the matter, baby?"

She looked up. It was her mother, her eyes full of hurt and concern. They had never looked so open, so accessible. She wanted so badly to say something, to fall into those eyes and cry—

Cry what?

Where were you, Mother, when I needed you most? Where were you when I was growing up? Why do you care what's happening to me now? You're just upset because you want to be my bestest buddy now and go shopping and hurt Daddy with another big credit-card bill, but I don't want to. I don't care. And you wouldn't care either because I'm—

Pregnant.

The word made her reel. She had never dared to even think it before because she was still a virgin. But she knew she was pregnant; she felt it in her heart. And when she threw up in the morning and anxiously crossed another day off the calendar without her period having arrived, it only fueled her fears. She had even bought one of those home test kits, and it had given her a death sentence. *It had turned blue.* Four out of five doctors would have taken that as gospel that she was—

Pregnant.

But how? She had never even let a boy get his hand on her panties, let alone been in contact with any of that awful sperm. *Watch out,* one of her girlfriends had said, *because it comes out fast and it's sticky and it gets everywhere even into places you didn't know existed, and if you're not careful it's wham! bam! thank you ma'am! you're knocked up.*

She stared into her mother's eyes, and the color left her face. She tried to think of a logical explanation. The swimming pool. A toilet seat. But there was nothing that any reasonable physician would take seriously.

She reached out for her mother, sobbing, and fell backwards into a black well of despair.

Her bare back hit something cold and slick. She screamed *No!* and kept her eyes shut tight, but she knew where she was. She could feel their hands on her, could feel the gaze from their dead black eyes moving slowly across her naked form. And though she was fighting hard not to look, she could see what was happening in her mind's eye, as vividly as the letters, purple and florid, that they were putting in her head.

"I'm *not* your child!"

The hovering creature was over her again, she knew, the silver bullet in its hand coming down, down, closer to her belly. And then the shock shot through her and she arched her back up from the table, the air in her lungs forming a half-scream as it pushed out of her throat. She had been here a half-dozen times, she remembered, and every time it had been different.

Each time had gotten worse.

And now, this was the ultimate. She was numb from the waist down, but it didn't stop her from feeling the tingling and the tearing sensation that told her something was being pulled from deep inside her.

Suddenly it stopped. Air rushed out of her lungs and she collapsed onto the table.

WE ARE DONE WITH YOU NOW. THERE WILL
BE NO MORE PAIN.

She kept her eyes closed tight. "You were the ones,"
she whispered.

YES.

Her eyes opened and tears spilled down her cheeks.
She looked down to see the bundle in her arms, the
strange baby peering up at her, as if studying her features. Moving one hand, she wiped at her face and
sniffed.

"You picked me up all of those times."

The creature straightened its head. YES.

"You poked me and prodded me and you stuck things
up inside of me. You made it so I didn't want to be
around boys."

YES.

"I was really worried about myself. You made me
wonder what was wrong with myself."

REGRETTABLE. BUT NECESSARY.

"You made me feel like I was pregnant."

THAT WAS UNAVOIDABLE.

"Because I *was* pregnant."

YES.

"And then you came for me again. And you sucked
the baby out of me."

YES.

She turned toward the glass walls. "Then you put it
in one of those jars and let it finish growing."

YES.

"So now—" She looked down at the wriggling bundle. "Now you want me to finish the job and be this
thing's mother."

NO.

She reeled. "No? After all you've put me through?"

YOU COULD NOT SUSTAIN THIS CHILD. YOU
COULD ONLY LOVE IT. IT WOULD DIE.

"How dare you!" she choked. "After the horrible way you made me feel? Do you have any idea of what I've been through? To think I was pregnant and then have you come in and suck the life out of me and not even explain—"

THAT IS WHY YOU ARE HERE NOW. OUR TIME WITH YOU IS FINISHED. WE CANNOT LEAVE YOU UNTIL WE HAVE MADE YOU COMPLETE.

"Complete."

The creature nodded. YOU HAVE EXPERIENCED A SERIES OF CONFLICTING EMOTIONS BECAUSE OF THE WAY WE HAVE USED YOU. WE MUST RESOLVE THESE NOW.

"By what? Putting this ugly little baby doll in my arms and telling me I'm a mommy?"

YES.

"You're lying!"

FORGIVE US, BUT WE ARE NOT. WE HAVE TECHNOLOGY THAT FAR SURPASSES YOURS, BUT WE ARE STILL IGNORANT IN THE WAYS OF THE HUMAN HEART. YOU MUST TRUST US WHEN WE SAY THAT AFTER THIS YOUR FEELINGS OF AMBIGUITY WILL BE RESOLVED.

"You think so?"

THAT HAS BEEN OUR EXPERIENCE.

A chill ran up her spine. "You mean there have been . . . *others*?"

The creature looked toward the wall of incubators. ALL OF THESE HAD MOTHERS.

"They're not all mine?"

NO.

"There were other women? Girls? And you did the same thing to them?"

YES.

"Why?"

IT IS A COMPLICATED ISSUE, CHILD. SUFFICE IT TO SAY THAT THE MALLEABILITY OF YOUR GENETIC STOCK IS USEFUL AND IMPRESSIVE FOR WHAT WE DO.

She stared for a moment in silence. "And just what is it that you do?"

The creature looked straight at her. WE SEED OTHER WORLDS.

"Other worlds. Planets?"

YES.

She raised the baby to her shoulder and turned away, as if trying to shield it from her host. "You're telling me that you're building Adams and Eves in here?"

IF THAT IS THE WAY YOU WISH TO THINK OF IT. WE HAVE LITTLE TIME IN WHICH TO WORK. WE MUST SALVAGE AS MUCH OF YOUR GENETIC MATERIAL AS WE CAN.

"Salvage?" she asked, alarmed.

The creature stared. YOUR RACE HAS MANY UNIQUE TRAITS. ONE OF THESE IS THAT YOU DEVELOP TECHNOLOGY BEFORE YOU ARE MATURE ENOUGH TO USE IT.

"Technology? Mature? Really, how responsible do you have to be to drive a car?"

THOSE ARE TOYS, CHILD. SUFFICE IT TO EXPLAIN THAT WE BEGAN OUR COLLECTION EFFORTS AFTER THE CITY OF HIROSHIMA WAS DESTROYED.

Suddenly she felt weak. She leaned against the glass wall, the baby tight against her shoulder. "You mean, we're really going to do it? Someone's really going to push the button and we'll be wiped out?"

NOT IN THE SENSE YOU ARE THINKING. BUT THE ATOM IS A TOY COMPARED TO WHAT YOU WILL SOON FIND.

"What? What is it that's going to destroy us?"

IT MAY NOT HAPPEN. IT IS POSSIBLE YOU
WILL MATURE IN TIME.

"You've got to tell me what it is so I can warn people."

YOU HAVE BEEN WARNED ALREADY. YOUR
PEOPLE HAVE DULY NOTED IT AND PUT IT IN
WRITING.

"Where? Where is it written?"

Nothing.

"Tell me!"

Now the creature did something different, something
that chilled her to the bone.

It shook its head.

She reeled back and wrapped her hands around the
bundle, holding it away from her body. "Tell me or I'll
smash this little monster."

NO.

"I'll do it—"

But it was no use. The words choked off in her throat
and her arms began to flex. One foot moved ahead of
the other until she was next to the creature. Then she
bent at the waist and leaned down, her fingers released
from their clutch, and the infant rolled gently into the
creature's hands.

YOU WILL NOT SEE US AGAIN.

"Just like that? You thank me for my womb and kick
me loose so I can go home and face the end of the
world?"

YOU WILL NOT SEE US AGAIN.

"You won't get rid of me that easily. I'll remember.
I will. And I'll tell everyone."

YOU WILL NOT REMEMBER. YOU WILL NOT
WANT TO.

The creature shook its head again. As it did, the door
to the hallway opened to reveal Joey, standing and waiting patiently.

"C'mon, sis," he said. "Time to go."

"And you don't care what happens," she snapped at him. "You play along with whatever these guys say." She shook her head at him. "I don't want to see you anymore. Not ever again."

"You will not see us again," said Joey.

"Good!" she snapped. "Now get me out of here. I won't forget."

"You will not remember," Joey said. "You will not want to."

He took her by the hand and led her away, into the hall, then down into the woods. She glared up into the light as the ship hovered above her, biting her lip and cursing softly under her breath.

"I will remember. I will. I *will*."

Fog swam before her eyes and words burned.

ROSABELLE BELIEVE.

She would not remember.

She couldn't.

She couldn't even remember the reason for her tears.

CHARIOT OF FIRE

WASHINGTON, D.C. / APRIL 1999

**THE VIEW FROM HERE
by Mick Aaronson**

April 12, 1999— Did you ever get the feeling that you were banging your head against a wall and had no apparent reason for doing it?

I've been banging my head twice a week now for nigh onto forty years. Through nine presidents, a couple of wars, some really juicy scandals, and dozens of useless fads (those of you whose age is showing, remember removing one's clothes and running through public places?). I've written a couple million words on the workings of the public psyche and how it affects our national politics.

After all of that, you'd think I had a pretty good handle on the way things work, right?

Wrong.

After a career spent putting nearly two million words before you in this twice-weekly column, another million words in the nation's magazines of political consequence, and two million words' worth of books about the subject, I'm ready to chuck it all.

That's right. Forty years and five million words, and yours truly is finally admitting that I don't know a thing about how politics works.

Other than the fact that it doesn't work.

And I think that I'm the first person to figure that out.

I mean, look at us.

In just a few days, we're going to open a vein and give until it hurts to our federal government. And we complain about it all the way to the bank, saying that the government needs to quit spending money it hasn't got and get its hands out of our pocketbooks. We even elected—and may re-elect—our President based on his promises to do something about this very problem.

Yet who did we send to Washington to help him carry out his threat? Only the biggest collection of larcenous big-spenders in the history of our government. Sure, the term limits that have swept our nation over the last decade have weeded out some of the all-time champions.

But we replaced them with the sons, cousins, spouses, even a son-in-law, of the people we ousted. We returned to Washington the practitioners of the philosophy we abhor.

You see, we've become a nation of parasites. We need to sacrifice, and we need to make changes, and we need to cut spending and turn this country around before it goes to the theological place of eternal damnation in the proverbial wicker container.

And we're all for whatever it takes to get it done, as long as it's being done by someone else.

That's why I am giving up. It's impossible for me to look at human nature and see it capable of anything other than the base behavior it is known for.

P.T. Barnum is well known for the dictum about the birth rate of the chronically gullible. Less known, but just as important to those of us in this line of work is the *other* great truth of life, stated by H.L. Mencken:

That is, that nobody ever went broke underestimating the intelligence of the American public.

And that, my dear friends, does include those we have sent to Washington as our elected leaders.

JOHN DRURY

There had been a time when John Drury's life had been better than good.

The world had been served up to him on a silver platter. He was the young lawyer whose quick wit and ruthlessness had catapulted him quickly to dizzying heights in the nerve center of American government. He had moved through three law firms in five years, shedding each like old skin, until he had ultimately landed a corner office in a prestigious firm. It had positioned him between big-name politicians and the political action committees that financed them.

There had been twelve-hour days and six-day weeks. His single-day weekends had been times of revelry. Life could be grand if you had the right pharmaceuticals.

But things had started to go slowly wrong. First a Monday-morning hangover, then Monday-morning drunk. Then missing Mondays altogether. And finally getting caught at a briefing with white powder crusted around his nostrils.

He had flown so high. And he had fallen so far. It all seemed so very long ago.

People no longer cared about whom he had been.

The only person who had paid any attention to him was a street preacher who annoyed him by falling on his knees in front of him, molding his hands into a prayerful position, and wailing, "Turn back, oh man!"

Drury slumped his back against the brick facade of an adult bookstore and slid down to the sidewalk, feet splayed out in front of him. He blinked slowly and tried to focus on the dark streets. Traffic was slow, almost nonexistent. It was late, but late no longer mattered. All he wanted to do right now was finish drinking and bring on the fog.

His hand reached under his battered greatcoat until it touched the slick surface of his Night Train bottle, but a commotion from down the street made him freeze. He turned to his right and saw a pack of black youths approaching, laughing and swearing, swatting and punching playfully at one another.

Drury withdrew his hand and laid it on the coolness of the sidewalk. It was better to wait until there was no risk of losing the precious bottle. He knew there were gangs that would just as soon kill him for sport as for a half-bottle of cheap wine.

The boys passed without even glancing down at him. Drury waited until they turned the corner and their voices faded, then slowly pulled the bottle from under his coat. He removed the cap with great deliberation, put his nose to the mouth of the bottle, and sniffed. He hadn't actually smelled anything in years. The chemicals had burned out the bone, or whatever it was that separated the two sides of his nose, and now he was left with no sense of smell or taste.

Well, he could still see and hear and touch. He could still get enough wine into him for the fog to carry him away. Wrapping his hand around the neck of the bottle, he lifted it to his lips, ready to tip it up. But before the liquid could splash his lips, a loud buzz startled him and the bottle clattered to the ground. His hand shot out instinctively to grab it, but when the tip of his finger touched the glass, he heard a sudden ripping sound. His head snapped toward the sound.

A pinprick of light was forming in the side of the liquor store across the street, pure and white hot. Drury looked at it in astonishment, wondering why it wasn't melting the surrounding brick. Then he realized the light was coming from *inside* the building.

But that couldn't be right, either, because the inside of the store was dark.

Now the beam of light split into two points amid more buzzing and the crackling of static electricity. One point moved up, the other down, but they remained connected by a thin filament of light.

Drury tried to move back, away from the light. The sight was scaring him, and for the first time in years, his face felt flush with the heat of an impending sunburn.

The points of light spread until they were almost six feet apart from top to bottom. Then the thread began to waver. Random shots of static electricity snapped between the points, whipping back and forth, producing an almost-musical whine, like a set of tinny windchimes playing in a minor scale.

At a point midway between the two points, the thread began to separate. A piercing blue-white light poured out of the breach, accompanied by a hot wind that struck Drury full in the face. He squinted and put his hand to his face. The air felt hot. It irritated the inside of his nose and felt as if something slick and oily had coated the inner parts of his mouth.

Now there was noise, an impossibly loud tearing sound that rattled the very bones in his chest. His skin was tingling now, and his hair felt alive, as if it were standing on end.

The light was now shaped like the iris of a cat's eye. The center point was spreading apart, spilling blue fire into the street. Drury screamed as he saw the streetlights dim. His fingers tried to claw into the concrete of the sidewalk.

Then—for a heartbeat—everything on the street was still.

A shadow emerged from the other side of the opening and began to spread across the street. It looked as if it were chasing the wind that came from the light, kicking up dust and debris into small storms along the avenue.

Then, at the point where the shadow entered the bright iris, Drury could see another shape, slight and showing almost skeletal in the brightness of the light behind it. It came up to the very edge of the opening, then cautiously brought a skinny foot up, then out, then down until it was touching concrete. It turned back toward the opening and methodically brought its other foot out.

Pausing for a moment to study the place from which it had just stepped, the shape touched its midsection, causing the static and the ringing to start all over again. There was wind again, this time into the strange portal, as if it were trying to suck the filth right off the city street. There was a final burst of static and maroon light. Then the iris closed; the points rejoined as one. Silence returned.

Drury blinked at the liquor store and the figure that now stood before it. It was strangely pale under the amber streetlight, its head too big for its skinny body, and it wore a suit that shone like crumpled aluminum foil. It looked around for a moment, and then its dark, unblinking eyes fixed on Drury.

Drury gasped, realizing the situation. He groped for his bottle of Night Train to use as a weapon. His fingers raked across the tip of the bottle, but succeeded only in knocking it away and spilling the precious liquid into the gutter.

"What do you want?" Drury shouted as the figure began to move toward him.

The figure stepped off the curb into the street, cocking its head at him as if it didn't understand.

"What do you want?" he shouted again.

Now the creature was on the sidewalk next to him, just a few feet from him, and he could see how ugly it really was. Its head looked like the bleached skull of something deformed and misshapen, planted unceremoniously onto the body of a tall, emaciated child.

Drury tried to scramble backward, but his shoulders were already pressed flat against the brick of the adult bookstore. The creature leaned down, peering with those wide, soulless black eyes.

Drury screamed. But the scream choked off in his throat. There were letters inside his brain, bright green, hovering above the blackness of his fear.

DO NOT BE AFRAID.

"Why?" Drury managed in a squeak.

I AM HERE TO HELP YOU.

"Me?"

YOUR RACE.

"Leave me alone. I swear I won't drink anymore."

The creature squatted down, its face inches from his. It studied him for a moment, then reached down and touched the silver buckle on its belt with a slender finger.

YOU ARE HURTING.

"They said it would be bad." Drury wept now.

THEY?

"At the Salvation Army. They said if I didn't stop, I'd have these things, that they'd get worse and worse." An animal cry of pain slipped from his lips.

I NEED YOUR ASSISTANCE.

"I'm ready to die now. Oh, please—"

YOU WILL NOT DIE. DO I FRIGHTEN YOU?

Drury nodded.

I AM SORRY. I MEANT TO DO THIS BEFORE.

Drury watched in awe as the creature ran its fingers over its belt buckle. There was a loud *crack!* and the creature rolled its eyes in agony. This was followed by a series of loud pops, each of which staggered the being before him. The thing began to change shape. Its fingers began to shrink and its body filled out. The abrupt angles of its head smoothed; the basic outline became rounder. A soft fuzz began to grow across the top. The eyes narrowed and shrank and dilated, then started to change color. A nose began to emerge from beneath the eyes, and below that a slit appeared, with lips, teeth, and a tongue.

The process slowed, then stopped altogether while the creature rose to its full height and looked carefully at him. It ran its fingers through its new hair and shook its head. Then its lips parted and it spoke to him in a thick, indefinable accent.

"Is this a more pleasing physiognomy?" the creature said to him. "I know it is crude, but it is the closest that I can approximate on a physical level."

Drury blinked. He felt dizzy now, and his eyes were starting to burn. "Just take me to hell," he slobbered.

The thing tilted its head and looked at him. "There is no need to fear me. I have tried to approximate your form."

Drury lolled his head back and banged it against the building. When he shook off the blow and looked up, he saw the creature leaning over him, studying his eyes intently in the light of the street lamp.

"I understand you now," the creature said, holding Drury's head in its cold hands. "You are impaired."

"Impaired?" Drury burbled.

"You are a chronic consumer of artificial substances for the sole purpose of impairing certain brain functions. I have researched your type."

"What do you mean?" Drury whined.

The creature reached down to its belt buckle again and manipulated it. "Your race is going to try my patience before this is over. To say nothing of my energy."

"Where'd you get those wild clothes?" Drury asked. "You going to a party?"

The creature tapped the buckle. "This will take only a moment."

Drury felt the fog rising from his brain, then felt himself lift off the sidewalk and float into a wonderfully warm, sleepy daze. But suddenly cold spikes of pain drove up his legs, through his gut, and hammered hard into his brain. When it subsided, he felt alert and alive. He realized that he was cold and dirty and was sitting in a puddle of his own urine. His stomach rolled over in disgust.

The creature grabbed his chin and pivoted his head. "I need your assistance."

"I don't know how I got here," Drury said. "But you can bet that I'm going to get out of here fast."

"Could you please tell me where the White House is?"

"The White House?" He looked at the ugly man. "Why? You a Russian spy?"

"Let's say I'm an authority figure with an important message for your President."

"Oh," Drury said, as if this had been the answer that he had known all along. He opened his mouth and directions came spilling out, a shortcut through five blocks of back streets that would take the ugly little man straight to 1600 Pennsylvania Avenue.

"Thank you," the man smiled. "You have earned your pay this evening." With a nod of the head, he turned and started walking.

"Hey," Drury called. "Did you say *pay*?"

"Is something wrong with that?"

Drury thought about it. Pay. The word resonated happily in his head. "I guess not," he said. "What am I being paid?"

"You've already received it." Then the man turned and began walking, disappearing around the corner according to Drury's instructions.

John Drury stared down the street after the eccentric little man. Even though Drury felt as if he had received something, he couldn't quite put his finger on it. But soon the nagging question was pushed out of his mind by an overwhelming urge to shower, shave, and start looking for a job.

LORENZO NORTH

With a job like this, you knew what kind of a night you were going to have.

Most of the time, it was warding off drunks or cranks who felt they had to make a personal statement to the President. Occasionally, you got innocents from Iowa or Indiana who thought they could drop by for a friendly word. It didn't matter what the hour was. The leader of the free world supposedly never slept.

Ironically, Lorenzo thought, the scariest time to guard

the White House was by day. Some of the protests went on and on and on, making him realize just how whacked out the country was getting to be.

His granddaddy had once told him, "Son, there's a big, fat behind to fit every chair," and he had seen the truth of it on this job. Every cause, from the most serious to the most frivolous, seemed to draw thousands of followers to the nation's capital. Early on, Lorenzo thought that the gays were the nuttiest, but they had long been surpassed by the animal-sacrifice crowd, the animal-rights gang, and the Society for Legalized Pederasty. And lately, within the last six months or so, the millennialists had started to emerge from the woodwork.

The millennialists weren't bad folk. In fact, most of them struck him as being good people.

It was just that their beliefs seemed a little . . . well, unbelievable.

According to them, on December 31 of this year at 11:59 P.M., the show was over. God was going to ring down the curtain, collect the faithful few, and move on to other galactic engagements.

Lorenzo didn't know what it was about the number 2000 that made people crazy for the Lord's return. His only regret was that these people's sudden interest in their relationship with God didn't inspire such intense devotion the other nineteen hundred ninety-eight years of the cycle. Ultimately, of course, the joke would be on them, because it was a biblical fact that not even the angels in heaven or Jesus Christ himself knew when the end was coming. That was written in God's own hand, on a calendar that only he could see.

Tonight had been easy duty. A handful of Japanese tourists had taken turns photographing each other standing in front of the night-lit White House, and he had posed with them as an authentic African-American.

Then a starry-eyed pair of naïfs had handed him a gift-wrapped bottle of wine brewed from grapes in their own backyard. Lorenzo agreed to pass it on to the President personally, knowing that it would never get past the Secret Service.

Now it was late—that hour when the night seemed darkest and the sky bleakest. Lorenzo turned his chair so he had a clear view out the window of his little shack, then leaned back and opened the Tom Clancy novel he had been perusing.

He had not gotten far—Jack Ryan was just starting to get in a fat lot of trouble—when out of the corner of his eye, he saw the figure approaching. It was a man, and he would have been hard to miss even in broad daylight, given the shiny suit he was wearing.

Lorenzo rolled his eyes. This guy was destined to come up to him. After sixteen years on the job, he had developed a sixth sense. Here came a nut who thought that casting a ballot gave him the privilege of meeting with the President of the United States. Lorenzo closed the Clancy novel, crossed his arms, and waited.

Interestingly enough, the man did not stop at the guard shack. He walked straight up to the red-and-white barrier and paused to look at it, as if calculating the best way to get around it.

Lorenzo watched him for a moment. Occasionally, when there was a science-fiction convention in town, someone would pull a prank like this. He cleared his throat with great deliberation.

The man looked up. There was something wrong with his face. He reminded Lorenzo of someone with Down's syndrome, but the face wasn't quite right.

"Sir, the President has already received a courier from the cosmos. So why don't you soar off to save another small and insignificant planet?"

"The President," the man said. "This is where your

President lives? I have the right place then." He lifted his leg to swing over the barrier. In two steps Lorenzo was up to the man, hand clasping his shoulder. The shiny material of his suit felt slick to the touch. For the first time, he realized how short the prankster was.

"Excuse me, sir, but you can't go in there now. The President is asleep now, unless he's up watching an old Jimmy Stewart movie. In any case, I don't think he's expecting you."

"He will want to see me. I have an urgent message for him."

"So do half the people in this country. And I'm afraid you're going to have to go through channels like everyone else."

"Very well." The man nodded his head. "Could you tell me where I could find these channels and how long it will take me to see your President?"

"Try a letter. If you have a computer, there's a bulletin board available. And if it's a White House tour you want, they start at ten tomorrow morning, although it's a long shot that you'll even see the President."

"But I have a message for him. It is very important. I have come a long way to deliver it, and I am exhausted from my journey."

Lorenzo looked the man over. "You've come a long way, huh?" He squinted at the man. "Millions, maybe even billions of miles?"

The man smiled. "You know?"

Lorenzo bit his lip. *Not another one!* If there was anything worse than the science-fiction conventions, it was the UFO conventions, which filled the capital with seers who carried galactic messages from supposed superior intelligences. They were the types who sat on their roofs during meteor showers, waiting for the mother ship. "You need to move on."

"You don't know what you're saying," the man said.

"Oh, yes I do." Sharpness crept into Lorenzo's voice. "It's not funny anymore, pal. You're starting to get on my nerves. I don't want you messing up my night with a bunch of paperwork, buddy. And that's exactly what's going to happen if you make me bring the Secret Service out here to talk to you."

The man's eyes widened.

"If you want to give your message of intergalactic harmony to someone, you get in touch with Geraldo or Donahue or that lady with the red glasses."

The man's features fell, and his eyes lowered to the ground.

It worked, Lorenzo thought. He gestured over his shoulder with the thumb of his free hand. "See that camera up there?"

The man glanced at a long device hanging from one of the eaves of the guard shack. He nodded.

"That's sending your picture to everyone in Washington. And with it is a message that if you're caught anywhere near here again, you're going to be shot on sight and your body will be hung on the fence as a warning to others. Got that?"

"I must see your President. It is important to the survival of your race."

"Listen, buddy," Lorenzo growled. "I want you to pack your message into that fancy aluminum suit of yours and get out of here."

The man thought for a moment. "I suppose I'm going to have to prove my intent to you—" His hand fell toward an oval bubble that looked like the buckle of a belt that didn't exist.

There was a loud click. Lorenzo had pulled his 9mm and leveled it at him. "Get your hands away from your belt. Then get out of here and don't ever let me see you around here again."

The man slowly turned and started to walk away,

back across the walkway and out to Pennsylvania Avenue.

Lorenzo took a slow breath as he holstered his weapon, wondering what kind of trauma would have caused a person's face to look like that. Had it been drugs? Had he been turned out of a mental hospital whose funding had been cut? The country sure had its share of casualties, and Lord only knew, Washington was a magnet for them.

But this man who was disappearing so quickly into the night was different. He seemed so desperate, so vulnerable . . . So out of it.

He knew he couldn't be charitable to every case that came to the president's gates. But, for the first time, Lorenzo North wanted to do something for a stranger on the street.

Reaching for his wallet, he started down the walk, looking in the direction the man had taken. He looked into the darkness all around him, but except for the sparse 3:00 A.M. traffic, the street was deserted.

"Oh, well," he sighed. Then he turned back toward the guard shack. "There'll be another one tomorrow night."

GHOST

Control.

Control was the word, and the word was control.

You couldn't lose it, not even once. You had to keep control. Control of your life. Control of your surroundings.

Shark was trying to control Ghost. Trying to take him over. That was bad, man.

Ghost couldn't let that happen.

If he had to, he'd kill Shark.

Maybe he could do something like Alex had done in that old movie, *A Clockwork Orange*.

Yo.

Now there was one righteous dude who was way past cool.

A Clockwork Orange was Ghost's favorite movie. He had first seen it years ago, when he was just starting to run for the local clockers. He'd been over at the house of a friend when it had come on the cable, and was shocked by the sight of bare breasts and phallic statuary. But he was galvanized by the violence.

And he knew right then. That was the life he wanted to live.

Two weeks later, at the macho age of fourteen, he had ripped off a local video store. He and three dudes in a stolen van had hit the place for $23,000 worth of tapes, laser discs, and players, then fenced it all for ten cents on the dollar.

Everything except a Sony TV and laser-disc player, and the disc of *A Clockwork Orange*. In the three years since, he had watched it hundreds of times. And while he disdained the bowler hat, mascara, and white codpiece that made up Alex's costume, everything else Ghost had done with his life had been an effort to emulate what he thought Alex would do—right down to listening to classical music. This music had brought him nothing but scorn, however, so he retreated from it, changing to hard-core metal and rap. But deep inside, he maintained a love for that music, and he treasured it above anything else he was exposed to.

Ghost licked his lips and kept up his pace down the Washington back street, while the others lagged just behind, Shark taking up the rear. What to do about him? He knew what Alex would do. There was an instructional scene in the movie where he stomped his gang just to prove he was still boss.

Ghost would love that. He would love to stomp Shark. The problem was, he wasn't sure he wanted to take on the others. He wasn't sure it was necessary.

Besides, Alex's gang had gotten their revenge later in the movie. He didn't need any of that. And he certainly didn't want Shark around, nursing a grudge.

No. Shark had to die. Plain and simple. Before he corrupted any more of his gang. Already Piggy Boy had been talking back, being mouthy, acting like he wanted rank and respect. There was no way that piece of jive turkey was getting over on Ghost.

Off Shark and stomp Piggy Boy. But first he had to scheme on Shark, put him up to burglary, maybe, of someone who kept a gun and wasn't afraid to use it. Maybe get him running scams with some of those mean dudes from New Jersey, then chill the deal and have them take him down.

Ghost almost missed it when Goldie said, "Yo, don't look now, but here comes fresh meat."

"Yo," Shark echoed.

Ghost looked up. Approaching them from down the street was a small figure in some kind of suit that picked up the color of the street lamp.

" 'Bout to dirty his pants where he stands," Squeak said.

"Let's see he does," said Shark.

"Wait for it," Ghost said to the others, looking down the street.

The man wasn't retreating, but heading straight for them.

Ghost couldn't believe this. The dude had to be a preacher or plain crazy.

"Gentlemen"—he waved one hand—"I need your assistance."

The idiot was actually wanting to talk to them!

"You lost?" asked Piggy Boy.

"We give you assistance." Shark grinned menacingly.

"Maybe you don't know what time it is," said Squeak.

"Maybe you don't know where you is," said Goldie.

"I'm in your nation's capital," the man said matter-of-factly. Ghost cocked his head and studied the man. God sure give some folks their share of ugly.

"What, you from out of town?" Squeak asked him.

"You could say that," the man said.

"What you lookin' for?" Ghost asked.

"I'm looking for someone important."

"Like who?"

"Someone who will listen to the most important message in the life of this planet in two millennia. Someone who will do something about it. Someone with the power to take action."

"Sound serious," said Goldie.

"Life or death," said Shark.

"End of the world," said Ghost.

"Precisely," said the man. "The end of the world."

Shark closed in and the others surrounded the man. "Now, what kind of all-important message you gonna give this dude?" he asked.

The man turned, looking at each of them. Not in fear. In earnest. What kind of loony tune was he?

"Your planet is in great danger," he said.

"Ho, right," Piggy Boy said.

"You from the moon or something?" Goldie asked.

"Escalating moral decomposition is corroding your Gaiasphere. Maybe you've noticed the manifestations. Increased volcanic and seismic activity. Repeated patterns of flooding previously seen only in century-long cycles. Disrupted and chaotic weather patterns, resulting in—"

"Even talks like he from the moon," Goldie said.

"Yeah," said Piggy Boy. "Speak English, huh?"

The man looked at them. "I am sorry. I am afraid I am rather anxious to convey this message. I was turned away by your President, and I am rather at a loss. I must find someone to take this message."

"We take yo' message," said Shark.

The man studied them. He started to shake his head. "No. No, I don't think so. I'm afraid not."

"Why not?" Shark asked.

"I'm afraid you're not in a position to do anything. You are members of the chronically neglected and undereducated part of society, which is another manifestation of the basic cancer that is eating away at—"

"You jivin' us?" Shark asked, moving even closer to the man.

"I need someone with more societal influence," the man said calmly.

"I got a dance'll burn this whole town," Shark hissed. "Done it, too, two years ago. Maybe you saw—"

"I doubt you were personally responsible for that unfortunate incident."

"You callin' me a *liar*?" Shark shrieked in mock outrage.

"I am merely expressing serious doubts as to the validity of your claim."

"He call you a liar," Squeak said.

Ghost dropped his arm down and rotated his shoulder. The metal rod he kept hanging under his arm dropped neatly into his outstretched palm. It was a move he had practiced ever since he had first seen Alex wail on his entire gang armed only with a cane.

"Let the dude go," Ghost said. "He ain't in his right mind."

Shark glared at him. "Looks like you fearless leader ain't so all-fired fearless."

Ghost felt himself tense. This was it—the power play, the move he had been expecting and dreading.

"Maybe he like this skinny little white boy," Shark challenged him.

"Maybe they in love," Piggy Boy said.

Shark reached out and grabbed the man by the collar of his tinfoil suit. He started to pull him in, his other hand whipping so the blade of his knife clicked into place. Ghost spun the pipe in his fingers, caught it in the web of his thumb and forefinger, then grasping it tightly, brought it down hard on Shark's weaponed hand. The impact resounded on the empty street. The knife spun onto the asphalt.

"I said no," Ghost growled.

Shark flexed his injured hand, keeping the small man between himself and Ghost. "Cuttin' me some payback, my man," he said. "Gonna see you bleed."

"This is not working out," the man said. "I came to bring peace, not have this—"

"Shuddup," Shark yelled, and he shoved the man hard at Ghost, pouncing right behind. Ghost rolled up the pipe and brought it across the side of the man's head, knocking him to one side, and in one smooth motion, continued the turn, brought up his left foot, and planted his Nike-clad heel into Shark's stomach. Shark grunted and went down hard. Ghost finished the spin, planted both feet on the ground, and swung the pipe with both hands. Shark was trying to sit up when the pipe connected with the bottom of his chin, sending a spray of blood and teeth into the air. He fell back and rolled into the street. Ghost leaped to his side, planting one foot squarely in the middle of his chest.

"Now"—he looked down at Shark—"you gonna chill, or do I put this ugly-stick upside yo' ugly head?"

"Do it!" Squeak squeaked. "Mess him good."

Piggy Boy glanced at the others. The wind was not blowing Shark's way. "Finish him. Mess his ugly face."

Squeak bent double to examine Shark's shattered face. "He dead?"

"He wish it, he see his ugly face in the mirror," Ghost said.

"This one dead," said Goldie.

Ghost spun.

Goldie was kneeling beside the man, who was curled up into a ball on the sidewalk.

"No way," Ghost said. "I just shove the man out of the way."

"You lay that stick upside his head," Goldie said.

Ghost walked over to the man and peered down. Goldie had his hands around his neck like he was trying to choke him.

"They ain't no pulse."

"No way!" Ghost took his pipe, raised it in the air, then let it fall and tapped Goldie's shoulder. "I hit him no harder than that. Love tap, git him out of the way."

"And killed him dead." Goldie rolled the body onto its back. "Looky here." He pointed to a welt on the side of the man's head that ran from temple to chin. "Don't know your own strength."

"He got a soft head."

"Looky," Squeak said in awe. "Ghost killed him a white dude."

"He ain't dead!" Ghost shrieked. "Man, he's out, don't you know it?"

"No pulse." Goldie wiped his hands as he rose from the pavement. "I know dead."

"Ghost gonna burn."

They turned. Shark had managed to get to his knees, and he was cupping his jaw in his hand. Ghost knew it was hurting Shark to talk, but he was doing it anyway.

"Ghost toasted a white boy. Now The Man gonna

come and get him and fry him up like a flapjack." Shark looked carefully at Piggy Boy and Goldie and Squeak. "He gonna come for you, too."

Piggy Boy was the first one to break. He set off at a dead run down the middle of the street, a choir of imaginary sirens dogging his heels.

Squeak went next, following Piggy Boy at first and then peeling off onto a dark side street.

Goldie went last, fading into the shadows and disappearing in the opposite direction.

Ghost stood and faced the bloodied Shark, boy to frightened boy, like gunslingers in an old western.

"You boss all right," Shark slurred. "Boss of nuthin'." He turned and walked away, in the same direction that Goldie had disappeared.

Ghost looked down at the crumpled little man and felt fear wash over him. This wasn't what he wanted. He'd tried to save the little runt, and he up and died on him.

It was the end of *his* life he was looking at. Alex was going to prison. It was full of faggots. And now there was AIDS.

Or maybe they would barbecue him, like Shark had said.

Far off, in the distance, Ghost could hear a siren.

Shark! Had he found a working phone and called it in already?

He looked down at the man in the tinfoil suit.

With clothes like that, someone would know who he was right off the bat. Probably a rock star or a movie actor.

Ghost fell to his knees, his fingers clawing at the strange clothing. There were no fasteners, no zippers. The only item of note was an oval-shaped smooth kind of rock that would have served as a belt buckle if the suit had only had a belt. He tugged at it, and it came away from the suit with a wet sucking sound.

The rock was heavy in his hand. It was cold and slick, and it reminded him of mercury, with its silvery, glistening finish. Ghost turned it over. There were no fasteners on it, and there was nothing on the suit to even indicate it had been attached.

Ghost slipped it into his pocket and began tugging at the suit again. The thing didn't have any seams, but when he pulled on the hood, it gave and stretched, even though the fabric didn't feel like elastic. He cried out in triumph and pulled some more. The suit's collar opened right up. He worked it down the man's pale shoulders, then eased the arms backward out of the sleeves, rolling the suit off, wadding it between his fingers as he went.

Oh, no! he was thinking. *I kill me a white dude! They fry up my butt for sure.*

As worrisome as that seemed to Ghost, nothing had prepared him for the shock when he rolled the suit down over the man's hips.

He let out an involuntary yelp when he looked down at the man's crotch.

The dude was a woman.

No. No, that wasn't right.

The dude was neither. There was nothing between his—*its* legs where there should have been something. There was just smooth skin, bare and pale.

Ghost pulled the suit the rest of the way off and turned the body over. No, this was impossible. The man had no butt, either. It was just as smooth as the other side.

He stuffed the suit under his arm and looked down at the strange body. He had hoped to get all of the identification off it, but now he didn't know. A body like that, so misshapen and ugly. It had to come from somewhere where people would be missing it. Maybe the CIA. They was always messin' with things like that.

Maybe worse. Maybe someplace even more secret and scary than the CIA.

Maybe the DEA.

Ghost decided that the best way to cover his butt was to torch the dude. But there was no place around he could cop some lighter fluid, and the sirens were growing louder, nearer.

With a last look at the dead monstrosity, he shook his head and said, "Sorry, my man. Whatever you is, I was only trying to help."

As the sirens increased their urgent plea, Ghost turned and ran.

FRAN MARKOWSKI

The Kojak light on the dashboard strobed blue as Fran Markowski mashed the accelerator pedal to the floor and careened across the empty Washington streets. McKeown was going to kill her for his, she knew, but business was off tonight. Maybe it was the chill in the air, but everybody on the streets seemed to be behaving themselves. Her attire—the leather jacket and miniskirt, vinyl boots and red silk bustier—attracted a horny senate staffer coming out of an all-night porno. And that was good for a time-consuming bust that led nowhere because one phone call to a well-placed friend meant that the arrest would be effectively expunged from record.

Washington, D.C. Where money meant nothing. And everything.

She was supposed to have been staking out a strip bar whose owner was suspected of pimping for the dancers.

He'd set up a slick operation. Overprice the drinks, spike them with grain alcohol, get the girls to rub their breasts on the customers' faces. Get them all worked up. Take them upstairs to a makeshift set of rooms and get them so drowsy from a postorgasmic glow that they'd never notice their wallets had been cleaned out.

And with the high embarrassment factor involved, nobody was talking.

Washington, D.C. Where character and morals meant nothing. And everything.

Fran had been standing across the street from the bar, one perfectly formed leg propped up on a fire hydrant, her hands seductively pulling the stocking up her leg, when her earpiece crackled and the call came in for an assault in progress less than three blocks away. She raced around the corner to her car, pulled the Kojak from under the seat and flicked it on, then started the engine and was on the way before the first distant sirens began to wail.

"Markowski, two-fourteen. I'm thirty seconds away," she barked into the microphone.

If Lieutenant McKeown was listening, he was having a litter of kittens right now.

Well, screw him. There had been a lot of gang activity in the neighborhood lately, and innocent civilians were getting caught in the crossfire. The battle for the inner-city raged on.

The intersection leaped out ahead of her, and she cranked the wheel. The tires bit at the damp street, and she slid around the corner. Her foot hit the accelerator again, and her headlights framed a tiny figure crumpled in the gutter.

"Markowski, two-fourteen. I'm on the scene. One person down, scene clear. Call an ambulance."

Fran slammed the car to a halt and jumped out, her right hand pulling the LadySmith from inside her boot and cocking it. She turned a complete circle as she approached the body. Nothing. Nobody. Then she stepped up to the body for a closer look.

"Holy Mother!" she said and crossed herself.

What was it? A midget? Or was it a dwarf? Just a small man with that disease—what was it, the disease that gave you a huge jaw and a deep voice? But the fingers and arms and legs were so skinny, drawn pitifully into the fetal position.

Fran drew a deep breath and reminded herself to be professional. There was no pooling blood, no cuts or punctures that would indicate a gunshot. She knelt down, touched the man's shoulder. It made her gasp.

The body was cold.

She pulled off her leather jacket and laid it over the inert figure. Then it twitched, and she reeled back in fright.

The strange creature sat up.

The blood drained from Fran's face.

"I don't understand," it said in a thin, reedy voice. "I just don't understand."

"What ... what don't you understand?" she stammered.

"Why am I being turned away?" it asked plaintively.

Fran swallowed to flush the fear back down inside her. "Who's turning you away?"

"Everyone. Has your Gaiasphere become so corroded that it clouds even your minds?"

She bit her lip. *He's delirious.*

"Why you're treating me like ... like ..."

"What?" Fran asked.

The man looked at her and gave her a bitter smile. "You're treating me like one of your own." He turned away. "I should be flattered. The aborigines are merely treating me in the same grand manner as everyone else—with hatred and malevolence. Oh, I fit in so well here—"

Fran looked up. She could hear sirens rising in the distance. "Sir, help will be here soon. You're going to be all right, but you need to help me so I can help you—"

"I don't understand," the man said weakly. His hands fumbled around his waist. "I need my . . ." His voice faded.

Shock, Fran thought. *He's slipping away. Got to do what I can before he loses it.* "What do you need? Is there something I can help you with?"

"Perhaps I should return and take the punishment due me. I deserve it. I should never have left." He turned his head and addressed the night. "Perhaps my colleagues were right. Your race has taken an evolutionary detour. You have bypassed your destiny and forgotten your purpose. I have risked everything to come here, and it means nothing. I am a failure."

Fran gritted her teeth and gripped the man's shoulders. *"Sir—"*

"Perhaps I should just stay here and share the judgment with you arrogant creatures. What is that idiomatic expression you have to describe it? *Spend one last night in Gomorrah?"*

The sirens were loud in Fran's ears now, and she could see red and blue light strobing off the corners of the buildings.

"But first," the man said, "I must escape from your insistent hospitality."

The air split with the roar of rubber on asphalt, and an ambulance bounded around the corner, flanked by two squad cars.

The man jerked in her arms, then went still.

"No!" she screamed and shook him.

The cars aimed straight for her, blinding her with

their lights. She plunged her hand into her bustier and removed a thin leather wallet, flipped it open with a practiced move, and flashed the badge inside at the oncoming vehicles.

"Markowski. Detective Sergeant. Vice," she called out as uniformed men rolled out of the vehicles.

"Rossi," said one of the uniforms. "Whaddya got, sarge?"

Fran stood, looking back at the still body. "A mess. This guy looks like he was hit in the head with something."

"Deader?"

She nodded. "He was shocky when I got here. Lived long enough to babble incoherently. I don't think there's anything worth mentioning."

"We'll have a look."

"Rossi," said Fran.

The officer stopped and looked back at her.

"I think this guy was a foreign national. He had a weird kind of accent, and he kept talking about other races and punishment. Like he was expecting this to happen to him."

"We'll have to bring in the suits on this one," Rossi said.

"Not yet," Fran said. "As far as I'm concerned, we've got an unidentified body. Just make sure your boys catalog every piece of lint within three hundred yards of the body because they'll want it all when this hits the fan."

"You got it." Rossi nodded and turned to his colleagues, who had fanned out around the body. "Guys!" he yelled. "This one's got to be by the numbers. The suits'll pro'bly be in on this one."

He was acknowledged with a chorus of assorted profanities.

"Any ID in the coat?" Rossi asked.

"The coat's mine," she said.

"I'll get it back to you. Lemme get some pictures first," he said, and started plodding toward his squad car.

Fran watched him go, then turned as another car, battered and generic looking, pulling up on the scene. She turned and walked toward it.

A redheaded barrel of a man hopped out of the driver's side and strode up to her, an invisible chip perched prominently on his shoulder.

"So you did it again, Frannie."

"I was thirty seconds away, lieutenant."

"You were assigned to the Red Velvet Lounge," McKeown said.

"The place was dead. There's nothing happening there tonight."

"How do you know we weren't five minutes away from something happening?"

"I didn't make sergeant for nothing, sir."

"You won't keep the rank with nothing either, Fran. You've got to stay focused on what you're being paid to do. You're not on patrol anymore. You're not Wonder Woman, trying to clean up the town from one end to the other. Now you're down in the trenches, chiseling away at the hard stuff."

Chastised, Fran nodded as Rossi approached.

"Sarge," he said, handing her the leather jacket. "We got something interesting. That foreign national of yours must've been some kind of circus freak or something."

She and McKeown turned to look at the young officer.

"He's got no—" he looked at her and blushed—"sexual apparatus."

Fran looked over at the body. One of the other officers was photographing it. "He's a woman?"

Rossi shook his head. "He's an *it*. Got no . . . uh, no organs of sexual identity at all. We can't even figure out how he—uh—it—went to the bathroom."

Fran looked quizzically at McKeown, then shrugged. "I guess the guys from homicide will figure that out."

"Oh no," McKeown said. "If the Red Velvet Lounge can't hold your interest, then this one's yours. You caught it, Frannie."

"But this isn't even—"

"You should have thought of that before you answered the call."

"McKeown, it's probably a foreign national. You know what that means?"

"It means," McKeown said coolly, "that it's going to cause you enough grief so that next time you'll keep your nose on the vice team, where it belongs." He turned and started to walk back to his car.

"And Fran," he said, pausing as he climbed into the waiting vehicle. "I don't want this investigation interfering with your regular duties." He slammed the door, gunned the engine, and drove off into the waning night.

She watched him leave, then went with Rossi to have a closer look at the body.

DR. GEORGE UNDERWOOD

Knife wounds. A prostitute with thirty-two stab wounds to her neck, chest, and abdomen, administered by her pimp. The pimp himself was carried in hours later, his throat cut from ear to ear, both carotid arteries sliced open.

Gunshot wounds. A fifteen-year-old clocker who was taking the product, stepping on it one more time on his own, and building a little nest egg. He wouldn't live to

spend it. A drunken white male who, in a show of bra-
vado, shoved a pistol into his belt, accidentally emascu-
lating himself in the process. A nine-year-old girl who
happened to be walking past a dispute over who owned
what to whom, paralyzed from the waist down.

Other wounds. A man whose wife had backed the car
over him while he was trying to secure the muffler with
a coat hanger. That one actually may have been accidental. A seventeen-year-old black kid whose jaw had
been shattered by a metal rod of some kind. Three
months of milk shakes for him. A torched wino. Crispy
critter—call the morgue. Why was he even here?

George Underwood had wanted to be a surgeon ever
since he had first seen *M*A*S*H*. The idea of saving
lives inspired him. The idea of racing against time to
save those lives was the ultimate thrill.

George Underwood, trauma surgeon. He loved the
idea.

And when he graduated with honors, he could have
gone to any hospital in the nation. He narrowed it down
to two: Henry Ford Hospital in Detroit or George Washington University Hospital in Washington, D.C.

Combat zones. Life and death. The Grim Reaper was
turning over the meter and letting it run.

When crime in the nation's capital began to spiral out
of control, the final choice was made for him. He went
where things would only get worse. And when he first
found himself up to his elbows in blood and viscera, he
knew he had found himself.

His first wife had called it "living on the edge." But
to Underwood it was rock and roll—loud, anarchic, and
confusing. And on occasion you were worshiped for
your deeds.

It was killing him, giving him ulcers, making him un-
fit for the company of a woman. But he loved it. He
thrived on it. It was all that he lived for.

Like tonight, for instance. Another rock-and-roll evening in D.C. Eight life-or-death cases, and there were still three hours left until the end of his shift.

People were vacating the capital. Even the politicians were loath to remain in the city after dark. And people weren't just moving out to the suburbs. What was happening here was the same thing that had been happening in New York City since the middle of the decade. They were moving out of the city, out of the suburbs, out of the state.

In their wake, they left the desperate and the depraved—and George Underwood. Him and Death, going toe to toe.

Stepping back from the gurney, Underwood pulled off his gloves and threw them into a bucket on the floor.

"Take her," he said, and two nurses gripped either side of the portable bed and wheeled her out of surgery.

"Whaddya think?" asked Heywood, another surgeon.

Underwood looked down at the silver bowl into which he had dropped three mushroomed slugs from a .38 special. He had repaired so many gunshots that he could tell with 90 percent accuracy the caliber of the bullet he was removing.

"She's young," he said, "and kids that age are resilient. The left femoral artery is a mess, but if it holds, she'll keep the leg."

"What are you going to tell her parents?"

"I don't know, Woody. I'm sure you'll think of something."

He heard Heywood swear as he walked out of the trauma room.

Underwood was halfway to the emergency-room operations desk when Veronica, the head trauma nurse, turned the corner and accosted him. "Dr. Underwood, you're wanted in room 4a. There's a head trauma case that the police want you to take a look at."

The police. Great. Wonderful. Time to see what kind
of favor he could do the boys in blue—maybe thank
them for all the business they'd been sending his way.
He turned toward 4a, stopping only to give his hands a
quick scrub and pull a pair of gloves from a dispenser.

"Can you give me a quick history?" he asked her.

Veronica checked her clipboard. "The victim is unidentified, and was found laying in the street. The only
mark was a welt from an apparent blow to the head . . ."

Underwood pushed through the door of 4a to see a
large black bag laying on the gurney. Swearing bitterly, he turned to the nurse. "I don't handle stiffs, Veronica. You know that. You want someone to handle a
body, call Woody. Or better yet, get Begelman up from
the morgue because—"

"I want *you* to take this one, Dr. Underwood."

Underwood turned. A woman dressed like a D Street
hooker was looking at him, and she was accompanied
by a uniformed officer. He rolled his eyes. "Look, lady,
if I had to cave in to every person who read that
write-up about me in the *Post*, I'd never get to do what
got me written up in the first place—"

The woman held out a wallet at eye level. It fell open
to reveal a badge. "Markowski, Detective Sergeant.
Vice. This is my associate, Corporal Rossi. Are you the
lead surgeon here tonight, Dr. Underwood?"

"I am. And that's why I don't have time—"

"Then you will appreciate that we need to have you
involved with this case. We need it done right. Especially with the CIA becoming involved."

Underwood looked over at the body bag. "The CIA's
in on this?"

"It's possible. What we apparently have is the death
of a foreign national. But until we can determine the
identity of the deceased, we have to follow procedures

carefully. There may be a lot of notoriety attached to this case, so we must have the best."

The woman had him by the ego. The fact that she was dressed so provocatively was icing on the cake.

"All right, sergeant," he said. "I'll see what I can do for you."

She nodded, and the uniformed officer closed the door. Veronica assisted Underwood in putting on his gloves.

"He wasn't DOA, was he?" Underwood asked.

"Dead at the scene."

"How long?"

"I'd like your opinion," she said.

Underwood nodded at the nurse, who unzipped the body bag and pulled it open. The surgeon whistled.

"He's gotta be a foreigner. We don't grow them that ugly here."

"Your opinion on the deformity?"

Underwood shook his head. "I'm no expert in fetal development or mutations in human physiology. It could be any one of a number of things. Acromegaly. Hydrocephalus. Maybe his parents were cousins." He reached his hand in and grabbed the corpse's wrist. "Judging from temperature, I'd say he's been gone between three and four hours."

Fran looked at her watch. "I talked to him forty-five minutes ago."

Underwood dropped the hand. "Impossible!"

"If he's been dead as long as you say, then where are the signs of lividity?"

Underwood grabbed the wrist again, brought it up, and examined the underside. "You found him lying on his back?"

"On his right side, in a fetal position."

He put the left wrist down and picked up the right. "You're right. Someone gone that long, the blood would have settled, and the right side would look blue, swollen."

"He was cool when I first found him."

"And you say you talked to him?"

"Actually, he did most of the talking. Mostly paranoid ramblings."

"If he was in shock," said Underwood, "that could explain a cool, clammy feel to the skin."

"But not that cold."

"Nothing I've seen in my experience."

"It gets better." Fran pointed to the towel around the corpse's waist. "Check it out."

Underwood stared at her.

"I don't think he'll ... it'll ... mind."

In his years in the ER, Underwood had seen his share of damaged genitalia. Man's pursuit of sexual gratification seemed to know no limits. The pursuit of revenge could be just as creative, and even more humiliating. But with all he had witnessed, nothing had prepared Underwood for what he was about to see. By the time he realized he was staring speechless, it occurred to him that he had been doing so for a good long time.

"Where are the genitalia?"

"I was hoping you could tell me," Fran said.

Underwood took a deep breath. "Once, when I was an intern, I saw a genuine case of hermaphrodism; someone with both male and female genitalia. There's nothing like that here. There are no exterior genitals, no genital openings, no development of pubic hair. It's incredible." Underwood placed his hands under the knees and back of the corpse and turned it over. He swore once, loudly.

"Now you know why we covered, uh, it with a towel."

"There's no—"

"Yes?"

"There's no cleft between the gluteal muscles. There's no anus." He cocked his head at her. "Is this somebody's idea of a joke?"

"I wish it was," Fran said.

Underwood looked down at the body. It was impossible for him to keep from staring. "This guy had some major problems."

"You can see why we need your help on this one, doctor."

Underwood nodded, then looked at Veronica. "I'll need a camera," he said thinly. "And a—uh, tape recorder."

"Certainly." The nurse left the room.

"I don't want you to do an autopsy," Fran said. "I want a thorough examination, well documented, and your expert medical opinion. Do whatever you'd normally do to try and save this person's life. Blood tests, X rays, you name it. I want to be able to say we did everything we could up to the point of actually slicing and dicing."

"Sounds reasonable."

"If anything beyond what I've just said happens to this body, I'll lose my badge, and I'll take your license with me."

Underwood nodded. "Got it."

"And if he does turn out to be some hick from the sticks whose parents were first cousins, I promise you can be the one to sell the story to the *National Enquirer*. Fair enough?"

"Make it the *Journal of the AMA* and you've got a deal."

"Done." She smiled. "It's a pleasure to be working with you. We'll leave you to your work now."

"Thank—uh, thank you," he croaked as Fran left.

"Are you all right?" Veronica asked when she returned.

"Fine." He toweled his forehead. "You, uh, understand the need for strictest confidentiality in this matter?"

She nodded. "Dr. Underwood, you think this could be a Chernobyl baby?"

"That, uh . . . that remains to be seen."

"I've heard stories that the old Soviet Union used to experiment with genetic manipulation of human fetuses, and that some of them lived. And now that some of them are old enough, they're trying to get here for help."

"That's why we have to be very, very careful with this, Veronica." Underwood looked over the equipment she had brought in, the camera and a Sony microcassette. "All right. Let's go."

GHOST

Ghost cursed as he examined his loot. He was certain it was worthless. The suit was some kind of weird cheap plastic—not even metallic, as he had first thought—and the rock that had been the belt buckle resembled some of the rocks he had seen at one of the city's New Age shops.

The weird suit? He'd take it to his fence. Henry might not give him much for it, but it would be out of his hands. As far as the rock was concerned, well, maybe he'd keep it. He liked the slick, cool feel of it when he held it in the palm of his hand. He liked the way the streetlights reflected off it, giving off a strange glow that made his stomach knot up. Strangest of all, when he rubbed the thing, he felt almost horny, as if there was something more that should be happening to him, but he wasn't quite sure what it was.

He folded the suit and stuffed it under his T-shirt, then dropped the rock back into the pocket of his jeans. Then he went back to the scene of the crime, just to assess the situation.

When Ghost saw the scene from two blocks away, he was horrified. It was a regular convention, flashing lights all over the place. Two—no, three cop cars. An ambulance. Uniformed men everywhere, keeping news crews away. In the middle of it all, two uniformed men and a woman dressed like a hooker were zipping the little man into a black bag.

Ghost had seen enough to know what that meant.

He hurried away from the scene, lost himself on the dark city streets, and for a time crashed out on a bench in the park. There was no sense in going straight home. Even with his face broken up, Shark might be waiting, maybe even to rat him out to The Man.

Finally, as dawn was breaking, Ghost could take it no more. He hurt from his ill-planned nap, he felt sick to his stomach from lack of sleep, and he wanted desperately to get to his own place, lay down on his own mattress, and sleep for a hundred years.

Giving in to his physical cravings, he dug some change out of his pocket, bought three crullers from a doughnut shop, and headed for home as the street lamps were shutting down for the day.

And no sooner had he rounded the corner to his apartment building than he saw Amos sitting on the steps, reading the morning edition of the *Post* and sipping coffee from a McDonald's cup.

He swore again.

Amos was one of those cops who lived in the neighborhood and made friends with all of the little kids. Amos would buy them ice cream and get them tickets to ball games and lecture them plenty on keeping their pants zipped, not using drugs, and not working for the neighborhood clockers, even if it meant never being able to plunk down cash for a pair of Michael Jordan Atomic Basketball Shoes.

As far as Ghost was concerned, Amos was an Oreo, and the sooner the neighborhood figured that out, the better off it would be.

Still, Ghost didn't think it was worth it to challenge Amos. Not today. The cop knew how to be tough when he wanted. Hunt and Trigger had tried to jack him around one Sunday afternoon, and Amos had taken them both down without even breaking a sweat. He had them on the ground, cuffed together, with tears running from their eyes before they knew what was happening.

"Hey, Kit," Amos called.

Ghost felt his stomach turn at the sound of his real name. If he were just bigger and meaner, he'd make Amos pay for that.

"Hold on, Kit. I want to talk to you."

Ghost turned to see him approaching, paper folded and under his arm. The coffee cup had been left behind on the steps.

"You gittin' home kinda late?"

"Yessir." The compacted suit was beginning to stick to his chest and itch, and the rock felt warm against his thigh.

"Kit, did you know that Clarence was admitted to the hospital last night?"

Ghost shook his head.

"His face was pretty messed up. You know anything about that?"

"Should I?" he mumbled.

"As I understand it, you and Clarence are pretty tight. You're in some sort of club together, aren't you?"

Ghost hated this man with every inch of his being. Once he got a notion in his head, he hung onto it with the tenacity of a bulldog. No amount of shaking or evasion would make him let go. If you tried to lead him one way, one well-placed question or statement would bring you back to the subject so fast you didn't know what hit you. And his way of understating things made him furious. It made everything that Ghost did and lived for seem so . . . *insignificant*.

"I guess," Ghost mumbled.

"Strange thing is, Clarence didn't want to say anything about what happened to his face. And I thought, since the two of you were so tight, you could offer me a little insight as to what happened to him."

Ghost shook his head.

"I'm sorry, son. I didn't hear you."

Ghost cringed. Two more reasons to hate the man. He made you talk to him, and he called everyone "son."

"No."

"That's strange. He claims that he has no memory of the incident, but he seemed certain that you were witness to what happened."

"Didn't see nothin'."

"Just as well," Amos said. "It's probably best if you didn't see anything this evening."

Ghost could feel beads of sweat forming on his forehead. Amos was just too slick.

"Because there was a foreign dignitary killed early this morning between here and the White House. It's all pretty ugly. Probably turn into an international incident. But, well, you know what people been sayin' about the city. They been sayin' it for ten years or longer by now."

"Yeah," Ghost said. "Guess it's true, ain't it." Circling, circling. When would he leap?

"It's just as well that Clarence has amnesia about the little incident. Maybe he can convince people he doesn't remember who else was there when it happened. I guess the poor little guy put up a fight. Messed up Clarence's face. But, in the end, I guess Clarence whipped him good. Even took the poor little guy's clothes."

Now the rock was on fire in Ghost's pocket. He managed to nonchalantly put both hands deep into his pockets. The rock rolled into one hand, and his palm tingled the way it did when Heidi pushed it onto one of her breasts.

"If you can help him come clean, Kit, it would sure help him out. If you can help us convict him, we could save him."

"From what?" Ghost blurted out.

"I'm not at liberty to say. But certain foreign nationals—I'm not allowed to say who—are very distressed that their man in Washington was killed under mysterious circumstances. They want his killer sent over right away, so they can do justice their way."

Ghost felt dizzy. He was falling into Amos's line of questioning, but there was just enough truth to it to make it sound real. He gripped the stone hard in his palm, hoping its coolness would spread; but instead its electric feeling went straight to his crotch.

"Of course, we'd never extradite someone for a crime committed on these shores," Amos said, "but these foreign nationals are very vindictive."

Ghost tried rubbing his thumb on the rock, trying to work off the sexual agitation he was feeling. It didn't work.

"We can't monitor every one of them coming into the country. So we don't know which ones are coming here to mete out a little justice of their own."

Ghost's throat was getting tight and he was losing his breath now.

"So it would be pretty difficult for us to protect Clarence—Or you, for that matter, Kit—"

"I don't know nothin'!" Ghost shouted. "So just shut up and leave me alone!"

Amos said nothing. He gave the boy a long blank stare, then turned and walked away, leaving his coffee on the apartment steps.

Ghost tilted his head back and sucked air into his lungs. "That was too close." And then it occurred to him that he had just experienced a first. He had crossed Amos, shouted him down, and won. Amos had given up and walked away. And this wasn't just a first for Ghost, it was a first for anyone in the neighborhood.

He put his hands on his hips, surveyed the neighborhood, and for the moment, felt like the king of the world. Then he bolted up the stairs in anticipation of some hot food and sleep.

He didn't notice that sexual stimulation was gone.

MEANINGLESS, SAID THE TEACHER

WASHINGTON, D.C. / APRIL 1999

THE VIEW FROM HERE
by Mick Aaronson

April 15, 1999—Yet another year has gone by and once again I find myself obligated to make out a check to our friends at the Internal Revenue Service and deposit it in a mailbox at 11:59 P.M.

Yes, I said "friends." These are just a bunch of guys with families who have a job to do, like cops and cabdrivers. They do what they have to do to put food into the mouths of their children, much as I have done these last forty years.

But this year, I may rebel. I may not deposit the envelope until 12:01 A.M. and say, "All right boys, come and get me."

And when they did, I'd tell them a thing or two.

I wouldn't come down on their occupation. After all, what child ever grows up saying, "When I grow up, I want to be a member of the tax police!" Like so many other professions in this life, that of the IRS agent is accidental.

What I would do is give them a message for their bosses.

You know the ones I'm talking about. Those five-hundred-odd members of our government who, like some kind of doctor of old, keep their fingers on the economic pulse of the nation. And when it gets too strong, they bring out the jar of leeches.

What is so upsetting about all of this is that for going on ten years, these so-called caretakers have turned a deaf ear to our pleas to ease the burden and follow the simple rule of economy that every American family must follow.

Don't spend more money than you take in.

However, this is the city of power and money. One of them corrupts absolutely. The other is the ultimate aphrodisiac. No amount of proud idealism and campaign promises can make a newcomer immune. Not for long.

Our leaders have made themselves a ruling class. By suing their own constituents over things like term limits, they have entrenched themselves more solidly than Britain's royal family.

Only ours are more obsolete and even more expendable.

Maybe it's time for a new revolution. But with most Americans now receiving some kind of money from the government dole, that doesn't seem likely. Why bite the hand that feeds them?

That's what I would tell these stern-looking men who are only doing their jobs. And I would tell them one other thing.

I would have them tell their bosses to go ahead and say what they've been dying to tell us for years.

They can finally say, "Let them eat cake."

SUSAN HILL

Green phosphor letters stared at Susan Hill. Susan Hill stared back.

The trick was to make something of them; to arrange the words so they entertained and informed and motivated. It wasn't easy to write Pulitzer Prize prose, however, about a woman who had just published the fifth in her series of books about fuzzy animals.

Susan swore to herself and reached for her soda.

The life-style page. Why write about life-styles when there was so much other stuff, real news, going on in Washington? She had signed up for this internship in order to study under the great Mick Aaronson. She had been promised the chance to see investigative journalism through the eyes of the king of the muckrakers, the last paladin of his breed in America.

But that promise had turned out to be a crock. She had been here six weeks and had seen the man only once, when he had called her in to congratulate her on being chosen for the position. He had seemed as docile in person as he was a curmudgeon in print. He had been gentle and soft-spoken, promising her an inside look at every section of the paper.

But where had it actually gotten her?

After a disastrous two weeks trying to report sports, she had been moved to life-styles. The White House Easter egg hunt. A has-been TV actor who was on the dinner-theater circuit. What today's new designs in Paris meant for American women tomorrow. And now, the climax of it all; the fuzzy-animal lady.

Wonderful.

All of this when there was surely another Whitewater out there getting ready to break.

She was able to pacify herself by tagging along when one of the other reporters—real reporters, she had started calling them—went to a presidential briefing or press conference. That was what had kept her going through all this, and if she survived fuzzy-animal city, it would be through their benevolence.

Susan looked at her lead sentence. *Ask any child who their favorite tree-chewing critter is, and they'll name Bizzy Beaver and all of the other furry friends who live on Paducah Pond.*

"Stupid fuzzy animals!" She cracked her knuckles. She stretched her fingers and started typing. *It's just a shame that Bizzy and all of his little friends have ended up with their heads stuffed and mounted on the walls of Big Ed's hunting lodge.* Her lips turned up in a smile.

A hand clapped her shoulder, and she gasped.

"Trouble finding a lead, Susan?"

"Uh, just getting the creative juices flowing."

"Just as long as your sarcasm doesn't accidentally make it into print." Julia Roman, the editor of the lifestyle section, patted the intern on the shoulder.

"Right," Susan said quickly. Her fingers flew over the keys of her terminal, highlighting the offending sentence and then deleting it.

"Frankly, I'm a little disappointed, Susan."

Susan looked up at Julia. Her stomach plunged.

"I always thought Bizzy and his little friends should end up as the main course at the Road Kill Café."

Susan burst out laughing with sudden relief.

"Bizzy's creator has a friend high up in the Department of Education," Julia said. "That's why the schools are crammed with that woman's books, and that's why she thinks she should get a headline story whenever she puts out a new one. When you get to be the reporter you've always wanted to be, promise me you'll investigate her."

"Sure." Susan smiled.

"And speaking of reporters, Susan, the big man asked me to send you up to his office."

"Who? Mr. Aaronson?"

"None other." Julia put her hand lightly on Susan's shoulder. "Don't get too excited. You still owe me that piece on Bizzy and his woodland friends, no matter what happens."

"I will. Thanks."

Susan hurried toward the elevator and took it to the seventh floor. Mick Aaronson's floor. The door opened, and she stepped into a world different from the one she had just left. Instead of the densely packed cubicles, the din of ringing phones and constant rattle of fingers on keyboards, there was a hushed quiet. She was walking on a carpeted floor, past spacious offices with big desks and window views. This was where the big boys lived and played.

Someday. Someday she would be here, too. A big girl holding her own here in the grown-ups' club.

Susan slowed as she approached the corner office. It was standing open, the brass nameplate heralding the occupant as MICHAEL AARONSON. She slowed and quietly stepped up to the door.

The pendulum of a large wall clock filled the room with a soft ticking sound. The clock was surrounded with framed newspaper stories and awards. On the opposite wall was a photograph of a younger Aaronson in uniform, shaking hands with Harry Truman. And off to the right were more photos of the same man shaking hands with every president since. Straight ahead were bookcases from floor to ceiling, all filled to overflowing. And in front of it was the large desk behind which the man himself sat.

The top of his head was covered with short-cropped gray hair. He wore reading glasses on his nose and used one hand to adjust them as Susan stepped forward to announce her presence. But Mick Aaronson already knew she was there.

"Come in, Suzanne," he said.

"Thank you," she said, crossing the threshold.

"Close the door, please."

She pushed it shut. It closed noiselessly.

"Have a seat. Please." He looked up at her with a wrinkled, round face and smiled, motioning to an over-stuffed chair.

She pulled at her skirt and sat, sinking into the chair.

"You wanted to see me, Mr. Aaronson?"

He looked down at the paper he had been studying. A red pen was balanced between two fingers.

"Yes. I've been keeping careful track of what you've been doing for the life-style section."

She squirmed in the too-soft chair. "Well, Mr. Aaronson, it's not exactly the kind of writing that I feel I'm cut out for."

Aaronson nodded. "And I don't see you as being cut out for any other kind of writing if you don't lose this attitude of yours, Miss Hill."

"Attitude?" she gasped.

"Suzanne, it's clear to me that while you're doing your best at the assignments I've given you, you've done so with an enormous chip on your shoulder."

"Assignments *you've* given me?"

"Every article you've worked on since starting your internship here has been given you with my approval. In a couple of cases, I even handpicked them."

Susan's mouth dropped open. "You mean this whole thing has been a setup?"

Aaronson smiled. "All a part of the program. You were a complete failure in the sports department, but I can hardly blame that on you. It's my opinion that sports writing is the hardest kind of writing known to man. It takes a special kind of person to do it at all, let alone do it well."

Susan smiled weakly and nodded. "You're being kind."

"However,"—he pounced—"you should be more than capable of doing life-style writing, and you have made a complete mess of that, too, my dear."

Now her face burned. She wanted to say, *Don't call me "my dear," you sexist pig, and while you're at it, you may refer to me as "Ms. Hill,"* but then her eyes fell to what he had been working on. They were photocopies of her articles, and his liberal use of red ink made them look bloodied.

"Let's start with your Senate-chili-recipe-cookbook story, shall we?" He cleared his throat and, to her horror, read her opening line with the authoritative tone of a latter-day Walter Cronkite. "The hard-luck dish known as chili has become America's favorite food. And while this may chagrin our Republican leadership, some clever Senate wives have decided to capitalize on this by collecting the Union's best-loved chili recipes into a single volume."

Susan looked at him with wide eyes.

His eyebrows knit into an angry glare. "For pity's sake, Suzanne, this is about a recipe book, not the 1999 budget."

"I thought it was a good lead," she said.

"For the *Post*, maybe." Aaronson searched through the stack of articles and pulled up another one. "Here's your piece about the annual Easter egg hunt." He cleared his throat. "The President tossed a bone of appeasal to members of the religious right during the White House Easter egg hunt yesterday. During a prehunt speech, he called for all Americans to be leaders in this nation's 'return to a more stable form of morality.' "

She looked at him with her best poker face.

"Suzanne, this is an insult to everyone who calls themself a Christian."

"But—Mr. Aaronson——"

"But nothing, Miss Hill. The President, who is a Christian himself, I might add, and somewhat more devout about it than his predecessors of either party, was merely making a statement reflecting the views of a great majority of his constituents. The statement he made over Easter was designed to cut across differences in theology and background and have a unified appeal. With a few well-chosen words for what was supposed to be a piece of fluff, you have reduced it to an act of demagoguery."

Susan bit her lip and frowned.

Aaronson's eyes fell to the stack of papers and began reading again. "While McCallister has not maintained the popularity he achieved when his television series *Here Comes Daddy!* was at its peak in the early 1960s, he has been an active and unashamed spokesman for the current administration and has become active in the President's reelection campaign."

Susan sat, listening to the ticking of the clock.

"You want to tell me what in heaven's name this little factoid is doing in a story about a man who is appearing in a dinner-theater production of *The Odd Couple*?"

"It's the truth," she said.

"Susan, if you hung these words around that poor man's neck and dropped him in the Potomac, he'd sink like a stone. First you tell us he's a has-been——"

"He *is*," she said defensively.

"Then you weigh this fact with loaded words like 'unashamed.' Do you sense a pattern forming here, Suzanne?"

She looked away from him and tried to shrug.

"Are you registered to vote, Miss Hill?"

Her mouth fell open. "Of course."

"How, may I ask, are you registered?"

She glared. "That's personal."

Aaronson laughed. "That's all right. You don't have to tell me. I already know."

"You might be surprised," she snapped.

"You're registered as an independent, Miss Hill."

She gasped. "How did—"

"Because you'd die before stooping to the cheap device of registering Republican, and to register as a Democrat would be a dead giveaway, don't you think? By registering as an independent, you give the impression that you have chosen your position in exactly the middle of the road, therefore making you an unbiased journalist."

Susan opened her mouth but was unable to speak.

Aaronson waved his hand. "Save it, Miss Hill. You can't hide your bias under a label. I'll let you in on a political secret. Like it or not, in the future we'll see even more Republican presidents, and they'll all survive young, naïve, and idealistic journalists like you. Now do you understand what I mean by 'attitude' and 'chip on your shoulder'?

"Suzanne, when you signed on to take this internship, you told me that you wanted to pursue a career in investigative journalism. Does this still hold true, or have I put too much fear of God into you?"

"I still want to do it," she said, adding weakly: ". . . In spite of you."

He chuckled. "Suppose you were digging a ditch, Miss Hill. Would your political orientation influence what kind of ditch you were supposed to dig?"

She shook her head.

"If you were flying an airplane, would your voter-registration card determine which destinations you choose?"

"No," she said softly.

"Very well. Then why should this job that you're seeking so earnestly be any different from any other vocation? Why should your political affiliation make a difference?"

"It doesn't," she said.

Aaronson slammed his hand down onto her stories and crumpled them in one swift motion. "Then how can you sit at your terminal down in the bullpen and let your bias creep into your stories? Forget what all of your heroes in the world of real reporting are doing. Forget about the bad examples that the American media has set for you. If you're an investigative journalist, Suzanne, what is the one thing over all that you should be interested in finding out? The one thing, over all other things, that is the most sacred of all?"

She sat there, frozen. There was a huge lump in her throat that she couldn't swallow.

"The *truth*, Suzanne!" he thundered. "The truth! And it doesn't matter whether it will bring down your favorite president or elevate him to the status of King of All He Surveys. With your nose and your pencil, you're digging for the truth. And Republican or Democrat doesn't matter. Shouldn't matter. *Can't* matter.

"Understand, Suzanne, that I couldn't care less about how you are registered. Go Communist. Go Fascist. Go New Age Transcendentalist for all I care. Just don't lose sight of that one precious thing. The truth."

"But isn't the truth a relative thing, Mr. Aaronson?"

Aaronson rolled his eyes and threw his hands into the air. "Heaven help me, you've been reading the work of those young turks, haven't you?"

"But it is, isn't it? Look at how things have changed, even so history itself is relative. Take Columbus, and how he was once held in regard as a hero, and now—"

"Don't start with him!" Aaronson growled. "What has happened to him is a symptom, not a cure."

"But that's my point, Mr. Aaronson. There are degrees of truth, and a journalist merely sorts the truths surrounding an incident. When that is done, and the key truths are published, a clearly visible picture emerges. Is that what you call a bias?"

"As a matter of fact, I *do* call it a bias," Aaronson said.

"But it's a necessary evil of the profession. Don't you see?" She stopped, out of breath. The room was silent save for the clock's announcement of the quarter hour.

"If it's an evil," Aaronson said finally, "then it most emphatically is *not* necessary."

Susan rolled her eyes. "Jesus, sir—"

"Watch your mouth!" Aaronson said sharply, pointing two fingers at her. "The gang in the bullpen might talk like that, but you never know who you're going to offend using language like that in the course of an interview. Be careful where you talk like that, I'd recommend not using language like that at all. It's too easy to slip."

She flushed red and looked down. "Yes, sir."

"You need to learn the value of the truth, Suzanne, so I'm taking you off of the life-style assignment."

"You are?" She tried not to sound too excited. There was no telling where she was going to end up.

"You're going to be working with me from now on."

Despite the fact that she had been duly chastised by the man, her heart leaped.

"But you still owe Julia the Bizzy Beaver story."

"Yes, sir!" She held back a grin.

"Now that you've had your share of crow, it's time for some red meat." Aaronson reached across his desk to the in basket and pulled out a manila file folder. He tossed it in front of her. "This may turn out to be nothing, so don't get too excited.

"Fact number one. A couple of our stringers who monitor the police scanners, reported that a mystery victim was killed on the streets the other night. The police band was alive with it, and then all of a sudden it stopped. Dead. No mention of it anywhere, and nothing in the briefing the following morning."

"Maybe it was a John Doe," Susan said.

"Then they'd be asking for our help to ID the corpse.

"Fact number two. The body was allegedly taken to George Washington University Hospital; but again, nothing was reported during the routine briefings.

"Fact number three. It has been leaked to us that a foreign national may have been killed at a time which coincides with this alleged homicide. There are no further details available, other than a report that the case was given to someone on the vice squad, and the body was marked for special treatment by the police.

"Fact number four. We've received an anonymous tip from the hospital that a body has disappeared from the morgue. The circumstances of this body's arrival were rather unusual. It was a DOA that went into the ER rather than the morgue, on police orders. Just a cursory examination was made—no autopsy. It was sent to the hospital morgue with orders not to touch it until further notice was given."

"Je—" Susan looked at Aaronson. "Gee whiz!"

"These may be four separate threads, Suzanne. They may not amount to anything. Or they could weave an intriguing little story."

Susan swallowed. "It's already a story, sir. That body belonged to someone. It had to have a mother or father. There's a reason why it's missing. If I find the body, I'll find the story."

"Very good, Miss Hill," Aaronson smiled. "Very good. Now just remember the one golden thing you're after."

"The truth," she said.

"Yes. Whole and unvarnished. Whether that body is Republican or Democrat. It may bring down the President. Or it may bring down your favorite rock-and-roll idol. It doesn't matter. I want the facts as they are—not as someone might want you to believe they are."

"Yes, sir." She rose from the chair, file in her hands, and started for the door.

"Oh, and Suzanne—"

"Yes, Mr. Aaronson?"

"Be honest with yourself. When you get the chance, change your voter registration to your true party affiliation."

She smiled broadly. "I'll do that, Mr. Aaronson. I will." And then she turned and vanished down the hall, with the speed and conviction of someone on a mission from God.

HARRY LAUTER

The key was finding the right place to testify.

On one street corner, they would let you stay as long as you liked. But across the street from that same corner, you might be chased off by yuppies or hooligans or even the D.C. Police.

Too close to the White House, and they would think your cause was political and ignore you.

Too far away, and they would think you were a religious nut and ignore you.

Harry Lauter had found what he considered the perfect place. It was near the Lincoln Memorial, with a view of the Washington Monument and reflecting pool. Not so close that he'd be chased off by the park police, but close enough that visitors to the monuments still had their mind on God and his blessings as they walked by.

Honest Abe. He had a way of making people think about how blessed they were. And Harry was determined to capitalize on that feeling.

In the beginning, he had carried a small plastic milk crate on which to stand, in order to put himself above the passing crowds. It was a great attention-getter. People actually would tend to linger and listen to a man on a milk crate. It literally had the effect of preaching on a soapbox.

Unfortunately, a judge had told him that the difference between standing flat-footed and on a milk crate was the difference between the First Amendment and creating a public nuisance. Harry thought the judge had been persecuting him because of his message, especially when he found out this same judge had ruled for choice in abortion cases and in favor of homosexuals in gay-rights cases.

Nevertheless, Harry Lauter had been commanded to testify, and testify he would.

He stood still on the street corner, looking up into the morning sky. The sun was warm on his face. It was a beautiful day for delivering the message—the first really nice day since winter had broken.

Yes, this would do quite nicely, he thought. Then he filled his lungs with Washington's exhaust-choked air and began to testify.

"My dear friends, brothers and sisters, you've seen the message on TV, you've heard the message on radio, and you've read it in the papers. You've heard a lot of people talking about the message of late, and you're going to hear a lot more about it before this century ends. Well, I want you to open your ears and your hearts to me once more. I want to challenge everything you believe in and I want to challenge everything you've been taught in Sunday school. I even want to challenge what you *never* learned from your parents. I want to challenge the things that maybe you should have learned. And I want to warn you that things are not quite what they seem to be."

He looked around for a moment. So far, nobody had stopped—nothing but a few curious looks. But people were hearing him, were listening to what he was saying. He could tell by the way their gaits changed when he spoke. It wasn't just the let's-hurry-up-and-avoid-the-crazy-preacher step he was seeing. It was the slow-down-look-busy-don't-act-like-you're-listening step.

That made all the difference in the world.

"What is the message? I'll tell you, my friends. A lot of my self-proclaimed brethren on TV are telling you that, come the change of the century, come the year 2000, our Lord and God is going to close up the factory and go home. They're telling you that at midnight on the morning of January One, 2000, Jesus, King of Mercy, is going to appear in the sky on his sacred white stallion, his sword of justice in one hand and a scroll of mercy in the other. They're telling you that he's going to separate us like wheat and chaff. And they're saying that this will all come to pass because the year 2000 is when God has set the alarm on his great clock. And that two thousand years of sin and suffering is all he's going to let us sit through; that there will be no evening show, just this matinee of misery.

"My friends, my brothers, my sisters, I'm here to challenge and warn you about all of that! I'm here to tell you that the time is nigh and that the time is *not* nigh! I'm here to bring you a truth that nearly cost my life!"

He had a small handful of people around him now. A heavyset black woman glared at him and said, "How dare you tell me that my King Jesus ain't comin' back for me!"

Harry smiled at her broadly and sincerely. "But my dear lady, Jesus *is* coming back for you!"

"But you just said—"

"What I'm saying, my dear lady, my dear friends, is that you don't want to bet your soul on the timetable of man! God has his own clock, and if you read in your Bible, you'll see that not even his sacred Son knows the day and the hour of his return. I'm saying that if our Lord and Heavenly Father were going to return for us after two thousand years, he would have been here already!"

"Say what?" someone challenged.

"Look it up in your history books," Harry told them. "Roman history. A devout man of God devised a calendar which began at the year of our blessed Savior's birth! And while he worked at it diligently, he was only human, and what human has not been in error? So when he determined the date of our Lord's birth, he missed it by four years!"

People were gathering now. Some tried to look skeptical. After all, they were standing and listening to a street-corner preacher. But the key to it was that *they were listening*!

"So what you're tellin' me, preacher," said the woman, "is that Jesus ain't comin' 'til 2004?"

Harry smiled and took her by the shoulders. "No, no, no, my dear woman! I'm saying that the Lord has been here, come and gone! That poor monk posted the birth of Jesus Christ four years too late! So God's great alarm clock would have wakened him in *1996*!"

"If the Lord's done been and gone," the woman said, "then how come we're still here? How come the sun still comes up every morning?"

"That is my point exactly." Harry beamed. "The Lord is still with us, and I'm sure he's having a good laugh over the foolishness that's being proclaimed in his name over the waves of our televisions and radios."

"Then when is he coming?"

"Five minutes from now."

There was a laugh of disbelief from the crowd.

"Tomorrow afternoon."

The sound began to rise.

"Or a hundred years from now. Go home to your Bible and look it up, my dear woman. No man knows the day and the hour of our Lord's return. It is a secret that even the angels in heaven long to know. That's why we've got to live each day, each minute of our lives for him! Because the world is still running, and at any moment God may punch the clock and demand payment. Don't set your watches by the faulty estimates of man, my friends! We are imperfect timekeepers against the perfection of God's universe."

Harry looked around. A primary crowd of about a dozen had congealed around him by now. There was a secondary layer of lingerers beyond that, and a third layer of people passing by who slowed as they neared, to hear what was going on. Transition time, he told himself. Time to take this goodwill you've earned and get out the message.

"And friends," he continued. "Brothers. Sisters. As surely as the entire, vast universe is God's singular creation, so there are many incredible and wonderful elements of his creation that we have not yet seen. Things that will be revealed to us in the twinkling of an eye, as surely as God's return, yet on a schedule known only to him.

"And *that*—*that* is what I am here to proclaim to you today, on this fine morning of God's creation! I have devoted half of my life to the pursuit of God's word, God's truth, God's wisdom, and from my travels I have brought back riches that make those of this world pale by comparison!

"Dear friends, I have crossed a thousand miles through shifting, burning sands on the strength of my own two feet. I have traveled the outback of the Holy Lands on the back of a donkey. I have eaten the food of the infidels and ridden their camels through the nations of the Middle East. And these nations have made me pay for what I have learned.

"My friends, what I have learned so angered the Turks that I was imprisoned and beaten on the soles of my feet. I suffered electrical shocks to the most private places of my body at the hands of the Iraqis. I was drugged and interrogated by agents of Israel's Mossad. In each case, all of them wanted to suppress the truth I had found. And, in each case, the hand of the Lord reached down and covered me, so that I might bring this truth to you!"

Harry stopped for a moment to catch his breath. The torture talk always got their attention. In the few short seconds it took to describe it, the crowd had doubled.

"What is it?" cried the black woman. "What have you come to tell us?"

Harry smiled benignly.

"I am here to tell you that the agents of the Lord are coming here to watch our lives and test our faith. And they may even be among us now!"

"Alleluia!" cried the woman.

"*Angels?*" another asked.

"No," said Harry, lowering his voice to a confidential tone. "My friends, I have seen things that the governments of the world do not want you to see. I have seen the scrolls of old, brought up from beneath the sandstone flats of the Dead Sea valley, preserved in dark, dry caves since the times of antiquity, their messages clearly defined in ancient Aramaic, a message of hope and warning given to us by prophets whose bones have long since turned to dust."

"And what do they say? What do they say, my brother?"

"They say that God's messengers are coming! My friends, they may already be here among us! They are not angel nor cherubim nor seraphim, but are nonetheless of God's magnificent creation! Be there any among you who are so jaded and selfish as to believe that our Father created this great, vast, infinite universe solely to confound us? Do you believe that he is a practical joker of profound proportions?"

"No!" cried the woman. "He is a god of love!"

"That's right!" Harry shouted. "Listen to the woman, my brothers and sisters, for she knows and understands the true nature of God. And I'm here to tell you that while great, impassable gulfs separate the stars, it is only because our great and magnificent Lord intended to keep his individual creations separate! Yes, he did!"

The woman closed her eyes and raised a hand into the air. "Yes, yes," she murmured hypnotically. "That's right, Lord. Thank you, Jesus."

"And I'm here to tell you, dear friends, that those of God's creation who have met with his favor have been given gifts beyond our wildest imagining! They can span the distance! They can travel the stars and reach other galaxies! They can close the infinite gulf until it is meaningless!"

There was a skeptical snort from the back. "More of that *Star Trek* nonsense." A tall figure turned and walked away, joined by two others.

"My friends," Harry said, raising his voice more to keep the others from leaving, "they travel on beams of light from place to place doing his will! And they are coming here, my friends, to watch us, to judge us, and to work with us if we are found worthy! And if we are found to be so worthy, they will share with us the bountiful harvest of God's love and creation!"

"Praise be to King Jesus!" the woman exulted.

"What will they bring us?" asked a goggle-eyed teen in thick glasses.

"The most precious thing God has given us. *Knowledge!*"

"Will we be able to go to Mars?"

"My brother! Mars, Jupiter, the Pleides, Andromeda—"

"Are they superior beings?" came another voice from the back.

"Not spiritually, my friends, for there we are all equal in the eyes of the Lord. But they have been granted technological gifts the likes of which we cannot begin to imagine."

"Will they have pointed heads like you?" a voice shouted.

There were hoots of laughter, and the crowd began to disperse.

Harry bit his lip. He was tempted to cry out and beg them to stop. Instead he pointed, moving his outstretched finger in a wide arc across them.

"Scorn and derision!" he shouted. "The weapons of Satan, who seeks to keep us from our destiny of ultimate enlightenment! But, my brothers and sisters, you must not fall into these evil snares! We must abase ourselves—

"We must do our God's will and fulfill our cosmic destiny! We must stand up like the grand creation we are and take our rightful place in the galactic scheme of things!"

The woman who had been echoing him opened her eyes and lowered her hand, ending her reverie. "What you say?"

"We must lift ourselves up into a greater phase of being. By evolving, ourselves, we will receive what has been promised us and will become—"

The woman began wagging her finger at him.

"Shame on you!" she hissed. "You go addin' to the Word of the Lord with that New Age stuff and nothin' gonna save you from the lightning that's gonna come out of the sky and burn you down! Nobody who adds to the Word of the Lord gonna live to tell about it!" With a snort, she turned and began to walk away, taking more of the precious thinning crowd with her.

"But this is what your government wants you to think! This is how they want you to act!"

"Render unto Caesar," the woman snapped without turning around.

"This is forbidden knowledge," Harry shouted in protest. "I was tortured by the Arabs. I was drugged by the Israelis. I was jailed by our own government. But they couldn't stop me because they can't stop the intransmutable will of God!"

Harry turned. He was alone now. "I walked a thousand miles through the shifting, burning sand. I went to Jerusalem on the back of an ass—"

He stopped suddenly. A man was standing there, staring at him, dressed in doctor's greens that hung loosely from his slight frame.

"You were back to the part about the camels."

Harry nodded, trying not to stare. "I ate with the infidels, too." With a shrug, he added, "It was like a big barbecue."

"Your heart is not in this," the man said.

"Tortured. Beaten. Drugged. Imprisoned. All for a bunch of ingrates."

"You must continue," said the man.

"Why," Harry asked, his shoulders slumping. "You yourself said that I'd come full circle."

The man raised his hands to indicate the passing crowds. "They need to be told."

"I've told them. They don't listen."

"I know," the man said. "I truly know."

The preacher's eyes narrowed. "What do you mean by that?"

"I mean that you are right. What you have seen is truthful and accurate. Try to remember the feeling, the burning in the breast you felt when you first read the words and understood what they were saying to you. Reach down. Deep in. It is there, somewhere. Something that the beatings and the drugs and the shocks could not take out of you."

Harry blinked. His eyes were gritty and burned. "How do you know what I saw?"

The man stared into his eyes. "I am one of whom you speak," he said. "I have sought an audience with your esteemed leader. I brought a message of great importance. I was turned away. Now I wait."

"For what?"

"Judgment."

Harry paused and licked his lips. "Listen, friend, I appreciate what you're trying to do, but you're just heaping coals on the head of a tired old man who everyone thinks has had the sense burned out of him."

Harry shrugged his shoulders and rolled his eyes. "Good-bye," he said.

The man looked around. "But I'm not going anywhere."

"Then I am." With an air of finality, Harry spun on his heel and stalked off. He needed to give this up once and for all. The government agents were finally leaving him alone, but it just wasn't worth it. The intimidation and disinformation that had been invoked against anything sounding even vaguely ... *extraterrestrial* ... had been effective. Nowadays, the only people who listened were the types who never missed an issue of *Weekly World News* and asked him questions about Elvis Presley. It didn't matter how biblical he made it sound. Perhaps that was the wrong approach, but he had seen the scrolls with his own eyes, translated their message out of the original Aramaic. He couldn't be wrong. He just couldn't.

Harry stopped at a water fountain and wet his lips. From the corner of his eye, he caught a glimpse of the man in green. He hadn't moved from the spot and was looking around, turning slowly, watching the tourists.

Then, slowly, he raised his arms and opened his mouth. The people passing around him slowed to listen briefly before hurrying on their way.

Harry watched in fascination as the man failed to draw a crowd, thinking that it took all kinds to make the world.

And then he thought again, *no*. That wasn't the case. In this case, it took all kinds to *end* the world.

Shaking his head, Harry Lauter started on the long walk home.

GHOST

Ghost sat on his bed, his fists clenched and teeth grinding.

Twelve bucks.

That was all the old man at the pawnshop would give him for the aluminum suit. He'd rubbed the fabric with his fingers, stretched it and snapped it. But, in the end, he had shaken his head and said that it was nothing more than a weird Halloween costume.

"Fifteen dollars."

"Fifteen? Hey, it's worth a hundred if it's worth a dime."

"Fourteen," the man said.

The belt buckle felt heavy in Ghost's pocket. He ignored it. "Don't you play games with me, old man. I'll go easy on you since my old lady's sick and I got to have the money for some penicillin. I'll take fifty."

"Thirteen."

Ghost threw his hands into the air in exasperation. "All right. All right. Fifteen bucks it is."

"Twelve," said the man. "Providing it isn't hot."

The rock shifted as if under its own power.

"Hot? A Halloween suit? You jiving me, man?" Ghost had said as he accepted a ten and two ones from the man.

"Anything else for me today?"

His hand went to his pocket, to the rock, and he scooped it into the palm of his hand.

Twelve bucks for the suit. What would the rock bring? Three? Five? He could guess what the old man would say. *Well, it looks like something shined up in a kid's rock polisher. Five bucks, my top offer.*

It hardly seemed worth it. Besides, when it came right down to it, he didn't want to get rid of the rock. It was too . . .

Too what?

Ghost reached into his pocket and pulled it out, rolled it into the palm of his hand. He let it sit, waiting for the change. It began to grow warm, warmer than when it rode in his pocket. Then it grew slick in his palm and began to shine, as if the surface had become liquid.

He reached out with a fingernail and tapped it. It was solid.

Fascinating.

No, this was worth more than five dollars. It was something like nothing he'd ever seen, nothing he'd ever felt. He thought maybe he should take it to a jeweler or a geologist. The man he had killed had been weird. Maybe he was a foreigner. Isn't that what Amos had said? But then, that was Amos's game, wasn't it, the kind that he was so good at playing in order to get someone to confess or blab something that was supposed to be a secret?

Or maybe this time Amos was telling the truth, and

the government would get on his butt because this foreigner had some kind of special rock that they were interested in.

He tapped the rock again and listened to his fingernail clicking on its surface.

Well, if it was something special, the last thing he wanted to do was start showing it around. What he wanted to do was . . .

Hide it. Hide it deep in a secret pocket, somewhere that only you know about. And don't tell a soul about it . . .

Ghost shivered and stood. What was wrong with him? Here he was, alone in his room, but worried sick that someone was going to catch him and nail him to the wall.

He gripped his hand tightly around the rock and imagined throwing it into the middle of the Potomac River. As he did, he heard the click of the front door. His hand sought his pocket, and the strange rock fell inside.

"Kit?"

Ghost rolled his eyes and cringed.

"You home, Kit?"

A small, dark girl appeared in the doorway, hair in cornrows, her face puffy, her clothes faded and baggy. Not even three months along, and she was already wearing maternity clothes. Trying to make a point with him. Her condition had made her crazy, like it did all women, and this was her way of sending him a message.

Well, he had a message for her. She would be out the door when the sex stopped or the kid came, whichever came first.

"You all right?" she asked.

" 'lo, Heidi," he nodded.

"Amos came into the shop this morning. Said he was worried about you. Said he thought maybe you was sick, or maybe you got into some bad stuff and was goin' a little crazy."

"He knows I don't do it," Ghost said.

"He catch you sellin', you goin' away."

Ghost turned to face her. That didn't help. Her jaw was set and there was fire in her eyes.

Marriage. That's what she wanted. That was what they all wanted, eventually.

As if drawn by a magnet, his hand sank into his pocket and scooped up the stone. His thumb mashed the surface.

"Kit, I been meanin' to talk to you about something. I think you know what it's about."

"Don't call me that name," Ghost mumbled. "You know what I want you to call me."

"You changin' the subject again," she said flatly.

"Don't start with me, girl."

Heidi put her hand to her temple and swayed, as if something had suddenly given her a headache. "You got an obligation we need to talk about."

"You heard my obligation. I give you money, you go to the doctor. End of discussion." Ghost's hand reached back into his pocket, seeking the comfort of the stone's smoothness.

"But Kit—"

"But nothing," he shouted, finger cradling the rock as if he was pulling a trigger. "I tole you a thousand times you be callin' me Ghost."

Heidi's tone went flat again. "Ghost."

He whirled to face her. She had never, *ever* called him Ghost. That had been the one sore point between them. She had insisted that using a street name was make-believe, like little boys with sticks playing army. He stared at the blank expression on her face and wondered what she was up to.

"Say it again."

"Ghost."

"Again."

"Ghost."

He turned away from her. This was a trick. It had to be. Without turning back, he said, "Tell me the truth now, woman. What you want to talk about?"

"I got this baby inside of me, Ghost. It's yours. You need to be a father to this baby. I need you to be a husband. We need to raise this baby together, Ghost."

The words made his face burn. He clenched the rock hard in his fist. How dare she challenge him, confront him in that dead tone of hers?

Time to fix it for good. One well-placed sentence, and she would be all over him, screaming, yelling, cursing. Then he'd do it. The fist. Once. Twice. Maybe three times. He'd make sure he broke her jaw.

"Girl, you want me to marry you?"

"Yes, Ghost."

"You think you'll make me a good wife?"

"Yes, Ghost. I think you're smart—too smart to be hustlin'. You could do better than the street."

The rock gave weight to his fist. Ghost relished the coming violence. "Let's see what kind of wife you'll make." Then he said it—the one thing that would flip her out, drive her crazy. "Get yo' butt in that kitchen and do my dishes."

His fist, his arm, his shoulder tightened. He heard her move. He spun quickly, cocking for the first blow.

She was gone.

Breath jumped out of his lungs as if he'd been kicked in the solar plexus.

"Heidi?" He said it so softly that he could barely hear himself.

Then, from the kitchen came the sound of running water.

No. It was impossible.

His arm still ready to strike, he eased out of the bedroom and through the small living room. A rattling came from the kitchen. Another few steps, and he could see her, not lying in wait with a greasy skillet, but obediently stacking dishes into a sink that was filling with steaming water.

"Heidi," Ghost said from the kitchen entrance, "what you think you doin'?"

"Dishes," she said flatly.

"Why?"

"You told me to."

He wanted to hit her anyway, right then and there, for doing this to him, for trying to humiliate him this way. But there was something about her voice and the way that she was going about her work that told him that something was wrong.

She was doing it, but it was almost like she was . . . *fighting it*. Her motions were sloppy, jerky, almost like—

A puppet on a string.

Ghost shivered. "Heidi. Stop."

She stopped.

"Put down what you're doing."

She put the dish in her hand into the sink.

"Turn around."

She turned around.

Let's see, he thought. *Let's see what's going on in that little mind of hers.*

Ghost gave her one more command. And it wasn't until she was kneeling on the floor in front of him that he lowered his arm and realized that he was unable to take his eyes off that smooth, slick, electric rock.

MAX KIERNAN

Max Kiernan sat at his desk, hand on a coffee mug which bore the words SUPPORT MENTAL HEALTH

OR I'LL KILL YOU. He stared at the headlines which were pinned to a cork-covered wall in his office. SPACE ALIENS RESPONSIBLE FOR ATLANTIS SHUTTLE DISASTER, said one. THE TRUTH ABOUT MARS: WHAT THE CIA DOESN'T WANT YOU TO KNOW, heralded another. A third revealed: "2001" MONOLITH MAY BE A REALITY, NEW LUNAR SURVEY SAYS—*HOW MUCH DID AUTHOR CLARKE REALLY KNOW?*

The board was cluttered with blurry photographs of strange colored lights half-hidden by clouds and cattle lying dead on the ground. Other photos were of scorch marks in fields of still-green barley, and there were pencil sketches of strange, thin, emaciated-looking shapes with large dark eyes. There were schedules and records of movements of various individuals. And in the center was a map of the United States, riddled with colored pins. Some rural areas had been pinned so many times that the map surface had turned into confetti.

Kiernan smiled and sipped his coffee. If someone had told him twenty years ago that he would make his living collecting and analyzing such nonsense, he would have laughed. And if they had told him that his work would have the full funding of the United States government, he would have turned hysterical.

Still, here he was, head of a government agency that didn't officially exist. One so secret that it didn't even have a name. One that handled matters so sensitive that, when asked about his profession, he was compelled by law to lie and say that he worked for the CIA.

He wouldn't have believed any of it, none of it at all, if he hadn't seen the frozen corpses in Dayton. Only one had been left more-or-less intact. The others had all been sliced and diced in the decades since their recovery in New Mexico.

Even then, he might still have denied the reality of it all had it not been for his mother's note.

As if hypnotized, Kiernan stood and walked to the cork wall. At one end was an old photograph of a woman who had been classically beautiful for her time. Married in '58. Pregnant by the end of '59. Chronically depressed by '64 because of her inability to conceive any more children. Dead in '71. A ten-year-old Max had found her and the note she had left. Even then, he knew the words did not make any sense. So he had hidden the note away, pulling it out from time to time and studying it carefully, trying to understand what had happened.

The search had brought him here. The understanding still eluded him; but with each passing year, with each new headline or photograph, he felt closer to it.

Someday he would know for sure.

There was a knock at the door that shook Kiernan out of his reverie. "Yeah," he growled. The door opened to reveal Kevin Wrampe, Kiernan's second-in-command and acting secretary. There were no official secretaries here because the fewer security clearances, the better. It meant typing their own memos and answering their own phones, but they made it work.

"I'm sorry," Wrampe said. "If you're busy, this can wait."

"What do you want?" Kiernan asked.

Wrampe held up a Federal Express envelope. "We just got in the latest from Gallagher. I thought you'd want to take a look."

Kiernan strode across the office in three quick steps and took the package from Wrampe, thanking him with a nod. Wrampe walked out, closing the door behind him.

Kiernan slit the envelope open and pulled out a tabloid-sized magazine, folded in half, with a piece of goldenrod-colored paper clipped to it. The page was half of what had once been a garage-sale flyer. On the blank side was written:

Boss—

All's going well. Nothing new on this end. Couple of leads, but they turned out to be soaked in moonshine. Or old 60's acid casualties.

My latest work enclosed. Think you'll be amused. Got the front page this time! I'm as proud of it as I can be, under the circumstances.

Best to the gang.

—C.G.

Kiernan read the note without emotion then set it aside, pulling the clip off of the magazine and opening it. It was the latest edition of the *Weekly World News*. The headline read JOHN LENNON KIDNAPPED BY UFOS! Below it was a picture of an emaciated man with stringy hair, a beak of a nose, and round-lensed wire-rim glasses. Gallagher had attached a yellow sticky note to it which read: *This guy's a house painter in Tuscaloosa (SP?), Alabama. Got him to pose for $50 and a bottle of JD.* Next to the picture was a smaller headline. ALIENS PICKED UP PEACE VISIONARY AFTER "FATAL" SHOOTING TO BECOME OUR FIRST GALACTIC AMBASSADOR.

Kiernan flipped through the magazine looking for the story. On his way through, he found another sticky note. *This one's mine, too. Could you tell?*

The headline read, HALLEY'S COMET REALLY AN ALIEN SPACE PROBE, PROMINENT NASA SCIENTIST SAYS.

One side of Kiernan's lip turned up into a smile.

Gallagher was having a good time with his job. Kiernan was proud of himself for singling him out for the position, prouder still for having come up with the idea of infiltrating the magazine in the first place.

Where else would Mr. or Mrs. Six-pack go to tell their story of having been abducted by an alien? A UFO magazine? Certainly not. They were run by head cases. The government? Hatred and distrust of the government was at an all-time high. One of the news magazines? The disinformation campaign had been so successful that legitimate news bureaus wouldn't take them seriously.

That left one outlet: one that was known to pay big money for such sordid tales.

Chris Gallagher sorted through the stories that came across his desk in Lantana, Florida. Field agents, posing as reporters, would check out the story, pay the people for permanent exclusive rights, and promise to tell the story "if there was room."

Of course, the story would never see the light of day. Instead, Gallagher would create cheap fiction from it and run it as a true account of a UFO phenomenon.

What a great world this was!

There was another knock at the door, and Wrampe stuck his head in again.

"Brickell's here to report in," he said. "Should I take it, or do you want to see him?"

Kiernan looked up from the tabloid. "Send him in." Wrampe started to disappear, but Kiernan barked him back. "Do me a favor. Send a message down to Gallagher. Tell him he's doing a great job, but to ease up a little 2on his stories. Theyre getting a little *too* crazy."

Wrampe shrugged. "How can you tell?" And then quickly appended, "I'll pass it along." He darted out the door and in a moment, Brickell bounded in, a wide fullback of a man with a high forehead and a toothy smile.

He didn't expect any formalities, and Kiernan didn't extend any.

Brickell eased down in the bigger of the two plush chairs in front of Kiernan's desk and pulled a Churchill-sized Cuban cigar from his breast pocket. He bit off the end and with his tongue, shoved it between his cheek and gum, then pulled a lighter from the pocket of his sport coat. He looked up at Kiernan, thought better of the ritual and replaced the lighter quickly without firing it. He chewed the end of the cigar instead.

Brickell stared for a moment, then said, "You're going to make me talk first, aren't you?"

"What have you got for me?" demanded Kiernan.

Brickell rolled the cigar between his lips with his thumb and forefinger. "What makes you think I have something for you?"

"If you didn't, you'd send me a carbon of your movements."

"Fenton and I have spent the last week tracing the Preacher's movements. He's keeping close to Washington, just like last week, and the week before. I think he's planning on staying."

"All right. What else?"

"He's smart. He's got a tie-in from the Bible to draw crowds. Which it's getting easier for him to do. All this millennial nonsense. With the end of the century getting closer, people are starting to think more about the world coming to an end. The latest sunspot activity hasn't helped. The aurora borealis was seen as far south as northern New Mexico last week. People think it's another sign from God."

"Tell me something I don't know."

"He gets into his sermon and then slowly switches into his New Age mode. Some people catch on, but the thing is, more and more people are starting to stick around after they figure out that he's talking about

ETs. Either the parks are filling up with kooks, or something's got them spooked."

"Or," grumped Kiernan, "we're evolving into a society with a hive mentality."

"It's still easy to let the air out of his sails by heckling him. You get in a few good shots, and some of the people leave. He sees people leaving and starts losing his nerve and his will to keep talking. He gets discouraged and doesn't realize that more and more people are staying to hear what he has to say.

"Yesterday, he was really hard core. He was talking about how he'd been tortured and beaten by the Arabs and the Israelis."

"Now," said Kiernan, "you're getting to the point."

"Fenton's on him today. I called on contacts in a couple agencies and did some research. Our friend may not have been tortured by every country in the Middle East, as he claims, but he's been arrested by most of them."

"Elaborate," Kiernan said.

Brickell reached inside his sport coat and pulled out a small pad. "Israel arrested him for proselytizing in public, then suddenly let him go but put him on the first plane out. His passport says he was on an archaeological expedition."

Brickell turned over a page in his notebook. "The Iranians picked him up because they said he worked for the CIA. The Iraqis threw him out because he was an Israeli spy. The Saudis accused him of posing as a Muslim so he could slip into Mecca. Egypt suspected he was an antiquities smuggler. The Turks claimed he was trying to buy hashish in bulk. The Lebanese—" Brickell stopped to laugh. "The Lebanese said he was trying to find his way into the homosexual underground to seek out some forbidden aphrodisiacs."

"Your opinion?"

"This guy's not a very welcome person in the Middle

East. He seems to make people nervous over there. It's possible some of them did give him the once-over."

"If he's that annoying, why wouldn't they just kill him?" Kiernan asked.

"Fenton and I speculated on that," Brickell replied.

"And you concluded that he had some hold on them, something that made them let him go."

"The scrolls, maybe."

"But don't the Israelis control the scrolls?"

"Boss, you know that ancient scrolls and parchments have been found all over the Middle East."

"The question is, what scrolls is he talking about?"

"I'll bet he's got copies—copies of something," Brickell said. "Somehow he got copies. Microfilm, something. He smuggled them out. He has some kind of arrangement so if he doesn't come back, they get splashed all over the place. For some reason, the Arabs and Israelis alike have a vested interest in his staying alive."

"So what's his game?"

Brickell shook his head. "That's where we're stuck. Too many things don't make sense. If he's got something, why is he preaching on the street? Why is he doing all of this millennial doom-and-gloom stuff?"

Kiernan shifted in his seat. "He might have part of something. Enough to make, say, the Israelis nervous. He may be here, posturing, trying to get enough clout to go back in and pick up the missing pieces."

Brickell placed the cigar between the palms of his hands and rolled it up and down. "All because of some scribbling on a goatskin."

"That the Israelis don't want anyone to know about."

"Why?"

"You tell me," Kiernan said.

"Maybe they just want to see them first? If it's something buried in their territory, they're going to have sovereignty over them as a national treasure."

"Or," said Kiernan, "their contents could seriously challenge the history and heritage of the Jewish nation."

"What could possibly do that?" Brickell asked.

"Think about it," Kiernan said. "Why are we interested in this guy?"

"Because he said the magic word. Extraterrestrial."

"Remember the biblical prophet Elijah?" Kiernan asked.

Brickell shook his head. "I barely remember Noah and the ark."

"This is one scripture you may want to become familiar with. Elijah was taken up to heaven in what is described as a 'chariot of fire' that came down in a whirlwind. As you might guess, some New Agers have put their own twist to that story. They claim that Elijah was abducted by aliens."

Brickell clucked his tongue. "Maybe I better start reading the Bible."

Kiernan continued. "Now, let's take this one step further. If God could take people away in a space chariot, then what's to say that he didn't bring people here the same way. Like Adam and Eve."

Brickell nodded. "We need to know what Harry Lauter has found."

"You and Fenton work on it," Kiernan said. "But be careful. You make the wrong move, and you'll have the Mossad on your tail so fast you won't believe it."

"Here?" Brickell said in disbelief. "In Washington?"

"The Israelis have spied on us," Kiernan said matter-of-factly. "When the Soviets were still around, the Israelis traded our secrets to them in the interests of maintaining their own national security. They've attacked our ships. If they thought you and your partner were stepping on their sovereignty, they wouldn't hesitate to make wet work out of you.

"Where we're concerned, we don't care about the

current state of the Middle East or what the politics of these scrolls are. All we care about is content. So proceed. With care. If you think you're starting to be shadowed by someone, try to get in touch with me. I'll keep you from ending up on the bottom of the Potomac."

"You've got it." Brickell rose from the chair. "I'll be in touch."

Kiernan immediately refocused his attention on the tabloid.

"By the way," Brickell asked, "what's the latest from Gallagher?"

"John Lennon lives." Kiernan smiled.

"Rock and roll," Brickell said and started for the door.

"Brickell," Kiernan called before the agent was out the door, "the disappearance of the body from George Washington U. Is that anything we should be looking into?"

Brickell shook his head. "To be honest, we don't know. Word has it that there was a foreign national involved. The CIA must have thought it was someone special because they beat us to the hospital. Didn't leave us with so much as a matchbook to work with."

"Figures," Kiernan said. "And the way they are with records, we'll never get to see them, either. Unless . . ."

"Unless?"

"Unless I make a couple of phone calls," Kiernan said.

SERENA BLAKE

Wake up, time to die.

The words resonated, throbbing along with the pain in her head.

They were appropriate, but where had they come from? There was a cloudy memory in her mind, of a few beers with some of her friends; of then sitting in the back of a theater with a boy who was all hands. She was woozy from the beer and disgusted by the violence on the screen. Her distraction had let him get his hands on her breasts. She had stopped him with a roundhouse slap. He got up and left, but returned later with a box of Junior Mints. She turned to the screen and watched as Harrison Ford was threatened by the aliens he had been sent to kill.

One of them had said, "Wake up, time to die."

That had been years ago. Probably half of her lifetime ago. She had liked the phrase and had remembered it. But it was pushed out of her mind by more pressing things.

Until college. Until the booze and the drugs and the hangovers.

Wake up, time to die.

Now the phrase haunted her and taunted her on mornings like this when sleep was the preferred refuge from the reality of morning; when suicide was more appealing than dragging oneself out of bed.

Suicide. Now, there was a fascinating thought. You could use a gun and get it over with fast. A razor blade or car exhaust would take a little longer. Or you could put stuff down your throat and up your nose, and it would take years.

Serena Blake almost laughed at this epiphany. Suicide wasn't a choice, it was a way of life.

She looked up at the clock on her nightstand and saw that she was two hours past the time when she should have been up. She swore bitterly and sat upright in bed. Her stomach became a fierce knot. Folding in half, she flopped back down onto the bed. Pain spasmed her belly, and her legs pulled up, drawing her into a fetal position. The motion turned her around, and she rolled unceremoniously off the bed.

Serena stayed on the floor for only a moment. The twisting and churning in her stomach told her that there wasn't time for her to wait for the room to stop spinning. Flailing her arms and legs, she found her way to her knees and managed a frantic crawl to the bathroom. She pushed the toilet lid up just as her stomach convulsed and emptied itself of the poisons that hadn't yet been digested.

The spasms finally ended, and Serena slid to the floor, her cheek resting on the cool tile. Her teeth, she thought. She had to brush her teeth to keep the stomach acid from getting to them. Women who were bulimic had bad teeth because the stomach acid being brought up constantly wore on their teeth. And she had been sick enough lately that the likelihood of her teeth going bad had become a very real concern.

In a minute. She would get up in a minute and take care of it. It felt so good there right now, there on the cool of the floor. She would just give it another minute—until the world stopped its badly skewed movement.

Her eyes popped open and her lips parted to let out a panicked moan. She had gone back to sleep, and now she had the dull ache of chill down to her very bones.

Worse yet, she saw as she struggled to her knees that even more time had passed, and she had now not only gotten up late, but she had slept past the time when she was due at work.

Serena reached over and flushed the toilet, then pulled herself up next to the sink. She ran the water cold and splashed her face, halfheartedly ran a comb through her hair, and then brushed her teeth carefully, giving ten strokes to each surface of each tooth.

There was still a tremor in her legs as she finished, but she managed to walk back to her bed, sit heavily on it, and open the drawer of her nightstand.

Until recently, her morning solace had been the generally accepted Bloody Mary. But now she went for the active ingredient, the anesthesia. She pulled the bottle of vodka from the drawer and uncapped it in a smooth motion that had become second nature. She took a long drink from the bottle. At one time the raw stuff had made her gag, but the reflex had long been subdued by the need to suppress other pains.

The liquid burned when it hit her stomach. That would be the reaction of the ulcer, but that too would stop before long.

Soon she was fortified enough to stand up without wobbling. She returned to the bathroom to rinse the vodka out of her mouth with Listerine and then palpated her nose in front of the mirror to see if she still had a septum.

She had heard that people who do a lot of coke burn out that piece of cartilage that separates the halves of their nose. Was that another of those stories or was it true? She didn't know. She did know that she hadn't had any nosebleeds yet, and she planned to quit after the first one; but she wasn't sure whether a burned-through septum would bleed or not, because wouldn't cocaine cauterize the damage as it went?

She didn't know. That had become her mantra. There were so many things she didn't know, and most of it had to do with what she was doing to herself.

Her septum felt in place, if that indeed was what she was feeling. She looked all right now, dressed and ready to face work and the world. A quick breakfast, and she could go out, find where the others were working, apologize for being late again, and get on with the business of her life.

A check of her kitchen put an end to the idea of breakfast. An egg would certainly make her vomit again. As would the bacon, the peanut butter, the cold carry-out chicken, the highly sugared breakfast cereal, and the Pop-Tarts.

She ended up with a piece of dry toast, which she carried out the door and ate on the bus to the downtown office building. On the way in, she stopped off in the ladies' room to recheck her appearance, then took the elevator to the tenth floor and a small office labeled CITIZENS WHO CARE.

The office was empty except for Tiffany, the secretary. "Everyone's gone," she said coldly.

"I know," Serena said. "Where are they today?"

"Making a survey sweep of the parks. They're probably down by the reflecting pool by now. If they're not there yet, you can probably catch them there if you wait."

"Thanks," Serena said softly.

Serena suspected that they hated her—all of them, everyone at Citizens Who Care. It was as if they hated her money, the hundred grand a year she put into the place, without which they would be as homeless as the derelicts they were trying to help. Or perhaps they hated the fact that it wasn't really her money; she got it by virtue of being born into the right family.

Or maybe it wasn't the money at all. Maybe it was what she was doing with it. Find a charity, her accountant had said. After pondering the national causes, Serena had decided to go with something local, something that was easy for her to keep tabs on. And here was this impoverished little nonprofit group trying to help the homeless by surveying and taking tests and doing research. Demographics, they called it. Find the demographics of the homeless and find out what makes them that way.

It seemed reasonable enough, and their credentials were good, so Citizens Who Care became the official charity of the Blake fortune. When Serena had told them the amount, they were overwhelmed. They offered to send her regular reports so she could see how her donations were being spent. That was fine, Serena had said, but she was also looking for something to occupy her days. Would they mind if she hit the streets and helped them with their work?

At first they were delighted. They were short on manpower, and volunteers were always at a premium, especially for an obscure project like this. One of them had joked that it was almost too good to be true; someone actually paying to work with them.

That lighthearted remark soon became a point of derision among them. She knew how they felt. Serena Blake, the young socialite with too much time on her hands, the cokehead with more money than was good for her, was trying to assuage the guilt that came with her decadent life-style. Buying her way into heaven—that's what she was trying to do.

Maybe they were right.

They didn't have to look far to get the lowdown on her lifestyle. It was all over the pages of the *Post* and the *Times*. All you had to do was look in the Lifestyle section, and you'd find a picture of her coming out of some nightclub or trendy restaurant with a young actor or some junior senator.

It didn't take them long to decide that she was too coked out to be of much help.

Well. Forget them. She could pull her money and find some other place that would be glad to have it. She'd heard about EMILY's List from some of her feminist friends, and it sounded interesting. But they were a political action group, which meant she couldn't write off the gift on her taxes. Some of her Republican friends had tried to get her involved with one of their splinter groups, but the idea of being a pro-choice Republican sounded like a contradiction in terms. In truth, she had no real convictions. Her desires were simple: making the Citizens Who Care like her and making her nights as pleasurable as possible.

The cab pulled to a stop within walking distance of the reflecting pool. She tossed the driver a twenty and told him to keep the change, then started to walk toward the Washington Monument. Strolling along one side of the pool, she finally spotted three of her colleagues sitting on a bench, passing out sandwiches from a large grocery bag.

Serena stopped for a moment, straightened the lines of her dress, then strode forward as if nothing was wrong.

"Hello," she said as soon as they made eye contact. "I'm sorry I'm late. Where did you leave off?"

"Right here," Gregory said. "We were working our way toward the monument. You can see who's not eating." He pointed his thumb at a large box at his feet. "See that they get something."

With the side of her foot, Serena moved the box away from Gregory, then leaned down and picked it up. "No sandwiches to the ones in designer suits. Right?"

She turned and walked past a clutch of people with briefcases and umbrellas, eating yogurt and drinking soup from wide-mouthed Thermoses. A group of yuppies munched on hot dogs, hunching into their London Fog jackets as the wind picked up.

There was one man by himself, sitting at the edge of the pond, staring into the water as if searching for the meaning of life. He had a three-day beard and a knitted wool cap. His arms were crossed to keep his military jacket closed.

"Excuse me, sir," she said to him.

Nothing.

"Sir . . ." She reached out and touched his shoulder. His head snapped around to look at her. His eyes were large and brown, sad and wild at the same time.

"What do you want?" he growled. Then his features softened as he saw he was speaking to a woman. "Sorry, miss. Ma'am."

"Call me Serena."

He shook his head. "You mistake me for someone else?"

"No," she replied. "I'd like to know where you live, if you don't mind."

"Right here."

"Where in Washington, sir?"

"I told you, ma'am. Right here."

Serena felt a sense of satisfaction. She still had the talent to pick them out, no matter what the other Caring Citizens said. "I want to know when you last had a good meal."

He shrugged. "Define 'good meal.'"

"Something balanced. All the major food groups." She reached into the box and pulled out one of the paper bags. "Meat, cheese, cereal, fruit. A little sugar. You like turkey bologna?"

"Ma'am, I'll take anything at this point."

She handed him the bag. "Two sandwiches with meat and lettuce," she said. "Some string cheese and an apple. Fruit juice. Oh, and something sweet. A candy bar or chocolate-chip cookies, depending on which bag you get."

The man smiled and nodded at her appreciatively. Half a sandwich was already in his mouth.

"Are you a vet?" Serena nodded at his jacket.

He swallowed with a gulp and washed it down with juice. "Yes'm."

"Where'd you serve?"

He was silent for a moment. He was staring at the apple as if he had never seen one before. Then he took a massive bite out of it and looked at her. "Desert Storm," he said, chewing. "Somalia. Bosnia."

Serena nodded. "You must have seen a lot."

"Too much," he said, spraying bits of apple out of his mouth.

"Forgive this next question, but can you read and write?"

Another bite of apple. "Yes, I can read and write."

"Then I need you to do me a favor. Inside is a questionnaire and a pencil. When you're done eating, I'd like you to sit down and fill it out, then return it to me or one of my associates." She tapped the CITIZENS WHO CARE button that was pinned above her left breast. "We're all wearing these."

He was starting on the second sandwich now. He nodded in acknowledgement of her instructions.

"There's also a dollar bill clipped to one of our business cards. I want you to keep them, and if you should decide that you want to change your life, give us a call. We'll do all we can to help."

He nodded, pausing over the Snickers bar in his hand.

"We could come here and plead with you, but you have to want out."

"Hmmm," he said, licking chocolate from his lips.

"You have to take that first step. You have to come to us. Understand?"

"Ma'am, for this food I'd bear your child."

"All right." She smiled, then put her hand on his shoulder. "Have a good day."

"Thank you, ma'am," he said, his mouth still full.

Serena continued on toward the monument, passing some young women who guzzled milk shakes. Her eyes scanned ahead and locked onto a forlorn figure sitting on a bench. He was slouching, hands folded in his lap, head turned away to stare at the monument. The posture and the motionless gaze were perfect, but the hospital clothes he wore looked too clean for someone living on the streets. Maybe he had just been turned out of a hospital or was a walkaway.

Serena slowly moved up to the bench and set the box down next to the man. He didn't move.

"Excuse me," she said.

Nothing.

"Sir—" She reached out and touched him on the shoulder. He turned and looked at her, and she gasped.

His face. And the look in his eyes. They made her want to cry.

He had the eyes of a child and a face that wasn't exactly hideous, yet clearly wasn't normal. The word *deformed* came to mind, but was pushed out quickly by a strange, overwhelming sensation.

She knew this man from somewhere.

She knew him well—in an intimate way that hadn't yet become sexual. Or had it? The feelings that were overwhelming her were vague.

The only thing she knew for certain was that she was in love with him.

The man said, "Yes?"

"I—" Serena stopped and took a deep breath. It helped to still the turmoil inside her. "I'm sorry, I didn't mean to stare. I—You actually remind me of someone I know." It wasn't exactly a lie, but that was how she felt. The only problem was *who*?

"That is all right," the man said.

Serena stared. She couldn't help herself. "Haven't we met?"

"No."

"Are you sure? Are you absolutely certain?"

The man sighed. "In the scheme of things, it is extremely unlikely."

Suddenly Serena flushed. Her face burned, and she remembered why she was there. "Well," she said, "I'm here to help you."

"I am beyond your help."

The Caring Citizens had taught her to ignore negative statements, so she did. She held out her hand to him. "My name is Serena Blake."

The man looked down at her hand as if he was unsure of what to do.

"What is your name?"

The man spoke, and it startled her. "Klaatu."

Serena screwed up her face. "Excuse me?"

"I'm sorry," he said quickly. "Some things are still difficult for me. Let's just say I'm just a visitor." He looked down again, then wrapped a cool hand around hers and shook it.

"Well. Victor," she said tentatively, hoping she had heard him right. Maybe he wasn't damaged. Maybe he was just slow. Dull. Not very intelligent. It's nice to meet you, Victor."

"You think quite a lot of yourselves, don't you?"

"We're just trying to help. A few people at a time." That was the slogan on the Citizens Who Care letterhead.

"I'm talking about your race," he said. "You are continually building monuments to yourselves."

"Just about every culture does that. Actually, we build these to honor our dead leaders. Our honored dead. In ancient Egypt, the leaders built the monuments to themselves while they were still living."

"Where I come from, we do no such thing."

That brought Serena back to her work and her next question. "Where do you live?"

He shook his head. "You wouldn't be able to pronounce it."

"How long have you been in Washington?"

"Not long. One day. Two days."

"Where are you staying?"

He turned his gaze from the tower to the pool. "I spent the night in one of your parks under one of your trees."

Serena moved the box off the bench and sat down in its place. She reached in and pulled out one of the carefully constructed lunches and a questionnaire. "When was the last time you had something to eat?"

"Not since I arrived here."

"Here." She put the bag gently in his lap. "It's not much, but it's balanced."

He picked up the bag and put it on the seat between them. "Thank you, no. I don't eat these things."

"You could take the meat off, if you're a vegetarian," she said. "There's fruit, lettuce, chips—"

The man tilted his head back to look at the sun and closed his eyes. "I get my nourishment in other ways."

"Where was it you said you were from?"

"Dear lady," the man said with sad eyes, "you really don't want to know that."

She tapped the piece of paper in her hands. "It's for our, uh, research."

"Research?" The man shifted uncomfortably.

"We're researching the backgrounds of . . . of people like yourself."

His eyebrows rose. "You are?"

"Yes," Serena said. "We're trying to find out why you are the way you are. If there is anything beyond socioeconomic factors which is influencing you to, uh . . . be here."

"Why I am here," the man said. "You want to know why I am here."

"That's what we're hoping to learn," Serena said.

"Foolishness. It's all foolishness."

"You are from . . ."

"You will not get an answer to that."

"You have been here in Washington a day or two?"

"Correct."

"How did you get here?"

"I walked."

"To Washington, I mean."

The man thought about it, then smiled. "Individual transportation."

"Do you still have your car?"

He looked at her. "My transportation is not currently available to me. Things were taken from me when I arrived."

"So you're stranded?"

He nodded.

"Have you applied to Traveler's Aid?"

"They would not be able to help me, even if I wanted them to."

"They could help you get home."

"No. I cannot go home. Not now."

Serena's face burned, and her heart was beating faster, but she wasn't sure why. She stared at the paper, trying to focus on the next question.

"Have you finished with me?"

"No—" she choked on her churning emotions, eyes scanning the long list of questions. "There's . . . I've . . ." She took a deep breath. "One more."

"At your leisure."

"What—" she started, the paper beginning to crumple under her grip. "What brought you to Washington?"

"What brought me to Washington?"

"Yes."

"I thought I already answered that."

"I mean—" She looked at the paper for refuge but she could no longer read the letters on it. "Why did you come here?"

"Why did I come here?"

"To Washington."

"I came . . ." He turned away from her. He looked down at the pond, then at the monument, then up at the sun, where he stared without blinking. "You want me to be honest?"

"I would appreciate it."

He looked her squarely in the eye. "I came here to save you."

Serena's hand went to her chest. Everything returned. Everything she had been trying to hold back since meeting this man; the uneasiness, the vague desire, the strange familiarity.

She opened her mouth and spoke. What she said shocked but did not surprise her. "Victor, do you want to come home with me?"

He cocked his head at her.

"You don't have anywhere else to go. You don't have anywhere to stay." Hesitantly, she reached up and touched the large bruise on the side of his head. "I don't think you're cut out for a life on the street. Not if your car was taken from you as easily as I think it was. Not if your idea of survival is sleeping in the park under a tree."

"I do not wish to be a burden."

"You're not going to be a burden. I've got plenty of room and more money than I know what to do with."

"You don't understand. I came here with a purpose, and I have failed, miserably. All I wish to do now is die."

"Then," Serena said, "we have something in common." She grabbed his hand and stood, pulling him to his feet and leading him down the sidewalk, away from the Washington Monument.

"This is not in your best interest," he protested.

"Nothing I do is."

"I am going to die."

"Aren't we all." She stopped, dropped his hand, and turned to stare at him, so ugly, so loveable. "One thing you have to understand, Victor. All of us are terminal. The only choice in life we have is the way we go."

He cocked his head at her, eyes uncomprehending. "A choice of ends? I don't think my culture has such a thing. A death is inherently filled with embarrassment."

"You must believe in one of those whacked-out eastern

religions. Well enough of that. This is America, home of
Jack Kevorkian and Camel cigarettes. As they used to say
in the old cowboy movies, 'Name your poison.' "

"Poison," the man echoed.

"Alcohol. Cocaine. Ecstasy. Heroin. Cheeseburgers
and a side of fries with a melting pat of butter on top."

"Ah," the man said, smiling. "Life-style toxins."

Serena smiled.

This is better than your hometown. "This is Washington, D.C." She took his hand. "Come on. I'll show you
the sights."

The man's cool fingers wrapped around hers. "I think
I understand this now," he said, following as she led.

Serena Blake felt a warm surge of happiness. When
she realized she was happy, tears came to her eyes because it had been so long since she had experienced any
real feelings. It only made her strange longing worse.
She wanted to laugh. So much the better if she could,
because the hurt in his eyes seemed to mirror what she
had felt inside for so long.

She led her prize out of the park to the street where
she flagged down a taxi, oblivious to the strange stares
she was getting from a small handful of Citizens Who
Cared.

SUSAN HILL

The bar was dark, and the music was ancient. The male
patrons were too loud. The women looked hard. They
matched the men, drink for drink.

If Susan had wandered into this place off the street
unknowingly, she still would have pegged the place as
a cop bar.

The dead giveaway were the girls, the ones who

looked like they didn't fit in. Their looks were vacant; their heads were empty; their chests were full. They had to be cop groupies.

All the place needed was a line of animal heads mounted up by the ceiling. Then the image would be complete.

A barmaid in a PROTECTED BY SMITH AND WESSON T-shirt stopped at the table to ask Susan what she'd have. Susan asked her for a Coke, and the barmaid glared. She knew Susan didn't belong here.

When it finally came, the soda was in a can—warm—and there wasn't enough ice to cool it. Susan asked the barmaid for more ice, and some pretzels or chips, or something salty. The barmaid disappeared, annoyed. A man staggered over to the jukebox and started to pump in coins. A handful of others shouted angrily at him, but it was too late. "My Generation" blared from the speakers amid a chorus of hoots.

"Not *again*!" someone shouted.

"I thought *you* were watching him!" came the reply. They dragged the man away from the jukebox, and one man stayed with the jukebox, bumping it with his buttocks so the disc inside would skip. Susan got her ice, along with a bowl of pretzels, which was slammed down on the table so hard that a few of the crunchy nuggets bounced onto the floor.

She looked toward the door, wondering if she should make a quick exit, when the person she awaited walked in. It was a woman with close-cropped hair, a black leather jacket, denims, and motorcycle boots. She scanned the scene until her eyes locked onto Susan. She shrugged out of her coat and draped it over a vacant chair. "So what can I do for the *Washington Tribune*?"

Susan pulled the reporter's notebook from her coat pocket and tossed it onto the table. "A couple of nights ago, you responded to an assault a few blocks from the White House."

Fran put her hand to her head as the barmaid appeared. She ordered a whiskey and water. The barmaid ignored Susan.

"The victim was declared dead on the scene," Susan continued, "and was sent to George Washington U. Then the body disappeared. I was just wondering what other details you could give me about this incident."

Fran slumped into her chair. "I didn't think that story was released."

"It wasn't."

"Then how did you find out about it?"

"Trade secret." Susan smiled. "You want to talk to me about it?"

"Depends. You going to quote me as a source?"

"Not if you don't want me to."

"I don't."

"All right," Susan said, biting one end of a pretzel. "Now that we've reached an understanding, what can you tell me about it?"

"There's nothing to tell," Fran said. "He was dead at the scene and had no identification. I sent him to the morgue. It was my homicide for all of two hours before the suits came and took it out of my hands."

"Suits?"

"Feds of some kind." The barmaid returned and laid down a napkin and Fran's drink. Fran picked it up and sniffed it. The look on her face told Susan that she wasn't sure why she had ordered it. "FBI, CIA, DIA—I don't know. One of those alphabet-soup outfits. I suppose the deader was a foreign national of some kind, and they wanted to handle it in their own way. We're getting a reputation as bad as Florida, you know. Anyway, you'd be better off going to the hospital, asking around there."

"I have."

"Then what do you need with me?"

"I just wanted to know if there was any insight you could give me on this incident, since you were at the scene."

Fran shook her head.

"Nothing at all? You're absolutely certain?"

"What do you mean by that?" Fran asked.

"According to your department's own statistics, the 151st person killed in Washington this year was apparently a foreign national, who was pronounced dead at the scene. You were the first one at the scene."

"Don't remind me," Fran said, feeling the whiskey.

"The foreigner's body was given a cursory examination by a Dr. George Underwood and then was sent to the morgue for storage."

"You *have* done your homework," Fran said.

"I'm taking this very seriously, and I'd like to know how seriously you took it."

"Very. I was the one who requested the exam," Fran said.

"So you were there," Susan said. "And you met with Dr. Underwood."

"Yes." Fran studied her interviewer. There was something about this line of questioning that she didn't like.

"The next thing that happens is that the body has vanished from the morgue, and nobody at the hospital wants to talk about it. By the time I get to the hospital to check things out, there's a regular epidemic of amnesia. Nobody knows anything at all about a body, missing or otherwise."

"Wait a minute," Fran said. She looked at her whiskey and set it down slowly. "What happened at the hospital?"

"I went into their PR office yesterday afternoon and told them I'd like to know more about this incident. Maybe a big write-up in the *Trib* would help them solve the mystery. I mean, maybe the body was Amish and was swiped by the family because they didn't want to have anything to do with our ways."

"Amish," Fran said. "That's good. I wish I'd thought of that."

Susan folded her hands and frowned. "The lady at the office told me there had been a misunderstanding, that nothing had disappeared from the morgue. I pressed her a little harder, and she said that a body had been misplaced, but was found later in one of the ER treatment rooms. There had been some kind of screw-up and some guy whose job it was to wheel patients back and forth on gurneys was fired."

"This story sounds reasonable to me."

"But not to a girl who is trying to impress Mick Aaronson," Susan said.

Fran shifted in her seat and glared. "Mick Aaronson? How do you know Mick Aaronson?"

"I'm working with him on this story," Susan said bluntly. "Now, then, my next priority was to contact Dr. George Underwood. The only problem is, he doesn't seem to exist."

"Sure he does," Fran said. "I talked to him."

Susan shook her head. "According to the PR department and the person I talked to in the human-resources department, there has never been a Dr. George Underwood working at George Washington University Hospital."

"That's crazy. Who did I talk to, then? An impostor?"

"If you want my opinion, I think you *did* talk to Dr. Underwood. I think he's the one who performed the exam, as you requested. Because this person was important to somebody I think the mysterious Dr. Underwood got yanked and sent off on a little vacation."

"You've been reading too many spy novels."

Susan flipped open her pad and ran her finger down

a line of notes. "I located an Underwood, George, physician, in Laurel, Maryland. I called the place and got a recording that said the number was no longer in service."

Fran shrugged. "So?"

"What about the ambulance crew?"

Fran shook her head. "I didn't know any of them."

"Do you know which service handled it?"

"No."

"Doesn't matter," Susan said. "None of them will admit to having handled the call. I talked with every service in the area, and then some."

Fran finished her second whiskey. The barmaid asked if she wanted a third, but Fran said no.

"That leaves you."

"I don't know anything," Fran said.

"Your report said as much. I suspect that's why you haven't been touched. See, it seems that everyone who had more than a passing contact with this body has either disappeared or has clammed up about it."

Fran shrugged. "I got there, the guy was dead."

"Dead or almost dead?"

"Almost."

"How did you know he was almost dead?"

"You see enough bodies, you know."

"What gave you the first clue? Blood?"

"There was no blood. You read my report."

"Then how did you know he was dying?"

"He told—" The answer jumped from Fran's lips before she realized it. She stopped short and looked at Susan, hoping she hadn't heard.

"He told you as much."

Fran said nothing.

"Is that right?"

Nothing.

"Is it?"

Fran nodded.

"What did he say?"

"He was delirious."

"But he still said something that made you think he was dying. What was it?"

"He said—" Fran thought for a moment. "He said something about returning home to take his punishment. And something about how nobody showed him any gratitude. And that was it. You know, people in shock sometimes say screwy things like 'Help me, I forgot to feed the cat.' Only this time I thought he was just ranting."

"Assuming that this body didn't walk out of the hospital under its own power, would it be safe to say that it was stolen from the morgue by someone with the power to make people disappear?"

"Or make their own records disappear," Fran said quickly. "Like George Underwood. That would make sense." Susan said nothing, but stared at Fran, waiting.

Fran said, "This body was a foreign national. Or so I thought. It seemed familiar, but I couldn't place his accent, and usually I can do that, you know? His English was okay, the grammar was fine—sometimes you can tell where they're from by the grammar—but there was something funny about the accent. There was something else about him, too. His body was deformed. He ... it had no ... you know ..."

"Parts?" Susan asked. ". . . Genitals?"

"Yeah. None at all. When I was filling out the paperwork, I called the hospital to talk to Underwood, and they said he wasn't there. So I mentioned the case, the deformed John Doe. I was on hold for a long time, and then someone came on the line and said, 'Oh, yeah, right, sorry we didn't tell you, but this guy was a British national who was a Thalidomide baby.' They said the body had been sent back to England."

"Sent back to England?" Susan asked. "That's a long way from disappeared."

"I like your theory."

"Theft?"

Fran nodded.

"Who?"

"Who else?"

Susan thought about it. "Underwood? You think Underwood pulled the vanishing act and took the body with him?"

"It makes sense," Fran said. "Maybe he saw his career being made with a strange body like that, and he wanted to do a detailed study on it. There was no ID at all on the body. Convenient all the way around. That would explain Underwood's disappearance and the hospital's sudden reluctance to talk about him."

"You think those suits know about this?"

"That would explain why none of the records on this seem to be available."

"So they would be on it to prevent an international incident of some kind."

"Maybe. If you want to break this open, you have to find whether there's actually a missing body."

"And if I find George Underwood—"

"You can find out what happened to that body I'll bet," Fran said.

"Well," Susan said, closing her pad and slipping a twenty onto the table. "I've certainly enjoyed your company, Sergeant Markowski."

"My pleasure," Fran said. "And Susan—" she waited for the reporter to turn before continuing—"I know I'm officially off this case—"

"But you want me to keep you up to date on what I find."

"Exactly. And when you find Dr. Underwood, I want

to talk to him before you blow his cover. The way I see it, I've got every right to smash his skull in."

CHRIS GALLAGHER

Paradise didn't get any better than this.

Sure, Florida was like the inside of a boiler. But Chris Gallagher had money now. Enough to do what he wanted on the weekends. He was an hour's flight from Havana, where he could bask on the beach, drink fine rum, and smoke good cigars. For a couple of hundred extra, he could buy the company of a clean fresh-faced woman who would be cook, translator, tour guide, and more for the entire weekend.

Then he could come back to a job he loved.

Two jobs.

One paycheck came from Kiernan, filtered through the IRS. An extra ten percent was added to the check, because he hadn't really wanted to come here. His move to Florida had been called a "relocation into a hazardous area." For that he received a nice differential.

But the topper was his other "job," the cover that paid him yet another check. It was this check that he devoted entirely to his red Miata and the weekend trips into Cuba.

Gallagher leaned back in his chair and stared at the screen in front of him. He puffed smoke from a *Revolución Dos* cigar which the fawning Maria had given him last night before returning to Miami. *Remember me, Señor Chris, when you return.* A woman with real initiative.

"You're either dreaming up a masterpiece or thinking about getting laid," said a gravelly voice behind him.

Without turning, Gallagher said, "Guilty."

"On which count?"

"Both." He turned and grinned. Lashley, the senior editor, was squinting at Gallagher's terminal, trying to read the glowing, flickering letters.

"That smokescreen you're laying makes it hard for me to read."

"I couldn't read, either, if I was old as you. Get some glasses, Lash."

Lashley growled, "The least you could do is bring me one of those Havanas from time to time."

Gallagher stuck the cigar in his mouth and grinned. "What for? You can walk into any *no habla ingles* 7-Eleven and get as many as you want."

Lashley shook his head. "It ain't the same. Back when you couldn't get the suckers, that made them special. Now anyone can buy them in the store. It only has meaning when someone brings them to you."

Gallagher blew smoke at him. "Sentimental, huh? I'll think about it."

Lashley squinted at the screen. "What you onto now, son?"

Gallagher rummaged through the debris on his desk and pulled up an 8×10 glossy. "This."

Lashley rolled his eyes. "Not again."

Gallagher took the cigar between two fingers. "I got a hot idea, Lash. Gimme a minute."

Lashley tossed the photograph back down. "Son, since we been printing, that rock formation has been Elvis Presley, George Washington, Richard Nixon, and Curly of The Three Stooges. Seems like we claim it's someone different every two years or so, when we got nothing better to run."

"C'mon, Lash."

Lashley looked down at his watch. "Sixty seconds," he said. "But it better be more than hot. It better be *nuclear.*"

Gallagher grinned. "Moses."

Lashley's eyes narrowed and one eyebrow went up. That was a good sign.

"You know, they show *The Ten Commandments* on TV every so often. It was on last night, and—"

"Get to the point, son."

"The point is, Moses and the Jews wandered all over the place for forty years waiting to get into the Promised Land. They must have gone *everywhere*."

"But *Mars*?"

Gallagher pointed out the fine points of the story with the tip of his cigar. "Think about it. These people are going to wander, leaving evidence of every place they've been. Forty years, they could have gone around the world in that time. Fathered nations, different languages. And it all led to the Tower of Babel. You know."

"Son," said Lashley, "the Tower of Babel was *before* Moses."

"Okay. So we skip that part. Anyway, say that God didn't want them tromping around all that time, messing with other tribes."

"But that's exactly what happened."

"Give me a break here, Lash. This is good. What does God do but zap them to Mars for a while. It would be the definitive Mars mountain story. We could retire it after this."

"That would be killing the golden calf," Lashley said.

"Goose," Gallagher corrected.

"Whatever." The senior editor looked longingly at Gallagher's cigar. "You get this from an expert we can quote?"

"A Bible expert," Gallagher said. "He's got a Ph.D. after his name, and we can stick 'Reverend' in front of it to make it look really good."

"What makes you think he'll testify on behalf of something this ludicrous?"

"If I pay him enough, he'll swear that the Virgin Mary ran a brothel. He's trying to raise money to get back to the Holy Land."

Lashley scowled. "How much we gonna give him?"

"*I'll* pay him. If the story works out, you can reimburse me."

"Up to seven-fifty," Lashley said. "Go ahead. Run with it."

"Cover page?" Gallagher asked.

Lashley looked at him. "It better shine."

Gallagher settled back down in his chair. He drew deeply on the cigar and blew, wishing he could sculpt the smoke into a mushroom cloud.

"New-clee-ar," he said.

A hand clapped on his shoulder. Gallagher looked back up. "What did I say?"

"It's what I *didn't* say," Lashley said. "I want you to be in charge of sightings."

"Sightings," Gallagher repeated flatly.

"You know. Some rotund housewife from Kankakee, Illinois, calls in and says she saw Elvis inhaling a Double Whopper at the local B.K. You take her name and number and say, 'Yes, ma'am, we'll get on it as soon as we finish tracking down John Lennon.'"

Gallagher studied his cigar. "I thought Riggs was doing sightings."

"Riggs is gone. *Newsweek* offered him a job. Can you believe it?"

Smoke ran up from Gallagher's cigar and formed a ball just above his head. It hung in the air—a mini-mushroom cloud. "What's it pay to cover sightings?"

"Pay?" Lashley scoffed. "I thought you'd do it because you love this job so much."

Gallagher studied the cloud. It was nice. And not looking at Lashley made him seem more aloof, he was sure. "Riggs loved his job, too."

"An extra hundred a month."

Gallagher broke into a fit of coughing. "Excuse me," he laughed. "I thought you said a hundred a month."

"Two hundred a month. But you have to get a story a month out of it."

Gallagher shoved the cigar in his mouth and shook Lashley's hand. "Sold," he slurred.

"Okay," said Lashley, walking away. "Now send Moses to Mars."

"Aye, aye," Gallagher said, saluting the senior editor's back. Then he slouched back in his chair and stared at the screen, grinning. Lashley had just made his job that much easier. Both jobs, in fact. Because along with Elvis and Lennon and dead Kennedys, sightings included aliens. UFOs. Extraterrestrials.

On top of that, he was getting paid more for doing it. He wondered if he could get a raise out of Kiernan, too.

Life sure is sweet, he thought. *It's absolutely nuclear.*

THE TASTE OF THE SCROLL

WASHINGTON, D.C. / APRIL 1999

**THE VIEW FROM HERE
by Mick Aaronson**

April 22, 1999—I recently went into a well-known consumer electronics store to indulge in a new electronic gadget I'd been reading about—a hand-held automatic book that reads everything off a little silver disc.

I was interested because the disc book never wears out. I'll admit that my age was a factor in this, too. The literature said I could make the print as big as I wanted for a comfortable read.

And for once in my life I wanted to be at the forefront of modern technology. I was the last person I know to get a VCR, a telephone-answering machine, and a fax. Three years ago, while I was on vacation, my colleagues here at the *Tribune* replaced my trusty Underwood typewriter with a computer. I'm just now warming up to the thing.

So I picked out a nice Sony Readman and a few

discs—*The Compleat Works of Shakespeare*, *20 × 20: The Works of Twenty Twentieth-Century American Poets*, and *Ten Classic Translations of the Bible.* I handed them over to the sales assistant along with my VisaMax and made myself several hundred dollars poorer.

He put my purchase into a big bag and handed it to me. Feeling proud of this major step, I thanked him for all of his help and held out my hand for a shake.

The miserable cretin stared at my hand like I was a waiter that he hadn't planned on tipping.

What has happened to this country?

Once upon a time, deals were made and financial empires were built on nothing more than a handshake.

Last week, the Supreme Court ruled that a signed contract is not necessarily a legally binding document, but a loose set of guidelines to govern behavior.

That must mean if I scan my ten-translation Bible to the book of Exodus, I'll find Moses going up the mountain to retrieve The Ten Suggestions.

Now, it seems, we cannot even be counted on to stick our own necks out for our fellow man.

Not even in a gesture of friendship.

Not even if your fellow man has made it possible to put bread in the mouths of your children.

They say the handshake originated when two soldiers in ancient times approached one another. Since their swords were carried in the right hand, when two right hands gripped, it was a sure sign that the sword was safely in its scabbard.

It was a sign of security. A sign of trust. And, over the years, it came to represent friendship and bonding.

I don't know what it means now.

All I know is that the handshake is a part of our species' history that has

gone the way of the zep- How sad. How very, very
pelin.   sad for us all.

GHOST

It was time for a test.

Ghost walked down the street, taking his time, the rock burning fiercely in the palm of his hand.

A test, yes. Of the rock and how strong it really was. A test that would also take care of any problems he had with the others once and for all. A test that might even prove he didn't need the others.

He continued on toward his destination, stopping to casually peer through the barred storefronts, thinking about his plan. It was a good plan, and part of it called for him to be late.

Late enough for Shark to start working the others against him.

Of course, he hadn't told Shark about the meeting. But he had told Squeak, knowing full well that he'd go straight to Shark, unable to keep his mouth shut. And Shark, who was bent on revenge, would make a point of getting there early to brainwash the other troops, like he had done with Squeak.

Ghost knew him. He knew the others. That's why he was the leader. Shark didn't care about the others. All he wanted was the power and what the others could do for him. Ghost felt he was different. He had taken the lot of them and molded them into something that was fearsome to behold.

Shark wanted to mess all of that up.

Not for long.

Ghost paused in front of a liquor store and looking in the window, he spotted the tall, shapely figure of Patrice. His breath stopped short and he swallowed. He found himself trembling. Patrice, who was always presiding over his wet dreams.

He walked into the store. A bell tinkled as he did, and Mr. Freddy, the old man behind the counter immediately began to shout.

"You! Kit! You get out of this place! You ain't old enough to be here."

The rock warmed in Ghost's hand. "Am too."

Mr. Freddy's mouth flexed as if the words had been cut off at the source.

"Fact, I'm twenty-two," Ghost said. "I been comin' in here a whole year to buy from you. You'd swear to that, wouldn't you, Mr. Freddy?"

"Yes," Mr. Freddy said flatly.

"All right." He dropped the rock in his pocket and bounded down an aisle in pursuit of Patrice. He found her looking over a display of wines. She was wearing a slick red raincoat, a leather mini, and black go-go boots. And she was tall, her breasts coming to his eye level. She held a bottle of something in her hand and blinked at it. Her face was tired, her eyes red and in need of sleep.

Ghost sauntered over to a cooler, opened it, and began to pull out cans of Colt 45. "'lo Patrice," he said.

She looked over at him and rolled her eyes. "Hello, Ghost."

"How you been?"

She put the bottle of wine back on the shelf and pulled down another. "Ghost, you get found in here, you gonna bring a world of hurt down on yourself. Not to mention Mr. Freddy."

"When you gonna let me have some, Patrice?"

She turned toward him and glared. "We been through this, already."

"I give you twice what you get from them white guys."

Patrice looked at Mr. Freddy, who had buried his head in a racing form. She said in a coarse whisper, "I ain't gonna do you, Ghost, no matter how much you give me. I don't do no one from the neighborhood, no matter how much money. I used to babysit you."

"You just like them white lawyers and politicians."

"They's some brothers, too," she snapped. "Now get out of here before I have Mr. Freddy kick you out."

Ghost juggled the cans of Colt in one arm and shoved his hand into his pocket. He drew a deep breath. "I think—"

"You thinkin' nothin', Ghost. You get your horny little thing—"

"I think you hurtin' inside Patrice. Deep."

Patrice gasped. The wine bottle slipped from her fingers and exploded on the floor.

Mr. Freddy looked up. Ghost turned to him. "You ain't seein' nothin', Mr. Freddy."

Mr. Freddy turned his gaze back to the racing form.

"Fact, Patrice, I think you gettin' the cramps. Bad."

She cried out.

"I think you gonna be too sick to work for Julius tonight, don't you?"

Patrice pitched forward and caught herself on the counter.

"Don't you, Patrice?"

She nodded.

"Fact, there's only one thing I think's gonna make you feel better. You know what that is?"

"No," she said.

"You want me to tell you?"

"Yes, Ghost. Please, please tell me."

"First you get on home and call Julius, tell him you're not working tonight. Got that?"

She nodded.

"Then you go to the D Street Motel and get a room. The one with that big whirlpool thing in it. You know which one I'm talking about?"

She did.

"You wait for me there. Maybe get some sleep. I'll be along when I feel like it, I give you the cure you need. But it may take a while. Maybe all night. You got that, Patrice?"

Another nod.

"I didn't hear that."

"Yes," she said, swallowing hard. "Ghost."

"I'll be seeing you," he said. He turned and started to walk away.

"You!" Mr. Freddy called out as the bell tinkled. "You didn't pay for those, Kit!"

Ghost turned. "Why, sure I did, Mr. Freddy. Don't you remember?"

"Don't start—"

"I paid you, Mr. Freddy. In fact, you forgot to give me my change, you stupid old fool."

Ghost walked up to the counter. Behind him, the bell tinkled again as Patrice made her exit.

"You open that machine right now and give me my change."

The cash register was one of those ancient things with the big keys and the big white numbers in the window. It made a satisfying *ding!* as Mr. Freddy punched it open.

"Well?"

Mr. Freddy's eyes welled up with tears. "I can't . . . I can't remember what you gave me."

Ghost rolled his eyes dramatically. "I gave you a hunnerd-dollar bill."

Mr. Freddy was relieved to know this. He counted the change into Ghost's open palm, put the cans of malt liquor in a paper bag, then returned to his chair and his racing form.

Ghost walked out, trembling and triumphant. The sheer feeling of power making him light-headed and horny.

Well. Patrice would be waiting. And he was certain that she'd wait until he got there.

But first things first.

His plan called for the gang to meet at the old warehouse near Union Station that had been their official hideout. On arriving, Ghost slipped through a break in the chain-link fence and walked around the back. There was a door that looked boarded but wasn't. Ghost pulled at the boards and got them open enough to squeeze through into the musty interior.

Inside, they were all waiting. Squeak, Goldie, Piggy Boy, and Shark, their conversation cut short as he entered.

"Santa's here," he announced, pulling a can of Colt out and lobbing it into the air toward Squeak. He gave cans to Piggy Boy and Goldie, then took the last one for himself, shaking his head at Shark. "Heard they wired you mouth shut. You try drinkin' this man's stuff, you be chokin' to death on you own puke."

Shark growled and parted his lips to reveal a mass of bright chrome wire.

"They got you all pretty, Shark," Ghost said. "Your teeth gonna be all nice and straight in time for the prom?" He popped the top on his can and took a long drink.

Shark slurred, "We got somethin' discuss wi' you."

"S'cuss away," Ghost mocked.

"We been talkin'," Squeak offered.

"That's why I called this here little meeting," Ghost said. "So we could all talk." One by one, he looked them in the eye. "So what do you want to talk about?"

Goldie took the can from his lips and swallowed. "We been talking about that guy you did. We got some real troubles comin' down on us, Ghost."

"What you mean?"

"Amos comin' down on us. Hard," Piggy Boy said. "He been to see each one of us. Talkin' to our mamas, too."

"Yo' mamas," Ghost said. "Amos, too. He one dumb old spook, sellin' his brothers out to The Man."

"He puttin' a lot of heat on us. Think he wants to get to you."

"Me?" Ghost tried to sound outraged. "Why me?"

"He think you done the guy."

Ghost stared daggers at him. "Where he get that idea?"

Shark looked away.

"Lemme tell you 'bout Amos," Ghost said. "He jump my butt that morning, before I even got home, 'bout that dead guy. I said, 'Fool, I ain't done nothin' like that,' and he ain't been back since."

"He been seein' us," Piggy Boy said.

Ghost stood in the center of them all and tipped up the can of Colt 45, guzzling and choking, liquid running down his chin. He didn't stop until he was sucking air. He crumpled the can and threw it across the warehouse.

"He been sayin' this guy you dusted was a foreigner," Goldie said. "He sayin' if he don't find who done it, then the feds gonna get involved. FBI. CIA. Maybe Interpol, or guys from the country he was from."

Ghost laughed. "That it? You think James Bond gonna come after us?"

Goldie continued, "We just been thinking, maybe it

ain't such a hot idea to be hanging around you right now."

Ghost knocked the can out of Goldie's hand and pushed him to the ground. He spun to face the others as they started to close in. His finger pointed accusingly at Shark. "You been listenin' to *him*?" he shouted in disbelief.

"He didn't kill anybody," Squeak said nervously.

"You're saying that you guys rather follow Shark than me?"

One by one, they nodded in consensus.

Ghost spat. "I suppose you can all go with him, then. But you remember I be braver than all you put together."

"You garbage," Shark sprayed.

"You no man," Ghost said.

Shark lunged. Goldie and Piggy Boy held him back.

"You wanna prove something?" Ghost said. "Right here and now?"

Shark nodded.

Ghost shoved his hands in his pockets. In one of them, the rock was waiting. "All right. Just you and me. One on one. We gonna prove for everyone here, all right?"

"Fine by me," said Shark.

Ghost's thumb rubbed. "You packin', ain't you Shark?"

"Yeah."

"Let's see it," Ghost said. "Let's see the piece."

Shark hesitated, then shoved his hand down into the front of his jeans. He pulled out a snub-nosed revolver, blue steel, with wooden grips.

Ghost smiled and caressed the stone. "Nice. Real nice, Shark. That a thirty-eight?"

"Three-fifty-seven," he slurred.

Ghost let the stone fall into the bottom of his pocket.

"Shark, we got a small problem here. So we gonna see how much of a man you are. You man enough to stick that man's gun in you mouth? Up to you wired-up teeth?"

"You fool," Shark said and slid the gun between his lips.

"You man enough to cock it?" Ghost eased his hands into his pockets and touched the stone.

Click.

Ghost stared at him. He had to play this right. Shark might seize the moment and turn the gun on him.

"Shark?"

The answer was indecipherable.

"You man enough to pull that trigger?"

Shark's expression started to change. His eyebrows knit together, and his lips started to curl up around the barrel of the gun.

Ghost grabbed the rock.

"Pull the trigger!"

Suddenly Shark's expression changed. His eyebrows arched and his eyes went wide, full of raw fear.

Then his head exploded with a roar. His body snapped back and hit the ground with a grunt, limbs thrashing wildly, legs kicking, torso twisting.

Ghost's ears rang from the shot. He looked down at Shark. The top of his head was gone, and his spasms were spraying blood across the floor.

"It worked!" he said in an awestruck whisper. He turned to share the moment with the others, but the three had broken and were running toward the door.

"Stop!" he shouted.

They stumbled and froze.

Ghost walked to them, shaking his head and wiggling his fingers in his ears, trying to shake the insistent ringing. He stopped between Goldie and Piggy Boy, clapping a hand to each shoulder.

"Where you boys going?"

"Nowhere, Ghost," they chorused.

Ghost looked back at Shark. He slipped the rock into his hand and tossed it into the air, letting it fall into the palm of his hand. "That Shark, he one crazy animal."

"Yeah, Ghost."

"Sure was."

"Now you two, neither of you gonna remember any of this, you got that? Anyone ask you about what went down here, you gonna have a big case of amnesia. Got it?"

"Yes."

"Yes."

"Get out of here."

They ran.

He turned to Squeak. "C'mere, you."

Squeak walked over.

Ghost held the stone tightly between his thumb and forefinger, gazing at it admiringly. "I got a job for you, Squeak."

"Yes, Ghost."

"You go get that gun and you put it in a nice, safe hiding place. And don't you forget where it is. Understand?"

Squeak trembled and his eyes filled up with tears. "Yes, Ghost."

"When The Man come and he ask you 'bout Shark, you show him where he is. They ask you why he dead, you tell them he threatened you mama. And you took that man's gun of his and put it in his face and pulled the trigger. It was just you and him here. Got that? No Goldie, no Piggy Boy. And I was a million miles from here. You understand?"

The tears spilled down his cheeks. "Yes, Ghost."

"Now go on. Do what I told you."

Squeak walked toward Shark's body, slowly, hesitantly, as if he was being pushed. Ghost walked away and squeezed out of the door, blinking in the sunlight of spring.

Money, he thought. He had just under a hundred dollars in his pocket, but he needed more. Lots more.

After all, he had a date.

SERENA BLAKE

The television was tuned to a dead channel.

The sound was up, loud.

Serena preferred it that way. The entertainment had ended as evening faded into early morning. The energy from the coke had long since ebbed, and the bright luster that the alcohol had given the night had faded.

The ringing in her head was so loud it kept her awake. Unless she disguised it with the television static.

Serena was lying on the couch, her eyes staring at the white static, unfocused. The bottle of prime ingredient for a Bloody Mary was on the floor, inches from her limp hand. Next to it, the remote control.

She blinked and fell into a moment of strange lucidity, which was braced by common sense. The moment said, *If you keep this up, you're going to die.*

At the moment, death seemed so abstract to her. She still believed she could continue the abuse. She'd quit, she told herself, and soon. When she finished her pursuit.

Pursuit of what? What's out there, Serena? What are you chasing? Or is something chasing you?

She groaned and lifted her arm to test her mobility. The effort hurt. Still, it didn't fill her with the nausea she had experienced earlier. She would live. She might even be fit company by noon.

She blinked at the whiteness coming from the television screen, trying to lose herself in its sight and sound. As she did, a pair of faded green cylinders speared, cutting her view into bands.

"Are you all right, Serena Blake?"

She looked up. "Victor." She smiled. "I'm sorry if I woke you."

"Your body is distressed, Serena."

"You noticed." She moved to sit up. It hurt every inch of the way, but she managed. "Next year I'm quitting. I'm giving up everything. It's my promise to the new millennium."

"And until that time you continue to abuse your body in this way? It does not make sense."

"What does?" She stretched. Every cell in her body was contributing to the dull ache that covered her. "You should have been there, Victor. It was a great party. One of the Kennedys was there."

Victor stood, staring.

"I really wish you'd come with me. I think you'd have a great time. You could see how the other half lives."

"The other half?" His eyebrows tilted.

Serena shook her head. It hurt. "It's one of those . . . what do you call it?"

"Idiomatic expressions."

"Yeah. And it means . . ." She thought about it. "Come to think of it, just what *does* it mean? I don't know."

Victor remained still. "Let me see if I understand this. You wish me to go with you and share in the process which puts you into an altered state of consciousness."

"Something like that."

"Yet the aftermath is the deplorable state in which you now find yourself."

"Yeah. Well. Nothing's perfect."

"A condition which is clearly self-destructive."

"Whoa." Serena pulled herself to her feet. "Don't you start on me again."

"I don't understand how you take such rapid offense at me when all I was attempting was a simple observation."

"Simple, nothing. You're on my case, Victor, and I don't appreciate it." Dizziness began to creep up on her. She sat back down.

"This consistent use of idioms. It is difficult to keep up—"

"Don't change the subject."

"I wasn't changing the subject."

"Who taught you how to fight, Victor? They didn't do a very good job."

"Fight," Victor repeated. "I thought we were having a conversation."

Serena cradled her head in her hands. "I've got enough noise in my head right now. You're so literal minded that you drive me crazy."

"Would you like me to leave, then?"

"No!" she shouted. "Please don't leave. Please—"

Victor crouched down so he was at eye level with her. "Is this strange behavior of yours due to your obvious conflict of emotions?"

She glared at him. "No. I was this self-destructive before I met you."

"And you want me to witness this?"

"No," she said bluntly. "I want to share it with you."

"That is why I should leave, Serena Blake. Because I would feel a moral obligation to prevent you from destroying yourself."

Serena looked at him down in that strange squat position. Not even looking uncomfortable. Staring without blinking.

What was it about him?

She wanted to say, *How can you make me feel this way, you ugly little man, and yet be so practical and depressive yourself?*

Instead, she felt the residue of the previous evening's entertainment welling up inside of her, trying to extinguish what she was really feeling. "You know what your problem is, Victor?"

"I have many, but they're irrelevant."

"There's where you're wrong," Serena said. "There is one that's relevant. You have a serious messiah complex, you know that?"

Before he could protest, she quickly ticked off her evidence. He had been here in the apartment with her, what—three days now? And in that three days he hadn't done much except watch CNN and read the papers. And when something particularly poignant caught his attention—like the woman who tried to sell her unborn child to a fetal-tissue processing center—he would nod his head loosely and say that this was typical, that the whole moral fabric of the planet was coming unraveled, at a rate much faster than even he had calculated. The beheading of extremists who had tried to smuggle a suitcase nuke into Jerusalem got him to talking about the timetable, and how it had to be accelerated now, that things were coming apart faster than at any other time on record.

She had said something to him about it on the first night he was there. *If you're so all-fired insightful, why don't you do something about it?*

And he had turned back toward the television, rested his head back, and explained that he had tried to go see the President about the situation.

Serena had responded with laughter. He had become sullen and withdrawn.

Now he said he was leaving. He was not doing any

good here in Washington, in general, and in Serena's apartment, in particular. If his device hadn't been stolen, he said, he could do something for her. He could help her with her dependency problems.

Normally Serena would have snapped at him, saying that she didn't want any help and that the vices she had were proudly her own. But she realized that she was terrified at the thought of being alone.

No, that wasn't it.

What scared her was the thought of being without him.

She had quit going in to Citizens Who Care within twenty-four hours of taking him home because she couldn't get him off her mind.

Who was this guy?

Victor reminded her of someone, but she couldn't remember whom. And while his appearance and distant gaze was unusual, his whole demeanor was not typical of the average homeless victim. He seemed to know a lot about Washington and America, but was blatantly ignorant about the stuff of everyday life. He must be from abroad, but she couldn't determine where. His English seemed flawless enough, but he spoke with neither the cultured tones of the British, nor the broad accent of the Australians.

Where, then?

On arriving at the apartment, Victor had seemed shy around her, so she had let him have her bedroom. She had made subtle hints, but he seemed oblivious to the fact that they were sexual.

So the next night Serena made her intentions as clear as she could. Dinner had been a cold salad, which he had refused politely, as he did the really good wine, the one she called her seduction vintage. She realized, in fact, that she had never seen him eat anything, and there never seemed to be any food missing after one of her absences. Well, maybe he was a devotee of fast food.

But that was no matter. Not at the moment. They passed dinner, as usual, with her eating and him talking about the news and asking questions about American culture. Afterward, she asked him if he wanted to watch a movie, offering him a choice of *9½ Weeks*, *Basic Instinct*, and *Lost in the Rain*.

He chose *Lost in the Rain* seemingly at random and would have watched it without comment had Serena not solicited his opinion of the goings-on during the infamous taxi scene. His evaluation was, "This gentleman has an almost-adolescent preoccupation with seeking the stimulation of his genitals."

Maybe, Serena thought, *this movie just isn't the right one for him.*

After the movie, Victor announced his intention to retire for the evening, although Serena had never really seen him sleep, either. She watched him go into her bedroom and shut the door, then stripped down to her blouse and panties. She unbuttoned the blouse, then knocked on the bedroom door.

"Is it all right if I come in?"

She opened the door without waiting for his reply. Victor was sitting on the edge of her bed, looking out the window. Strolling in casually, she took off her blouse and bra and tossed them on the dresser.

"Sorry," she said. "I need some clean things for tomorrow. I hope I'm not disturbing you."

"Oh, no."

Serena rummaged through her drawers to make the act look convincing, grabbed a few things, then turned to face Victor with her fists on her hips.

"What do you think?"

Victor was looking at her. Or rather, he was looking her way. No, he was looking *through* her.

"Well?"

His head jerked and he made eye contact. "Hmm?"

"What do you think?"

He smiled, seemed pleased. "Oh. Thank you. I didn't know you were interested."

At last! she thought.

"I was pondering the impact of light bending when in proximity to strong gravitational fields. It has a disruptive effect on navigational calculations. For example, if you had two virtually identical photons of light energy traveling side by side, and both passed equidistant to the event horizon of a singularity, the end result could not be predicted. One may drop and the other may continue on. Both may travel straight, or bend. They may collide and go careening away in different directions. Now, if there were a way one could calculate such effects of chaos—"

"Oh, shut up, Victor!"

Serena rushed out of the bedroom and sat down hard on the couch, her face in her hands.

Why, why, why couldn't she reach him? He quite literally did not have a clue as to what was going on.

Well, maybe it wasn't his fault. Maybe he was gay. That would be just her luck. He could be mentally disturbed. Or maybe he had gotten his thing shot off in the war. That had happened to guys in Bosnia, she knew. That would explain his striking features and some of his other obvious quirks.

Whatever his problems, Serena didn't care. She wanted him around.

As if on cue, the door to her bedroom opened, and she heard his footsteps approaching on the carpeted floor. When they stopped, she lowered her hands and looked. He was there, kneeling in front of her.

"I have erred in dealing with you. I apologize."

"That's okay," she sniffed.

"There is something I can do for you."

"No. Really."

"If I had my device, I could instantly make things better for you, Serena."

"That's all right, Victor."

"In the absence of the device, I can help you best by continuing to develop our interpersonal relationship." His cool hands gripped hers.

"That's fine, Victor. That's fine."

"You expressed a very specific need to me and I failed to notice it. What is it you require of me, Serena?"

She gently pulled her hands from his grip and put them around his neck, pulling him close to her.

"Just don't leave, Victor. Stay with me."

"If you wish."

On thinking it over, she realized that whatever it was she needed from him, it certainly wasn't sex.

And it wasn't love.

She knew it wasn't love, even though she wasn't sure what love was.

But whatever it was—or wasn't—scared her.

"Will you?" she asked softly. "For how long?"

"Until the end of this world."

But now she was arguing with him again, or at least trying. He didn't fight or argue. It was frustrating. If she got in a good lick, he said that he would take her point under consideration, then walk away.

In fact, Victor was doing that now. He said, "I fail to see what this has to do with my alleged delusion of being a messiah, but—"

Serena cut him off before he could tell her he'd think about it. "Then let me spell it out for you, Victor. Everything you see you think should be fixed, and you talk like you're the fixer. But what are you doing about it? And don't give me that line about trying to get into the White House."

"I have tried, in a manner that is beyond your comprehension." He stared at her without blinking.

"You tried to save the whole world, all at once. Am I right?"

"Isn't that how it is done?"

"Only in the movies." Serena slid off the couch, turned off the television, and sat cross-legged on the floor. "I don't know anything about being a messiah, but I do know a little bit about Jesus. Not as much as I should, I guess, but enough to know how a messiah should behave."

Victor smiled. "Oh, yes. Jesus." He eased himself down to the floor and duplicated Serena's posture.

"You know, you get these guys on the TV with their Rolex watches and their million-dollar Cathedrals of Prayer and Commerce, and they get the crowds worked up and stick their fingers in the ears of actors who say they've got a nicotine demon living in them, and they tell everyone that if Jesus were around, he'd be right there in the middle of what they're there doing."

"Yes." Victor nodded.

"Well, I say if Jesus were there watching what all those people were doing, he'd get mad. He'd start throwing chairs. He did that once, threw chairs."

"Did he?"

Serena nodded. "I saw it in a movie. Anyway, Jesus wouldn't be fooling around with all those old toads. You know where he'd be?"

"Tell me, Serena."

"He'd be down there laying his hands on drug addicts and people with AIDS and the guys who got gassed in Bosnia. He'd be down there on the corners, taking guns out of the pockets of twelve-year-old kids, and he'd be telling them, 'Man, what are you doing with this big and nasty weapon? You should be out playing cowboys and Indians or watching cartoons.' He'd say, 'I'll bet you don't even know the words to "Jesus Loves Me." ' And then he'd teach them the words."

"Can I hear it?" Victor asked.

"Later," Serena said. "My point is, why would Jesus want to mess with a bunch of people whose lives were okay because they thought they were saved? He'd be out there taking care of the people with the most screwed-up lives in the world, because they're the ones who needed him the worst."

Victor was staring again.

"You see what I'm getting at, Victor? You can't just walk in to see the President and save the whole world. And you can't do it by watching CNN and complaining about how bad things are getting, and where the world is going and how it's going to get there. If you want to save the world, you've got to do it one person at a time. You start with one and you save him. Then the two of you go out and save two more people. The four go save eight, and so on."

"Exponential multiplication," Victor said.

"Whatever you want to call it," Serena said. "Then, maybe when you get the numbers, then people will start to listen to you. Jesus started out with twelve guys. But it wasn't until he had hundreds of followers that the Romans sat up and took notice and killed him off."

"Before he could finish," Victor said.

"No," Serena said. "By the time he was killed, it was too late. Jesus had already set the saving into motion, and there was no stopping it. The people took it over after he died."

"What happened then?"

"What? To the world?"

"Yes."

"We quit listening," Serena said.

Victor looked away.

"What's wrong now?"

"What's wrong is that you are right," Victor said.

"Are you going to 'take this under advisement?'"

"There's no use. I have failed you, Serena. I have failed you by coming here too late."

"What do you mean by that?"

"There isn't enough time left to save the world one person at a time."

"It must not matter that much to you, then—"

"It means more to me than you can understand, Serena."

"Then prove it, Victor. If you can't save the whole world before it ends, then you cut your losses and save what you can."

"And where would I begin this process, Serena?"

She took his hand and pressed it to her chest so he could feel her heart.

"I understand," he said. "And if I had—"

"I don't want to hear another word about that missing device, Victor. Before you save me, you've got to be my friend. Come with me. Let me show you my life."

"I—"

"You don't have to do what I do. Just watch me. Be with me. I'd rather have you with me, even if you can't do a thing for me. I'm out there at night, trying to forget everything, and I can't get you out of my mind." She dropped her grip. His hand stayed on her heart. "I can't get you out of my mind." One corner of her mouth turned up, almost a smile. "I'm a regular party girl, and I'll show you a night you'll never forget. You might even stop your brooding."

"I understand."

"One last night in Gomorrah," Serena said.

HARRY LAUTER

For the second night in a row, the couple in the room next door was engaging in a marathon, and the audio was coming right through the thin walls. Judging from his triumphant shouts, the man was giving orders which seemed to lead to great results. Over a period of forty-five minutes or an hour, the commotion would build up to its logical conclusion, then fall silent. After another hour or so, the show would start again.

The eerie thing about it was the woman's continued silence. Even when the springs were protesting and the bed was banging against the wall, Harry heard nothing but masculine sounds. Even if she was a prostitute, Harry thought she should at least demonstrate her acting skills.

But there was nothing.

The night before, he had idly wondered whether there were two men in the room. But as he left his room this morning, he had encountered a woman with a bagful of groceries keying her way into the room.

There had been an uncomfortable moment as they exchanged glances. Her eyes were sad and tired and distant. The stare said she knew that he knew what had been going on, and it disturbed her.

But she said nothing. The moment faded, and she disappeared into the room.

That woman needs Jesus, Harry thought as he listened to the banging and thrashing. *And that guy with her. He needs to be kneecapped with a Louisville Slugger.*

The noise suddenly stopped and Harry closed his eyes, hoping that sleep would overtake him before the rumpus started up again. He was just beginning to drift when there was a sudden clanging in his right ear. Harry rolled to his side and picked up the telephone.

"I hope I woke you up," a voice said before he could speak. "You're one hard person to find."

Harry sat up and cleared his throat. "Chris?"

"One and the same. I knew I'd catch you. Even the drunks at Union Station aren't receptive to the Gospel at this hour."

"Actually," Harry said, "I was thinking of witnessing to the people next door. You remember that old Paul Simon song about the guy in the cheap motel?"

"Lincoln Duncan," Chris said. "But hey, Harry, you're gonna be able to move to the Omni Georgetown when you hear what I've got to tell you."

"If I had that much money," Harry said, "then I'd be on the first plane out of here."

"The Omni in Jerusalem, then."

"What do you want, Chris?"

"First of all, I want to put your name on something."

Harry rubbed his eyes and turned so his feet were flat on the floor. "I'm afraid to ask."

"Moses on Mars."

Oh, no. Not another one.

"Harry? You there?"

"I wish I wasn't."

"It's really simple. God didn't want the Israelites tramping around Earth for forty years, so he whisked them to Mars for a while. While they were there, they built a monument to Moses. They knew how to do it because they'd built all of the Egyptian pyramids."

"Not that mountain face again," Harry grumbled. "I thought that was supposed to be Elvis."

"George Washington, but that was a couple of years ago."

"Chris, it's a great angle, but that story is full of holes. Anyone who opens a Bible to check it is going to—"

"Who's going to check it, Harry? The people who

buy this magazine see aliens on their way back from tapping a jug of 'shine off the still."

Harry stayed silent.

"It pays two hundred fifty bucks."

"For something like that? My price on this one is a thousand."

"Three hundred."

"It's my name on this one," Harry said. "Nine."

"For nine I could get Billy Graham. Four."

"You need a name for this thing to fly. Six."

"Five hundred dollars," Chris said. "And for that you have to come down here and lay your hands on my boss, because he's going to have a heart attack when he hears how much I spent to get a name for this story."

"Make it a money order," Harry said. "I'm having some personality conflicts with the IRS."

"I'll overnight it in the morning. Thanks."

"That's not going to get me very far at the Omni."

"That's the other reason I called. I've got some more good news for you."

"What could be better than discovering a statue of Moses on Mars?"

"I've been put in charge of sightings. So any leads you can give me, I can slip some extra bucks your way. If you can get me a full-fledged story with pictures, I can pay you big-time."

"Sightings?" Harry asked.

"Elvis, Kennedy, Lennon. Bigfoot, Nessie, UFOs."

"That's too easy," Harry said. "All I have to do is walk a couple of blocks, and I'll find people who see those things all the time."

"You know what I mean," Chris said.

"I know what you mean."

"All right. Thanks a lot, Harry."

Harry signed off and hung up. Things were looking up now. All he had to do was keep his eyes and ears open, and he was certain to find someone with a story for Chris—someone who was fairly lucid.

Harry walked to the kitchenette for a drink of water. Yes, he reflected, God was certainly good to him.

In the other room, the marathon was beginning again.

AMOS WHITE

In the dozen years since he had joined Washington's police force, Amos White had never been inside the FBI building. He had come close a couple of times, when The Job had gotten to him, and he thought that he would be better off with a federal badge and a transfer to some backwater jurisdiction like South Dakota, working the reservations.

That was back before Charles Barkley had said he wasn't a role model. Although Amos was a die-hard Bullets fan, he had admired Barkley's style. How many professional basketballers were there in the country? What were the odds of a ghetto kid making it to the pros?

On the other hand, how many cops were there in the country? Not enough, he knew. And if a kid kept his grades up and his nose clean, then he might one day wear a badge.

From then on, Amos became the role model, moving back to his old neighborhood, plying the kids with ice cream and Bullets tickets and stern words about staying away from all the vices on the street.

He liked doing it. And on the wall of his office cubicle there were plenty of plaques and certificates of appreciation as proof that the community liked what he was doing.

And now the Feds wanted him for something. The

word had come to him from the chief: be at the Federal building at ten o'clock sharp. The chief had no idea what for, but didn't seem concerned. He knew that Amos was a good cop and kept himself clean.

Amos couldn't imagine what they wanted, either. Unless the FBI wanted to recruit him. He would have to see what the salary would be, he told himself. But he would probably tell them that he had long since talked himself out of the idea of being posted in South Dakota.

He arrived at the building at 9:58, badged his way into the lobby, and showed his ID to the receptionist. She flagged down an agent to escort him through the building. He ended up standing in front of a set of double doors. A sign indicated that the conference room on the other side was occupied.

"Through here," the agent said.

"You coming?" Amos asked.

The agent shook his head. "Not allowed. Don't have the clearance."

"What about me?"

"You're invited."

Amos looked at the door. *What am I in for now?* he thought, as he opened it.

He was relieved to find a friendly atmosphere inside. A small group of business-suited men were standing around drinking coffee from Styrofoam cups. A large box of doughnuts lay open on the center of a large table. There was also a large white screen and an overhead projector connected to a small notebook computer.

All heads turned his way as he closed the door behind him. "I hope I'm not late," he said. "I'm Sergeant White, D.C.P.D."

A short man put down a cruller and stepped forward to shake hands. "Agent Kemper," he said. "I'm coordinating this little project." He turned and pointed to the others in turn. "My assistant, Agent Carlisle. Agent

Dawson from our psychology unit. Agent Lawrence, our crime-scene expert. And Max Kiernan, a special liaison agent from the Internal Revenue Service."

Amos shook hands with them all. "I've paid my taxes," he said to Kiernan. Kiernan said nothing.

"Mr. Kiernan is here as an observer," Kemper said. "And you, Sergeant White, are hopefully our expert witness."

"Me?" Amos asked.

"Let's sit down, shall we?" said Carlisle, placing himself in front of the tiny computer. When they were all seated, Kemper dimmed the lights and Carlisle tapped keys on the computer. The FBI logo filled the screen, along with the words SPECIAL INVESTIGATIONS FILE—CONFIDENTIAL.

"Sergeant White," Kemper continued, "we are currently working on an investigation of a particularly sensitive nature. It's important for you to understand that what you see and hear in this room stays in this room."

"I understand."

"We are aware of the rapport which you have with the central-district residents. This investigation involves one of them, so any help you can give us would be of use."

"I'd be glad to help any way I can," Amos said.

Kemper nodded. Carlisle fingered the keyboard. An image appeared on the screen. It was a mug-shot series, frontal and right profile of a scowling black youth.

"Sergeant, do you recognize this person?" Agent Lawrence asked.

Amos nodded. "I was there when that picture was taken. That's Ghost."

"Ghost?" Kiernan asked, shifting in his seat.

"That's his secret name. His real name is Kit Washington."

A new image appeared.

"William Golden," Amos said.

"Does he have a street name?" Lawrence asked.

"Goldie. He runs with Ghost as part of his gang."

The image changed again and again until he had inventoried the rest of them. Piggy Boy, Squeak, and Shark. He felt as if he were back at the police academy taking Suspect Identification 101, telling the instructors what they already knew.

"These are all members of a known street gang?"

"They're not a full-fledged gang," Amos said. "Ghost is a clocker, the footman running the drugs for some of the big guys in the neighborhood. And in turn he's grooming some of the others to be his lieutenants."

"Are they involved in anything other than trafficking?" asked Dawson.

"Not that I know of," Amos said. "They're just a bunch of screwed-up kids who want to get money for Nikes."

Lawrence said, "If that's all they are, then why are they in hiding?"

"Are they?" Amos asked.

"We were hoping you might know," Kemper said.

"Gentlemen, I don't see them every day," Amos told them. "Maybe twice, three times a month. I'm working on them, but they're a little far gone. I concentrate more on the younger ones."

"Would you know where we can find any of them?" Dawson asked.

"There's been a dispute over leadership, and Ghost busted up Shark's face pretty good. Had to have his jaw wired up, in fact." Amos looked at them intently. They all stared back.

He said, "Gentlemen, I know that I'm not telling you anything that you don't already know. And unless I miss my guess, you want information on something specific that you're reluctant to talk to me about."

Carlisle laughed. "Your chief told us you were sharp."

Then it clicked. Amos said, "This is about that alien, isn't it?"

Kiernan lurched forward in his chair. "What alien?" he demanded.

"The foreigner that got whacked last week near the White House. He was British or German or something, I don't really know. All I know is that the incident had Ghost's handwriting all over it, so I rattled his cage. You know, he seemed eaten up with guilt when I asked him about it, but he said he wasn't involved.

"Foreigner," Lawrence said.

"I don't think the Bureau is handling that one," said Kemper.

"Would they tie together?" Dawson asked.

"Would *what* tie together?" Amos pleaded.

Kemper looked at the others. "Gentlemen, I think we're going to have to lay our cards on the table." Amos noticed that Kemper glanced at everyone, but held Kiernan's gaze. After a moment, he said, "Carlisle, let's show him the video."

Carlisle began to type. "What you're about to see, sergeant, was taken two days ago by the security cameras at the main branch of the Liberty Loan Bank in Georgetown. I must remind you of the confidentiality of what you're about to see."

"Fire away," Amos said.

The image was clean and sharp, and in full color. Amos appreciated that. It wasn't too long ago that security cameras had provided blurry, jerking images that were useful only occasionally. This digital stuff was amazing.

"Give him the sound, too," Kemper said.

A few keystrokes, and the sounds of commerce filled the room.

It was a busy day at the bank. The lines were short but steady, and the tellers were kept on their toes.

Then it happened. A tall kid swaggered in through the doors and stopped in the dead center of the bank lobby, then shouted "Everybody freeze!" He paused for a second, turning slowly in a circle. When he was content that everyone was cooperating, he stepped up to the nearest teller cage and tossed in a pillowcase.

"Give me all the money," he said to the woman behind the counter. "And no funny tricks. No silent alarms. None of them exploding dye cans or marked money. All I want is U.S. Government currency." He leaned toward the teller. "Got that?"

The teller nodded and started putting money in the pillowcase.

"And the same rules go for all the others, too. You get all your clean money in the sack, and you pass it to the left. I don't want no tricks from any of you."

The scene was bizarre. The line of tellers obediently passed the pillowcase from cage to cage, down to the assailant who waited at the last cage. The robber collected the bulging sack and started to leave. Then he stopped and turned back, pointing to one of the tellers.

"You in the red blouse. C'mere."

The teller circled around to a side door and emerged.

"You lookin' good. You be comin' with me. The rest of you we be seeing later." With that, he gave a sarcastic salute and walked out the door with the teller on his arm.

"That was Ghost," Amos said as the image faded to black.

"Did you notice anything unusual about this event?" Kemper asked.

Amos nodded. "I'd be blind not to. He never once

showed or implied he had a gun. He just waltzed into that bank like he was king of the world and asked for what he wanted."

"Very good," Dawson said. "How do you think he did it?"

"You're the psychologist," Amos said. "Don't you have any theories?"

"We'd like to hear *yours*," Kiernan said.

"Maybe he had his gang standing out of camera range with machine guns. But I doubt that's the case. You've probably got a reverse-angle recording that shows Ghost acted alone. Besides, if it had been the whole gang, you'd have picked them all up by now."

Kemper nodded solemnly.

"The question is, gentlemen, what do you want with me?"

"Your expertise in finding this man."

"He's no man," Amos scoffed. "He's a boy. That's all. Just a scared little boy who never had the chance to grow up right."

"What you saw him commit there, Sergeant White, was a felony." Kiernan said brusquely. "That's a man's crime."

"I'm with you on that. And he should pay for it."

"Mr. Kiernan," Kemper said. "If we're going to give Sergeant White a true appreciation for the gravity of this situation, we have to be more candid than we have been. I can do that only with your permission."

Man, Amos thought. *The IRS has their fingers in everyone's pockets now.*

Kiernan dropped his eyes for a moment, then looked at Amos, then at Kemper. He nodded.

"Thank you," Kemper said. To Amos: "Sergeant, your assessment is correct. Kit Washington acted alone."

"What can't be explained," Dawson said, "is that his

instructions to the patrons and personnel of the bank were followed to the letter. The silent alarm was not tripped. Existing marked money and dye canisters were not used, even though there was ample opportunity to use them. Two armed security guards had clean shots at this man, but did nothing to stop him. The only reason this robbery got called in was because someone about to go into the bank saw Washington running out with his sack full of money, and called 911 from a pay phone."

"Everyone was still standing there when the police arrived," Lawrence said. "One of them finally had to shout out an order to relax before they returned to anything resembling normalcy. Everyone inside that bank was like a zombie. We asked them what happened, and we got an identical story from everyone. 'This black kid came in and told us to freeze. We did. He took the money and the teller and left.' Like they're all reading it from a script."

"One more thing," said Dawson, "they all seem to be unusually susceptible to suggestion, although this tendency is fading as time goes on."

"What about the woman who left with Ghost?" Amos asked.

"After the robbery, she used her Visa card to check into the Jacuzzi suite at the Georgetown Holiday Inn. That's within running distance of the bank. Yesterday morning, the day clerk saw her standing out front looking up and down the street. He thought she was waiting for a taxi. Then she stepped in front of a bus." He slid a file across the table to Amos. "She was twenty-six."

Amos opened the file. The first page was a blown-up photocopy of a Virginia driver's license. The next page was the beginning of an autopsy report. "Semen everywhere," he said. "Vagina, mouth, under her nails, on her breasts."

"A marathon," Carlisle said.

"We're thinking maybe this could be a weird inside job," Lawrence said. "Maybe she was in with this guy Ghost, and they planned this together. Maybe she promised the tellers and the guards a cut. The crowd froze because the guards did. It makes some sense."

Amos flipped through the file pages. "How many tellers on duty?"

"Five," said Lawrence.

"And two guards. How much money did he get?"

"Just over twenty-three grand."

Amos drummed his fingers on the table top. "You think all these people would risk their jobs and jail for less than three thousand dollars apiece?"

"That's what we're asking you," Kiernan said.

Amos turned back a page in the file. "That woman was twenty-six years old and lived in a house in Arlington. Married to a nice lawyer, had two kids. That a successful woman of color would want anything to do with a scumbag like Kit Washington is unlikely."

"Do you have a better theory?"

Amos shook his head. "Did you ask your zombies if they saw a weapon?"

Lawrence shifted in his seat. "Not one person saw a weapon."

"Well, then." He spread out his hands. "Maybe they just decided he was a poor kid trying to work his way out of the ghetto, and *deserved* the money for showing a little initiative."

"That's not funny," Kemper said.

"I'm not trying to put you down, but you white folks with suits seem to think that black folks all know each other and belong to some kind of secret club," Amos said. "That's why you were willing to believe that everyone in the bank cooperated with a common criminal. Most of them were black. The guards were black. The tellers were black. One of them even went with him."

"Tell you what. Instead of hoping that I can read the mind of a criminal, why don't you go straight to the source?"

"That's just it," Kemper said. "We can't seem to find Mr. Washington."

Amos laughed. "Come on. You're the feds." He pointed to Kiernan. "You've got the Internal Revenue Service on your side. Between you there's no safe place to hide. Ghost would have to be invisible for you not to catch him, and even then, you still might."

Lawrence shook his head. "That's just the thing, sergeant. He might as well be invisible. Nobody seems to have seen Ghost or any of his accomplices in the last two weeks."

"No way," Amos said. "I talked to him last week in—"

He stopped. *In connection with the murder of that foreigner.* Now it was starting to make sense. The spooky guy from the IRS, the FBI jumping into things. Ghost had graduated to a more heavy-duty line of work. There was only one thing that didn't make sense.

"What are you thinking, sergeant?" Kiernan asked.

"I was thinking, about how Ghost got his name. See, he was always a slick little hustler, even when he was starting out as a clocker. He could get in and out of places quick as you please—there one minute, gone the next.

"But the thing is, while he's sharp, he's no genius. And he's got a few fatal flaws. So what you've got is a kid who's loved and respected by the drug community, but the rest of the neighborhood would spit out the window if he died tomorrow."

Lawrence said, "When we say that nobody has seen him in two weeks, we mean nobody."

"We canvassed his neighborhood yesterday," Kemper

said. "You're the first person who claims to have seen him during that time."

Amos stood. He placed his palms on the tabletop and leaned toward all of them. "Look, the only way the people around that little dirtbag are going to stand up for him is if he's got a nuclear bomb hidden somewhere and is threatening to set it off.

"It can't be as hard as you're saying to find him."

"But you have to know where to look," said Lawrence. "And we don't."

"Please understand." Kemper stepped forward and placed a business card on the table in front of Amos. "We're not asking officially for your help. But a phone call would be appreciated."

Amos picked up the card, read it, nodded.

"And of course, any help you could give us would certainly be kept in mind if you ever wanted to make a career move."

Amos laughed. "Where were you seven years ago?" He shook his head. "I'm too much a part of the neighborhood now, Mr. Kemper. I want to stick around. But as the saying goes, if I scratch your back . . ."

"Just give me a call."

"And Mr. Kiernan. If my tax return looks a little strange this year . . ."

Nobody laughed.

"Just kidding." Amos stepped away from his chair and pushed it in flush with the table. "Gentlemen, if you'll excuse me, I have to go catch a ghost."

MAX KIERNAN

"You wanted me, boss?"

Kevin Wrampe was standing in the doorway of

Kiernan's office. Kiernan had been glaring at notes he was making on a legal pad. When Wrampe spoke, Kiernan removed his reading glasses and looked up.

"Yes." He stood up holding the legal pad. "I have a scenario to bounce off you." He walked to the dry-write board and picked up a pen. He wrote APRIL 13—BODY in big green letters. "In the early-morning hours of April thirteenth," he narrated, "the Washington police got the report of an assault in progress near the White House. The responding officers arrived to find the victim, an unidentified white male of undetermined age, dead at the scene." He grabbed another pen and wrote DEAD in red. Then in black he wrote WHITE HOUSE and drew a short line which terminated at GEO WASH HOSP.

"The body was taken to George Washington University Hospital. According to the ambulance crew and the attending physician"—in blue, he wrote EMS CREW and UNDERWOOD—"a Dr. George Underwood, this victim was not your typical *Homo sapiens* stock."

In red, he cataloged the list of symptoms as he recited them to Wrampe. "Possible hydrocephalus. Possible acromegaly. No navel. No visible genitalia. No body hair. Then, sometime on the thirteenth, the body . . ."

In big letters he wrote: DISAPPEARS.

"What are our options at this point?" he asked, uncapping a brown pen.

"The most likely explanation," said Wrampe, "is that he was a functional but malformed American citizen. The disappearance could be explained by the Amish theory. Or perhaps nobody could get a proper vital sign on him because of the deformity. Or maybe he somehow faked his own death and escaped."

"Good," Kiernan said. He wrote GENETIC, USA, AMISH?, ASSUMED DEATH, ESCAPE.

"Another possibility is that he was a foreign national.

Thalidomide would mean British. Radiation would mean a Chernobyl baby or a Kazakhstani. Or one of the Chinese experiments."

THALID - UK, RAD - CHERN, KAZAK, EXP - CHINA.

"Or . . . it could mean an ET. But we don't have any compelling evidence for that."

"Now," Kiernan said, writing with the brown pen APRIL 22—ROBBERY. "On April twenty-second, a two-bit hood named Kit Washington walked into a bank in Georgetown and made off with twenty-three grand. He apparently carried no weapon, yet everyone cooperated to the letter. He even took one of the tellers with him for marathon sex. And nobody who was in that bank could explain what happened."

In black: G'TOWN BANK.

In blue: KIT WASHINGTON, TELLERS, GUARDS, CUSTOMERS.

In red: $23 + K, 100% COOPERATION, AMNESIA.

"Explain it," Kiernan challenged.

"Incredible charisma," said Wrampe. "Liberal guilt. Hidden weapons. Mass hysteria. Mass hypnosis. A security camera that didn't record the entire event." He shook his head helplessly.

Kiernan recorded the options in brown. "I didn't even think of mass hypnosis," he grunted.

"What do I win?" Wrampe asked.

"One of Brickell's cigars. Now. Are any of these things connected?" he asked Wrampe.

"They must be, or you wouldn't be grilling me like this."

"Guess who's the main suspect in the assault near the White House?"

"Kit Washington."

Kiernan drew a line from KIT WASHINGTON to

BODY in blue. Along the length of the line he wrote the word ASSAULTED.

"You have no proof of that," Wrampe said.

"Stay with me," said Kiernan. He stabbed at the word BODY and some of the blue ink rubbed off on his finger. "In what condition was the body found?"

"Dead."

"No," Kiernan corrected. "Naked."

"That's not fair," Wrampe said. "You're withholding information."

"It was in the police report. One of the officers on the scene covered it with her jacket."

"Have we talked to her?"

"Brickell did." Kiernan took his index finger and rotated it next to his ear. "She was out of it. Not paying any attention. Stupid."

"And he believed her?"

"The report alleges she threw her coat over the body and went in pursuit of what she thought was the assailant. She lost him and came back to the body as backup arrived."

In red, Kiernan wrote NAKED. "Motives for assault."

"Fear? Revenge? Self-defense . . ." His voice trailed off.

"Tell me what you're thinking, Kevin."

"Robbery."

Kiernan gave him a thumbs-up. Next to ASSAULT he wrote ROBBERY.

"I see it," Wrampe said. "Washington robs this strange little man on the street, and within ten days he pulls off a robbery in a way that nobody can explain."

"Then he drops from the memory of the people in his neighborhood." Kiernan picked up the red and wrote DISAPPEARS again, then in blue connected it with the one under BODY. "Do you see a pattern forming?"

"This is more than a scenario," Wrampe said. "We may have something."

"More than just something," Kiernan said. "We may have technology involved. What's the status of our file on this body?"

"The CIA gave us the records. We've also picked up the doctor and the two EMS technicians. They're on the way to Dayton."

"Move them to the New Mexico unit," Kiernan said. "What about the cops?"

"I talked it over with Fenton and Brickell. They're not a risk."

Kiernan said, "Where do we start looking?"

Wrampe walked to the board and pointed to DISAPPEARS. "Right here. If Washington relieved the victim of what we think is technology, then how did the victim get out of the hospital?"

Kiernan bit his lip and stared at the board. "Ever check out of the hospital AMA? Against medical advice?"

"You put on your clothes, you walk out. But he had no clothes."

"Scrub greens," Kiernan said quickly. With the pen in his hand, he drew a line and wrote the two words.

"A homeless man in scrub greens," Wrampe said.

Kiernan looked at him.

"Well he doesn't have any money."

"Point," said Kiernan. "Alert Brickell and Fenton to keep their eyes open. Get them checking the shelters."

"What about Washington?"

Kiernan smiled. "The FBI's on him. And when they get him, he'll be coming straight to us." He picked up a blue pen, then turned and gave a heading to the scenario that had grown on the board.

VISITOR.

SUSAN HILL

Skeletons. Digging. That was Mick Aaronson's response when she had described feeling stonewalled in her investigation. None of her phone calls were being returned, not even from Fran Markowski. Aaronson had listened to her frustrations and then said, "Get more bones. And when you've gathered enough, I'll let somebody help you flesh them out."

That was why she was sitting in a battered Rent-A-Wreck, outside of the apartment building that was home to Dr. George Underwood. She wore the coat and hat of a Domino's Pizza delivery person, and a Domino's flag was magneted to the top of the car. On the seat beside her was a pepperoni pizza inside one of their insulated blankets.

She shoved a stick of gum in her mouth and ground it between her molars. "Nobody's going to fall for this."

She grabbed the pizza and walked up to the door of the complex. Looking at the row of buttons, she chose the one below Underwood's and pushed it.

"Hullo?" a woman's voice squawked.

"Domino's," she said, cracking the gum. "Got your pizza."

"I didn't order a pizza," the voice said.

"What?"

"I didn't order a pizza."

"I'm sorry," she said. "I can't understand you." Susan waited. The lock buzzed. *So far, so good* she thought, opening the door.

Susan went up the stairs and was met at the second floor landing by a curler-haired woman in a housecoat. "I didn't order any pizza," she said.

"Large pepperoni, thin crust?" Susan asked, chewing.

The woman shook her head.

"Underwood? Apartment 26A?"

The woman rolled her eyes. "We're 26B."

"Oh. So sorry." Susan managed a sheepish grin. "Guess I hit the wrong button."

"Yeah." The woman grumbled as she turned to go back into her apartment. Susan strode down the hall to the door labeled 26A and raised her fist to knock.

"That won't do any good," the woman said.

"Huh?" Susan cracked her gum.

"He's not home. I think he's on vacation."

"Oh," Susan said haughtily. "Like you know all about him, right?"

"He plays loud music in the mornings when he gets off shift," the woman said. "I haven't heard it in a while."

Susan looked straight at her and knocked.

"Okay. Don't believe me." The woman shut her door.

Susan waited.

She knocked again.

She waited.

Nothing.

She pressed her ear to the door.

Silence.

She walked down the hall and knocked on 26B. After a moment, the door cracked open, and the woman peered out cautiously.

"Look," Susan said, "I'm sorry. You were right. Looks like I got scammed. You want this pizza?"

"No," the woman said.

"Free?" Susan asked.

The woman shook her head.

Susan let her shoulders slump. "Thanks anyway."

Susan went down to the first floor and pulled a flat-tened duffel bag out from under her jacket. She took off the jacket and cap and stuffed them and the pizza blan-ket into the duffel bag. She slung the bag over her shoulder and took the stairs into the basement, where she knocked on the apartment manager's door.

When the door opened, the sounds of a basketball game spilled into the hall. She was standing eye-to-eye with a weary, balding man in a Washington Redskins shirt.

"Yeah?" he asked flatly.

"You have got to help me," she said, exasperated.

He cocked his head at her. "Who are you?"

"You don't know me," she said, "but I'm sort of, uh, *friends* with George Underwood. You know, 26A?"

He nodded.

Susan ran her hand through her hair for effect. The move strategically shifted her breasts under the T-shirt. The manager noticed immediately that she was braless. "Well, you know, we sort of met at the hospital. And I, well, I sort of left some things in his apartment. Some really important things."

"Things." His eyes narrowed. "You mean like *pills*?"

Susan rolled her eyes. "Don't use them. If you must know, I left my medieval history books there along with my final term paper. If I don't get that paper in on time, I'm going to lose a letter grade on it. And he promised he'd be home tonight."

"Maybe he stepped out," the manager said.

She waved the box under his nose. "Then why'd he have me pick up the pizza?" She lowered the box and went into her pout again. "I think he's avoiding me."

The manager looked her up and down. "Just like a doctor," he said. "After the physical, he's out the door."

Susan stepped forward and let herself brush against him. "You'll help me, then?"

In less than a minute, the keys were jangling in his hand, and she was following him up the stairs.

"He seemed like a nice guy, y'know?" she said.

"Uh-huh."

"And I mean, I'm *selective*, you know?"

"Uh-huh."

"So I thought, this guy, he's a doctor, he should be *safe*, you know? And maybe I could even get hooked up with him for a while."

The manager stopped at 26A. "I do this, you gotta disappear and not come back, okay? You see Dr. Underwood again, you go the other way."

"Okay," Susan said.

He slid the key into the slot and turned the knob. The door drifted open. Susan carefully stepped inside, feeling for the light switch. Her finger touched it, and she flipped it.

"Oh, no!" she said.

Except for the overpowering scent of a strong disinfectant, the apartment was empty.

"I know how you feel," the manager said. "He didn't even give me notice."

Back in the car, Susan slipped on a Georgetown U. sweatshirt and dug a slice of pizza out of the box. She chewed it dejectedly as she thought about how thoroughly the apartment had been cleaned out. The manager had said it was the cleanest a tenant had ever left one of his apartments. There wasn't even a matchbook left in a closet corner. Even the dust bunnies had been sucked out of remote corners. And then there was that overpowering smell, the disinfectant.

"At least I got his deposit," the manager had said.

Whatever was going on, it couldn't be over something as simple as a Thalidomide baby. This was nobody from Chernobyl or China. It was bigger.

Susan tried to imagine what. Plague, perhaps? The disinfectant smell had been so strong that it had stung her eyes and nostrils. Maybe the CDC was tracking down a foreign terrorist with a bioweapon.

A bioweapon, she thought. You're eating pizza after

chasing someone who might have been up to their neck in germs. She curled her upper lip and tossed the remainder of the pizza aside.

Bones. Keep looking for bones. Think of another goofy trick and try to get more information until the skeleton is complete.

HARRY LAUTER

"If you look through the Bible, my friends, you'll find that Satan has many names. He has many, many names, and none of them are good. They all describe with terrible accuracy the foulness of this fiend whose only reason for being is to abscond with our precious souls!

"Brothers and sisters, I'd like to talk to you about one of those names—'Deceiver.' It says a lot, doesn't it? This fallen angel, this overlord of evil, this abomination, this ruler of the netherworld wants to cheat you out of your everlasting soul.

"And how does he do it, my friends? Well, it depends. Most of the time, he shows you his watch. And what I mean by that is, when you're down and you're out and you've decided that there's no place left for you to go but the loving and merciful arms of the Lord your God, Satan pulls out this pocket watch and shows it to you, and he says 'WHAT DO YOU WANT TO DO THAT FOR? YOU HAVE PLENTY OF TIME TO TURN BACK TO GOD!'

"He's doing that even now, my friends, by spreading the word of the coming millennium. 'WHY DO YOU WANT TO REPENT NOW?' he's saying. 'YOU HAVE EIGHT MORE MONTHS BEFORE GOD RETURNS. EIGHT MORE MONTHS TO DRUG AND DRINK

AND GAMBLE AND WHORE. LIVE IT UP WHILE YOU CAN!'

"Brothers and sisters, right now there are people roasting in hell because they bought this lie. There are people roasting in hell because they took one more slug of whiskey or inhaled one more line of cocaine. There was one more good-looking woman in the bar that they just had to have. And then there are all of the others who have been lost because of accident or sudden disease, precious souls who were led to believe that there was time enough to put off that critical decision.

"And now friends, as we approach the millennium, the Deceiver has one more trick up his sleeve. One more devious ploy to capture your soul and condemn it to an eternity of purest darkness. And this is the most sinister thing he has ever done, my friends. Why? Because he is telling you, TIME IS SHORT, SO RUN TO GOD AND EMBRACE HIM!

"That's right! You heard me right, my friends! Satan is saying run to God and embrace him!

"But what kind of god is he telling you to run toward? Ah, that is why he is the Deceiver! He is telling you to run toward whichever god suits your needs! From the foulest and most insidious cults to the New Age concept that we are all God—to the ancient Gnostics who felt that God was cold, distant, and unknowable—he is telling you to be ready for the coming crisis by means of this deadly embrace!

"He wants you to run, RUN! to your destruction now! Hurry! Hurry! Hurry! My brothers and sisters, you have to watch out, you have to be careful—because the Prince of Darkness will snatch you up!"

Harry Lauter paused and brought a plastic bottle to his lips. He squeezed, and sweet water shot out of the straw into his mouth. This was remarkable, he thought. This was his biggest crowd ever. He had them where he wanted them, and they were *riveted.* He thought, *Thank you, Lord, for giving me the millennium to scare them with.*

Now, if he could keep it up. If he could get to the real message, the scrolls, without losing them. He had to build up to it slowly and hit them with it quickly. And if someone heckled him, he would have to keep going, ignore it, or give as good as he got.

He stood for a moment, swallowing and looking at the crowd. Some of them stood motionless, their palms raised to the morning sun, their eyes closed, their lips spilling out *Thank you, Lord* and *Praise Jesus!* They looked like strange, basking lizards. But, Harry thought, even a lizard soaking up sun on a rock looked happy.

Harry took one more long squirt of water from the bottle and cleared his throat, getting ready to go back to the Amen-ing crowd, when a single voice rose above the others.

"Praise, brothers and sisters! *Praise!* I say it again, praise God and all his creation."

Harry put the bottle down and looked through the crowd. There, pushing toward the front was a tall, pale man dressed in Salvation Army chic.

"Sing praise with all your might! This is a new day, and all things are good which come from the Lord!"

Harry squinted. His eyes weren't what they used to be, that was for sure. Maybe it was the beatings or the interrogational chemicals that had done it. He needed new glasses, but who could afford them when you were saving up to go back to the Holy Land?

The man came closer, but even then Harry couldn't pin down who he was. He looked strangely familiar and apparently knew Harry, because he stepped right up to him and embraced him with a mammoth bear hug.

"You listen," he said, turning to the crowd, keeping his arm around Harry. "You listen to this man. He speaks the truth, and the truth shall set you free. He spoke the truth at me, time after time after time, and I wouldn't listen. It was only through his interceding prayers that I was saved. God reached down from the top of his mountain and grabbed me by the lapels. He shook me by the lapels of my rotting suit and said, *TURN BACK, O MAN!*" The man shouted this last part, and it thrilled Harry's audience. Hands shot up into the air as it filled with shouts of praise and admiration. Harry could only stare with an open mouth.

The man looked at Harry, grinned broadly and said, "You don't recognize me, do you?"

Harry shook his head sheepishly.

More laughter. "That's because I'm not wallowing in my own filth! Praise God for his salvation! Harry"—he took Harry's head in both hands and brought it close to his—"I'm John Drury."

Harry squinted. He tried to imagine the face with a shaggy beard and mustache, covered with grime.

"I imagine I smell better than I did last time you saw me."

Yes, Harry thought. *It's him. It's really him!* Astonished, he took a step backward. "John," he said in awe and offered his hand to shake. Their hands connected, and then they pulled together for another embrace. The crowd cheered.

Harry turned to address the crowd. "Brothers and sisters, just as God turns those deep in sin over to the consequences of their actions, so I had done with a man named John Drury. I thought he was so stained and scarred that nothing would ever get through to him. But God had other ideas for him—like showing me that nothing is beyond his reach!"

They embraced again. More cheering and praise. And within moments they were both working the crowd like a tag team, entreating and encouraging. The crowd grew, and the atmosphere reminded Harry of a tent revival meeting on a hot summer night, where the shirt stuck to your back, and the passion of the souls inside multiplied with the mugginess outside. There was shouting and yelling. Two people fainted. Another claimed that the nicotine demon had been driven right out of him. And when someone tried to heckle the two of them by saying that they wanted to hear about space aliens, you would have thought that Old Scratch himself had shown up, only to be reviled and turned back with tongues that hissed a hundred different verses of scripture.

Harry broke the meeting up only after the park police started to become agitated. He felt wistful as he watched the crowd dissipate, but they would be back, he knew. John Drury's appearance and witnessing was a full-fledged miracle, the likes of which many would have paid money to see.

Then John said, "These are the days, aren't they, brother?"

Harry nodded. "So many souls. So little time."

"You got through to me. That should count for something. It means you've effectively doubled your number."

Harry looked at him. "I can see that. But I meant what I said about leaving you to your sin. I wasn't just giving the people a good show. I had given up on you, John. And now I can't imagine what I may have said or done that turned you around." He looked him over. "Or at least started you on the way."

"I'm on the way," John said. "I haven't had a drink in over a week. The clothes aren't much, I know, but I've signed on with a legal-aid group that provides services to the poor. I think I've still got a decent legal mind, if I haven't fried too many brain cells."

"So tell me," Harry said. "What turned you around?"

"I'm sure your influence had something to do with it. I mean, last time I saw you, you said you were going to pray for me, right?"

Harry nodded. He had said something like that, but it had been a while ago. He had even dropped John's name from his prayer list, counting him among the "miscellaneous others" he always mentioned at the end.

"Well, your prayers went up as a pleasing aroma before the Lord, Harry, because Jesus himself came down to heal me."

"He did?" Harry tried not to sound too skeptical.

"Indeed he did. And he spoke to me in words that burned pictures in my head. And then he healed me. After I thought about it, I realized whom I had seen, and I realized the need to repay the debt. So I got a Bible, and I've been studying, Harry. You'd be proud of me. And then, when I saw you here proselytizing to the others, I just had to do it. I just had to come forward and share with the others how Jesus had made me feel."

"That's wonderful," Harry said, patting John on the shoulder. He didn't want to put the man off his religious epiphany, but in Harry's experience, God just didn't work that way. True, powerful spirituality occasionally led to things for which there was no accounting. But the age of miraculous intervention had ended with the death of the last apostle.

Of course, he couldn't tell that to John Drury. Or to the man who had felt the nicotine demon leaving his body.

Whatever got you through the day, Harry thought.

"His grace is abounding," Harry continued.

"Isn't it, brother? Isn't it?"

Harry was torn between asking John if he wanted to go to lunch and quietly going his own way. He had had a long night, what with the neighbors pulling another marathon, and he wasn't entirely sure he wanted to be around the burning zeal of a new convert.

He looked at John, who was saying, "This is a good day for the Lord."

"It is," Harry said. Then the thought was there, presenting itself fully formed in his mind. "Listen, I want to make sure of something. You said that Jesus appeared to you in the flesh and healed you."

"Amen to that. Amen and amen."

"What did he look like?"

"Not like you would think, Harry. In fact, I think he at first made his presence hidden to me, just like he did to the apostles after his glorious resurrection."

"You're sure it was Jesus?"

"I wouldn't have come to thank you if it hadn't been."

Harry swallowed. He hated to do this next part, but his mind wandered back to the desert, the cave hidden in the sands. The smell of tanned animal hide thick in the air, undisturbed for centuries. Opening the scrolls and reading them. Taking the pictures, only to have the Israelis find them when he was trying to clear customs. "You want to spread the joy you've found? I mean really, truly see that it gets around?"

John's head nodded loosely. "Everyone should feel this way, Harry. Everyone."

Harry continued slowly, "I have a friend. He works for a national magazine. He might be interested in your story. If he is, he'll put your story out to millions of interested people. Does that sound like something you'd want to pursue?"

"Yes," John said, without hesitation.

Harry paused. There was still time for him to back down and walk away from this and leave John and his faith intact. But there it was again: the smell of the scrolls, hidden away for centuries, waiting to be unearthed when the time was right. And here he was, Harry Lauter, the instrument of their deliverance, marooned in Washington, D.C. Sometimes it took the sacrifice of one to save many. Even God understood that. "Well, then," he said, "I'll give him a call. If he wants to talk, I'll get in touch, make arrangements for the two of you to get together. That sound all right?"

"Absolutely." John smiled the smile of an innocent.

"All right." Harry reached out his hand, and they shook. "It's good to see you, brother. And I'm happy for you."

"Thank *you*, Harry. You'll never know what you've done for me."

Harry thought about saying, *That goes double for me*, but thought it would be a bit too sardonic. Instead he said, "How can I get in touch if this goes through?"

"You'll know how to find me, Harry."

Of course. What else would John be doing with his free time now, for every waking moment of his life until his heart stopped or the sheen from his saved feeling wore off? The exact same thing that Harry had been doing.

Forgive me, Harry thought as he watched John go.

AMOS WHITE

Amos was sure he was being followed.

He had no proof, only a feeling that raised the hair on the back of his neck, and it was based on the strange shadows he kept seeing in the mirrors of his spy sunglasses.

Years ago he had seen the glasses advertised in a catalog that sold books about mercenary work and "tools for surveillance." He had bought them thinking that they might someday save his life.

In the upper part of the outside of each lens was a tiny concave mirror. He had practiced with the glasses enough that with a natural-looking sweep of his head, he could scan the entire area behind him.

What he had just learned was that whoever was following him was good at it. Even when he did something subtle like stopping to look in a store window, the predator knew enough to duck into a store or behind a passing bus.

Amos knew that he wasn't the target. Whoever was following him knew that Kit Washington would be at the end of the trail.

When Amos had returned to work after his visit to the FBI, the chief called him in again, rolling his eyes, and asking what Amos had gotten himself into.

Nothing, Amos had said. What was the problem?

The problem was that the chief had just gotten a call from someone at the Bureau saying that Amos White was to be put in charge of finding Kit Washington. And the phone call was supposed to be kept confidential.

"Then why are you telling me about it?" Amos asked.

"Because you're not stupid," the chief said. "What do the feds want with him?"

Amos could only shake his head.

And so he started his investigation by retracing the steps the FBI had already taken. It was no surprise to him that nobody in Ghost's family knew where he was. Mama had kicked him out a long time ago, when he had started dealing and had impregnated some nice little cheerleader.

Heidi, the girl Ghost had taken up with recently, was even more of an enigma. Amos tried to draw her out about his whereabouts, but she insisted adamantly that she hadn't seen him in two weeks. That didn't ring true to Amos. She had been living with him in that apartment, and it had been only a matter of days since she had returned home to her mother. Amos thought he could see something in her eyes, something desperate and haunted. It was a look he usually saw in the eyes of attack or rape victims, but he knew that Ghost and Heidi had been doing the nasty on a regular basis. Besides, Ghost wasn't a beater, at least not of women. That wasn't his style.

It was nothing he could take to the bank. Or to the FBI, for that matter. Amos gave Heidi a card and told her to get in touch if she wanted to talk. She probably already had a hundred of his cards, but he felt he had to do something.

Things got strange after that. With the exception of Shark, who was another family outcast, the families of the other members of Ghost's gang reported that their sons had not been seen in two weeks. They volunteered that they had not seen Ghost, either, but Amos suspected that Ghost had been there and scared them so completely that they weren't talking.

Even though it looked like he wasn't getting anywhere, Amos felt a pattern forming in the haunted looks and the stammering denials. If he didn't know better, he would have sworn that those he talked to had been intimidated in some strange and forceful way. It was something that the feds would never sense because they weren't familiar with the neighborhood, didn't know the people.

The mothers of Piggy Boy, Squeak, and Goldie were all sure that Ghost had taken the boys off somewhere—to New York City or Miami, maybe, to seek their fortunes in the drug trade. Amos knew this was empty speculation, conjured up by worried mothers to help them get through another night of worry.

No, Amos was certain the other boys weren't with Ghost. Ghost's solitary action in the Georgetown bank had confirmed that. He had moved into a new line of work and had shed the baggage of the gang in doing so.

Well. It was clear there were lots of things that the feds didn't know. If Amos was going to be tailed, he was going to show his unwanted guest just how much he or she didn't know about life in the nation's capital.

He drove past Union Station to the abandoned warehouse that had been a magnet for Kit all of his life—the place where he had taken his first drink, the place where he had first had sex, and where he had conducted his first drug transaction. Amos parked, and before he got out, pulled the Glock .40 caliber from his shoulder holster and chambered a round.

It was easy enough to get through the fence, but finding the way into the building was more of a trick. Goldie had told him about it a couple of times, but Amos had never actually had the occasion to go in. It was a matter of finding the right loose boards, moving them aside and squeezing through.

Amos knew something was wrong the instant he was inside the building. Even though the building was massive, his nostrils picked up a scent that made his throat contract. He sucked air through his teeth and slowly made his way in. It was made of filth and sour food, something he had smelled more times than he cared to think about during the course of his career. But it was tainted with something else, something even more insidious that Amos recognized at once.

It was the smell of death. Old death.

Amos stopped, pulled a handkerchief from his pocket, covered his mouth and nose, then continued on. It wasn't long before he found the source.

The body was bloated and oozing, but Amos knew right away that it was Shark. Amos blinked the water from his eyes and knelt down for a closer look. The back of the boy's head had been blown away, and what was left of his brain had leaked out and formed a congealed puddle on the already-stained concrete floor.

Amos stood, unsure of what to do next. His thoughts focused on the Glock in his hand, primed and ready to go. Holster it, he told himself. There's no reason to be cautious now.

Amos drew a large breath and held it, then opened his coat to holster the weapon when there was a clatter from a far corner of the warehouse. Instinctively, his arm shot out, aiming the Glock at the source of the noise.

"No!" a voice cried.

Amos took big steps. His aim led him to a large pile of rags heaped in a corner. As he closed in, he could see a mass of opened tin cans and pizza boxes scattered across the floor. In another corner, rolls of toilet paper and piles of what could only be human waste.

Amos stopped a dozen feet from the pile of rags and said, "Come out."

The voice said, "You come to take me away?"

"Depends," Amos said.

"I'm ready to go."

"Come out and we'll talk about it."

The rags began to stir. Amos took a step back and sighted down the barrel of the Glock. It wasn't Ghost under that pile, but it wouldn't hurt to be cautious. But when he saw who it was, he was shocked. He was expecting a strung-out vagrant to appear in the sights of the weapon. Instead, Squeak emerged, haggard and skinny, not at all alarmed by the gun. He looked almost relieved.

"Franklin?" Amos's tone was one of disbelief.

"H'lo, Amos," Squeak said. "I'm ready to go to jail."

Amos exhaled loudly and slipped the Glock into his holster. "Why would I want to take you to jail?"

Squeak broke eye contact with the officer. The words came out in a monotone. "I did Shark. And I got the gun hid right here." He reached under his coat and pulled out a revolver with two fingers, holding it out to Amos.

Amos hesitated for a moment, then stepped forward with his hand outstretched. Squeak dropped the revolver into it. Amos stepped back and thumbed out the weapon's cylinder. It was a .357 magnum, Smith & Wesson, with a two-and-a-half-inch barrel. It held six rounds. One had been fired.

"You?" he asked. "You did Shark?"

Squeak gave a robot's nod. "He threatened my mama, Amos. So I took that man's gun of his and put it in his face and pulled the trigger. It was just me and him here. Goldie and Piggy Boy weren't here. And Ghost was a million miles away."

Amos snapped the cylinder of the .357 back into place. "This was Shark's gun?"

Squeak nodded. "I took that man's gun of his and put it in his face and pulled the trigger."

Amos took another step back. "Franklin, if Shark had the gun, how did you get it away from him?"

"I took it. He threatened my mama, Amos. I did it. It was just me and him here. Goldie and Piggy Boy weren't here. And Ghost was a million miles away."

"I didn't ask you about Ghost, Franklin."

Squeak said nothing.

"Did Ghost do this?"

"Ghost was a million miles away."

"Did Ghost tell you to confess?"

"Ghost was a million miles away."

"Did he tell you to tell me that he was a million miles away?"

Tears spilled from Squeak's eyes. "Ghost was . . . Ghost . . . He . . . I . . . I . . ." A moan spilled from his lips and filled the building. His eyes rolled up into his head, and he fell back to the floor with a thud. A tremor shot through his body. His hands twisted into claws. Amos swore violently and dropped to his knees next to the boy, cradling his head in his hands to keep it from striking the cement floor.

Amos felt his mind spinning as the boy's convulsions subsided. He had no problem believing that Ghost was the one who had robbed the bank. As to his methodology, his sheer brazenness might have accounted for the behavior of the bank patrons.

But this. This was something entirely different. Amos didn't believe in telekinesis or mind control or even hypnosis, but Ghost was obviously into something.

He had no doubt that Ghost was involved in Shark's murder. Maybe he had done it himself and made Squeak take the rap for it. Or maybe Ghost had manipulated the two of them into the deadly encounter. It might have even been true that Ghost and the others weren't even around at the time of the killing.

Still, if that was true, why was Squeak so willing to volunteer the information?

Amos tried to put it all together. Ghost. The foreigner. The FBI. That strange Kiernan fellow. The bank robbery. Shark's murder and Squeak's confession. It was like the parts were all there but something fundamental was missing.

What was it?

Amos thought back to his boyhood for a moment, when he would pay twelve cents for a comic book at a magazine and sweet shop near the Capitol Building. The place had long since become an adult bookstore, but the locale still had a sentimental meaning for him. Once a month he would buy *Green Lantern* and

The Incredible Hulk, and either a Dr. Pepper or an Oh Henry! bar. And he would sit on the bench outside the store, lost in the gaudy four-color adventures.

What fascinated him most about the comic books were the ads they ran, for strange and mysterious objects that would give you powers almost equaling those of the superheroes you were reading about.

There was one in particular that had caught his attention. The hypno-coin. Carry it in your pocket, the ad had said. Keep it handy. A million laughs for all occasions. Great fun at parties.

No, he told himself. That was just a cheap gimmick to cheat young boys out of their allowances. The hypno-coin when you were ten or twelve, and the X-Ray Spex when you were fourteen or so.

It was weird, he told himself. Too, too weird.

It seemed to take forever for Squeak's convulsions to stop. When they did, Amos waited, watching. He had seen his share of grand mal seizures, and most of the time when they were through, the victims regained consciousness slowly, rolling their eyes, and trying to pierce the fog that had enveloped their brains. The paramedics who had trained Amos in first aid had told him the name of that phase, and it had been on his final exam, but for now it escaped him.

Squeak did no such thing. While he did seem to calm down and his breathing resumed a normal rate, he remained unconscious.

Amos opened the boy's shirt. The kid stank to high heaven. How long had he been living here, without a toilet or a shower, surviving on canned foods that he had obviously pilfered from one of the neighborhood stores?

With the knuckle of one finger, Amos rubbed the boy's sternum. Nothing. He pressed harder and tried it again. Still nothing. Not only was he out, he was out for the count.

Amos scooped up the .357 and slipped it into the pocket of his sport jacket. Then he stood, squatted, grabbed Squeak by the arms and pulled him up, throwing the boy over his shoulder in the classic potato-sack carry. Then, with one arm around the boy's waist, he started for the boarded-up door.

When Amos got to his car, he radioed for backup and an ambulance. While waiting for them to arrive, he laid Squeak down on the ground, elevated his legs, and covered him with a blanket from the trunk of his car. He was looking at the revolver again as the first sirens reached him. It was a black-and-white unit, lights flashing. Amos pulled out his wallet and flipped it open to show his badge as the car pulled up next to his.

The driver was out of the car immediately, a thin, pale officer with a worried look on his face. His passenger, a stocky sergeant, took his time in climbing out of the vehicle.

"What have you got, detective?"

Amos flipped his wallet shut and slipped it back into his coat. "I need you to take this as a crime scene. There's one dead, inside the warehouse. Juvenile male, about sixteen." He pointed out the door and told them how to get in.

The sergeant motioned to Squeak. "This one the suspect?"

"He confessed, but I don't think he did it. We'll have to see."

The sergeant motioned to his sickly-looking charge and said, "Let's get started on this." The young officer started toward the door.

Amos said, "The two of you should know something."

They stopped to look at him.

"He's been dead a long time."

The sergeant nodded. "Thanks." Then, to his associate: "You up for this?"

He nodded uncertainly. "Gotta do it sometime."

"Good attitude. Let's go."

They vanished into the building as more vehicles arrived, the ambulance, another black-and-white, and an unmarked. Amos met the ambulance crew and explained what had happened to Squeak, and they immediately set to work. The officers from the new black-and-white asked what they could do. Amos told them that there was another victim who wasn't going anywhere, and that their sergeant was already on the scene. The pair opened their trunk and began to lug bags of equipment into the warehouse.

Amos pulled out his handkerchief and blew his nose, trying to get the scent of the warehouse out of his head. He walked to the unmarked car and rapped a knuckle on the roof. The door opened and Jack Mardell climbed out, rolling his arms and shoulders to adjust the fit of his suit coat.

"You got it under control here, Amos?"

Amos looked at him. "I wish I could say that. This is just the tip of the iceberg."

"What do you mean by that?"

Amos looked toward the warehouse. "How much do you know about what I'm doing, Jack?"

"Chief told me you're on a special assignment to find Kit Washington 'cause some federal types want to talk to him real bad." He reached inside his suit and pulled a slip of paper from his breast pocket. "He also asked me to give you a message. We put the word out on Kit and his gang, and someone from an outfit called Citizens Who Care called and told us they had a homeless kid who fit the description of William Golden. So we nabbed him."

"Anything?" Amos asked.

Mardell laughed. "Get this. He says he's got a case of amnesia. Those are his exact words. 'I don't know nuthin', man. I got a case of amnesia.' " He pulled a cigarette from inside his suit coat and started to light it. He stopped when he saw the detective looking urgently toward the warehouse. "What's wrong, Amos?"

"Did Goldie say anything about having seen Kit Washington?" Amos said quickly.

Mardell shook his head, blowing the first puff of smoke. "He wouldn't even give his own name. Amnesia, you know."

"And Ghost was a million miles away," Amos said.

"What are you talking about?" Mardell asked.

"I wish I knew, Jack." *Another piece of the puzzle,* Amos thought. *Another victim of the hypno-coin.* "I need to see him right away."

"You got a crime scene to manage, detective."

"You've got to catch this one for me, Jack. This is important. I can fill you in on the particulars later."

Mardell blew smoke in disgust.

"Call the chief to clear it if you want. He wants this thing off my desk, and I want out from under it."

"You're not just doing this because you've got a ripe deader in there, are you?"

"Would I do that to you, Jack?"

"Any day of the week."

Amos climbed into the car and gunned it out of the warehouse parking lot. Inside of fifteen minutes, he was parked at the battered precinct building. With an air of urgency, he headed for the entrance, but he was stopped by an urgent shout.

"Hey, brother, wait up."

Amos tried to ignore it, but as he hit the stairs, a hand tagged him on the shoulder. Rolling his eyes, he turned to see a heavyset man clad in lime-green silk, gold toothed, with a mustache and a soul patch in bad need of trimming. The figure was wearing enough gold jewelry to sink him to the bottom of the Potomac River.

"Julius," he grunted. "I told you to never show your face in this neighborhood again."

Julius held his hands up defensively. "Hey, brother. Don't get so mad. I'm here on official business."

Amos pointed a finger into the man's face. "Wha'd you do, make bail? I told you if you ever got busted around here, I'd break both your legs. You're lucky I'm in a hurry."

"I want to call a truce, brother Amos, because I need your help," Julius said smoothly. "You always tellin' folks, they need help, come to you because you're the man who cares."

Amos bit the inside of his lip. Leave it to Julius to remember that particular promise. "You have two minutes."

"One of my ladies is missing."

"I'm sorry, Julius, that's not—"

"Patrice," he said.

Amos froze. "Patrice?"

Julius nodded. "Last time I saw her, I sent her to Mr. Freddy's to buy some nice wine for a dinner we was gonna throw."

Amos looked over Julius's shoulder and down the city street, thinking. He had always hoped that Patrice would turn out right. She almost had. Then she had met Julius. "Well," he said slowly, "maybe she finally smarted up and got out. You're just going to have to find a way to make up the income, Julius."

Julius shook his head. "I think she was snatched."

"Don't give yourself that much credit, Julius. Maybe, like last time, she ran off to take a breather."

"Brother Amos, she left Denzel behind. I don't think she'd leave him behind, either way."

"She might," Amos said.

"Then I wish she'd come get him," Julius replied. "Stupid thing chewed up one of my best shoes and wet all over my carpet."

"You're supposed to walk him, Julius."

"I wouldn't be caught dead walking that thing. Gimme a Dobie any day, or a mastiff. Denzel, he ain't more than a little rat; but Patrice, she loves him more than life itself."

"All right," Amos said. "You've got your truce." He pointed to the steps, and the pimp started up toward the door.

"Thanks, brother," he said. "Man, I hope you ain't got her in that morgue of yours."

Amos thought of the clipboard in his car with the listing of recently recovered Jane Does. "I don't think anyone with her description has been brought in. What was she wearing?"

"Mmmm-mmm," Julius said, shaking his head. "She was dressed to kill that day. Had on this red vinyl number, with black go-gos and fishnet stockings. Her hair was—"

Inches from the door, Amos stopped. "What did you say?"

"I was gonna say she messin' with this new hair-do—"

"What was she wearing?"

"I told you. This red vinyl thing, and it turned all the right corners, if you know what I mean. Then these black boots—"

"Red," Amos said. "She was dressed in red."

"Amos," Julius said, his lower lip trembling, "tell me you ain't got pretty little Patrice in that cold old morgue of yours."

"So was the bank teller."

Julius shook his head. "Brother, you one confused nigger—"

Amos flew into action. He flung open the door and shoved Julius inside, shouting for the desk sergeant to drop what he was doing and take the man's statement. Julius, stammering and ready to cry, was left behind as Amos ran down the hall.

"I know where he is," he said, bursting into the chief's office.

The chief, in the company of one of the senior detectives, looked up from the cigar he was lighting. He glared at the interruption. "I thought you caught a deader."

"Mardell's handling it. Chief, I know where Kit Washington is."

The cigar came out of the mouth. "Where?"

Amos took two steps to the chief's desk and pulled a black Magic Marker out of an ancient coffee mug. Then he stepped to a wall that held a giant map of the district.

"What are you doing, White?" the chief shouted as the detective began to draw.

"Georgetown was an aberration," Amos said. "He went there because he never goes there. He stays east of Rock Creek and this side of the Potomac." The marker squeaked under the guidance of his hand. "West of the rail lines as far north as McKinley High. South of Union Station, as far east as the Anacostia River. But never west of 395."

"What are you doing?" the chief repeated.

Amos stepped back from the map and pointed with the marker. "This," he announced, "is the range of Kit Washington's movements. This is his turf, the territory he knows the best. Where he's comfortable."

The cigar was now in the chief's mouth, smoking furiously. "Get to the point, detective."

"You're going to think I'm crazy," Amos said, slapping the outline with his hand. "Are there any red motels in this area here?"

FRAN MARKOWSKI

From the rear, the man looked grotesque. The mop of hair on his head was ill-fitting, and the back of his neck was a web of raised ridges and too-smooth skin. He was short enough to be a kid, but the bouncers had let him in. Fran Markowski didn't look forward to seeing him from the front.

Besides, she was more curious about the tall blonde he was with. She was drunk now, tossing her head in time to the beat of the music, hair tangling around her face. She would whistle and yell each time the music stopped, calling the table dancers one by one to perform for her companion. The man would look up at a dancer who would look down and then tactfully away from his face. He wouldn't raise a finger. All he did was watch. And when the dance was over, the blonde would stuff a tip into the dancer's garter and motion for the next one.

This ritual was interrupted only by the blonde's frequent trips to the ladies' room. She would return energized and ready for another round, ready to procure another dancer for her man, pausing only to wipe her nose on her sleeve.

Fran suspected that beneath the clingy cotton blouse the woman wore, she was probably skin and bones. No boobs at all, and you could practically count her ribs from clear over here. Add it all up and what did you have? *Major cokehead. Major, major cokehead.*

Fran wrapped her hands around the gin and tonic she had been pretending to drink and glared at the blonde. *I'm going to remember you.*

But at the moment, Fran's pressing concern was a man the papers were calling the Scarlet Avenger. He was a lunatic who had dropped a few bricks while on the way to a whacko-rights march and was attacking working girls with balloons full of red paint. He'd shout out something about Hester Prynne before heaving the weapon, which meant that he had either caught his wife in flagrante delicto one time too many or had overdosed on Nathaniel Hawthorne. The pattern of attacks seemed to center around this particular bar, and since it hadn't yet been blessed with a visit, Lieutenant McKeown had come to the conclusion that it was just a matter of time before the guy showed up here with his balloon-busting act.

So all Fran had to do was keep the male patrons of the place away from her, which wouldn't necessarily be an easy task considering the level of testosterone in the place.

Which was why she was caught off guard by a proposition from a working girl who had come in and perched on the bar stool next to her.

"Hey, honey," she said, "I think you got just what I need."

Fran didn't even look up. She kept her hand on her glass, eyes daggering the party blonde, and didn't say a word.

"Don't take offense, darling. I'm thinking you and me could do a little business."

"I don't do any of that lesbo stuff," Fran growled. "Even if it's just an act."

"Don't sell yourself short, honey. I think you and me could have a whole world of things to talk about."

Fran slowly loosed her grip on the glass and let her hands ball into fists. Then she started to turn, setting her features hard. A quick glance and she would know whether to handle the situation with a torrent of profanity or—

Instantly she tried to withdraw her anger but it escaped, hissing through her clenched teeth.

"What are you doing here?"

It was that reporter from the *Tribune*, dolled up for a night on the streets. Too much mascara, too much lipstick, too much cleavage showing and not enough bosom to make it worth the effort. A lot of leg showing, but what were those on her feet? *Reeboks?*

Fran grabbed her by the arm and jerked her off the stool. Turning to the bartender she said, "Excuse me, but my friend and I have to make a trip to the little girls' room. Would you be a dear and save our seats?"

Since the night was slow, the bartender nodded, and Fran Markowski dragged Susan Hill into the restroom and pushed her into one of the stalls. She latched the door behind her, then whirled on the reporter with a vengeance.

"You certainly have your nerve showing up here, and you've got a lot to learn about dressing the part."

"I turned down some very lucrative offers before I found you," Susan said.

"You could have been mugged or busted or a hundred other things. As it is, you're about to screw up my surveillance—"

"Fran, I've got a theory," Susan said, standing her ground. "Believe me, if there was any other way to get in touch—"

"Yeah? Ever hear of the telephone?"

"I've been trying to get in touch with you for days. I left messages at the precinct house, but they never got through to you."

"I never got any messages."

"That's my point. Fran, I think you're being watched.

I think it has to do with the foreigner whose body vanished from the hospital."

Fran leaned against the door. "What have you been smoking?"

Susan recounted the events of the last few days, concluding with her examination of George Underwood's apartment.

"That's it?" Fran said. "You went to all this trouble just to find me and tell me that some doctor went on the chicken run?"

"No," Susan said. "I'm here to tell you that there's a real possibility that your life is in danger."

"Really," Fran said.

Susan nodded. "How's your health, Fran? Are you okay? Have you felt any strange symptoms since you were in contact with that foreigner?"

"Nothing out of the ordinary aside from the urge to strangle a certain reporter with the *Washington Tribune*."

Susan said, "I think that whoever is watching you may be expecting you to become sick in the very near future."

"I'm being watched. I'm getting sick. You're not making any sense."

"I will in a minute," Susan said. "When I got into Underwood's apartment, the first thing I noticed was the smell of disinfectant. It wasn't like Lysol, it was major-league industrial-strength stuff. Maybe iodine based. Now why would that smell be in Underwood's apartment? Because he was up to his elbows in that mystery man, and the mystery man was host to some strange virus."

"That's a pretty big leap of the imagination." Fran shook her head in disbelief. "I think you're trying too hard to impress Mick Aaronson."

"Fran, if somebody thinks you had only minimal

contact with the guy, then they might assume you didn't get close enough to catch whatever they think he has. Or maybe they just haven't caught up with you yet."

Fran winced.

"On the other hand, maybe they've left you alone because you're a—" Susan stopped and looked around. "Because of your profession. You'd certainly be missed. And your peers would not take your disappearance lightly. I don't know. I think you should watch yourself."

"What would they think this guy had?" Fran asked.

"I don't know for sure. Maybe one of those extremist nut-bars in the Middle East has cooked something up."

"So they contaminated someone and sent him over here to set things off?"

"Could be, the way they're acting."

Fran stared off into space, then finally said, "No. It doesn't make sense. If there were some sort of plague, they would have grabbed me by now. Besides, there are more likely explanations. Like, what if that man left the hospital under his own power?"

"That's more likely? You told me he died in your arms."

"But I didn't tell you what his last words were."

"Sure you did. Something about going home to take his punishment."

"He said something else, Susan. He did some ranting and raving, so I thought he was in shock, but then he suddenly became lucid and said that he had to escape from our hospitality. That was how he put it."

"So you think he faked his own death and walked out of George Washington U. after his own autopsy?"

"Maybe."

"But how, if he'd been all sliced open?"

"He wasn't," Fran said. "Dr. Underwood just did a cursory once-over. He didn't get into the in-depth stuff."

"How do you know?" Susan drilled. "All of the records vanished."

"I told Underwood not to cut," Fran said. "I was afraid the guy was a foreign national, and if he died under bad circumstances and we dropped the ball in handling it—"

The door opened and the pair waited while someone walked into the room. There was rustling and clicking, a moment of silence, and then two loud sniffs. Someone cleared her throat, ran water, sniffed again, then walked out.

"That woman is going down hard," Fran said.

"Never mind that. You think that this person *pretended* to be dead, just to get away from you? That he did some trick like an Indian fakir?"

"He would have had to fool the ambulance crew and Dr. Underwood, too," Fran said.

"Even if he fooled all the people who checked him, there was an ambulance involved, too, with equipment that measures vital signs. I mean, there's an old magician's trick that makes it look like you've stopped your pulse, but this guy would have to stop *everything*."

Fran gave her a long, hard look. "You're really filling my life with joy—you know that?"

"I hate to be the bearer of bad tidings, but George Underwood has vanished from the face of the earth, and I'm thinking you could be next."

Fran stepped out of the stall, splashed her face with water at the sink, and then looked at Susan. "Don't worry about it." Fran slung her purse over her shoulder. "Listen, when this whole thing blows over and you get a little distance from it, maybe we should get together. You know, have lunch?"

"I think that would be great," Susan said. She moved forward and shook Fran's hand tentatively. "Thanks."

The door swung wide open, and they were framed by

light from the bar. Fran looked out, and instantly her mouth dropped open with amazement.

"Susan!" she screamed, grabbing the reporter's arm. "It's him!"

"Who?"

"The man! The dead man! He was the one wearing that stupid wig!" She bolted for the door, Susan behind her. "You were right all along! I don't believe it!"

"Fran!"

The detective took one step out. Something hit her chest in a wet explosion. She fell back into a shrieking Susan, her flailing hands covered with red.

A collective scream went through the crowd. They began to break toward the exits.

"No!"

Fran looked up. Susan had caught her under the arms and was trying to lift her up. Susan's face, her hair, and that ridiculous hooker costume of hers were covered in splatters of red.

That's funny, Fran thought. *I don't feel a thing.*

Numbly, she looked back at the crowd. A man with wild-looking eyes stared back at her.

"Harlot!" he screamed. "Defiler! You bring plague and pestilence among us!"

Susan gave one final push, and Fran stood. She blinked her eyes, stunned.

"Foul wench! Wear this, then, the mark of Hester Prynne!"

"Oh!" Fran said. Once she understood the situation, she acted accordingly, stopping the Scarlet Avenger's purple prose by breaking his jaw.

GHOST

He woke up disoriented in the middle of the night, unable to remember where he was. He was naked and was lying on the top of a bed that hadn't even been turned down. Something beneath him rustled as he shifted.

Then it came to him. It was money. The bed was covered with money.

Ghost sat up, money clinging to him as he did. He rubbed his eyes and peered around the small motel room. Patrice was on the floor, curled into a ball by the radiator, breathing heavily in sleep. And the guy next door who watched Holy Roller TV all night long was asleep, too, because there was no muffled talk of Jesus coming through the wall.

It was nice. Peaceful. Quiet.

Ghost lay back down.

Wrong!

He bolted upright and listened, straining his ears. There were no sounds at all.

That was wrong. It might be early in the morning, but there was still a lot of traffic out on D Street, and the hiss of the tires on the concrete was better for bringing sleep than counting sheep.

But there was nothing out there at all.

That could mean only one thing.

His heart hammering wildly beneath his ribs, Ghost rolled off the bed and down onto the floor, keeping the mattress between himself and the door. He shoved his hand between the mattress and box springs until he rolled his magic rock into the palm of his hand.

Okay, pigs. I'm ready for you.

On the opposite end of the room, Patrice stirred. Maybe if he sent her out of the room, screaming and yelling at the top of her lungs, she'd get blown away and give him enough time to get out the back window.

But they were too quick for him. Just as he was about to give her the order, there was a hammering on the door and guttural shouts.

"Open up! Police!"

Ghost trembled. He wanted to say, *Go ahead officers, come on in and we'll have a nice little chat,* but he was so frightened that he couldn't even draw breath. Besides, the door was locked and latched from the last session with Patrice.

Oh, well. Let them come.

And come they did. There were one, two, three loud blows from the door. On the fourth, the door gave way, swinging fast and smashing into the wall as uniformed men streamed into the room. Patrice screamed as they shouted a warning of their own.

"Freeze!"

Ghost crouched behind the bed, holding his breath inside his lungs. Beams of light played across the inside of the room.

"Kit? Get out here, boy!"

It was Amos. Well, that was it. It was time. He pushed the breath in his lungs hard against his throat and shouted as loud as he could.

"NO! YOU FREEZE!"

Instantly, silence returned to the room.

It worked, his mind raced. *It worked it worked it worked . . .*

He gulped air and pushed again. "DROP YOUR GUNS!"

He heard thud, thud, thud as they dropped to the carpet and the clatter of polymer on the asphalt outside.

Ghost pointed at one officer and said, "Turn on the lights." He squinted as they came on. They all waited patiently as his eyes adjusted. When they did, he singled out one officer who was about his size and demanded his clothes. The man stooped to comply as

Ghost picked one of the Glocks off the floor and walked over to Amos.

"You been one huge thorn in my side, Amos," he growled. "How'd you find me?"

"I used the consistent patterns in your behavior."

"Don't use no big words on me, Amos. Just tell me."

"You seem to be sexually stimulated by the color red," he said. "This motel is red."

Ghost scoffed. "So it is. Well, Amos. I got something I want you to do. You got one of them unmarked cars?"

"Yes," Amos said flatly.

"Good." Ghost smiled. "Patrice, get over here."

"Yes, Ghost."

He took the nude girl's hand and handed it to Amos. "Take it."

The officer complied.

Ghost waved at the bed. "Take that money with you. All of it. Then the two of you go get in that unmarked car of his and drive out of here. Go as far as you can on three tanks of gas. You got that?"

"Yes," they said together.

"Good. Then I want you to find a motel and check into it. Order a pizza when you get hungry. But I don't want the two of you to come back until you've done it a hundred times. Understand?"

"Yes," they echoed.

"Okay. Get to it, then."

They stooped over the bed and began gathering up bills. Ghost picked the other officer's clothes up off the ground and tucked them under his arm. Then he walked to the door and made a general announcement.

"The rest of you all can just forget you ever saw me here. Just get in your cars and go home." He laughed. "Take the rest of the night off."

The crowd began to disperse. Clothes still under his

arm, Ghost walked to the nearest squad car as the driver fired the engine to life.

"Get out and leave it running," he ordered.

The officer obeyed.

Ghost waved his confiscated Glock in the officer's face. "All of you carry this kind of gun?"

He nodded.

"You got extra clips for this puppy?"

"Yes. Two."

"Three, counting the one in your piece. Gimme them all."

Ghost tossed the clothes onto the front seat of the car while the officer disarmed. He sat down in the driver's seat, pulling the seat belt across his naked waist, then collected the clips. "Tell me something," he said. "What makes a brother like you want to become a cop?"

"I grew up here," the officer said. "I wanted to give something back to the neighborhood."

Ghost laughed. "You're all right, you know that? You go on home. All right?"

"All right."

Ghost held his hand up and gave the officer a high-five, then he slammed the door of the squad car and gunned the engine, squealing the tires and heading toward Capitol Hill. He turned the radio up loud, trying to make sense of the coded language coming over it. A quick series of turns followed, and before long he was barreling down Pennsylvania Avenue. Steering one-handed, he punched buttons until the lights and sirens were running. He roared past the White House, screaming and laughing hysterically, and hoping that his racket would wake the President of the U.S.A. himself.

"Look at me!" Ghost screamed out the window. "I'm Superman!"

Superman.

The word burned in his mind.

He was there, all right. He was practically Superman. As long as he had that rock, which was like some hypnotic version of Aladdin's magic lamp. *Only my wish is your command.*

That was it. He had the rock. He could have it all.

Then he screamed. "No. Oh, no!"

The suit!

He banged his fist on the steering wheel. *How could I have been so stupid? I sold the clothes!*

He had to have them. If they were anything like the rock, then they would have been brilliant. Who knew what kind of superpowers they would give him. Maybe they could make him bulletproof. Then he really would be Superman.

Maybe they could even make him fly.

That was it, then. He had to get them back.

But somewhere from beneath the reptilian raging of his brain, common sense called. *They'll be looking for you*, it said. *They'll be mad about the car. You've got to lay low for a while, brother. Find a new place to crash. Get a bottle. Get some more sleep. And do something to keep that rock closer by.*

Tomorrow, then, he decided.

Tomorrow.

Tomorrow it would be good-bye Clark Kent.

MAX KIERNAN

"Tomorrow."

"Tomorrow and tomorrow and tomorrow." Kiernan glared at Brickell. He drummed his fingers impatiently on the desktop. Brickell was staring down at him, his fingers rattling a brown grocery bag. "What have you got for me?"

"A story," Brickell said.

"About what?"

"About whom. Your friend, Amos White."

"What about him?"

"Fenton last had him headed west on 395 with—get this—a stark-naked hooker named Patrice and a bag of cash."

"Did Fenton put someone on him?"

Brickell shook his head. "He's out of the picture for now, unless we grab the pair in New Mexico."

"So." Kiernan nodded. "That is the latest twist in the Kit Washington story."

"Indeed it is. But first things first. You said Gallagher called you with a Jesus sighting?"

"Someone reported that Jesus walked out of a wall and healed his alcoholism. The timing fits."

Brickell smiled. "The jigsaw pieces are there. But when you see what I have for you, you're going to cry like a baby."

Kiernan motioned for Brickell to open the bag.

"Let me start," said Brickell, "by saying that Amos White is good. Really good. He made me from the moment I started tailing him. And he should have had that kid nailed eight ways from Sunday. The problem was, the kid has some kind of gift."

"Gift," Kiernan said, as if the word put a bad taste in his mouth. "Who from? Santa Claus or the Easter bunny?"

"I think he's got some kind of technology."

"What do you mean?"

"There are people with charisma," Brickell said, "and if their motivation is powerful enough, people will obey. Hitler had the German economy working for him. Jim Jones and David Koresh had the fear of hell on their sides. But no kind of charisma can make a cop run off with a hooker, or give you his clothes and gun, or make your enemy blow his own head off. Rasputin never even had such charisma."

"I think you'd better tell me exactly what you're talking about," Kiernan said.

"I'll do better than that." Brickell brought up the grocery bag and unceremoniously plopped it on Kiernan's desk. With a wave of his hand, he invited him to open it.

Kiernan unwrapped the top of the bag and stuck his hand in. After a moment of probing, he pulled out a handful of silver fabric. He held it in one hand and cast the bag aside with the other. "What's this? John Travolta's suit from *Saturday Night Fever*?"

"You're holding alien technology, boss."

"This is a kid's Halloween costume."

"O ye of little faith," Brickell said. He stood and took the fabric from Kiernan's hand, holding it between his hands and jerking them apart. The fabric snapped. "Would you say this is pretty stiff stuff?"

"Made in Taiwan," Kiernan said. "Reynolds Wrap should sue."

"Could Reynolds Wrap or the Taiwanese do this?" Brickell sat in the chair and pulled the neck of the suit open. It stretched. He stuck one foot inside the costume. It went down to the foot-shaped ending which filled out to fit Brickell's size eleven shoe. He widened the neck farther and stuck his other foot in. Kiernan laughed. While Brickell's feet fit, the rest of the uniform was balled up below his knees. Unimpressed by his boss's mirth, Brickell reached down, grabbed the neck, and pulled. The suit cleared his thighs, his waist, and in a moment was up under his arms. Brickell stuck his hands down inside, and the sleeves expanded to fit his arms. The tiny hands at the end of the sleeves elongated as well. Brickell rolled his shoulders and the rest of the suit snapped into place, covering him from the tip of his toes to the bottom of his neck. "It's got a hood, too," he said.

"It's like a condom," Kiernan said. "One size fits all."

"You have to admit, it didn't feel like a miracle stretch fabric."

"Vince," Kiernan said impatiently, "this is the age of miracles. We manufacture them every day."

Brickell knitted his brows. "If this was a Halloween costume, would I dare do this?" He ripped a piece of paper off one of Kiernan's green pads and crumpled it. Then he grabbed the oak lighter from the desk and lit the wad, and closed his hand around it, watching the flames lick through his fingers as the paper burned to ash. "If this were a kid's Halloween costume, you'd be writing an insurance check to my mother right now." He smiled at his boss. His boss didn't smile back.

Brickell walked to the door of Kiernan's office and opened it. "Wrampe, come here."

Wrampe walked into the office sheepishly.

"Got your nine on you?"

Wrampe reached under his suit coat and produced a pistol. Brickell grabbed the weapon, chambered a round, and before anyone could protest, fired a round into his right foot.

Kiernan was out of his chair. *"Brickell, are you crazy?"*

Brickell handed the smoking gun back to an astonished Wrampe. He stooped over, picked something off his foot, then walked over to Kiernan's desk without even a trace of a limp. "Let's see your miracle stretch fabric do this." With the flick of his wrist, he tossed a mushroomed 9mm slug onto Kiernan's desk. "These guys have to wear *something*, boss." He pulled the suit from one hand and then the other. "They're in a hostile environment. A suit like this can protect them from the worst the human race can throw at them."

"Can I touch it?" Wrampe asked, eyes wide.

Brickell shrugged his way out of the suit and handed him the child-sized garment. "Maybe you could jump out the window and see if it lets you fly."

Wrampe flexed and crumpled the fabric in his hands. It crackled like a candy-bar wrapper.

"If the suit made our visitor invulnerable," Kiernan said, "then how did a two-bit hood like Kit Washington strip it off him?"

"Plain dumb luck. Our visitor must've had the hood down, or the kid's club hit him in the one place the suit didn't cover." He pointed to the side of his head.

"This is weird," said Wrampe. He stuck one arm into the suit and was flexing his now-silvery fingers. "It feels greasy and warm at the same time."

"You don't sweat when you've got it on, either. I did some experimenting last night."

"How did you get your hands on it?" asked Kiernan.

"Can you believe it? The stupid jerk pawned it. Fenton and I followed Amos to a warehouse where he found one of Ghost's gang with the back of his head blown away, and another in a catatonic state. Then we tailed Amos back to the station house, but before he could get inside, he was accosted by a pimp. I used the Electronic Ear to listen in and heard them talking about a hooker named Patrice. That set Amos off, and he dragged the pimp into the station.

"After about half an hour, Amos reappeared with half a dozen cops behind him. They went to Kit Washington's old neighborhood and canvassed the place, showing photographs of Patrice to anyone they could stop.

"One of Amos's stops was a pawnshop. He grilled the proprietor about the whereabouts of Kit Washington and this Patrice woman, but came away empty-handed.

The man behind the counter insisted he hadn't seen
Ghost since he pawned something a few weeks ago, and
Amos stalked out."

"That's when you went in," Kiernan said.

Brickell nodded and smile. "I flashed one of my bo-
gus badges and said I was an agent from the Federal
Trade Commission. I asked if I could see his books, and
after a couple of minutes I found an entry where a
K. Washington had pawned a silver child's costume for
twelve bucks. So I told the man his books looked all
right, then pretended to spot the suit hanging on the
rack, and shelled out twenty bucks for it." Brickell
laughed. "I told him my daughter had the role of
Tinkerbell in the school play.

"When I caught up with Amos, he was meeting on
the street with his men. They split up, so I followed
Amos's group to a fast-food joint on D Street across
from the D Street Motel. Fenton trailed the others and
caught up with me just before midnight. Finally, just after three o'clock, a bunch of squad cars closed off
D Street a quarter-mile on either side of the motel.

"Now, get this. The cops got into position. They
charged the motel with Amos in the lead. Amos made
it in; then everyone froze. They were standing around
looking every bit like a mannequin convention. Then
Kit Washington walked out of the room wearing nothing but a grin, a pile of clothes in one hand and a gun
in the other. He got in one of the squad cars, collected
something from a black officer, and sped away from the
scene. Before we could react, Amos came out holding
the hand of the missing hooker. The woman didn't have
a stitch of clothing on, either, and she and Amos were
carrying armloads of cash.

"Fenton tracked them well into Virginia until it became obvious they weren't coming back, not for a while

anyway. He called in another team to pick up the chase so he could come back."

"What about the other cops?" asked Wrampe.

Brickell shrugged. "They all looked like they were going home. They looked tired."

Kiernan eyed the suit. "*Idiots.* They were supposed to notify the feds if they found him. Next time we'll be ready. I'm going to activate the Team and have them stand by."

"Do you think that's necessary?" Wrampe asked.

"One government agency can't trust another to do its work. We tried going through channels, and it didn't work. Now, where did Washington go after all of this?"

Brickell shook his head. "Lost him. That's the bad news. I think if we stake out that pawnshop, we can get him when he comes back for the suit."

"Why would he come back for the suit?" Kiernan asked.

"He's not stupid. Sooner or later he'll figure that the suit and whatever he kept is a set. And he's going to want to put them back together for the full effect."

"All right," Kiernan said. "I want you to get back out there and scout out a place for the Team to wait in position. Counting the time it takes for them to get the signal and start their van, they should be no more than a minute away."

"Got it."

Kiernan looked at his watch and turned to Wrampe. "Kevin, I want you to lead them on this one. That means I want you in the store, staking it out, starting at seventeen hundred hours. Get a DEA badge from the vault and use it to intimidate the owner."

"Right, boss."

"And Wrampe . . ."

"Yes, sir?"

"This might be a good time for you to bring Rosie along."

Wrampe's lips parted and their corners turned up. "Yes, sir. Absolutely, sir. My pleasure, sir."

MICK AARONSON

The wind out of the north was cold, stirring the newly greening grass and causing the man to hunch down into his London Fog jacket for warmth. It never ceased to amaze him that the wind could sweep across this place, as sheltered as it seemed to be. Somehow, he just couldn't imagine this place as windswept some one hundred thirty-something years ago, when General Robert E. Lee had walked off the front porch to fight a war he could not possibly win.

He made his way among the headstones, all small and white and identical, except for the names engraved across their face. Finally he found the one he was looking for. From inside his coat pocket he produced a single red rose and laid it at the base of the stone.

"Hello, Suzanne," Mick Aaronson said to his wife. He straightened up and shoved his hands in his pocket, staring quietly.

"They're taking good care of you, I see. The grass is coming in nicely this year. I think it's going to make it this time. That's good. It's been only what?" He looked up into the sky. In spite of the cold, the sky was clear and brilliant.

"Three years. Yeah, it's been three years.

"You know something, I was walking past the Lincoln Memorial the other day, and there was this guy preaching to a crowd on the sidewalk. He said that everyone is getting worked up about the millennium for nothing. He said that if the world was going to come to an end two thousand years after Christ's birth, it would have come to an end in 1996. I thought about stopping and telling him that my world *did* come to an end that year, but I didn't."

He stopped. They were coming; he could feel it. The distinctive hardening sensation in his throat, the tremor running the length of his jaw. There were still tears there. How dare they surface now? He had put time between himself and the event. It was 1,096 days today. And it hadn't been as if he had been blindsided by her departure. There had been plenty of warning: four years of it for him to prepare for the inevitable, watching her live the life of the damned. All in all, 2,497 days since the death sentence had first spilled out of the doctor's lips.

He had been ready for it, but when it happened, it was still a shock. The final departure was something a person could never be ready for.

Oh no, he thought.

You could be ready for it and yet never be ready. And when it happened, you could get used to it, but you could never get completely used to it. Just when you thought you were doing fine and life was grand, a whiff of perfume or a note from a song, a photograph you thought you had put away or even a stray thought you had long suppressed would surface and leave you biting your lip and looking away from the people you were with, wishing you were anywhere else in the world.

Wishing it would finally and irrevocably be over.

Aaronson drew in the cold morning air and tried to continue.

"The only problem is I'm still here. The sun still comes up in the morning. I have to put words on paper so they can run them on Monday and Thursday.

"You know, you're the lucky one. I mean, I know it

wasn't great for you those last few years, but you're resting now. And what you went through physically is nothing compared to what you'd be feeling mentally if you'd beat"—he gulped air again—"if you'd beat the cancer."

That did it. The tears came freely now, and he did nothing to stop them. They formed streaks down the front of his coat, trickling down to moisten the grass at his feet.

Aaronson stopped for a moment to look around and make sure he was alone. "The country's gotten worse, darling. We didn't think it would, but it has. And I miss you so desperately, but I'm glad that you're not here to see it.

"I love this country. I gave it four years of my life. In return, it gave me my education. It provided the opportunity for me to meet you. And now it's taking care of you. It's given me a career, a pulpit that I've tried to use to make things better."

"You know, Mick," Suzanne Aaronson said. "You never stopped serving your country. You just changed your way of doing it."

That had been when he'd read her the letter, the one saying he'd won his first Pulitzer. He'd used the line in his acceptance speech and called on his audience to examine their lives and do the same.

"And there was a time when people listened, Suzanne. Remember the letters we used to get?" He laughed at the thought of it. "Remember how we used to try and answer them all personally? What a time that was! All we had to worry about then was the Soviets. Remember how they used to say that if there were full-scale war between them and us, the living would envy the dead? We're fighting that kind of a war now, a civil war. And it doesn't matter who's winning, because we all wish we were dead. Walt Kelly was right, Suzanne. We are our own worst enemy."

He stopped for a moment and looked out across the cemetery, at the endless rows of white headstones.

"You're resting with heroes, Suzanne," he said, turning back to her. "Heroes of every major war since the 1860s. But what makes it all so ironic is that while they died to keep us together and free, they also died for the freedom we're using to self-destruct. Maybe if they'd known how it would end, they would have put down their weapons and gone home."

The wind kicked up, and Aaronson stuffed his hands into his pockets, knotting them into fists to warm them. He stared down at the headstone, taking deep breaths, trying to calm himself. *Perhaps,* he thought, *I should open my coat and let this cold whip right through me. Maybe that would reinvigorate my senses.*

His lips formed into a half-smile. "Other than the fact that the land of our dreams has become a moral wasteland, things are fine. I know you thought I should chase after Christine Belmont after you were gone, but I told you that I'd never remarry. I'm too old to mess with that anymore. Too set in my ways. I make my tea the way I want it and don't worry about the coffee drinkers. I invested most of my life in you, Suzanne. I'm not about to sell you short now. Christine is with Don Selgrove now." He laughed. "I fixed the two of them up.

"Work is fine. The usual, anyway. Corey complains every time I turn a column in, says I'm getting too cynical in my old age. So I tell him, 'The Age of Innocence is dead. Long live the Age of Cynicism.' Then he lets me have my way. Sad but true, I've achieved journalistic godhood now. They might complain about what I write, but they run it word for word.

"Sometimes there's hope, though. They sent me this

little girl for our internship program. She's a Susan, too, and she reminds me a lot of you. She's got that head-strong idealism that says there's no problem in the world too big for her to solve. We were both on fire with that. Remember?

"And you know how for years I complained that no-body wanted to do investigative journalism for its own sake? That the truth in and of itself was what you needed to pursue—never mind what the viewer ratings, circulation numbers, and the Q index said? That you could trade in fame and money and ratings, but it would be worthless unless your end product was the truth?

"Now this Susan Hill . . . she's been listening to too many lectures by network news anchors; she thinks journalists are obliged to save the American people from themselves. But she's catching on to the impor-tance of the truth. I sent her out to follow a dead-end story, and the way she's tearing into it, you'd think the future of the planet depended on it.

"You know, if she saw me out here talking to you, she'd rush back to my office to measure it for curtains and wallpaper." He squinted at the stone and shook his head. "No, she's not that mercenary. She's on fire for the job. She has integrity. She just doesn't know what to do with it."

He stood silent for a moment, shivering against the wind. With two fingers, he pulled the coat from over his wrist and checked the time.

"Well. I've got to get back. I don't want to, but duty calls. I'm supposed to give a speech to the Washington Press Club this afternoon. They want me to say some-thing about the responsibility of the press in the twenty-first century." He laughed bitterly. "Maybe I'll lecture them on their responsibilities in *this* century.

"That I miss you goes without saying. There's not a day that goes by that I don't think of you. You were

such an important part of my life. You still are. And you
will be again. Just as soon as God decides when he's
done with me. So. Until then, Suzanne. Until then."

He took one final, long look at the headstone. Then
turned and slowly started to walk away, knowing that
he would be back again.

KEVEN WRAMPE

He was polishing Rosie when Kit Washington walked
in. There was no need to check the copy of the mug
shot he had brought with him. Even if the looks
couldn't be verified, the attitude would have been a
dead giveaway. The kid strolled in like he was king of
the world.

Brickell had read Kit Washington like a book.

Wrampe had only been at the pawnshop for half an
hour. He had shown up first thing in the morning, flashing a badge, claiming that he needed to check up on the
work of one of his field agents—could he please see the
records his agent had examined and have a private
space in which to work? The old man had grumbled and
put him in the back room. It had taken some doing, but
Wrampe was able to position himself so he could keep
his eye on the door.

He didn't have to wait long. Not long at all. And now
there was Kit Washington, a/k/a Ghost, the Emperor of
Everything, demanding that the old man give him the
suit.

The old man said, "What suit, son?"

"You remember," said the Ghost. "It was that flashy
thing, all silver like tinfoil. Looked like something out
of *The Wiz*."

Wrampe cradled Rosie and waited. It had to be the

right moment. Wait until the kid's hands are both visible and empty, Kiernan had said. Then take him down hard. He eased his hand into a pocket, found the small box inside, pressed a button.

"Man, I don't take no clothing here. Besides, you too young to be bringin' stuff in here."

"This was a costume, man. Like a space suit for a kid. Fancy. Glittery like. You gave me twelve bucks for it."

The proprietor looked away. "Doan remember."

"What you got, man, old-timer's disease? Weren't two weeks ago." He slowly turned, looking up and down the walls of the place. His face fell into a frown when he realized he couldn't find what he had come for. He rushed the man and grabbed him by the lapels. "Man, I want my—"

"You got your ticket?" the old man asked.

Wrampe jammed on the button again and then kicked his way out the door, took two steps, and aimed the Anaconda .45 caliber revolver right between Kit Washington's eyes. He pulled back the hammer and the weapon made a loud *click!* Kit's eyes went wide as he got a look at the weapon.

"Keep your hands right there," Wrampe said.

Kit glared but obeyed.

"This a shakedown?" the old man whined. "I knew it. You can't get ahead in this life. You just can't get ahead."

"Shut up!" Wrampe barked, then turned his attention back to Kit. "Keep your hands on the old man, but spread your fingers out wide."

Kit obeyed.

"Now slowly move your hands out and away from your body. I want to see you get wings like an airplane. You go for those pockets, and they'll be cleaning your brains off the wall with a wire brush."

Over Kit Washington's shoulders, Wrampe saw a black van appear and screech to a halt outside the window. The rear door flew open, and a handful of men in dark suits spilled out, all wearing dark glasses and carrying Uzis. *Perfect,* he thought. *Less than thirty seconds after the second signal. Great.*

The door smashed open and the Team filled the pawnshop. Kit looked back to see what the commotion was, and his eyes grew even wider.

"I wasn't doin' nothin'," he whimpered.

"Quiet!" Wrampe ordered. He nodded at the Team, and two men emerged, Fenton and Brickell. Brickell made a show of cocking his Uzi and placing the barrel against Kit's temple while Fenton slapped a handcuff across one wrist.

"I got my rights," Kit said as Fenton brought the other hand back and cuffed it. "I want my phone call."

"In a minute," said Wrampe, keeping the Anaconda trained. "Fenton. Check his pockets."

Kit Washington's expression darkened.

Wrampe's finger twitched on the Anaconda's trigger, but he consciously stopped it from pulling. Fenton was right behind the kid, trying to decide which pocket to check first. If Wrampe fired now, the slug that would remove Kit's head would do the same to Fenton. His lips pursed to shout out a warning.

But Kit Washington spoke first. "*Everyone* freeze!"

Suddenly Wrampe felt thick. The Anaconda now weighed a thousand pounds in his outstretched hands, but his muscles were locked into place, holding it out at this absurd angle, trigger finger a hairbreadth from igniting the chambered round. Nothing that left his brain produced any physical manifestation.

His thoughts raced. *Fire,* FIRE! *Just another fraction of an inch, PULL! Forget Fenton. We're all going to be dead in a minute,* WILL YOU JUST PULL THE TRIGGER—

"Y'all are getting to be a real pain," Kit said matter-of-factly.

Wrampe tried to move his eyes off Washington, but he couldn't. From the periphery of his vision, he could see the kid had them all: Fenton, Brickell, all the others. Even that old man was affected. But how? The speculation had been that the kid had a hand-held device and that some sort of physical contact with it was needed. They had studied the tape of the Georgetown bank robbery and noticed Washington's right hand clenched into a fist as if he were holding onto something very precious.

He didn't understand. There had been nothing in the kid's hand when he had nailed him. *Nothing.*

"You with the handcuffs. Get 'em off me."

With precision, Fenton removed his key ring and uncuffed Kit Washington. Wrampe wanted to shout and tell him to resist, to blow the kid's head off, but his mind felt trapped in his inert body. Even breathing seemed an effort.

"Just wait there a second," Washington told Fenton. He stepped away from the agents, rubbing his wrists and surveying the scene like he had all the time in the world.

Like he was the king.

He stepped over and grabbed the Anaconda by the barrel. "Leggo," he said and Wrampe obeyed. "Big puppy," he observed, weighing the weapon in his hand. He uncocked it and slapped it down on the counter.

Good-bye, Rosie. Good-bye. If only he had tried a little harder to pull the trigger. If only Fenton hadn't been in the way.

"All right," Kit Washington said, rubbing the palms of his hands together. "We're gonna play a little game here this morning. That is, everyone but *you*." He pointed straight at Wrampe, who still had his arms out straight from holding the revolver. "You get to watch." He turned to the other agents. "All of you got handcuffs? Lemme see them."

There was a rustling as the six agents reached into the pouches of their belts and held the cuffs out for inspection. Washington counted them off quickly, one through six.

"All right, here's what you're going to do. First off, everyone drop your handcuff keys on the floor."

Dutifully, the agents all started trying to remove one key from their key rings.

"Forget it, man. Just drop the whole thing."

There was a chorus of rattling as keys hit the floor.

"All right. Now I want you all standing side by side, and I want you to loop arms with each other. You know, a human chain."

There was some scuffling and discussion as the agents worked it out. Kit looked back at Wrampe.

"You their boss?"

"For this operation," he said obediently. It was a strange feeling. He could feel his lips moving and hear the sound of his own voice resonating in his ears, but he remained curiously detached.

"You know," Kit said, leaning in as if conspiring with Wrampe, "I could kill all these guys. I could make you do it with that big gun of yours. But you know what? I'm not."

Wrampe remained motionless. *If I could spit,* he thought, *I'd show you what I think of you.*

Kit scowled. "You sho' is ungrateful!" He stamped hard on Wrampe's left foot. Sensation filled the agent's brain. It wasn't pain, just a sensation, like the dentist's drill taking its first bit of a Novocained tooth. "You should thank me for sparing the lives of your friends. Say 'Thank you, Mr. Washington.' "

"Thank you, Mr. Washington." *I'm going to kill you. I'm going to jam Rosie in your chest and blow your heart out. I'm going to have your head on a stick . . .*

"You're welcome." Kit bowed. He turned to the line of agents. They were standing in line, arms interlocked, waiting for the next order. "Okay, boys. Take your handcuffs and cuff your own hands together. I want this chain so nothing's gonna pull it apart."

The rattling and ratcheting of the cuffs began. Kit stepped back, then again addressed Wrampe.

"You know about my little toy, don't you?"

"Yes."

Kit reached inside his collar and tugged at a gold chain. At the end was a silvery, shimmering stone, held to the chain with thin strips of duct tape. "Here it is." He grinned. "I found out it only needs to be 'gainst my skin to work." He turned away from Wrampe, took two steps, then turned and kicked out at the agent savagely. His foot impacted squarely between Wrampe's legs. Washington staggered back, caught his balance, and looked in amazement.

"That hurt you?"

"No."

"That's right. What's your name?"

"Kevin Wrampe."

"Well, *Mister* Kevin Wrampe. You're *unfrozen.*"

Pain exploded in Wrampe's brain. He folded in half and staggered backward, hitting the counter and twisting to the floor.

"You're still pretty ungrateful, ain't you? Say 'Thank you, Mr. Washington.' "

Wrampe was fighting nausea. He was suddenly slick with sweat, and his face was on fire. The pain was right there, all over him.

He gasped, "Thank you ... Mr. ... Washington."

Kit Washington began to laugh. Wrampe fought to stay conscious, pushing against the pain. *Stay awake*, he told himself, eyes tearing up. *Stay alert. You know Kiernan's going to want to know every detail of what this was like ...*

He sucked air into his lungs and blew it out. It wasn't working. He was about to be swallowed whole.

But then something caught his ear, something eerily familiar. It was a choir of men's voices, accompanied by the cadence of stamping feet.

"Heigh ho, heigh ho, it's off to work we go ..."

The bell over the door of the pawnshop rang, and the voices began to fade. Now Wrampe felt cold and began to shake, and he bit his lower lip until he tasted his own blood, trying to register as much information as possible for the lengthy debriefing that would surely come. He wanted desperately to leap to his feet, grab Rosie from her temporary resting place and, with six pulls of the trigger, turn Kit Washington into hamburger.

But for the moment all he could do was lay there with the room spinning around him. There he was, missing it all, but the tiny bit of reason left in his brain told him that he was going to emerge from this fiasco as the luckiest of all seven agents.

SERENA BLAKE

"Fun?" Serena asked merrily.

"Fun," intoned her guest.

"Admit it, Victor, You're having the time of your life. Aren't you?"

She watched him carefully, hoping for a reaction. They were in the backseat of a rented limousine. The liquor cabinet was open, and she had already killed half a bottle of Absolut. On the television screen flickered a worn video of *Beyond the Green Door*. Serena herself was wearing a filmy white blouse that highlighted the fact that she was again braless. Her matching white skirt had a slit in it that ran almost up to the waistband, and she lifted her foot and propped it on the edge of the seat, knowing full well that she was showing a lot of leg.

None of it made an impression on Victor. His only concession that evening had been to suck on an ice cube dipped in Absolut. Now he was sitting up straight in his seat, his lap belt on, perusing the magazine that Serena had just bought him.

Slowly leafing through the pages, he commented, "I don't understand this preoccupation with the display of the female genitals. It's something that happens in primates as a precursor to mating, but theoretically human intellect controls sexuality." He closed the magazine and looked at the title, splashed in red across the front. "And I fail to see the correlation between such displays and the mammal genus *Castor*."

Serena grabbed the magazine and tossed it to the floor. "Forget it, Victor," she barked. "Just forget it. I'm sorry I brought you here."

"You had your reasons. This is your city, and you're showing it to me. Obviously, this is a part of it."

"Right!" she fumed.

"I'm sensing frustration," Victor said.

"Oh, yeah?" Serena said.

"Is it because we haven't completed our tour, and it's now time to go to the party?"

Serena looked through the dark glass into the driver's compartment, locking onto the rearview mirror. The dark eyes of the driver were on her. She considered losing her temper, but instead became philosophical. *He's*

*given me more looks in one night than Victor has since
I met him.*

"No," she said, breaking eye contact with the driver.
"It's because—"

*Because what? Because you still want him and you
can't have him? Because you need release but he'd
rather talk about archaeological digs in the Middle
East?*

Shaking her head, she said, "I give up." And then, to
the driver: "Take us to Georgetown."

The limo lurched and pulled out into the traffic. Victor's eyes drifted to the screen. "Your video has ended,"
he said.

Serena did not answer, but let her gaze drift out one
of the side windows.

"I am trying to understand this malaise which has
settled over you," Victor said quietly.

"So am I, Victor."

"I know you are disappointed and frustrated with my
slowness. I know that I am supposed to be helping you.
But I cannot until I know about you, and I feel that I do
not yet understand you."

"What do you know about me, Victor?"

"By the standards of your society, you drink too
much alcoholic liquid. And you participate in the use of
substances which are illegal. But rather than submitting
to the standards of your society, you have sought out a
social substratum of people who engage in the same destructive behavior."

"I'm not giving up my friends," Serena snapped.

"I understand your need for companionship," Victor
said, "but it is my observation that you are not seeking
out this stratum for friendship. You seek it out to legitimize your own destructive behavior. They do not condemn your actions, nor do you condemn theirs. This

kind of passive libertarianism makes for a toxic relationship."

"They're the only friends I've got," she said defensively. "I don't seem to be able to keep the other kind."

"Then you need to reassess your definition of friendship."

"Yeah?"

Victor nodded. "A real friend would not let you continue on this course. A real friend would object to your behavior and help you change it."

"Is that right?" Serena challenged. "Well what do you know about friendship, Victor? Tell me. I mean, what have you ever done for me? You sit around my apartment all day and complain because the world is going to end, and then you follow me around all night and watch me do what I do because you say you want to understand it. But you never try it. You never do what I do so you can know what I'm going through."

"I don't have to participate in order to understand your needs," he said.

"My needs? What a laugh. The king of the Ice Palace is trying to tell me about my needs." She turned sideways in the seat and crossed her arms at her waist. Then, raising her arms, she pulled the blouse off over her head and tossed it into Victor's lap. "Tell me about my needs now."

Victor stared at her. Not at her breasts, but into her eyes. He said calmly, "You are equating sex with friendship. There is a great difference there."

"Wrong!" she snapped. "Sex is love. Love is friendship."

"Sex is not love," Victor said. "Sex can enhance love as a process of physical bonding. But friendships between the genders are not necessarily built on the physical."

Serena shivered. She was suddenly cold, and she

could feel the driver's eyes on her. She reached across to take the blouse from Victor's lap and cover herself. "Do you love me, Victor?"

"I don't think I'm capable of love as you know it, Serena."

"But you care for me."

"I am concerned."

"Doesn't that count for something?"

"If you had the ability, would you stop a stranger from drowning, Serena?" He waited for her nod. "The same principle applies here."

"I'm drowning."

"In a spiritual sense."

She closed the distance between her face and his. "You're like a lifeguard."

"The similarity escapes me."

"Are you sure," she said softly, "that you don't love me? Even just a little?"

"This odd attraction you have is something which I must resolve," he said.

"Odd attraction," Serena echoed. "Odd attraction. You call it that, Victor. But all I know is that I've never wanted to make love to someone as badly as I want to do with you."

With both hands, she grabbed his head and pulled it toward her. She met him with her lips, soft and moist, plying his for all she was worth.

But her passion evaporated. The kiss slowed, then stopped. His face was cool and dry in her hands. His lips were unmoved by hers. She retreated slowly, pulling the blouse on over her head.

Victor spoke. "If I love you at all, it is a brotherly love."

"I understand," she said. "I understand why you're resisting me, Victor." She drew in a breath and held it, afraid of breaking into tears. "This thing I'm feeling for you—it's not rational, is it?"

"No."

She brushed a hand down her arm. It was covered with goose bumps. "Driver," she said, leaning forward. "Would you give us some heat back here?"

"Certainly," he said. "Are you ready to stop at your Georgetown destination?"

She looked quickly at Victor. "Yes."

"Very good," the driver said. "Thirty seconds."

Serena rolled her eyes. How long had they been in the neighborhood with the driver circling patiently, eyes on her breasts in the rearview mirror, until she had decided she was ready to be delivered to the party?

The limo rolled to a smooth stop in front of the well-lit hotel, and in a moment, a stone-faced man in a red uniform coat was opening the door for her. She stepped out of the limousine onto a red carpet.

"Keep it warm," she told the driver quietly. "You never know if there's going to be enough to drink."

Without emotion, the driver nodded.

She watched Victor disembark from the limousine. She kept going through the same cycle of affection, then attachment, then outright lust. Followed by disappointment and hopelessness. A passionate animal one second, a hurt child the next.

The red-coated man closed the door, and the driver pulled the limousine away.

Victor smiled at her. *Charm. Lots of it. How does he do it: turn it on and off like that?*

She felt a tug at her arm. Bless his heart, Victor had taken her elbow just as he had seen a movie star do on *Entertainment Tonight*. He was leading her down the red carpet toward the door. Two tuxedoed doormen pulled the door open for them, and she could see from the periphery of her vision that the adoring crowd inside was applauding her. They were smiling and pointing, and for a brief, lucid moment, she could almost read their thoughts, crackling in her mind like the signal from a faraway radio station.

Aren't they beautiful aren't they wonderful aren't they special aren't they lucky don't you wish that you could be them?

It was something to die for, she thought. Something that she and her girlfriends, once upon a time ago and far away, had talked about happening only in their wildest dreams. And though Serena had passed through a scene like this many times in the last few years, it never had meant as much as it did at this moment. For now she was lucid enough to enjoy it. and while the Absolut was racing around in her system, it had brought on a warmth inside, instead of bringing on fever for the powder that would set her brain on fire.

Suddenly she felt cool. Confident. In control.

Maybe, for the first time in her life, she was truly in love. She tried to memorize the feeling because she knew that nothing lasted forever.

It was all so wonderful. The warmth of the spring evening. The noise from the crowd. Victor's coolness on her arm. The strobing of flashes.

She decided this was like something out of a fairy tale. A modern fairy tale.

So perfect.

So dreamlike.

She was sure it would never end.

THE WRITING ON THE WALL

WASHINGTON, D.C. / MAY 1999

**THE VIEW FROM HERE
by Mick Aaronson**

May 3, 1999—Remember the old tale of the monkey's paw? It was about a magical talisman that could make wishes come true in a literal way, and the moral of the story was that you should be careful what you wish for because you might just get it.

I'd now like to add a corollary to that old saw, one that is perfect for the state our species now finds itself in. That corollary is, when people become militant about something they want, they don't really want it.

For example, a battle has been raging back and forth between scientists over whether or not homosexuality is inherited. This is something which the gay-rights lobby wants desperately to prove, in order to legitimize their minority status with mainstream America.

But I suspect that those who would further the homosexual agenda would beat a hasty retreat from that stand if they took five minutes to think about it.

Think about it for yourself. Besides hair and eye color and the length of Dad's nose, what other things can you receive from the genetic legacy of your parents?

Hemophilia. Heart disease. Diabetes. Breast cancer. Lou Gehrig's disease. Certain birth defects.

Even now, many gynecologists and obstetricians act as genetic counselors for their patients, advising them on whether they should be fruitful and multiply or adopt, depending on what they may be passing on to their children.

You can answer this next question yourself. Would you choose to adopt if you knew that your genetic child would be predisposed toward homosexuality?

Or what if the "natural cause" of homosexuality is found? Would that not necessitate that the search begin to find a cure? Do

gay-rights advocates really want a cure for their condition, or would they live with their affliction in order to maintain their political clout?

A staple of the feminist plank is easy access to abortion. This is something which has brought us to the brink of a spiritual civil war.

Yet when you add ultrasound and other techniques which allow gender determination into this equation, it leads to unborn females being aborted more often than males. This is especially true in nations like China and India, where males are considered more valuable than females.

By now you can put the rest of the pieces together for yourself. For whatever reason, we let ourselves become convinced that there is something we need which will somehow preserve our way of life and that of generations to come.

Things like the national income tax. Social Security. Medicare. Sex education in schools. Socialized health care. Gun control.

But all we end up doing is costing ourselves even more money and restricting our personal liberties in ways that we never imagined or thought possible.

So the next time a smiling politician leans over at you from the back of his wagon and offers you a potion or poultice that will cure your ills, pay your bills, and make you irresistible to members of the opposite sex, beware.

Because if you let yourself get sold a bill of goods, you'll be getting everything you deserve.

FRAN MARKOWSKI

It was 4:00 A.M., and Fran Markowski still hadn't been able to wind down. She had gotten home just before 2:00, all wired from a highly successful series of arrests. The ensuing paperwork hadn't dulled her senses. So when she found *To Live and Die in L.A.* running for the umpteenth time on HBO, it seemed like the perfect diversion.

It wasn't.

She ended up staring at the TV with the sound off, trying to decide what to do next. Whenever she felt this way, it usually meant that she would get to sleep only by eating. Divert the blood, get it rushing away from the brain; give it a chance to start shutting down.

The refrigerator was conspicuously empty, and she cursed herself. She had been putting off her grocery shopping until after payday, but payday had been yesterday, and she had been too busy to cash her check.

Well, no matter. After all, she still had some cash. She put on her shoulder holster and leather jacket. Fifteen minutes later, she pulled into a run-down Denny's on the Maryland side of the river. After a moment of staring at the garish yellow sign, Fran told herself this was the right decision and got out of the car.

At the entrance, Fran stopped before a row of newspaper boxes. The Sunday editions were already out. She fished a handful of quarters out of her pocket and studied the machines. She skipped past the *Washington Tribune*. The last thing she wanted to do was run across the name "Susan Hill," so she fed the coins to the *Post* and walked into the restaurant.

Fran took a seat, ordered an omelet, then opened the *Post* and started scanning. She skipped over international affairs, preferring not to read about places she would never visit. She skipped the national section as well, since politics turned her off.

She spent a few minutes glancing over the sports section, selecting bits and pieces of information that she could use in conversation with the guys in the precinct.

Fran ate slowly, finally putting the sports aside and looking at what was next.

Style.

"Oh no." Fran's hand dropped and started to crumple the section's cover page, exposing what was beneath. She rolled her eyes again. *"No . . ."*

It was a picture of the stoned woman from the bar. The corners of Fran's lips turned up. *Now, what was this woman's name?*

She opened the section and ran her finger down to the photo's caption.

NEW MAN IN HER LIFE: Citizens Who Care benefactress Serena Blake is seen escorting an unidentified friend to a reelection fund-raiser in honor of Rep. Ty Cornell (D-Mass.) The fete, held last night at the Four Seasons Hotel, was also attended by . . .

Gotcha! Fran thought. *All right, Serena Blake. I've got your number now.*

She moved her finger up to the man Serena was with. Her mouth fell open, and she shrieked.

The inside of the restaurant went silent. She didn't notice. She got up from her chair, the style pages in one hand, and walked away from the counter. At the register, she threw down a ten-dollar bill, then dashed outside, where the first rays of morning were beginning to light the sky.

She shrieked again, her voice reverberating off of street and sidewalk.

The picture was unmistakable. It was Susan Hill's vanishing corpse, the man Fran had held in her arms while he died, the man in the silly wig at the bar.

So he wasn't dead, Fran thought, staring hard at the photograph. She could believe her eyes, which hadn't been playing tricks on her at the bar. This guy had fooled her. He had fooled the paramedics, and even the doctor. It was lucky that she had ordered only a superficial autopsy, or the guy would be worm chow right now.

Fran Markowski chuckled. *What do you know? I've got you—you and your coke-slut girlfriend. Now I'll find out what you've got.*

The thought jarred her.

If Susan Hill had been right about the body's disappearing from George Washington University Hospital, then maybe she was right about some of her other hunches. What was it she had been talking about? Disappearances? A plague? Some kind of government cover-up?

Suddenly Fran felt the street closing in on her. Her mind reeled as her hands crumpled the style page. She forced herself to walk to the nearest pay phone, rummaging in her purse for the *Tribune* business card that Susan Hill had scrawled her home number on, hoping she still had it.

She picked through her purse until she found it, along with her calling card. She started to shove the card in the phone, but thought better of it and fumbled back in her purse for two quarters. With trembling fingers, she pushed the coins in and punched Susan's number. There was a sharp click. Fran jerked the handset away from her ear to hang up, but she heard the line ringing at the other end. With great effort, she brought the handset back to her ear.

The phone rang nine times. Ten. Eleven. Finally, on the twelfth ring, it was picked up. A groggy voice said, "Hello?"

Fran froze.

"Hello?"

Fran closed her eyes and pushed the words out of her brain. "Girl?" she said in her best black accent.

"Yeah?" Susan said suspiciously.

"Listen," Fran said, trying to get the rhythm of the words right. "You know you had your eyes on that man at the bar the other night, and you were dyin' to meet him? But before you could introduce yourself, that weird guy sprayed us with red paint?"

"Yes!" Susan said loudly and suddenly. She had caught on.

"Well, I think I can fix us up. And I think he's gonna pay big-time, if you know what I mean."

"Great!" Susan exclaimed. How—"

"Same time, same place, girl. And don't forget to bring some of your latex friends."

Before Susan could answer, Fran slammed the handset into the cradle. The palms of her hands were slick with sweat, and her heart was hammering wildly in her chest. She was shaking with rage and fear.

She had him. She had that weird little man.

Did that mean she was going to die from some strange disease?

The street suddenly seemed cold. Cold and empty.

HARRY LAUTER

Something waited for Harry Lauter in his sleep. He didn't know what it was. He knew only that it was dark and faceless, that it drained the living color out of his dreams.

It was the same thing that so often kept him from his sleep.

It was dread. Pure dread.

He wondered whether this was another weapon in Satan's arsenal. Usually, when Satan came after him, he announced himself clearly, taking great pleasure in describing what a weak and worthless individual Harry was, and how he was going to enjoy dragging him off to hell. When Old Scratch went toe to toe with Harry Lauter, bluster was the order of the day because the subtle stuff never worked.

Like that hooker who had lived next door until a couple of days ago. There was no temptation in that. It was so obvious that Harry could see right through it.

He pondered her fate for a moment. Maybe this dread was related to her. She had so obviously needed Jesus, and Harry hadn't lifted a finger to help. And then one morning he had awakened to find . . .

That's it, isn't it, he asked the dread. *That poor*

*woman was being dragged off to hell before my very
eyes and I did nothing to stop it.*

But he couldn't make himself think about it now. He
tried to dismiss the feeling. *I must not become diverted,*
he told himself. *I have the scrolls to think about. I cannot engage in personal soul-saving. I must confine my
mission to the street corner.*

That was when the dread answered. *That's right,
Harry. Remember, even God allowed souls to slip
through his fingers when it suited his almighty purpose.
Sacrifice the one for the many.*

Harry replied, *No! God would do no such thing!*

Oh, yes, my sweet Harry, he does, the dread answered. *What about Judas Iscariot? God tossed him off
to hell so his son could be betrayed and die to save the
rest of mankind.*

Get behind me! Harry thought. Judas had a choice,
and he made it. And if he had thrown himself at the
Savior instead of hanging himself, he would have been
forgiven with open arms. But he let you into his heart,
and you blinded him.

Just as I have blinded you, Harry.

Never, Harry thought defiantly.

*Your betrayal of that woman was just an aperitif,
Harry. It served only to conceal your other betrayal, the
one that is now complete.*

"No!" The word slipped aloud from Harry's lips.

Yes, said the dread. *And I damn you to search, not
knowing, until you find what you have done. And when
you find it, I damn you again, to live the rest of your life
with the consequences of your actions always in the
back of your mind.*

"No," Harry screamed. *"No!"*

He found himself sitting up in bed, drenched with
sweat. The room was silent except for the ticking of his
alarm clock. He gulped air until his shaking stopped,

and then pushed more words out of his mouth, this time in a whisper.

It wasn't true. It couldn't have been. He had been so careful. The woman had been a fluke. The sacrifice had been necessary. There hadn't been any more. He had been doing what he was supposed to, preaching the word and scrambling for money to go back and finish recovering those precious scrolls.

But the dread echoed in his head. *There is another . . .*

Moaning, Harry rolled off the bed and onto the floor, head bowed, hands clasped between his legs. "I am so weak. Forgive me for the woman, my sin of omission. Give me strength. You have given me something mighty to do, and I must do it. But where is the line to be drawn between total compassion and global salvation? Give me the strength and wisdom of your Son in dealing with this. If I have transgressed yet another, forgive me my sin. And take from me this damnation that has been placed upon my head . . ."

The telephone rang.

A shock ran through Harry's body, and he screamed. The phone rang again.

Harry groaned and looked over at the clock. Was it really so early? Who would be calling at this hour?

"Hello?" he asked the telephone.

"I'm sorry. Did I get you up?"

"Well—"

"Good! You are one tough hombre to get hold of. Especially, it seems, when you're dealing in gold."

Harry breathed a sigh of relief. "Chris?"

"The one, the only. How's it going? You sound horrible."

"I seem to be losing sleep," Harry said.

"Well, hey, how about if I make it all worth your while?"

Only if you're an agent of God, Harry thought. *And I don't think you're qualified.* "What do you need now?"

"That old Harry Lauter mojo," said Gallagher, knowing full well that Harry hated the word. "I think you're onto something hot here, and if you've got anything more on it, I would love to have it. I'll make it worth your while."

Harry sat on the edge of the bed and rubbed his eyes. "Chris, I have no idea what you're talking about."

"I'm talking about Jesus returning to Earth and doing some impromptu healing," Gallagher said. "In case you hadn't noticed, Harry, in the next few months we're going to be changing the way we keep time on our calendars. It's got a whole lot of people out in Mr. Averageland really excited. This Jesus healing stuff is phenomenal. I mean, you can imagine the story potential. Jesus is coming back, but first he's making a few discreet visits to right a few wrongs."

"Chris—" Harry started.

"I know, I know. You don't really want to think about that. But my editor loves it. It's a gold mine. In fact, I'm overnighting you another grand because the boss thought so much of that last story that he didn't want you to get away."

"What?" Harry gasped.

"But there's a string attached," Chris said. "You find any more people that have had a close encounter with J.C., you get on the line to me right away. This stuff is gold, Harry. Pure gold. With the right play, it can carry us comfortably into the next century. And if it carries us, it's gonna carry you. Remember that, Harry."

Harry paused. "Chris, I'm overwhelmed."

"Well, don't be. That find was a stroke of genius on your part, Harry. Sheer genius. And we want to milk this, but not like the son of Elvis. We want to play this one straight. Only genuine cases. So keep your eyes open, your ears open. We'll make it worth your while."

"I'll do what I can," Harry said sheepishly, afraid to tell Gallagher that the whole thing had been a fluke. In fact, it had been a spur-of-the-moment thing because John Drury had told of his miraculous conversion, and the fund-raising had been going slowly, and—

Suddenly Harry went cold. His palms were slick with sweat, and he could hear dark laughter surrounding him.

Now you know, Harry. Now you know how complete your betrayal has been. And I damn you to remember this, and think of it in each of your remaining waking moments . . .

He yelped and dropped the phone.

"—better than gold," Gallagher's voice was buzzing. "It's platinum. Platinum with a uranium jacket. It's atomic, Harry. Absolutely nuclear."

The laughter returned, loud and rasping, until it drowned out Gallagher's inquiries. It ignited flames of torment in Harry's brain while he dressed and then fled out into the cool spring morning.

Outside, the streets were deserted. Washington had not yet wakened, and since it was Sunday, it would take its time doing so. The eerie quietness spooked Harry.

Harry headed for Pennsylvania Avenue, then cut toward the Washington Monument, turning north into a run-down residential area. His heart was working hard now, and he desperately wanted to stop, but he wouldn't let himself. Not yet.

Remember, he told his brain as he pushed on. *What was John's new address? Come on, Harry.* With great mental effort, he retrieved the street number from his memory bank.

It was a nothing place, John had said, a place to lay his head at night while doing the Lord's work.

Harry tracked the address through the urban jungle to

a set of three identical apartment buildings splattered with graffiti. The sidewalks shimmered with a rainbow of broken glass. Windows were cracked and taped; the lower ones were covered with iron bars. In spite of the early hour, rap music blared from an open window. If it weren't for the music, the place could have been a postapocalyptic landscape.

Harry ventured into the lobby of the middle building where the smell of beer and stale urine assailed him. Holding his breath, he went up the stairs, stepping around crumpled newspapers and garbage.

He found John Drury's apartment on the third floor. He knocked on the door, which drifted open from the impact of his knuckles.

Harry peered inside. It was dark. His nostrils caught the scent of something strong. Disinfectant, he thought. Like pine cleaner on steroids. No, Harry decided, this hygienic overkill wasn't John Drury. Something was wrong.

He went inside, finger tripping the light switch. "John?"

"Shuddoff da light!"

Harry jumped and spun. The living room had been cleared of the few possessions John Drury had managed to accumulate during his rebirth. A figure clothed in a pile of rags huddled in a dark corner, surrounded by empty bottles.

"John?" Harry asked again hesitantly.

"No," gurgled the voice. "He's gone."

Harry's stomach knotted. "Where?"

"Dunno." The bundle of rags took a long pull from a bottle and liquid dribbled down his chin. "Bugs tookim."

"Bugs?" Harry didn't know anyone with the street name Bugs. He knew a Big Bear, a Roadrunner, and a Shark, but no Bugs. "Bugs who?"

The creature leapt up, eyes wide and frightened. "Not Bugs Who. *Bugs! Insects!* Cock-a-roaches! Biguns, tall's me." He motioned with his hands to impress upon Harry the size of the monsters he had seen.

Harry stepped back from the descriptive advance. "How many? When?"

Rags shrugged. "Doan remember."

"What do you remember?"

"They told me not to tell."

Rage filled Harry's veins. He wanted to leap across the living room, grab this ragged creature by the throat, and throttle some answers out of it.

"Paid me not to tell." Rags pointed back toward his corner. Harry followed the gesture to a box with a hole unceremoniously ripped in the side.

"The bugs? They gave you—" Harry squinted. "They gave you a case of Everclear not to tell?"

Rags nodded as if his head was about to drop off. "Great stuff . . . it is. John . . . he brought me offa street, tried to bathe me. I take his food, but no bath. Hate his preaches. 'I was you once, but you gotta see Jesus. Open the door and let Jesus come in your heart.' " Rags laughed himself into a wracking cough. When he recovered, he leaned toward Harry as if to impart a deep, dark secret. "I saw what happen when you let Jesus in your heart. You open the doors and bugs, they come an' take you away."

Harry looked around the apartment. Light was falling into the bedroom, which he could see was empty. "Everything?" He looked at the creature. "They took everything he had?"

Another loose nod. "An' they spray gas around, too. But they gave me that not to tell." Another drunken gesture toward the case of Everclear.

A new dread began to grow inside of Harry. Not the dark, malevolent kind that had been tormenting his soul, but the dread that seizes a man when the noose tightens around his mortal neck. It was the same dread he had felt when the Mossad had appeared in his barren cell and announced they wanted to ask a few questions, and again when he had watched the jeep full of Turkish soldiers drive away after removing the handcuffs and shoving him unceremoniously across an invisible line until both of his bloody feet were inside Iraqi territory.

He sensed that he had just stepped across another line.

Harry began to back toward the door. "If the bugs come back, don't tell them I was here. You tell them you've been alone this whole time."

"What you give me to be quiet?" Rags demanded.

Harry tightened the features of his face and produced the best menacing look he could muster. "If you tell, I will come back and take your bottles away. You understand?"

Rags dropped his bottle. The liquid began seeping into the carpet. With a slobbering nod, he began stepping away from Harry.

"And I'll come and preach at you until the bugs come for you. Do you understand? *I'll make the bugs come for you!*" Harry thrust his hand out, pointing an accusing finger. The creature cowered, whimpered, and melted back into his corner.

Harry began to tremble as soon as he was out the door. He could guess what the bugs had been. Somebody in black uniforms, dark helmets, and breathing-filtration packs.

But why? Did it have anything to do with those scrolls?

No. That couldn't have been it. Nobody knew about the scrolls except himself and the Mossad. And maybe some Arab fundamentalists.

Besides, if it had been the scrolls, they would have grabbed him, not John Drury.

But John Drury had seen Jesus ...

Harry rubbed his aching head as he walked back toward the monument. His sleepless night had left him weary, and his legs suddenly felt as if they could no longer carry him.

He plopped down on the first bench he came to. When at long last a Metro bus showed up, he bought his way on board. Collapsing into a seat, he gazed out the window, trying to collect his thoughts. But the eyes of those riders behind him were boring a hole in the back of his skull, a sensation that made the old dread reappear.

They know, it taunted. *They know you're a traitor. You've betrayed a trust. The lowest level of hell is set aside for people like you ...*

Harry wanted to yell out against the intruding thoughts, but he fought back the impulse. He swallowed air and looked around. On the seat across from him was a disemboweled newspaper. He grabbed the top section and opened it, sticking his nose inside, trying to forget.

When his eyes came to focus, he wanted to scream. There it was now, all coming together and falling into place right before his eyes.

Within the crumpled remains of the style section of the *Washington Post* was a picture of the man he had met in the park—*what?* Two weeks ago? A month ago?

Harry had written him off as a crank.

Yet this strange person had talked as if he had known about the scrolls. He had mentioned them knowingly, though indirectly, as if playing a mental game. But something important between them had gone unsaid.

Suddenly Harry knew what had been unsaid, and what they had been too frightened to say aloud.

Who knew about the scrolls? He did. The Mossad. The Arab fundamentalists. And now this guy.

At that moment, Harry Lauter's mind made an intuitive leap. It was a conclusion that he couldn't substantiate. Yet it made sense. Heaven help him, it made so much sense that he couldn't shake it out of his mind.

This guy was the reason John Drury had disappeared.

But how? Why? What was their connection?

Harry Lauter's mouth dropped wide open when the answer came to him. That ugly face suddenly reminded him of Isaiah's prophecy that the Messiah would "have no beauty that we should desire Him." And then Harry spoke to the picture in the paper in a soft, reverent tone.

"Oh, Jesus. Sweet Jesus. It's you, isn't it? It's really, truly you!"

MAX KIERNAN

"Kiernan here."

"Boss. What are you doing there? It's Sunday."

"Then why did you call here on a Sunday?"

"You weren't home. I know you. Where else would you be?"

"I thought you would be in the hospital for another few days."

There was a pause on the other end of the telephone and the crinkling of paper. "Something interesting has come up. Fenton came over to laugh at my ruptured testicle and go over the debriefing on our recent fiasco."

"You mean major screw-up, don't you?" Kiernan growled. He knew it hadn't been Wrampe's fault, or Brickell's or Fenton's, or anyone else's. They had played the situation by the book. But it was humiliating to be outsmarted by a kid who had grown up on the streets. "Go on."

"Well. Fenton brought me a nice little care package. He told me the kid didn't take Rosie."

"True."

"He brought me some other stuff, too. A couple of Cuban cigars, which they won't let me smoke. A few Kit-Kat bars, which I've already eaten, and the Sunday *Post*. Have you seen it?"

"Yeah," Kiernan said. "And I still think Hobbes is too wise to be a figment of Calvin's imagination."

"Wrong section," said Wrampe.

"*The Wizard of Oz* is going to be on HBO for about the millionth time."

"Wrong again. Try the style section."

"Style? Kevin, you tell them to cut back on the pain killers." Kiernan rolled his chair back from his desk, leaned, and stretched his arm down to the wastebasket. "If you're down to the style pages, you must be seriously bored."

"I went through them twice," Wrampe confessed. "Good thing I did, too." Kiernan pulled the newspaper out of the wastebasket and spread it on his desktop. "All right, I've got the style section."

"Page J–3, boss."

Kiernan thumbed the page open. "What am I looking for? Wedding notices?"

"The photomontage, middle of the page."

"What? The Cornell fund-raiser?"

"You got it," Wrampe said. "There's a picture in the montage, kind of down by itself. The caption says 'New Man in Her Life.' "

"Yeah. Some bimbo with the ugliest guy I've ever seen. What about it?"

"Look at the picture, boss. Carefully."

There was silence as Kiernan looked more closely. After a moment he said, "You've got to be kidding."

"I'm not," said Wrampe, excitedly. "It's him."

"You can't be certain."

"But I am. Look, boss, I was the one who pulled the records from George Washington Hospital. I gave them a real good once-over before I digitalized them and sent them on to Dayton. *This guy is our visitor!*"

"Just a minute, Kevin." Kiernan turned to face his computer console and entered a new command. In a moment, he was keying his way through the montage of photographs that had been taken at the hospital. "I don't know."

Then Kiernan went silent.

"What's wrong, Max?"

"Nothing. Nothing's wrong. Why should anything be wrong?"

"Because I'm fighting to sell this to the man who'll chase after any sighting, no matter how ridiculous it may seem. Remember that July we spent in Manitoba searching for pieces of that French satellite because someone claimed that something had shot it down? I still have scars from the mosquitoes.

"Now we've got something that has every indication of being the real thing, and you're trying to pass it off as something insignificant. If I didn't know better, I'd swear this is a mystery you're not anxious to look into."

Kiernan drew a long, slow breath to settle his temper and soothe his nerves. "Kevin, you understand what this will entail. I just want to make sure that this is the genuine article before we go grabbing people off the streets."

"Do yourself a favor, boss. Believe this one. If this isn't the real thing I'll quit. I swear it."

"All right," Kiernan said. "I'll look into it."

Another long silence. "You've got to do more than that," Wrampe said finally.

That was it. Kiernan had had enough. "Rest easy, Kevin. And remember your promise." He hung up the phone and turned to gaze out the window. The capital was greening rather nicely this spring, but the tranquil scene wasn't enough to suppress his nagging anxiety.

Wrampe was right on the nose. The evidence was incontrovertible. They already had the silver suit. They knew Kit Washington was carrying some kind of powerful alien technology. And they could draw a straight line from him to the Visitor. All Kiernan had to do was pick up the telephone, and it would be done. Human capture of an extraterrestrial intelligence. *A close encounter of the fifth kind.*

So what was keeping him back? What was keeping his hand from the telephone? He paused and studied the picture of his mother, taken in another place and another time, neither of which seemed of this earth. So happy. Everything to look forward to. His mother seemed as alien to him as the ugly little man on page J–3 of the *Washington Post.*

"What now?" he asked the picture wearily.

The fact that he felt this way didn't make sense. This was the moment he had been waiting for all his career, when he could grab one of those little things by the lapel of its magic suit and shake it until its black almond eyes rattled in its head, growling out between clenched teeth: *Who are you? Who? Who? Why are you doing this? Why? Why?* He'd show the alien critter the files, the tragic list of names, mostly women, a few men, some children, all with two strange things in common.

They claimed they had been abducted by a UFO.

And they later died by their own hand.

"And this one"—he would say, showing the picture of his mother—"this one . . ."

Driven to suicide by the aftershocks of an alien abduction or run down by a taxi cab while crossing the street.

This was his chance. Yet he was hesitating. What was there to fear? Under the sanction of the United States Government, he was to capture an alien intelligence and negotiate a pact, an exchange perhaps of technology for raw resources.

What would be left to do then? Write memoirs. Hit the talk-show circuit. Hobnob with has-been movie stars. Start drinking. Blow your brains out on a warm summer day, just like Mom.

Just like Mom.

Kiernan swiveled his head to look up at the sky.

"Soon," he said to the hovering vehicles he knew were there. He didn't know what would happen, but he would not turn out like her. Even if it meant putting his .45 against one of their heads and blowing purple brains and green blood all over the wall of his office.

He had survived what they had done to his mother.

He had survived what his mother had done to herself.

He would survive this, too.

Kiernan picked up the phone and stabbed Brickell's number into the keypad. Brickell answered on the second ring with a snappy "Joe's Bar and Grill."

"Grow up!" Kiernan snapped. "I've got something I want you to do for me."

"Yeah?" His voice sounded muffled, as if he had a mouthful of food. "Fire away."

Kiernan snorted his laugh. "I know that you're next in line to do it, but I want Fenton to lead the Team. I think we may be making a for-real grab here in the next day or two."

There was muffled obscenity from Brickell, a pause, and then his voice cleared. He had swallowed. "But I've got seniority."

"I understand that, but you have to understand this. I'm going to be gone someday, but the agency will continue, and it could use someone like you to keep it alert, alive, and running. After all, you're a man after my own heart."

"What's that supposed to mean?" Brickell demanded.

"It means you have a character trait that I need for an upcoming project. Something that neither Fenton nor Wrampe have. Something that is required in dealing with the Kit Washington problem."

"Yeah? And what, pray tell, is that?"

Max Kiernan said, "You're not afraid to get your hands wet."

GHOST

He shifted on the ground, trying to get comfortable enough to go back to sleep. *Some rotten way to live,* he thought. *Here I am, king of the world, and I have to sleep outside in a park.*

Ghost didn't let himself dwell on that for too long. He might have the magic rock, but he also knew the rules of the game.

It was a game invented by white men.

And it went like this: when a brother started to get ahead in life, started to accumulate some money, some power, some admiration, then it was time to take him down.

It happened all the time. Look at what they'd done all through history. Paul Robeson, blacklisted. Muhammad Ali, shot him full of that awful disease that made you shake. Richard Pryor, they set him on fire. They tried that with Michael Jackson, too, and when that failed, they got him into that trouble with the kids. Not just any kids, mind you, but white kids.

And now that the Ghost was out there grabbing his handful, they were after him.

The bad part of it was, they were so obvious about it, as if they didn't care who saw them doing it. He'd first noticed it yesterday, coming out of the store. There was a strange black car cruising slowly down the street, followed by a black van with antennas sticking out of the top.

Ghost hadn't thought about it until he decided to do a quick sweep through the old neighborhood, maybe slip up to his apartment for a few essentials and use the rock to make everyone forget he was there.

But then he saw another car and another van parked outside of his building. Further reconnaissance of the neighborhood saw these strange pairs outside of his momma's place, across the road from the D Street Motel, and at the old warehouse where he'd left Squeak and Shark. They even had Amos's place covered.

Even when he managed to get cleaned up enough to try checking into the Four Seasons, the clerk slipped back into the main office for a suspiciously long time. Ghost produced the rock and ordered the clerk out, and the clerk emerged with a cordless phone in one hand and a photo of Kit Washington in the other. So he blanked out the clerk's memory of him, replacing it with Jesse Jackson, and then got out of there.

Back on the street, he started watching. Black car, black van. Always on the inside lanes. Going slow. Looking for somebody.

Him.

That was the game. And he knew what it was all about.

It was about a lot of things, but mostly it was about power, and keeping it out of the hands of the brothers.

The reason was simple enough. If they couldn't keep them as slaves, then they didn't want them around at all.

Now this rock—or whatever it was—gave him power beyond his wildest dreams. Not only would he be able to control the neighborhood's drug traffic, he now had the capability to crash into the Big Time.

As he lay on his back in the grass and the cold from the ground crept into his bones, Ghost became painfully aware that he was not moving fast enough. After all, how long had he had the rock? A week? Maybe two? And for all of his efforts, what had he gotten? All of the Colt 45 he could hold. All of the sex he could stand. And so much money that he had literally been rolling in it. It had been fun, but where was it getting him?

A suite in the damp grass that surrounded McMillan Reservoir.

It occurred to him that he was actually worse off now than he had been before finding the rock.

And now he was being chased by The Man. No, it wasn't The Man. It was the THE MAN, the one with those big black cars and antennaed vans, THE MAN who carried gigantic weapons and gadgets that could suck a brother right into secret machinery that would grind him into nothingness. It was an awful fate he faced, because not only would he be dead and gone, but it would be as if he had never existed.

"Kit Washington?" his friends would all say once it had happened. "Who? Kit who? Ghost what? Nossir. Don't know no nigger by that name. Never heard of the man."

Yes, he had power now, but there was a nightmare side to it, and with it a moral as clear and preachy as the lessons in those old superhero comic books. *There's something that comes with power, son, and if you abuse it, the fires of hell await you.*

Especially if you were black.

Ghost was in that hell now, and he knew it. His friends were all gone. Women made sure they weren't around when he was in the neighborhood. It hadn't taken long to dispose of his enemies, which had led to the discovery that the world was an extremely boring place without them.

Unless your enemies were everywhere. Like THE MAN.

He reached up and rubbed his eyes, forcing himself to think. What to do next. He'd dug himself into a deep hole. Now he had to find a way to dig himself back out.

Well. He had the power. All he had to do was figure out how to use it. The right way this time.

That meant getting away from THE MAN.

But how, when THE MAN was crawling all over the place?

He wrestled with the problem until he cast his newsprint blankets aside, and rose to see a beautiful young woman on the arm of the one man in the world who could help him.

SUSAN HILL

Susan Hill was sitting in a McDonald's restaurant two blocks from Serena Blake's apartment, inhaling a chocolate shake and nibbling on fries. Her nerves were on fire in anticipation of meeting the socialite. An open engagement like this made her nervous. But Fran had insisted. It was safer, she had said, than meeting at Serena's apartment. Susan had tried to argue. After all, it was their plan to get into Serena's apartment. But Fran had been adamant.

Susan had been glad to hear from the vice cop. She

was afraid she had lost all credibility with tales of vanishing bodies and disappearing witnesses.

Then two days ago, Fran had called with a cryptic request that they meet at a bar. Susan knew that she had to be onto something then.

So Susan had dug out her hooker outfit and gone to the bar where they had collared the Scarlet Avenger. Mick Aaronson would like this, she thought. And something this big could make her career.

But after waiting for almost half an hour, the glamour had faded. She realized for the first time that this story was now far too frightening to be much fun.

She sat at the bar, slowly nursing a couple of beers and fending off the attentions of horny lawyers and lobbyists. Fran finally appeared after an hour. She set a copy of the *Washington Post* down on the bar and ordered a whiskey sour.

"Sorry I'm late," she said. "Got tied up busting a French tourist for soliciting oral sex. At least, I *think* that's what he was asking for."

Fran gulped a mouthful of air.

"This is why I called," she said. "Everything we've talked about has been true. And now we have concrete evidence." She opened the paper. "Page J–3. In a story of no significance, the *Post* nearly scooped you."

Susan looked at the photograph and understood immediately. Her first impulse was to leap into action and corner Serena Blake at the first available opportunity. After all, if Fran had seen the picture, then heaven only knew who else had noticed.

"No," Fran said. "We need to do some homework first. Here's what we do."

Susan didn't like to be slowed down, but she let Fran speak.

"Call Serena for an appointment to interview her about her work with Citizens Who Care. Ask her to

meet in a neutral corner—somewhere crowded that
won't arouse curiosity like a McDonald's. The sooner
you can do this, the better. Take a photographer along
and persuade her to let you take pictures of her at
home."

"Sounds okay," Susan said. "I'll see about getting a
photographer from—"

"*I'll* be your photographer," Fran interrupted. She
slapped her hand on the bar, prompting the bartender to
bring another round. "I have the feeling I've been
scammed, and I'm going to get some satisfaction, one
way or the other."

When Susan called next morning to set up the interview, Serena had sounded less than coherent. But she had
agreed to meet Susan and a photographer at 7:00 P.M. the
following day. She couldn't imagine why anyone would
want to talk to her about Citizens Who Care, Serena protested, because she merely put the money up and others
did all the work. Susan made up something about getting
the story behind the story.

Now here she was, waiting for Fran and Serena both,
checking her watch for the hundredth time. Fran was
late again, and so was Serena.

To calm herself, Susan reviewed the plan in her
mind. Meet quickly. Get into Serena's apartment, start
chatting her up, and then spring it on her. *Look, I've
been scooped by the* Post. *It seems they ran a shot of
you on Sunday with someone. The two of you certainly
looked very happy together. Would you like to tell me
about him? Introduce us?*

Susan winced at the progression of thought. This was
investigative journalism, true, but she wasn't supposed
to do a *60 Minutes* and batter down the poor woman's
defenses. Better to slide in under them and let her expose her own soft underbelly.

She stared down at the reporter's notebook. What

scared her most was this man in Serena Blake's life. He
had fooled a team of EMTs and a doctor into thinking
that he was dead. What price might be on his head if
people who had come into contact with him were disappearing left and right? Was she risking her life to chase
this story? Was there a limit to how far she should go
to please Mick Aaronson? After all, some of Susan's
classmates had dismissed him as a dinosaur, but she
recognized the power he still wielded. She sensed that if
she pursued this story, she might learn too much. Then
even the great Mick Aaronson might not be able to protect her.

The thought made her shiver. She rubbed her arms
and looked up at the door, and as she did, a couple of
business-suited men walked in. Their Ray-Bans, cocky
smiles, and too-neat hair signaled only one thing. *Feds.*
Their idea of going undercover was taking off their ties.
They made their way through the restaurant and fell
into line, acting nonchalant. They laughed over a shared
joke. Then the shorter one looked *right at her*, only she
couldn't tell where his eyes were going because of the
Ray-Bans. Was it her skinny legs? Her breasts? Or was
it the panic on her face? *Did they know?* His lips turned
up into a smile, but Susan looked away.

That spooked her. She picked up her tray nervously,
shouldered the camera bag, and started to step away
from the table. A glance back showed that she'd left her
reporter's notebook behind. She turned and reached
down for it, closer, closer, and then—

"Susan Hill?"

She yelped and spun around.

"I'm sorry. I didn't mean to startle you."

Susan turned. The pale, weary-looking woman who
now stood before her could only have been Serena
Blake. Susan could see that the woman could have been
beautiful if she had taken the time to do something with

her hair and apply a little makeup. She had thought the picture of the socialite in the *Post* had been badly over-exposed, burning out the skin tones on both her and her escort, making them look pale and emaciated. But that was not the case. Susan now saw that the picture was overexposed because of Serena Blake's pale skin. *Girl, you really ought to get out in the sun more.* Then it oc-curred to her that the man in her life, the coroner-dodger, had looked ghastly, too. That could mean only that the two of them had to be sharing a coke spoon.

Sheepishly, Serena Blake said, "Look, I'm sorry I'm late, but I had to stop and pick up a couple of things. You know how it is. One thing leads to another."

Susan nodded, her hand grabbing her reporter's note-book. The feds, who were now ordering Big Macs, were a million miles away from her thoughts.

Serena clapped a hand to her mouth. "I'm sorry. I mean, you *are* Susan Hill, aren't you? I mean, you did have that notebook."

Susan realized that she hadn't yet responded to the woman. "I'm sorry." She offered her hand. "Yes. Yes, I'm Susan Hill."

"I'm Serena Blake. Officially." She put on a thin smile that seemed forced. "I'm sorry I was so late. Were you leaving?"

Susan looked down at the tray in her hand. "No. Not really. I wanted to get rid of this stuff, and I couldn't re-ally leave the camera lying around."

Serena glanced around nervously. "I thought you were going to bring a photographer."

"So did I," Susan said. "But she got pulled to cover something else at the last minute. All right, Susan thought. Maybe I can make this work. "So I guess it's up to me."

"You know how to use that thing?" Serena asked, looking apprehensively at the camera bag.

"All of my photographs are blackmail quality," Susan assured her. "Too dark, out of focus, and grainy."

Serena laughed again. Susan counted it as another victory. The feds reemerged in her consciousness now, but she decided that she had been paranoid. They wouldn't really interfere with her here, at a McDonald's, in front of God and everybody.

"So," Susan continued, forcing the words out as if she were on a first date, "can I get you something? Coffee? French fries? Mayor McCheese cookies?"

The laugh that came this time stayed, fading into a smile. "No, thank you. I thought we'd just have something at the apartment. I've got one of those electric coffee-bean grinders and a hundred kinds of beans that I never touch." She held up a gold-foil shopping bag fitted with black plastic handles. "And I picked up some light and insignificant cookies. If that's all right, I mean."

"Sounds fine," Susan said. She adjusted the weight of the camera bag on her shoulder and slipped the notebook inside. "Lead on."

Serena did just that, and Susan followed her out of the McDonald's, her eyes darting back and forth, hoping to catch a glimpse of Fran. This was supposed to have been Fran's show. Had Susan been able to set this up herself, she would have taken a completely different approach. As she followed Serena Blake back to her apartment, she thought of a line from a poem memorized eons ago: *Into the jaws of Death,/Into the mouth of Hell . . .*

Susan followed Serena into the lobby of a chrome and glass building. Serena stopped at the bulletproof security window to sign Susan in, and handed the reporter a plastic-laminated pass which she clipped to the strap of her camera bag.

"There's been nobody here to see you," the guard

told her with a glazed look. "I haven't seen anyone at all."

Serena said, "That's good. I didn't expect anyone." Then to Susan, "Follow me."

Susan did, glancing back at the guard. As soon as she was out of earshot she said, "I wonder what he's on," and then instantly regretted it. *You were right, Mr. Aaronson, you were right. I need to watch my mouth all of the time.*

"It's ironic," Serena said, pushing the button for the elevator. The door opened right away and she stepped into the car.

"What?" Susan asked, following.

"This is one of the few apartment complexes in the D.C. area that's had any luck in keeping the junkies and hard cases out of the lobby. But they can't do a thing when it comes to hiring them to work inside."

Or letting them in as tenants, Susan thought.

"I hate living here," Serena admitted. "But that's off the record."

"Then why do you?" Susan asked. The elevator lurched, and her stomach rolled in protest.

"When I was twenty-five, a rather sizable trust fund was rolled over into my name. One of the conditions for staying on the family payroll was to live in Washington, D.C., for ten years. Two more years, then I'm out of here."

"Your family some kind of sadists?"

"Washington wasn't this bad when they set it all up."

"Still, why would they set a condition like that?"

Serena shrugged. "My father designed half the buildings built in this town since the late seventies. So you can imagine what it's like having to live here. Two years, Susan. I'm marking time. And then I'm getting out. I'm going to go away. Far, far away."

The elevator jerked to a halt, and the pair spilled out into the hallway.

"And when I go," Serena continued, "I'm going to leave my bad habits behind." Then she sniffed, almost as if for emphasis, a subconscious admission of something which bothered her but was best left unsaid.

"But I'm going to continue my involvement with the Citizens Who Care. I mean, somebody has to do something to help." She pulled a plastic card out of her purse and reached out for the slot on the door. Then her hand pulled back quickly, almost as if her fingertip had been pricked by a burst of static electricity. "Look. I've done it again. I've been really distracted lately." She smiled warmly at Susan, and to demonstrate what she meant, pushed the door with her finger. It opened. "I'll introduce you to my distraction."

Susan followed her inside, her eyes drinking in the scene, making note of every detail. Mauve walls and carpet highlighted with splashes of deep red. Chalk white fur couch splashed with red. A surrealistic print on the wall of a half-nude man, fingers clutching his stomach and ribs, eyes open wide in a scream, a freight train billowing charcoal black smoke bursting from his open mouth. Splashed in red. And then the smell hit Susan's nostrils, that strong metallic tang that was overpowering—the undercurrent of potpourri and Lysol—and it all connected at once, her brain shouting, *Oh no oh no oh no get out get out GET—*

Serena Blake screamed.

Knowing too well what it was, Susan sucked in air and held it, then stepped around Serena, closing in, one careful step at a time, while Serena shrank backward, fists at her mouth. Susan's mind raced wildly. *Is it him, is it the guy, who did this, why did they do it, what have they done, now we'll never know—*

And then, she saw that it was worse than she had imagined.

The body was on the floor at the point where the living room hooked to Susan's right and became the kitchen. Blood pooling on the linoleum floor, clothing torn away, a series of gashes on the upper torso too numerous to count. A large knife was still dripping on the countertop, carbon steel, designed to chop leeks and quarter artichokes, anything but the evil for which it had been used.

The body's face was smeared with blood just starting to dry.

Fran Markowski.

A cry slipped from Susan's mouth—not a scream, but more of a low moan of denial. And now she was stepping backward, too, back towards the chalk white fur couch, fingers clutching her own stomach, waiting for the freight train to emerge, thinking, *telephone I know I saw a telephone in here somewhere . . .*

And then words. Clear, low, and icy.

"She had a magic little badge that got her in here. But it weren't magic enough to keep her alive."

Susan gasped and stood up straight.

"Freeze!"

The noise cut off in her throat, and suddenly she went into total brain lock. The telephone she knew was only inches away might as well have been on the other side of the moon.

Why had she done it? Why had Fran set her up this way?

A figure strode into the room from deep inside the apartment. Tall as a man, but with boyish features, spotted with blood and wiping his hands on a peach towel.

"Ladies," he said. His look was pure evil.

Susan's mind raged and boiled. She had taken defense classes and knew how to deal with men like this.

Throw the camera bag, shout *No!* Sink the knee into the groin, aim the palm for the bridge of the nose, the fingernails for the eyes, the elbow for the throat. She wanted to throw herself at this man, tear his heart from his chest, and hand it to him, still beating.

But she couldn't move.

"You-all can call me Ghost," he said, smiling with mock politeness. "Since I don't think either of you gonna live long enough to identify me to the police." He looked at Fran's body. "Not that they's a whole lot the police gonna do." Back to the two of them. "Let's try that out now, just so's you know who the almighty god and boss of this here situation is. Both of you say, 'I understand the terms, Mr. Ghost, sir.' "

Susan bit her lip.

Serena said, "I understand the terms, Mr. Ghost, sir."

Susan clenched her teeth and forced air out from between her lips. Anything but that. *Anything.* "F—f—fu—"

"I understand the terms, Mr. Ghost, sir," he repeated slowly. "You get it right, or you gonna be hurtin' bad."

"I understand the terms, Mr. Ghost, sir."

What was he doing to them? And how was he doing it?

"Very good."

Now he laughed. He told them both that he was glad they had come to an understanding and that if they cooperated, there would be a little fun for everyone involved before he had to kill them.

You're dead, Susan thought. *You're a dead man. And before you die, I'm going to hand you your fun, floating in a jar of formaldehyde . . .*

Ghost reached into the pocket of his Raiders jacket and drew out a blue steel revolver. "Courtesy of the Washington P.D.," he laughed, putting the gun on an end table. He reached in again as he turned to Serena. "You the Serena Blake that live here?"

"Yes," Serena said blankly.

He turned to Susan. "Who you, then?"

Susan bit her lip and tried not to answer.

"I hurt you if you don't tell."

"Susan Hill. Washington *Tribune*."

This interested Ghost. "You a newspaper lady?"

"Yes."

He pulled his hand out of his pocket and revealed a wad of paper. Unfolding it, he showed it to Susan. It was the picture of Serena and the man from the *Post*. "You take this picture, then?"

Susan closed her eyes. "No. Wrong paper."

"Oh. Too bad." Then, as if that was all the interest he had in her, he turned back to Serena. "You know this man, don't you?"

Susan watched as Serena answered. The socialite might as well have been a ventriloquist's dummy. "Yes," she said, arms by her sides, expression blank.

"Ha!" Ghost said at Serena's reply. "Thought so. You's probably doin' him, ain't you?"

"No," Serena said.

"Liar!" Ghost shouted. "Lemme tell you something, you gonna get the cramps hard every time you lie to me—you got that? Starting *now!*" He pointed an accusing finger at Serena, who stood calmly looking back at him. After a moment of silence he said, "I told you to tell me if you're doin' it with this guy. Are you?"

"No."

Susan watched his mouth drop open.

"You ain't?"

"No."

"You's what, then? Just friends?"

"I love him."

Ghost snorted. "Must be some kind of faggot if he's not gettin' any offa you. What's his name?"

"I call him Victor."

"Last name?"

"I don't know."

Ghost studied her. "I warned you about lyin' to me."

"I'm not lying."

He rattled the paper. "You know where this guy lives?"

"Here."

Ghost turned away from her, throwing his hands in the air in disbelief. Then he whirled on her violently and shouted, "You feelin' *pain*, Serena!"

She grabbed her abdomen and bent at the waist.

"Harder!"

Serena hit the floor with a groan. Susan's teeth clenched, wanting to leap the distance and kick, tear, and bite him. *Save it,* Susan told herself. *Save your strength. Wait for the moment. Make it count.*

"You tellin' me you don't know his last name, you's not givin' him any, and he's here livin' with you?"

"Yes." It came out as an extended hiss.

"You expect me to believe any of this? What's wrong with you anyhow?"

"I," Serena gasped, "am an alcoholic. I . . . am a co-caine addict."

Ghost shook his head. "Strike me blind." He looked around the room for a moment, searching for inspiration and finding it on the end table. "Get up, Serena," he ordered, grabbing the gun. "You ain't in pain no more."

Serena picked herself up off the ground as if nothing had happened. Ghost wandered to the sliding glass doors in the kitchen that opened onto the terrace. He spent a moment looking out over the city. "Nice view," he mumbled.

"Thank you," Serena volunteered. "My father designed this building."

Ghost turned back to them. "You know," he said, sauntering as if he was addressing a courtroom on a hot summer day, "they's nothing worse than a woman thinks she's got a sense of humor. Ain't a woman alive who can tell a joke right."

Susan pushed air hard against her throat. It came out in words. "The joke's on you." Then as an afterthought, "Mr. Ghost, sir."

Ghost snapped up the revolver and cocked it in one smooth motion, aiming squarely at Susan's head. "Don't you be pushin' me."

Susan forced a smile. "Go ahead."

"Wouldn't dream of giving you the satisfaction." He uncocked the gun and pressed it into Serena's hand. "She's gonna do it for me."

"No," Serena said.

"Shut up," Ghost snapped. "Now, here's the story. I'm gonna ask you some questions. And if I ain't happy with the answers I'm gettin', I'm gonna have you shoot up this reporter lady here, one piece at a time."

Susan strained against the paralysis she felt, but it was no use. It had been effort enough to verbalize the insult.

"Now, Miss Serena, this man's name is—"

"Victor," she blurted.

"And you don't know his last name."

"That's right."

"But he lives here."

"That's right."

"What about his stuff?"

"What do you mean by 'stuff'?" Serena asked. And then she added, "Mr. Ghost, sir."

Ghost rolled his eyes. "Miss Serena, raise up the gun and point it at your friend's big mouth."

The arm came up. The gun aimed.

"Any more lies like that, you gonna be shootin'. Got that?"

"I understand."

"By 'stuff,' I mean jewelry, fancy things like that. He bring any of that with him?"

"No."

"He didn't bring nothin' in here with him?"

"When I brought him here," Serena recited, "he was carrying only a lunch that I had given him. The only other thing he had was his clothing."

"Clothing." Ghost's eyes lit up. "Tell me about that."

"He was wearing doctor's greens. The words 'Property of George Washington University Hospital' were stenciled on them."

Ghost looked down dejectedly. "That's it?"

"That's it." Her arm, unwavering, held the gun on Susan.

"Where are they now?"

"Gone."

"*Gone?*"

"They were filthy. I put them in a paper bag and sent them down to maintenance to have them burned—"

"*Burned?*"

"Two weeks ago. Maybe three."

Ghost became a flurry of activity, stomping through the apartment, kicking the walls and knocking things over. "Woman, you know what you just done?"

"I'm sorry."

"You know where he is now?"

"Didn't you kill him?"

"What you think I am, stupid?"

"Yes," Susan blurted, ready to force his hand and be done with it.

"Kill her!" he ordered Serena.

The arm with the gun wavered.

"What's wrong with you?"

"I've never fired a gun before."

Ghost swore violently. "Don't you watch any television? You pull back the hammer. You pull the trigger. You watch her head explode." He watched her for a moment, burning with anger and frustrated by disbelief. "So do it!"

Serena brought her other hand up and pulled back the hammer with a dry metallic *click*. "Susan," she said. "I'm really sorry."

Susan closed her eyes tightly.

"Stop!"

Susan's eyes flipped back open. The voice was new, calm and soothing. As if in slow motion, Serena's hand opened and the revolver fell, end over end, until it crashed down into the carpet.

Ghost yelped. In one smooth motion, he jumped to the gun and scooped it up. He turned toward the apartment door, aiming the weapon. As he sighted it on the intruder his face changed suddenly, and Susan could tell from his expression that he'd found what he had been looking for.

It was the strange little man, the vanishing corpse. And he was every bit as ugly as Fran had described. He stood in the doorway of Serena's apartment, clad in the best casuals that Land's End had to offer, a copy of the *Tribune* under his arm.

He looked around at the carnage. Not a muscle on his face moved, as if he had seen such violence all of his life. After taking in the scene, he closed the door behind him and deposited the paper on the library table by the door. Then he walked calmly toward Ghost, seemingly oblivious to the fact that he was facing a man with a gun.

"*You* stop," Ghost growled, pointing the gun.

The man took another step toward him.

"No, Victor," Serena pleaded.

Ghost's free hand reached under his shirt. "I told you to *freeze*."

Victor shook his head. He took another step.

"How come you ain't frozen?"

Victor shrugged. "It's set for *your* brain frequencies, not mine."

Ghost nodded and stepped backward, toward the kitchen, keeping his distance. "You be the man," he said, smiling. "That's what I thought. Well, you ugly bastard, I'm needin' to talk to you. You got some things I need."

"I have some things that everyone on this planet needs."

Ghost threw his head back and rolled his eyes. "No, no, no! Not Jesus again! You don't understand, my man. You got the toys I want."

"I'm afraid I'm not following your line of thinking."

"You don't recognize me, do you?"

"Should I?"

"My man, I'm the one who busted you upside you head a few weeks ago. Took your fancy clothes. And this." He pulled a chain around his neck and something popped out, a stone of some kind with duct tape wrapped around it. "You recognize this?"

"Oh, yes. I'm happy that you've decided to return it. Thank you very much." He took two confident steps toward Ghost, who retreated and waved the gun until he stopped.

"Victor!" Serena said urgently.

Victor ignored her. "If you're not here to return it, then what are you here for?"

"I want more things like this," Ghost said. "Like the clothes you was wearing."

"You took those from me. You mean you didn't keep them?"

"If I'd known what they was, I would have," Ghost said angrily.

"That doesn't seem to be my problem."

"Awright." Ghost dropped the stone and shifted the gun in his hand, keeping the barrel pointed straight at the man's chest. "Forget the clothes. I want more things like this rock, only better."

"What for?"

"What you think, ugly? You startin' to get on my nerves."

"I don't have anything more to give you—"

"You said you had something for everyone."

"A message."

"More lies, my man. This rock here I took from you. I don't believe in magic or nothin', but I'm willing to say this rock has some kind of mind control."

"In your terms, it might be called an Empathetic Suggestion Amplifier."

"Whatever. I been playin' with it, and now I'm thinkin' maybe you're connected with the CIA. Wherever you're from, you're gonna get me some more of these toys, or I'll blow your lady's head off."

"You can't have any more," Victor said in a monotone.

"What you mean I can't have any more? Man, in case you ain't noticed, I'm the one with the gun."

Another step. "You can't have it because you're not mature enough as a species in general and as an individual in particular to handle our technology responsibly."

"I don't want to hear your excuses."

"Do you really want to bring upon yourself more of the misery that that little trinket has brought you already?"

"This trinket," Ghost shouted, jerking the chain out of his shirt for emphasis, "has given me the *power*!"

"You might have the power, young man, but you're

very alone with it. It happens whenever one of our little
'trinkets' falls into the hands of your species. Jim Jones.
David Koresh. But they can never handle it. And we always get our devices back." He took another step. "You
know, you're right. I have lots of other marvelous
things at home. Some of them you don't even have to
hold. You just look at them. Or think about them. You
would think that they were miraculous. But the price.
Oh, the price."

Ghost stepped back onto the kitchen linoleum and
drew in a deep breath. Then he spoke with slow and deliberate words. "I want it."

"I feel sorry for you. I could give you these miracles,
friend, but I promise that within a week you would be
quite insane."

Ghost stared at him for a moment, then let out his
breath. "All right, ugly. I'm gonna show you that I can
play this game the way white men play it." He swung
his arm and pointed the revolver straight at Serena. One
side of his lip curled up. "Watch *my* miracle."

Susan tried to shout out a distraction, but it wouldn't
happen. All she could do was watch Ghost's finger
twitching on that terrible trigger.

Then it happened.

The glass door to the terrace shattered, and there was
a wet *pop!* Susan cried out and staggered backward,
suddenly free but drained by her mental struggle. It was
clear that whatever Ghost had done to her—

Ghost . . .

Susan looked up and stepped back, horrified. The top
of his head was completely gone, with only the teeth of
his lower jaw left, curving in a sardonic grin that
gleamed with fresh blood. The mutilated figure spasmed
violently, tossing the gun, then started to fall. As it did,
the chest cavity exploded, spraying its contents across the
apartment.

Serena screamed and collapsed. Victor kneeled to see what was left of Ghost, reaching inside his shredded shirt to pull out the smooth-looking stone.

"No matter what happens," he said matter-of-factly, "they always come back to us. Always."

Susan fought back the nausea and dizziness and stepped through the kitchen to examine the spider-webbed pattern of cracks on the terrace floor. Behind her, Serena wailed.

"How did he get in here? How did that awful man get in here? And who is that horrible dead woman?"

Victor moved to her side and placed a comforting hand on her arm. "It's complex. The boy had something of mine." He showed her the strange stone. "He used it to get in here, but its power brought him back to me and destroyed him. It always ends this way."

"The woman was a cop," Susan said.

"What?" Serena asked.

"She was supposed to pose as my photographer. We had to get to you, Ms. Blake. This may seem obvious now, but you're in great danger." She stepped out onto the terrace and scanned the surroundings buildings. A screech drifted up from the street, drawing her eyes downward. Below, she could see vehicles converging on the front door of the apartment complex. Cars and vans. All black.

"Oh, no!" she said.

"What's wrong?" Victor asked.

"Trouble." Susan retreated from the terrace, bolted into the living room, and grabbed her camera bag. "We've got to go. We've got to get out of here right now."

"I don't—"

"You've got a lot of people after you, Victor. Government people, I'm afraid. And if we don't find a way out of here fast, I think we're all going to disappear." She reached her hand down for Serena, who grabbed it and pulled herself up from the floor. "And that sound means we're now in a hurry."

"Certainly," said Victor. "But first—"

But it was too late. He was cut off by the door bursting off its hinges. At least a dozen black-suited figures forced their way inside. They wore helmets and gas masks and carried weapons the likes of which Susan had never seen.

"Hold it right there." One man stepped forward and motioned with the muzzle of his gun. Susan took Serena's hand and stepped aside as the intruder went over to Ghost's body. Two others followed, unfolding a large black nylon bag between them.

The man probed Ghost's chest with the tips of his gloved fingers. "Where is it?" he asked.

"What?" asked Susan.

"You mean this?" Smiling, Victor held up the rock. Susan's extremities again felt too thick to move and it again seemed an effort to talk or breathe or even think.

Oh, no! Not more of this . . .

The lead intruder panicked at the sight of the rock, cursing violently and trying to bring his weapon to bear. But now his movements seemed sluggish and oddly comical, his fingers fumbling the bolt of the weapon, unable to bring it up, ultimately dropping it to the floor.

And then Susan realized that it was deathly quiet in the apartment.

"Well," Victor said confidently. "That's much better." He motioned to the other figures crouching near Ghost's body. "You three may stand if you're more comfortable."

In robotic unison, they all rose.

"Gentlemen," he said, "this is the arrangement. I cannot have you following me or my two friends. I cannot even have you identifying us. That's why I must insist that you remember nothing of the last twenty-four hours. Any attempts to remember anything from this period of time will result in severe pain. Are you all clear on that?"

Susan darted her eyes and counted heads as they nodded. There were thirteen of them.

"Very good. Very good. And now, ladies ... You know where to go."

And suddenly Susan was *walking*. The sensation was strange because she knew that her movement and direction were being controlled by something else. She wondered where she was going, then realized that she was following Victor. She did not resist; she felt strangely safe.

There were two more black-clad soldiers at the elevator. Victor waved at them as if he were greeting a favorite uncle, and they raised their weapons. Red lines streamed out from the top of the weapons, making dots on Victor's pale blue shirt.

"Freeze," they said.

"Freeze," Victor echoed.

They did.

Victor rang for the elevator. As he waited for it to arrive, he turned to the men and gave them instructions that would wipe out their memories of the last twenty-four hours, too. Then he told them to close their eyes and count to a thousand, then go down the hall to the room that the others had occupied.

In the lobby, two more soldiers were waiting inside the security office. Two others were standing by the main entrance, their backs to the door, and were waving away spectators and angry tenants. Victor gathered their attention politely and instructed them all to clear their memories of everything that had just occurred.

He started the two guards counting down from a thousand, then turned to Susan.

"Well?" he asked.

Her limbs jerked as she suddenly regained control of her body. "How do you do that?" she asked, impressed.

"Never mind. You need to get us out of here."

Susan looked up and down the street. "I thought you were in charge."

"My part was to get us out of the building. Now we need to leave the area."

"The farther away, the better," Serena said. The drying blood on her face made her look paler than before.

"You got a car?" Susan asked.

Victor shook his head. "Serena takes mass transit or a limousine everywhere she goes. Don't you have a car?"

Susan shook her head. "It's at the *Tribune*. I took the subway."

There were shouts. People were getting impatient with the guards, who were having trouble explaining their presence.

"Why can't we take the bus?" Susan asked. "You could make everyone forget that we were there."

"Control becomes taxing after a while," Victor said. "It is necessary to conserve one's mental strength or else side effects set in. Even in my species."

"Then," said Susan, "we'd better start walking."

"Wait." It was Serena. She was trembling now, looking as if she couldn't walk a dozen yards. "There're lots of cars right here. Let's take one."

Victor smiled and walked down the line of vehicles, peering inside. He stopped at one and tapped on the window. A black-clad soldier hopped out and drew a pistol. Victor had a few words with him. Then the soldier holstered the pistol, reached into his pocket, and handed over a set of keys. Victor waved for Susan, who wrapped her arm around Serena, and together they shuffled to the waiting car.

Victor had the back door open by the time they got there. They eased Serena inside and closed the door. Then Victor handed Susan the keys.

"Me?" Susan asked. "You want me to be the getaway driver?"

"I don't know how to drive," Victor said.

"All right." She took the keys, climbed into the driver's side, and jammed the key into the ignition. The engine fired as Victor climbed into the passenger's side. Putting the car in gear, she lurched out into evening traffic, nearly mowing down a priest. She drove aggressively, raising choruses of honks with her sudden lane changes and turns.

Victor sat back in his seat, fingers locked behind his head. "Very good. Very good, uh—"

"Susan," she said. "Susan Hill."

"Where did you learn to drive, Susan?"

"The movies."

He smiled. Susan nodded. Okay, now she could see how Serena might be attracted to this guy.

"And you're Victor, the new man in Serena Blake's life."

"Actually, I am more of a presence in her life. As she is in mine."

"You got a last name, Victor?"

He shrugged. "Serena hasn't given me one."

"Okay. Right." Susan flexed her hands on the steering wheels. "What's your story, Victor?"

"My story," he said flatly. "Oh, yes. You are with the *Tribune*, the newspaper of Mick Aaronson."

"Yes I am. Do you know Mick?"

"I have been reading his work. His points are valid, but he is going about seeking correction in the wrong way."

"Well, I work with him," Susan said. "And you were the reason I arranged the interview with Serena. I want to learn some things about you, like why these rejects from a Spielberg movie are after you."

Victor shook his head. "Technology, I suspect. That's usually the reason."

"Are they the reason you faked your death and then walked away from George Washington University Hospital?"

"You are very efficient in your work," Victor said. "Actually, I wanted to escape from a woman who had come to my aid."

Susan felt a lump rising in her throat. "Fran Markowski. She was the one who was murdered in your apartment."

"I see," Victor said flatly.

"Well . . . Victor. As you can imagine, I've got a lot of questions for you. But, right now, I'll restrict myself to the one which concerns our immediate welfare."

"Very well."

"Question number one. What's our plan, Victor?"

"Our plan." The monotone was back.

"Where do we go?"

"Where Serena said. Far away from here. The farther the better."

"Great." Susan slapped the steering wheel. "Which direction? North? South? West? We go too far east, and we hit the ocean."

Victor looked into the backseat at Serena. "I need a place that is secluded. A place with some privacy. I need to tend to some things which have traumatized Serena."

"I can think of a hundred places that fit the bill, but I need to ask one question. How much money have you got?"

"Money." His flat and lifeless tone was starting to make her crazy.

"Maybe you don't have cash. Do you have any credit cards? I'm sure these guys are feds, so they can trace the transactions, but it won't hurt us to get some cash with the cards if we do it right now. What do you say?"

He shrugged. "Serena handles the money."

"That doesn't help us a whole lot. You want privacy, you've got to have money to buy it with. Money is important if you want to gain distance." She reached up and tapped the car's instrument panel. "Uncle Sam left us with less than a quarter tank of gas. That won't get us very far, unless that weird little rock of yours can make us invisible."

"It can," he said. "But only for a limited amount of time."

Invisible? The story, Susan thought, *would never be believed.*

"Okay. Let me try a different tack. Do you have any other friends here who can help us?"

"No."

"Do you know anyone in town besides Serena?"

"No. I arrived only recently."

"Pardon my asking, Victor, but if you don't have any friends and don't know anyone, then what are you doing here?"

"I came here to deliver a message to your President," he said.

"The President?"

"The guard at the gate said he was too busy."

Susan slapped the steering wheel. "What did you want to tell the President?" She waited for it, like she would anticipate the punch line to a shaggy-dog story.

"Well," said Victor, "it is something which falls solely within the domain of the President. I could tell you, but what would you do with it?"

"I'm a newspaper reporter. Remember?"

"Perhaps that would be a good idea."

Susan shouted, *"Stop that, Victor!"* Then she took a breath to calm herself and said, "If what you've got is so important, then why are you living with—" She wanted to invoke some of Fran Markowski's vocabulary to describe the socialite who was prone in the backseat, but the thought of a disapproving Mick Aaronson hovered over her and she thought better of it. "With a woman who has as many problems as Serena Blake?"

"It was her idea," Victor said.

I should have known.

"She said if I could not save the whole world, then maybe I could save one little piece of it. Starting with her part."

"You're saving Serena?"

"I was trying." He held his rock up to the light. "But it was difficult without this."

"So Serena will be saved now, but you're going to blow off the rest of the world?"

"What was I supposed to do? Your President would not see me. And I cannot go home again. I would be disgraced if I did. I might as well stay here with the creatures I've spent my life studying."

"Wait a minute. What are you talking about?" *This guy has strange powers, but . . .*

"Your planet is under a quarantine, Susan. I violated that quarantine because I learned that Earth was about to be sterilized of all sentient life. I thought if I could warn your President, he could implement policies which would reverse the process and save your species. If I had succeeded, the High Tribunal might have forgiven me. But for me to return in failure means disgrace." His gaze drifted out the passenger window. "Your culture is so strange to me. The President's guard—a person of relative insignificance—stands in the way of your preservation."

Susan's mind was spinning. She would normally dismiss this guy as a crackpot. But there had been too many implausible events, too many imponderable mysteries, too much that was too hard to explain. Would the U.S. government send soldiers to apprehend a common kook? What about his miraculous recovery? His disappearing act? And his ignorance about things a seven-year-old would know? Then there was the biggest anomaly of all: that strange, hypnotic rock.

"Victor," she said in a halting voice. "Where exactly are you from?"

He shook his head. "You can't see it from here, Susan."

She swallowed hard. "With the naked eye, you mean?"

"Not even with a telescope. Not even your Hubble eye in space. It's obscured by what your astronomers call the Horsehead Nebula."

A shiver ran through her. "Oh, Jesus!" she exclaimed.

Victor smiled benevolently. "No. I'm not Jesus."

Susan's foot clamped on the brake, and the car fishtailed to a stop. Her mind was racing, her intellect trying to reject what her heart wanted to believe.

"Susan. What's wrong?"

"Nothing." She smiled. "I know what to do now."

She pulled her foot off the brake and stomped on the gas pedal. The car leaped back into traffic. At the first chance, she cut a U-turn across the middle of the road and sped back in the direction from which they had come. "You should know something, Victor. The President is not the only agent of change in this nation."

She navigated the car through the city streets to the beltway on the Maryland side. A few minutes later she took an exit that she had taken only once before, with a carload of young hellions from the *Tribune* who had decided to go out looking for the place. They had had the courage to drive past the place only once, but the directions had burned themselves into her mind. They came back to her as she retraced her steps. This time, instead of peering through the trees that isolated the dimly lit house from the road and most of humanity, she took a brick driveway until it ended in a closed garage door. Then she jumped out of the big black government car, hurried down a narrow concrete path, and rang a doorbell.

When a slightly hunched figure finally answered her insistent ringing, she apologized profusely for the late hour. And then she put her arm around the shoulder of the little man next to her and said, "Mr. Aaronson, I'd like you to meet Victor. I think he's from outer space."

HARRY LAUTER

Harry was walking quickly down the sidewalk. The clerical collar was itchy around his neck, and the rest of the costume was tight, contrary to what the woman at the costume shop had said about it fitting him perfectly.

He hoped that what he was about to do wouldn't be considered deception. And if it should violate the commandment against bearing false witness, he hoped that God would forgive him. After all, hadn't some of God's prophets practiced that fine art? Jacob had resorted to trickery to fool his father Isaac into blessing him for the birthright he had already bought from his brother Esau. On two occasions, Abraham had passed his beloved wife Sarah off as his sister, and God had made him the father of the chosen nation.

What would be the harm in practicing a little deception if the ultimate goal was to gain access to the scrolls? The more he thought about it, the less it seemed such a blatant deception. He was merely using the costume to symbolize his work.

And then the Doubt raised its ugly voice again, taunting him. *That's right, Harry. The end justifies the means. You just keep on lying to yourself, and I'm gonna get you.*

"Get thee behind me," Harry murmured, and for comfort, he clutched the cross that hung around his neck. He had bought it at a K Mart jewelry counter to add what he thought was the final touch to the costume, but now he found himself depending on its presence to get him through the doubts that assailed him.

And what do you think you're going to do with those crumbling old scrolls once you get them, Harry?

Harry's grip on the cross tightened and he brought up another verse: *Ye shall know the truth, and the truth shall set you free.* His pursuit of the truth had landed him in half a dozen prisons. If he were to be set eternally free, he must first set the truth free. "I'm going to release the one thing that you can't handle," he mumbled to the Doubt. "I'm going to release the truth."

We shall see, Harry. We shall wait and see.

There was a loud, echoing laughter that reverberated inside of Harry's skull and disappeared as he rounded the corner to his destination. He stopped. No, he told himself. It couldn't be.

But it was. A line of black vehicles was parked in front of the apartment building, all vans or large cars. A crowd was gathered around the entrance, and a line of figures in black were trying vainly to keep them back away from the door.

"Oh, no!" he said.

It was a replay of the scene at the motel a few days

ago. He had been wakened by what he thought was a crash and shouts from the room where the sad-eyed black girl was staying, but after a moment everything had gone silent and he had drifted back to sleep. He didn't know how long he had slept after that, but he had been wakened again by a knocking on his door. On answering it, he had faced a tall man dressed in black, a strange-looking machine gun across his chest. Over the man's shoulder he saw something that looked like a scene out of a sci-fi film—a bunch of police officers being rounded up by a small handful of men in these black uniforms. He thought for a moment that it had really happened, that the forces of the Antichrist had taken the city and were rounding up the faithful to send to concentration camps in some godforsaken place like Wyoming or Neveda.

But no, the man at his door merely wanted to know if Harry had experienced any contact with the couple next door. Harry said he suspected the woman needed God's love, and the man swayed on the balls of his feet, back and forth, trying to block Harry's view of what was happening outside. But Harry had managed to catch a glimpse of a black van with an antenna array mounted on top. It had been a van that looked like the one he was staring at now.

The black-clad troops were wearing masks over their faces. *Bugs,* Harry thought. A few soldiers had removed their masks and were sitting on the hoods of cars, heads tilted back, looking at the afternoon sky.

Harry stared at the scene for a moment, lamenting the fact that he was too late. Then he told himself that this had to be a coincidence. After all, what connection could that poor woman and her violent lover have had with the scrolls? None. This had to be one of those new surgical-strike task forces that went in without warning

and dragged drug dealers off to whatever perdition the
United States Government could arrange.

Perhaps there was someone inside who needed a man
of God to help them through a desperate moment. Well,
that was why he had worn the costume. To reach Serena
Blake and the strange, new man in her life.

Harry took a deep breath and thrust out his chest,
then started to cross toward the building. He took one
step off the sidewalk and heard a screech. One of the
black cars had pulled out of the line and was headed
right for him, burning rubber as it came. He yelped and
jumped back, knocking over a newspaper rack propped
outside a restaurant door. An anonymous soul helped
him to his feet with a concerned "Are you all right, Father?" and then he was on his way again, looking both
ways this time.

As the embodiment of the separation of church and
state, he ignored the soldiers outside the building. Much
to his surprise, they ignored him. Now that he was
closer, he could see that they acted addled. They
seemed confused, trying to preside over a scene of an-
archy.

Inside the lobby, a collection of curious people had
gathered around one of the soldiers. He told them
gruffly he had no idea why he was there. Harry stepped
up to the security window and asked a confused atten-
dant for Serena's apartment number. "We had an appointment but I'm running a little late."

The man looked blankly at the date book on the desk
in front of him, turning the pages back and forth, then
gave Harry a hurt look. "What day is it?" he asked.
Then he grimaced and waved his hands in apology.
"I'm sorry. She's in 15–G. If she's expecting you, she's
expecting you."

Harry backed away and started toward the elevators.
Halfway there, a hand landed on his shoulder, and he

wheeled around. One of the soldiers, his face a mask of pain and confusion, appealed to him.

"Father," he said, eyes welling up with tears. "You've got to help me."

Harry replied gently, "What can I do for you, my son?"

The soldier's mouth moved but nothing came out.

"Easy."

"I have sinned, Father. I have done something horrible."

An opportunity, Harry thought. "And what is it you have done?"

Tears began to spill down the young man's face. "That's just it. I don't know. *I just don't know!*"

Harry patted him on the shoulder. "Then go in peace."

The soldier grabbed Harry's hand and sank to his knees. "Bless me, Father. You have to bless me."

"My son—"

"For the love of God, Father, you have to bless me!" His hands locked around Harry's in an iron grip.

Harry sucked air through his teeth. He pulled the soldier's helmet off and laid his hand on his head. He held up two fingers of the other hand and began to move them in a cross-shaped pattern over the kneeling figure. *Here goes nothing,* he thought, and in a singsong voice chanted the closest thing to Latin that he knew, something taught to him by a man he had once shared a jail cell with down in old Mexico.

"La cucaracha ya no quiere caminar, Porque no tiene, porque le falta, marijuana por fumar."

The soldier released Harry's hand.

"Thank you, Father," he mumbled, his tone grateful. "Thank you, Father, thank you, Father . . ."

"Thank the Lord, my son." Harry continued toward the elevator, arriving just as the door was closing. He managed to step through in time to join a few grumbling tenants.

"Big Brother strikes again," said a man who got off on the third floor.

"It's a police state, I tell you," said another who got off on seven.

"This is completely ridiculous," muttered a woman who departed at nine.

After that, Harry was alone until the door opened on the fifteenth floor. He emerged into more soldiers and more confusion. Ten or more uniformed men were wandering around, milling aimlessly, asking each other questions. Nobody seemed to be in charge, and nobody noticed him.

He turned toward apartment G, and his heart sank. The door was wide open. As he got closer, he saw more soldiers inside.

I am too late, he thought. They knew about Serena and the man without beauty. The man who knew about the scrolls.

A bewildered soldier approached. Harry gritted his teeth.

"Ah, Father. Thank God you're here. There's somebody here who needs last rites." He stretched his arm toward the door. They were actually inviting him in.

A second later, Harry wished that he had never come. The inside of Serena Blake's living room was splattered with blood. The room started to close in as the soldier guided him toward the body of a woman, crumpled on the floor. Harry felt as if he couldn't breathe.

"Something wrong, Father?"

Harry tried to swallow but couldn't. "What happened here?"

The soldier shook his head. "I don't know, Father." He handed Harry the woman's wallet, "But this woman deserves your attention."

Harry opened the wallet and stared at the polished glare of a badge.

"I think she must've gotten into a shootout with that guy over there. What's left of him."

Harry followed the soldier into the kitchen. There was more blood, and a dark figure sprawled on the floor.

"But she needs last rites. Don't you think she needs last rites, Father?"

Harry's jaw trembled. He wanted to tell this man that last rites had to be administered while the person was still living. He wanted to confess that he wasn't really a priest. But most of all, he wanted to leave. Quickly.

"Father?"

"I'm sorry, my son, but I'm not that kind of priest . . ."

There was sudden commotion at the door, and another soldier burst in. In one hand was a bolt-action rifle with an elaborate scope. In the other was his mask.

His face chilled Harry Lauter to the bone.

It was one of his hecklers.

Harry remembered the face. When the soldier spoke, saying, "What's going on in here? Why didn't you grab the target when I took out the clocker?" Harry remembered the grating voice. He realized that recognition would cut both ways, so he had to work fast.

Harry turned away from the intruder to the soldier next to him. "There's nothing that says we can't pray for the soul of this dear departed woman. Pray with me now, son. Pray with me."

The soldier bowed his head.

"Son?"

"Father?"

"Your helmet. Let's show a little respect for the presence of the Lord."

"Of course." The soldier removed his helmet and

placed it in Harry's outstretched hand, then scrunched his eyes shut and lowered his head.

"First," Harry said, pulling off the collar of the costume with one hand, "a moment of silent prayer, that we might express our thoughts privately to God almighty." He put the helmet over his own head.

The soldier nodded, head down over the woman's body.

The man with the rifle was spewing out a torrent of profanity now, shaking soldiers and demanding to know what had happened. Harry slipped out the door and into the hall. He headed straight for the elevator, dropping the prayerful soldier's headgear into a pile of abandoned equipment. He had the shakes, now, brought on by the realization that someone in the government knew about the scrolls. The commandos obviously had been seeking the ugly little man who knew about them. The whole thing had Satan's fingerprints all over it.

Well. Wasn't that just like Old Scratch? Bad enough that he had turned the Arabs and the Israelis against him. Now he was working on Harry's own government. And he would keep it up until he had reduced the scrolls to ash.

But what if it wasn't Satan? What if it really was the United States government that was after the scrolls? Would that be so bad, Harry?

It depended on what the authorities did with them. If they released them to the world, it would be fine. But if the scrolls were locked up in the Smithsonian, hidden in a secret warehouse like the Ark of the Covenant in that Indiana Jones movie, if they never saw the light of day . . .

That mustn't happen. Not as long as he was alive.

The elevator stopped and disgorged Harry Lauter into the lobby. He stopped only long enough to call 911, and then walked back out onto the street, his jaw set, ready to do battle.

Judging from the mass confusion he had seen, Harry decided that the strange, little man must have gotten away. The confusion was too widespread, too unvaried to be explained by even the most spectacular bureaucratic screw-up.

The mystery man, Harry knew, was now the quarry of the United States government.

As Harry Lauter vanished into the Washington night, he prayed that he would be the one to find him first.

MICK AARONSON

"Victor, eh?"

Mick Aaronson lifted the whistling teakettle off the stove and strode to the table where Susan sat with Serena's guest. The government car was safely stashed in the garage, and Serena was dozing on the couch in the living room.

Having just returned from another encounter with Suzanne in Arlington, he really was in no mood to be bothered. But Susan's move had been so open and brash and . . . well, flattering. Here she was, two months past her twenty-first birthday, coming to him with an open can of worms, though by all rights, he belonged in the pantheon of has-beens.

So, because it was appealing to his male ego, and because Susan looked like she was at her wit's end, and because this man called Victor was so outlandishly ugly, he took them in.

"Serena calls me Victor," the man said evenly.

"And what would you be calling yourself these days?"

"I have no name. I would identify myself as a visitor."

Aaronson worked his tongue around his mouth. "Visitor. Victor. It's a leap, but I can follow it." He looked at the cup he had set before the visitor. "Put the tea holder in the cup. A tea isn't a proper tea unless the water is poured over the leaves."

The visitor, who had insisted that he didn't want any tea, looked up at the journalist. "You are such an insistent race," he said, complying.

"Victor, I want to tell you something. It is all right if I call you Victor, isn't it?"

"Unless there is something else you would rather call me."

"Fine. In my forty years as a journalist, I've seen a lot, and most of it had to do with deception. You see where I'm taking this?"

"Mr. Aaronson!" Susan protested.

He dismissed her with a wave of his hand and continued. "I've seen presidents lie to the people and get taken down. I've seen our elected officials do anything and everything they could to get reelected to another hitch on the old gravy train. I've seen respectable people lie, cheat and deceive to gain an advantage."

The visitor stared blankly as Aaronson poured boiling water over the silver tea holder that rested in the bottom of his cup.

"What I'm saying, Victor, is that for forty years I've seen every type of deception there is. It has been my job to cut through all the crap and find the rare, gleaming nugget of truth. So, here in my own house, I do not accept deception, no matter how noble the cause. I do not tolerate it. And those who do not comply, I destroy. Are you following me, Victor?"

"But he's not lying," Susan said.

"I understand that," Aaronson said. "He hasn't yet

said anything. You're the one who said he came from beyond the stars."

"He has never said it," Susan acknowledged. "But then, he didn't have to."

"It's my contention that proof of someone's alienhood goes beyond contrived patterns of speech and a reluctance to drink tea. It's going to take more than that to convince me he's a genuine spacefarer."

She turned to the visitor. "Show him your thing. That device. The miracle rock."

"It would take more than that to convince a stubborn man," the visitor said.

"The implication is that you do claim to be from beyond?" Aaronson countered.

The visitor waved his hand. "One of your writers once said that any technology sufficiently advanced beyond your own would be judged by you to be a trick. Any demonstration for the skeptical Mr. Aaronson, he will dismiss as black magic. I know you, Mr. Aaronson. I know what you have experienced and what you think."

"I don't believe in black magic," Aaronson challenged. "I'm paid to be an agnostic by six hundred and fifty daily newspapers, three monthly and two weekly periodicals, and a weekly radio program. The way I see it, Victor, everybody's got an angle, a scheme, a scam. My function is to judge their efficacy and whether the truth is in them—no matter how painful it is."

The visitor nodded, then looked at Susan. "You were right, Miss Hill. He is a very good candidate."

Aaronson cast a suspicious glance at the intern. "Candidate for what?"

The visitor smiled in a way that unnerved him. The way his features stretched produced a look that was almost . . .

"An agent of change," said the visitor. "One whose

influence can have an impact on great numbers of people."

"The numbers aren't what they used to be," Aaronson said.

"Don't let him kid you," Susan said. "He still has millions of people who accept his word as gospel. And just as many more who hate his words but read them religiously. I mean *religiously*—with a prayer that he won't write about them."

"Why do I feel that you two are conspiring to get me into some kind of trouble?" Aaronson snorted.

"Since when have you ever flinched at trouble in the pursuit of truth?" Susan demanded.

The visitor interrupted. "We have reason to believe that your government is after me."

"I see," said Aaronson. "But there could be any number of explanations for that. For starters, they might want their car back."

"They want to suppress the truth, Mick Aaronson. They are well intentioned, but their actions will seal the fate of your entire race."

Susan crossed her arms, tight and tense. "This is where it gets hairy."

Victor spoke again, straight-faced. "Considering the circumstances I have found here, it would seem that you may be the best chance humankind has of being saved. I have a truth to impart to you, and you in turn must broadcast it as widely as possible, by every means at your disposal."

"Let me tell you something." Aaronson sat forward, agitated. "Back in 1961, when I was still a little bit wet behind the ears, I put together a column cobbled from sources-who-knew which said that some Secret Service men had been arranging for physical interludes between Jack Kennedy and Marilyn Monroe. Against the advice of everyone, I went public with it, and it bought me nothing but trouble. It was the kind of news that nobody at the time wanted to hear.

"But ever since then, people have sought me out because I wasn't afraid of that, or any other truth. Lots of people. Hundreds, maybe even thousands of them over the years. Every one of them had a little piece of truth that they wanted me to broadcast to the world. Some were picayune; some were tantalizing, like the mating habits of certain presidents.

"Then there were the truths that really mattered. Like the third-rate burglary that brought down a president. Those truths are rare, and they can make or break careers.

"But the funny thing is, Victor, every person who comes to me thinks his truth will change the world. It might only be that the gas station down the street is watering down the eighty-nine octane, but whether it's a peccadillo or a state secret, the storm-tossed whistle-blower is sure that it will have global consequences."

He paused for a moment, took a sip of tea, and looked straight into Susan's eyes. "It's my job to determine the size and scope of the truth and how important it is for the public to know. There are times when a little truth matters the most. And there are times when a big truth is just too big.

"I may be the last man in America who processes the truth like that. The last one who offers it to the public without a hidden political agenda or moral stance. I would like to pass that attitude, that clean philosophy, on to young Susan here. But even as I try, I feel like I'm one of those ancient dinosaurs whose bones are now on display at the Smithsonian. I represent a time that has passed. I'm an old relic, an endangered species, waiting for extinction."

"You're not extinct yet," Susan said. "If you found

some incredible, important truth, you'd still be obligated to put the word out."

"Absolutely," Aaronson said. "But I couldn't guarantee the public's reaction. Nobody can."

"This is a truth they will want to hear," Susan told him. "It's one they need to hear."

Aaronson's gaze wandered back to the visitor. "You certainly have Susan convinced."

"Mr. Aaronson, if you'd seen what I've seen—" she pleaded.

The journalist held up one hand to stop her. "Please, Susan. Let's allow our guest to tell it."

The visitor looked from Aaronson to Susan and back. "No," he said.

"*No?*" Susan was out of her chair. "What do you mean? I thought you wanted to get this out to the world—"

"He doesn't believe," the visitor said.

"Does that matter?" Susan challenged.

"In this case, yes. You see, Mick Aaronson, you left out one important kind of truth. The truth that does exist, but goes unrecognized because those who learn the truth refuse to believe. During your youth, I believe there was an evil ruler who conducted genocide against the Jewish people. But because of the enormity, the magnitude, and the horror of it, the world refused to believe. And so the truth grew, unchecked, until it became the holocaust.

"That is the kind of truth that I am bringing to you, Mick Aaronson. As your protégée stated so clearly, I am from 'outer space.' And my message is that your species faces extinction unless drastic changes are made in the nature of your self-governance."

Aaronson shook his head. "Let me guess. You're one of these spiritual-revolution, apocalyptic types—"

"Hear me out before you condemn me, Mick Aaronson. Your agnosticism has made you grow cold to things that once would have warmed you. Perhaps this is what has kept you from doing the writing you most want to do. You would like to warn your country of the crisis that is boiling inside of her."

"Wait a minute!" Aaronson began. "How do you know—"

"But you have fixated on the negative. You await the inevitable collapse, so you can wallow in the misery you have predicted. Hear me speak, and you may see if this is a truth worthy of your attention."

Stung, Aaronson held his hand. "The floor is yours."

The visitor looked down at the tile floor for a moment, then smiled. "These idioms," he mumbled.

"To understand the message," he began, "you must first understand me and where I am from. The place where I live, as I have told Susan Hill, you cannot see from here."

"Convenient," said Aaronson.

"Shh," Susan hissed.

"It is a world like you have never seen, a world even your Steven Spielberg has not imagined. A world lit by twin suns. My world has been totally transformed by its inhabitants. We have recreated most of its surface, as smooth as glass and as black as the ocean at midnight. From beneath this surface our structures are grown. They have not been built, as yours have, but seeded and grown. We engineer the seed to grow whatever structure we need. Organic crystallography, which thankfully has not yet struck your species, for you lack the maturity.

"There is great beauty on my world. You might aptly describe it as heaven. The shine of it. The purples and reds and fiery golds of our structures. Our world is shielded by a veil of light which our technology can open at will. We can pass through it and travel by light ray to other planets. That is, in fact, how I came here."

Mick Aaronson delivered a large, purposeful yawn. "Come on. I'm no scientist, but I've watched enough of the Sci-Fi Channel to recognize some huge holes in your story. If your world is that far away from us, even at light speed it would take you millions of years to get here." He shook his head. "I'm not buying this."

"We do not ride in the light, as you would describe it. That would be, as you point out, too time consuming. When I step through the veil, I move outside of the continuum of the universe. The technology is quite complex. I do not fully understand it myself. But I am able to utilize it—just as you can operate a computer or a microwave oven without comprehending what is at its core."

"So what brings you here? What is this phenomenal message of yours?"

"By trade I am a xenologist. I study other sentient species. My specialty has been your species, *Homo sapiens*. I have grown rather fond of you as you struggle to perfect yourselves. You try so hard and yet you fail so miserably. Your persistence is admirable. I wish that the others could see the potential that I see in you."

"Others?" said Aaronson. "What others?"

"Other races. The Family of God."

"God?" Aaronson wagged his head and set his teacup down.

"You are still at the rebellious stage. You think your intelligence has risen to the point where you no longer need the concept of an omnipotent creator. And it is that puerile arrogance that has gotten you into such trouble."

"You mean a race as advanced as yours still believes in God?"

"No," said the visitor.

Aaronson smiled and nodded. "That's what I suspected."

"We *know* there is a God. Listen, Mick Aaronson,

and learn. Worlds without number lie beyond the reach of humankind, worlds that are constantly changing. Some are like mine and harbor species which have reached maturity and have taken their place in the interplanetary community. Others are like your world, where the sentients are still struggling to reach maturity before they can link with others and advance. Other planets are barren, but with the richness that will support sentience in the future. We seek out these worlds for seeding."

"Seeding." Aaronson rolled the word out of his mouth with incredulity.

"Extreme shortsightedness is one of the great failings of *Homo sapiens*. You see space as an inhospitable vacuum, yet it is abundant with the ingredients for the creation and development of new worlds. It is our job to engineer these new worlds and to bring forth sentient life. We even monitor this life as it matures. We do not interfere or even have contact with the sentients during their development. This maturing process is something which they must complete independently. It's a struggle, but they can progress only by gaining experience. And when they have matured fully as a species, we welcome them into the interplanetary system."

"Wait a minute," Aaronson said. "You're telling me that Earth is just a part of some galactic construction project?"

"The analogy is appropriate." The visitor nodded.

Aaronson looked at Susan. "How do you feel about this?"

"It's ... it's staggering," Susan said.

Victor continued: "I see many faults which you on earth must overcome to reach full maturity. Shortsightedness and xenophobia are the primary concerns. You believe that you are unique. You must overcome that.

"Look back on what I have said to you, Mick

Aaronson. Sentients without number. Worlds without number. An intergalactic society without number.

"This process of building never ends. There is a never-ending succession of physical renewal of resources and spiritual evolution of both the fledgling sentients and the mature species."

Aaronson jostled the cup in his hand, watching the tea slosh around the bottom. "So then your message is 'grow up and join the Family,' right? I guess that's not so bad. At least your dog isn't telling you to go out and shoot people in parked cars."

"Mr. Aaronson—" Susan blurted, outraged.

The visitor held up a hand, his face patient. "That is all right. Skepticism is to be expected, and at this stage it is healthy." Then, to Aaronson: "I only wish it were so simple. It will require much more than growing up and joining us. As you have observed in your column of late, the road to maturity is strewn with obstacles. While I believe you were referring to national regeneration, it applies to your spiritual progress as well. It has been my experience, through observing hundreds of seeded worlds, that in almost every case, these obstacles are created by the species themselves. And sometimes it happens that a species creates problems that are insurmountable."

Aaronson said nothing. Susan said thinly, "What happens when something like that happens?"

The visitor's gaze went to the window and stared outside at the blackness that surrounded them. With a resigned expression, he said, "Then the world is destroyed."

Susan shifted uncomfortably in her seat. "Just like that? Trashed?"

The visitor shook his head. "You misunderstand me," he said. "We do not dispose of the entire world. In most cases, the planet remains intact. It is a selective cleaning. All of the sentients are removed."

"Just like that?"

"It is more involved, but yes, that does basically describe it."

Aaronson finally set his cup down on the table next to him. "I know what you're going to say next."

"Do you?"

"I do. You're about to tell us that the Earth is on the verge of being scrubbed."

"Correct," the visitor said sadly.

"So how will this be accomplished?"

The visitor shrugged. "Unfortunately, I am merely a xenologist. I can tell you only that spiritual pollution has a powerful effect on physical forces. The inhabitants themselves are generating the destructive power that will cleanse the Earth."

"Are you telling me that sin causes earthquakes?" scoffed the columnist.

"That is an oversimplification," said Victor, "but essentially, it is true. Your seismologists will confirm that there has been a dramatic increase in the number of major earthquakes during the past two decades."

Aaronson snorted, "So these are the last days, you're saying."

"For your species, yes," said Victor, "unless the present trend is reversed."

"Why?" Aaronson's tone didn't sound inquisitive enough to indicate he believed what he was hearing. His tone was flat, as if he were still trying to draw the story out, looking for weaknesses and cracks, something to exploit and attack.

"Why?" the visitor echoed. "Because your species has failed. Earth is a lonely speck of warmth and greenery, populated by an insistently self-destructive species of sentients."

"So what did we do wrong?" demanded Aaronson. "Did we develop the atom bomb too soon?"

"Your maturity did not keep up with your technology, true," the visitor said bluntly. "Your species has become spiritually contaminated. You are addicted to wickedness and violence, to a degree unprecedented in the annals of our system. Your planet has been placed under quarantine to protect the interplanetary community from moral degeneration."

"Quarantine," Aaronson said.

"Yes," said the visitor. "So if you are looking for signs from the heavens and see none, that is why. We are not allowed to be here, for fear we would absorb your evil and spread it beyond this planet."

"Let me ask you this," growled the old curmudgeon. "If this is such a bad planet, if there's this intergalactic quarantine over the place, then what are you doing here? If all of this is really true, then doesn't your presence here belie your own story?"

"Very good," said the visitor. "You are thinking, and that is good."

"And you, my friend, are stalling."

"I will answer your question at the risk of losing your respect."

"You haven't earned it yet, pal."

"You might say I am a criminal."

"Yeah," Aaronson said. "I might."

"Because I defied galactic law to come here and warn you what is about to happen."

"Right. You're a renegade, so you can't produce anyone who can back up your story."

"*No!*" The visitor smacked the tabletop with the palms of both hands. "Your characterization of me is *not* true!"

Aaronson watched him carefully. The tone of voice and the gestures were clearly angry, but there were none of the other physical clues—the flushed or the paling face, the trembling, the darting or narrowing of the eyes, the rising and falling of the chest from increased respiration, the bulging, pulsing veins. A shiver slithered down the journalist's spine.

"You must understand! I am forbidden to intervene in the affairs of this planet. I came here at grave risk to save your species from destruction. I developed a compassion for *homo sapiens* from my studies of them. They ... you ... are worth saving. *That*, Mick Aaronson, is the reason I am here. *That* is why I defied galactic law. I am here to warn you of impending doom, and to tell how you may save yourselves. But you have this arrogance, this pride, this ... this ...

"I tell you, Mick Aaronson, unless humankind can overcome its evil nature and produce a righteous society, your wickedness will destroy the Earth. I repeat the warning. Moral corruption will beget physical corruption.

"Yes, physical decay as a result of moral decay. You are trying now not to foul your nest. But there is a factor you have not considered. Your spiritual degeneration has resulted in the contamination of the frail bonds that connect your spiritual natures with the elements of the planet.

"Has the sudden violence of Nature escaped your notice? Freak storms. Floods. Earthquakes. Tidal waves. Volcanic eruptions. Extremes of heat and cold, rain and drought. You have failed to connect the escalating geophysical violence with the escalating human violence. You may see no connection, Mick Aaronson, but there is. Oh, there is.

"One of your idioms says that the weather makes people crazy. It is not the weather that makes the human crazy. It is the human that makes the weather crazy. Spiritual and geophysical harmony makes this planet resilient. But your violence and corruption have infested the Gaiasphere, and now your planet is losing the ability to purify itself. Your world needs the lesser creatures, the plants and the bacteria, but the greater need is *sentience*. That is what your species gives it.

"But worse, spiritual sickness is contagious and could contaminate the other races of the galaxies. It could spread along the very light paths on which we travel.

"The symptoms are everywhere. The rampant millennial fever which you think is so annoying is not a conscious fear of the future. It is a direct manifestation of a much darker fear welling up in your race's collective subconscious. It is the fear that you are destroying yourselves. The fear is a dire warning, but you are too spiritually immature to understand it."

Aaronson looked at the visitor through squinted eyes. "People like you are always saying they've got the answer to the world's problems; but when it comes right down to it, there's some little personality flaw that somehow manages to prevent us from doing anything about it."

"But there *is* something you can do about it—"

Aaronson shook his head. "Not today, Victor. You can talk all you want, with conviction and articulation. But when it comes right down to it, what you're passing out is the same New Age nonsense. The packaging is a bit different, but once you open it up, it's the same stinking thing, foul and sour."

The visitor's mouth dropped open in a gasp of anguish, and he wheeled in tight circles on the floor. He spread out his arms, palms up, until he resembled someone who had been nailed to an invisible cross.

"I understand," he said to the ceiling. "I understand now the deep frustration of the Most High when considering the fate of this hard-hearted race." Then he let his arms drop, and he turned to Aaronson. "I understand, too, the deep frustration you feel in dealing with those of your own kind. I understand now why your language is filled with antisocial vulgarities."

Aaronson shrugged and rolled his eyes at Susan.

The alien's lips curled back from his teeth. He looked at the two journalists cautiously. "Damn," he swore. Then he shook his head. "It's no good. I'm not one of you, so I cannot derive the release or the pleasure that you get from it."

Aaronson stifled a yawn.

The visitor slapped his palms down onto the table again. "What do you want me to do, Mick Aaronson? What would you have me do to earn the respect of your belief? Levitate in the air? Transport you, as we did with Castaneda, to some far-off place where you can have your own personal spiritual reawakening? No. That's easy. It's much too easy. And it's written off too easily by someone like you who is determined not to believe.

"The reawakening that will save this world has to come from you, from inside you. It is something each individual must do, just as each individual species must struggle to mature on its own. Your own columns condemn your people's lack of insight, but you offer no prescription for the moral renaissance which you claim this nation needs desperately. What is needed must come from within the heart of the nation, from each individual in the nation. I guess it cannot be thrust upon you by someone from the outside, such as myself."

Aaronson chuckled. "I knew it," he said.

"What? That I was a fake? A fraud? A hoax? No, Mick Aaronson. Even if I perform some feat of an obvious advanced technology, you still wouldn't believe. To you it would only be magic. Hallucination."

Aaronson took a long and deliberate look at the watch on his wrist. "Victor, I believe we are at an impasse. And we're going in circles. This is territory that we've already covered—magic, hypnotism, hallucination. Why don't you quit mesmerizing the lovely Miss Hill and admit what you really are."

"Fine." The visitor reached into his pocket and laid the slick-looking stone next to the journalist's teacup.

"Yes!" Susan cried triumphantly.

"Pick that up and ask Susan to do something as outrageous as you dare. I'm sure she will consent to the experiment, under the circumstances."

Aaronson reached for the stone, and with two fingers, pushed it back at the visitor. "No."

"Why not?" Susan demanded.

"Because you want me to believe. You'd do anything I said just to convince me."

"Then let me use it on you." She reached across for the device, but the cool hand of the visitor pounced on her wrist and stopped her.

"That will not do, either."

Aaronson pointed at the visitor. "Anything that convinces me will have to come from him. It has to be devoid of trickery and deceit. It should be so pure and original that I have no other choice but to believe in the source of your information."

"Pure and undefiled," said the visitor.

"Exactly," Aaronson challenged. "Unimpeachable."

"Very well, Mick Aaronson, then that is what you shall have."

"Good luck. There's nothing you could say or do to convince me."

"Ah, but perhaps there is." He cocked his head at the intern. "Susan Hill, what time is it?"

She turned to look at Aaronson's microwave. "Nine fifty-three P.M.," she said.

"Very well. Make note of that time, my child." The visitor turned to Aaronson. "And you too, you foolish agnostic. For you will hear something that is so familiar to you that you should have known it all along. And the source, as you requested, is unimpeachable. I present to you, Mick Aaronson and Susan Hill, *the history of the human species*."

He spread out his hands. Susan shifted uncomfortably in her chair. Aaronson folded his arms, waiting for the little man to pick up a silk hat and produce a rabbit.

"I shall avoid the earliest history since our respective versions of the Creation may differ. So I shall begin with an era over which there can be no question."

The visitor clapped his hands together. Then he began to speak, rapidly, in a clear, high tone.

It was history, beginning with the Egyptians' first encounter with the fertile Nile valley.

But there had never been a history lesson like it. Victor cited intimate habits and obscure customs—small details that rang true to the ancient Egyptians. The flood of facts—tiny bits and pieces that clearly were real—overwhelmed Aaronson. He found himself wondering why history had missed so much.

The Druids, Victor said, were overrated, with nothing better to do than arrange stones in circles. The Roanoke colony had not been abducted by extra-terrestrial kidnappers, as many millennial alarmists were beginning to claim, but quite simply were assimilated by the surrounding aboriginal tribes. The breakdown of a cart had resulted in the American colonies choosing English over German as their official language. Custer, he revealed, was one of the first men killed at the Little Big Horn, shot off his horse as he led the charge, hoping that a victory would put him in the Oval Office. And Adolf Hitler. The visitor assumed the Fuhrer's shrill voice and frenzied mannerisms, bobbing and weaving and gesticulating through his terrifying, mesmerizing orations.

Victor described incidents from Egyptian, Babylonian, and Roman times. He continued down through the ages, drowning Aaronson in more historical details than he could possibly absorb. There were many tidbits like the secret of Damascus steel that Aaronson wanted to remember but he simply couldn't keep up with the influx of information. If his mind wandered for more than a few seconds, he missed a hundred years, a key formula, or a point of natural law. Aaronson thought it couldn't last, but it did. The visitor went on and on and on, even after Susan, who had initially been enthralled, gave up, wandered into the living room, and curled into a sound sleep on the La-Z-Boy.

Then Aaronson himself dozed fitfully, in the sitting-up half-sleep that he had perfected while in the marines. By then the visitor had added chemistry and physics and astronomy to the mix of things, and his droning included facts that the columnist couldn't comprehend even on a good day. The protons, neutrons, and electrons found in californium and molybdenum. The nature of quarks and superstrings. A nearby star about to go supernova.

Finally, as the first rays of morning began to warm the horizon beyond the kitchen window, the visitor was back on familiar territory, going on about the factors which resulted in the breakdown of the Clinton presidency, recounting such intimate facts and details that Aaronson could have believed that this man was a White House insider.

"Stop," he finally growled. "That last bit, about the Iranian nuclear arsenal. How did you get that? Those documents haven't been declassified yet."

"It is my job to catalog such things," the visitor said. "About this world, about this nation."

"All right." Aaronson stared at the alien's face. The rising sun had tinted everything orange, but the light had failed to warm his deformed features. "You've made your point. You're not from around here."

Victor's face changed. Was it a smile? The features brightened, though they remained ugly.

"It's obvious to me that you're *something* from out of this world," said Aaronson. "I haven't yet decided *what*."

"That is good," the visitor said, sounding pleased. "Very good. You are ready to consider what I have to say, then."

"Only as my intellectual superior," Aaronson said. "I think the jury is still out, Victor. But someone who knows as much about human history and human nature as you do is bound to have something worthwhile to say, so I'll hear you out."

The visitor rubbed his hands together, with satisfaction. "Despite the moral decline of your species, I have never in my long career as a xenologist observed a species with such a latent capacity for good. It is this potential that makes me believe you could overcome your inherent tendency toward evil. The hope of your world lies in a moral resurgence, a spiritual rebirth, which must begin in the United States. This is the message I wanted to bring to your President. But I was not allowed to deliver it to him."

"Why America?" Aaronson asked. "We're only a small fraction of the planet's population. Why not go to India or China? Why not Germany or Russia or Japan? Why America?

"Don't misunderstand me, Victor. I love America. She's a grand old lady. But her time . . ." He looked away wistfully. "Her time has come and gone."

The visitor shook his head in protest. "America has the power to revive this dying world, Mick Aaronson. Why is English the international language? Why is the dollar the international currency? Why is your economy the international cornerstone? Upon whose money are global transactions based? Whose technology has shrunk the size of the planet? What nation, above all others, has defeated disease and promoted free agency? What nation has been so successful in creating a political ideology that others have risked life, limb, and security to embrace? To whom do this world's desperate people turn for protection? Which nation disseminates its news to the entire globe, and has exported its culture to the far-flung sectors of the planet?

"You may feel this nation's time has come and gone, but it is still the jewel in the human crown. Now, what happens when this source of pride, courage, and human inspiration falls?"

Victor's look was stern. Aaronson knew he didn't have to answer. He could tell that his thoughts were being read.

"Why America, Mick Aaronson? Save America . . ." He extended his arm, his hand, and then pointed a long, bony finger toward Aaronson's lips.

". . . and you save the world," Aaronson answered, as if hypnotized.

That look crossed the visitor's features again, that triumphant smile that annoyed Aaronson.

The journalist crossed his arms and hunched his shoulders against the sudden coolness he felt. He was beginning to understand what Susan saw in this guy. He spoke with the passion and conviction of one utterly dedicated to his cause. And he seemed far too lucid to be delusional. For a brief, unnerving moment, Mick Aaronson actually found himself buying Victor's story. He forced himself to be objective. *What if this guy is just another charismatic lunatic? What if this charisma and conviction is just a part of his psychotic mania? What could this person say or do to convince me that he's worth believing?*

The answer hit him a heartbeat later.

Like the little man said, you're going to have to rely on faith and buy into this story or write him off completely. You're going to have to listen, as he said, and learn.

"So, Victor. Where do we go from here?"

The visitor nodded. "What is needed, Mick Aaronson, is a call to action for the inhabitants of this planet. It must begin here in America because, despite its decay, its people are still sovereign. Over the years, Americans have taught most of the world to be sovereign as well. The world will listen to what America says.

"And what America must say is that democracy is something to be worked at, not merely thought about. Something to be lived, not merely talked about. Democracy is the will of the people, but the people have abandoned their will in favor of hedonism. They must take back their will from political leaders, who can no longer be trusted to do anything but serve their own desires. Each individual American must turn. Then America herself will turn. America is the architect and high priestess of democracy. If she turns, the world will follow. America must speak by its actions because the world watches what she does.

"Your problem is simple spoiled complacency. Americans are a people who for too long have had too much good fortune that they did too little to earn. Too many Americans have forgotten the central place of effort and learning. That loss is suicidal for any civilization.

"Mick Aaronson, civilization and survival are a matter of morality. Hedonism and complacency have made you forget your moral roots. You are willing to forsake the inherent morality of liberty for the tyranny of security.

"What faces America is not a problem of power or

weakness; not one of politics or statesmanship. It is a question of right or wrong. Other nations at other times have forgotten this. They became victims of their own folly, of their self-inflicted ills. Simply put, your nation needs more service and less self. More trust and less deceit. More humility and less arrogance. More decency and less intolerance.

"You must strengthen your moral muscles or they will atrophy. You must reshape your lives or you will lose them."

"Fine," Aaronson grumped. "Are we supposed to push a button that reverses our polarity? Many of us see the problem but are overwhelmed by its enormity."

The visitor replied, "I believe that the people need to be stirred . . . stimulated . . . educated . . . reminded of a better way. They must know that they're not alone, that others have been purified before them."

"Your leaders have lost the trust of the people because they serve themselves."

"Then," asked Aaronson, "why did you bother to go to the President?"

"Many American still believe that a person who steps into the Oval Office is somehow transformed from a politician into a statesman. I shared their belief—maybe it's no more than a hope—that the President would have an eye on history . . . that he would put the welfare of the country ahead of petty politics."

"I've always kept *my* eye on Presidents," Aaronson said sourly.

"I think Americans have learned to believe what you write," said Victor, "though they may not like what you write."

"I would like to save my country," Aaronson said seriously. "To be able to pull it back from the brink. But I'm a tired old man. I can write the message over and over again, and people will regard it as an old man's bitching."

"You make a mistake in your writings. You emphasize the negative. That is not how this should be done. You cannot condemn. It will drive people to do worse. You must have a lighter touch. You must encourage. It will work, Mick Aaronson. Once the change begins, it will spread. Person to person. Neighborhood to neighborhood. City to city. On and on."

"How long do we have? Until the great destruction, I mean."

"That I cannot honestly say. But your species may not survive to see the millennium."

"So the doomsayers may be right!" Aaronson said, shaking his head.

"Without knowing what they say, they could be right."

Suddenly the old curmudgeon balked. "I can't. I don't have the words anymore. There was a time when I did, Victor. I honestly did. I believed that people still cared about the truth."

"They still do."

"Back when my Suzanne was still alive, I could do it for her."

"Then you must do it now."

"This may not even get past my editor."

"There is everything to gain by trying. And everything to lose if you don't."

Aaronson ran his hands through his thinning hair. "You'll have to get me started. Tell me what to say."

"I will tell you what to say, Mick Aaronson, but the words will be your own."

"I don't know. Maybe I should just let the destruction take its course and put all of us out of our misery."

"You may be old and tired, but that does not mean your species is. I have met some people here who would be very disappointed if they could not live up to their potential."

Aaronson said nothing.

"Do you have children, Mick Aaronson? Grandchildren?"

"Yes," he said.

"If not for your species, if not for your country, then for them. In that way, you will be doing it for your beloved Suzanne."

Aaronson gazed out of the kitchen. His eyes fell on Susan, asleep on his La-Z-Boy. After a moment, he set his jaw and nodded. "All right, Victor. What do you want to tell them first?"

THE LION'S DEN

WASHINGTON, D.C. / MAY 1999

**THE VIEW FROM HERE
by Mick Aaronson**

May 10, 1999——I have two words I'd like to say to the American people.

I'm sorry.

That's right. *I'm sorry.*

I'm sorry for using this space as a forum for the complaining I've done over the last few years.

Now, it would be easy to blame my behavior on any one of a number of un-wholesome things. I could say I was having mo-mentary depression be-cause of the passing of Suzanne, my beautiful wife of forty-two years. But that happened in 1996. I know people have been embittered by less, but Aaronsons are made of heartier stock than that.

No, I'm not going to blame this on anything. There's nothing I could say to you that couldn't be properly retorted by say-ing, "For heaven's sake, Mick, just pop a pill and get on with your life!"

So, as of right now, I am accepting responsibility for all of the vileness and bitterness that I have recently inflicted on you.

I'm going to get on with my life now.

Without drugs.

Now. The reason I'm offering this apology is so I can tell you this: Our nation is in big trouble.

So what else is new? I can hear you say.

That's why I want to make sure you read the next words to roll off of my fingertips.

Namely: *Friends, it is time to do something about it.*

The time has come for revolution. Not Republican or Democrat. Not capitalist or socialist.

It's time for an individual revolution.

We've gotten used to our politicians spoon-feeding us with social programs so all we have to do is sit back in our recliners, click on a professional wrestling match, and suck up a brewski.

If you'll indulge me one more piece of bad tidings. *Somebody's going to have*

to pay for all of this, and the bill is coming due.

Sooner, in fact, than you may think.

But the good news is that we can do something about it.

It's going to take a re-dedication to some things like common sense and old-fashioned morality.

But before you go grabbing your pen to write your congressman about not spending more than we take in, notice that the operative word here is "we."

That's you and me.

It has to start with us.

Our leaders won't listen to the people who elected them until the people themselves become an example. Those of you who still believe in the things that can make this nation a great place to live, it's time to get up out of your recliner and be counted.

I know you're out there.

But before you start with the "in-your-face" tactics of the extremists in our midst, just remember

that your children are
watching what you do.

Oh yes, we owe it to
our forefathers to safe-
guard the inheritance they
struggled for, sacrificed
for and died for.

But we also owe it to
our children to pass on to
them, intact, this precious
heritage.

Your country needs you,
folks. And believe it or
not, you can make a dif-
ference!

MAX KIERNAN

Things couldn't possibly get more screwed up than this.

Max Kiernan cradled his head in his hands and gazed
sullenly at the files scattered across his desktop. Most
were the required postmortem reports, written by the
troops on the scene. Except for the reports from
Brickell's sniper team, who never made contact with the
alien, they were all so murky and confused. The authors
could not understand why they should write about
something that, in their minds, had not happened. Whatever block had erased their memory of the incident had
been a dandy, Kiernan thought. The only useful information to have come out of this fiasco was that the
after-effects suffered by the Team were identical to
those suffered by the victims of Kit Washington's per-
suasions. At least that confirmed the connection between the clocker and the alien.

Washington's body was another issue altogether. The
sniper team had been ordered to take out their target, if
necessary, with a chest shot so they could run checks on
Washington's nervous system. But as the situation developed inside the Blake apartment, Brickell realized

what was at stake and opted for a neural shot instead. That cost them any use that the drug dealer's body might have been to them, along with the device that he had been using to control people.

No matter. What was left of Kit Washington was now on the way to the Wright-Pat unit. The initial autopsy had been disappointing. It had shown nothing unusual, but Kiernan wasn't sure whether or not that was a relief. Anything unusual might have provided an important clue. As it stood now, Kit Washington was just another stupid clocker who had gotten over his head in something he didn't understand.

Kiernan rubbed his eyes and re-read the concluding lines of Brickell's report.

My Team had been given specific instructions to isolate subject Washington, and was not advised of other Team movements in the area. My Team delayed isolation, resulting in the death of a Washington D.C., police officer. When it was realized that the target was threatening the apparent residence of VISITOR, the Team utilized extreme sanction to save the lives of others in the Blake apartment. Within two minutes of the event, the Grab Team entered and attempted to take control. This entire Grab Team was immobilized by VISITOR technology. I scrambled my Team to the Blake apartment to assess damage and take control. Because of tech-induced confusion, the secondary event was blown into high-profile status and outside agencies (D.C. Police, FBI, and NSA) became involved. NONE OF THIS WOULD HAVE HAPPENED IF I HAD BEEN TOLD ABOUT THE GRAB TEAM'S MOVEMENTS.

All right, Kiernan thought. So I distributed the information on a need-to-know basis. That was my prerogative. I gambled and lost.

He shuffled the papers on his desk and pulled up the evaluations that had been done on the agents who had been assigned to make the raid on the Blake apartment. Most were amnesiac, confused, anxiety ridden. One showed symptoms of full-fledged psychosis. Attempts to break through to the concealed memories with hypnosis and drugs merely caused profound psychic pain. Those who had been exposed to the visitor's influence seemed strangely bonded with their block.

He found it ironic that their best source of information was a female member of the Team who was one of the first ones in the apartment, then had disappeared until three hours ago, when she turned up at her mother's condo in Fort Lauderdale.

From her account, Kiernan concluded that the visitor's commands to the team had been directed in a gender-specific manner. The Team had been addressed as "Gentlemen," inadvertently exempting the female member of the squad. But in addressing Serena Blake and the unknown woman who was with her, the visitor had said ... Kiernan looked at the woman's report. There it was.

Ladies ... march! You know where to go.

And the woman on the Team had known exactly what that meant. She had been asking for time off to visit her ailing mother. Without authorization, she felt compelled to borrow one of the agency's cars and make the drive south. Upon arriving she had called in immediately, but she felt strangely motivated to stay and visit her mother.

Kiernan had sent Gallagher over to interview the absconding agent. She hadn't been subject to the memory-purging command addressed to the men and was able to provide more complete information. She positively identified a picture of the visitor from a collection of deformed faces that Gallagher had shown her. She identified Serena Blake as one of the women, but had no clue who the other woman was.

This was tolerable. A few mistakes had to be expected. True, a cop had died, but they could prove they had taken out the scumbag who had done it.

The problem was that someone had managed to land a complaint on the desk of Ty Cornell, the congressman who oversaw the agency and made sure it remained overfunded. The complaint was accompanied by the Washington P.D.'s homicide report on the dead cop and a juicy editorial from the *Post* about how the best apartment complex in the city had been turned into a shooting gallery.

Kiernan had just spent a blistering three hours in Cornell's office, trying to explain what had happened. And he had almost won, but then he tried to dismiss the whole thing with: *Actually, we lucked out. Our hands are going to be clean on this one.*

It had been a tactical error.

"Oh, you think we're lucky, do you?" Cornell had raged. "Try telling that to the family of Sergeant Markowski. Not to mention the company that owns the apartment building, or the other tenants. Or the mother of the kid whose head you blew off. She's talking to lawyers, trying to figure out who to sue.

"Now listen, Max. I appreciate what you've done with the agency and all, and I'm one thousand percent in favor of its existence. But there's an election next year, and to be frank, I'm a little spooked that somebody was able to link me with the project.

"We both agree on the importance of your project. We both know that someone has been watching us since we exploded the first nuke at Alamogordo. The surveillance intensified after Jack Kennedy announced we would put a man on the moon. Whoever was visiting us from space, he said, seemed to be friendly enough. But he wanted us to find out who they were. So the agency was born.

"Those were the days, Max. The Senate would take a break and my dad would come home, take me out in the backyard, point to the stars, and say, 'We know they're out there, Ty. Someday we're going to get in touch with them.'

"One reason I went into politics was to keep my dad's dream funded. I found you to take over the agency. But you're starting to act rabid. My advice to you? Don't. If we manage to grab a little green man and have to start making public explanations, I'm gonna become very, very upset."

Max had nodded and said with dead seriousness, "He's little, but he's not green."

"That's exactly what I mean. You've got to watch your attitude, Max."

They shook hands after that, but Kiernan still was not happy. Cornell was a good man, but he was still too political. When the rubber hit the road and the alien was actually in custody, Cornell would have the thing speaking to the President and appearing on David Letterman.

No, this job was best left in the hands of professionals. Even if they screwed things up once in a while.

Kiernan had been trying to piece it together. *Know your adversary, and you will know how to defeat him.* But in this case the adversary was so . . . *alien.*

The medical workups on the visitor that had been taken from George Washington University Hospital were full of notes and speculation on the strange nature of the blood chemistry—familiar looking, but not quite right. Chlorophyll-like. Did that mean this guy was a plant?

There was also the report from a member of the ambulance crew that had brought the alien to the hospital. The information seemed useless, other than the officer's wry comment that put a strange twist on the alien's distorted features; *subject looks as if head had been caught in a rice-picking machine.* The remark sounded strangely familiar, but mostly it was unsettling. It meant that, for better or worse, this creature could pass for some semblance of normal on the D.C. streets.

And Cornell would want to take it to state dinners and introduce it to aspiring starlets.

No. Kiernan would not let it happen. When the time came, Cornell would have to be handled. Kiernan wasn't sure what that would entail, but he would think of something.

Kiernan's eyes fell on the picture of his mother and he lapsed into the reverie that had consumed him a thousand times before. *What was she really like? What would have happened to me if They had never happened to her?*

The bleating of the telephone tore him out of his trance. He answered it with a grunt.

"Boss?" It was Brickell. "I'm out."

"Good. How'd you do?"

"A couple of the FBI people tried to jerk my chain, but they couldn't come up with anything conclusive. They threatened to watch me like a hawk, but that doesn't worry me too much."

"Good."

"Did your friend from Congress spin you over the coals?"

"He thinks he did. Let's say the stakes have been raised."

"So what's the plan?"

"As the agents come out of psych, make sure they're fit for duty and then put them to work turning the metro area upside down. I want an all-out search, every lead checked out."

"Any ideas where to start?"

"If you were an alien, where would you hide?"

"I don't know. New Jersey. Or Alpha Centauri. As far away from here as possible."

Kiernan forced out the laugh that told people he had caught them in the act of being wrong. "That's why *you* call *me* boss."

There was a silence on the other end of the line. Brickell was waiting for it.

"As I see it, our friend is a stranger here, and for some reason, he's being escorted by Serena Blake, who has lived here most of her life." Kiernan leaned across his desk and opened the file on the socialite. "Now, if you were a coked-out heiress whose whole life was Washington, D.C., where would you go?"

"The Motel 6 in Bethesda."

"All right, then. Get on with it. And Brickell?"

"Sir?"

"Don't get carried away. He's got to be taken alive."

Brickell had an afterthought. "One more bit of information for you, boss. My leak at the P.D. tells me that some hotshot reporter from the *Tribune* has taken a sudden interest in local missing-persons reports."

"Maybe she's doing a premillennial piece. You know, theorizing that these folks have been raptured."

Brickell snorted. "Rapture or not, there's a possibility that she may put two and two together. Especially if she discovers two plus two equals Little Ugly."

"Well, then," Kiernan said slowly, "I guess you have someone else to watch."

"I guess so," Brickell said. "And if she gets suspicious?"

"Discourage her."

"And if she knows?"

"You know what to do."

MICK AARONSON

He stared at the glowing screen and squinted at the words he had just created. *It's deceptively simple when you think about it. We must restore our faith in one another and take back the faith we have put into our government. If we need a helping hand, we must look not to those who have spent us to the brink of bankruptcy, but to the end of our own arm. We must rediscover self-reliance.*

Our species has evolved into a highly specialized predator, preying on the victims of happenstance and accident. The lawyer and litigation have replaced the stone ax and the bow and arrow. They are the weapons by which we destroy our friends and colleagues and neighbors.

It's time for the third step in the progression: strong selves, strong families, strong neighborhoods.

Aaronson thought, good. Very good. You've put his ideas into your own words, and they're palpable enough to the average citizen whose brain was destroyed by our education system. Schools were next. He'd start on that tomorrow.

From the corner of his eye, he saw his office door glide open. He looked up to see Corey, the managing editor, creep in with a fat manila envelope tucked under his arm.

"To what do I owe the honor of this visit?"

Corey waved his hand when Aaronson's eyes connected with his. "No, no," he said. "Keep working. Don't let me bother you."

"You're sure?" As he spoke, Corey approached him, head cocked to one side and locked in a stare. Aaronson touched his lower lip consciously. "What? I forget to shave?"

Corey shook his head. "Just checking your nose."

Aaronson pulled at it.

"Your nostrils, to be exact. I'm looking for residue."

"Residue?"

"Of the happy powder you've been sniffing."

Aaronson glared.

"No happy powder?" He picked up the journalist's mug and sniffed. "I know. I'll bet those special tea leaves of yours came straight off the Prozac tree. Is that it? Or maybe it's that intern of yours. Mick, are you getting laid?"

Aaronson rolled his eyes. "Corey, you seem to be the one with a substance abuse problem. What's going on?"

"The columns."

"What about them?" He leaned back in his chair. "You don't like them?"

Corey smiled. "I love them. And so does the public. We're starting to get phone calls from the papers who carry you, five-to-one in favor of what you've been writing the last couple of weeks. And the syndicate says you're picking up papers for the first time in years. But that's not all. This will absolutely blow your mind." The editor took the manila envelope from under his arm and turned it upside down over the desk, spilling out an avalanche of letters. "Look at this, Mick. People are writing to us. God bless them, they're actually putting pen to paper and *writing*. I mean, this is actually freaking me out."

"Don't get carried away. I may ask for a raise." Aaronson idly picked up one of the envelopes. The return address was Silver Spring.

Corey held his hands out helplessly. "I have to tell you, the boys on the editorial board were starting to wonder whether you were growing dinosaur feet ... whether your clock was running out. There were even suggestions that we should buy out the rest of your contract so you could retire. Then we could use this office for something useful, like storing vacuum-cleaner bags. I mean, more than once I stood up for you and said no, Mick Aaronson is the last living Real American."

Aaronson slid his thumb under the flap of the envelope and tore it open. He pulled out the letter inside, written in a steady hand on cream-colored stationery. Clearing his throat, he read, "May 21, 1999. Dear Mr. Aaronson. God bless you! It's about time somebody came out and said that America still has it! My dad served in Vietnam, and he always told me that while he got treated bad because he volunteered, he was so proud to serve his country. Now nobody wants to serve their country anymore and they're talking about bringing back the draft. I think that's so sad." Aaronson looked up at Corey. "He wrote 'so sad' in block letters and underlined them twice." He turned back to the letter. "Next time this year I'll be graduating from the U of Virginia. I had planned on going to Wall Street and grabbing everything I could while I was young. But after reading what you've had to say recently, I've changed my mind. This *is* still a great country and I owe it something. So I'm going to join the army, and maybe apply for officer's candidate training. Again, God bless you, and thank you."

"See what I mean?" Corey said. "Even I was beginning to have doubts about you, and I'm the most tolerant person in the world."

Aaronson chortled.

"But now . . ." Corey focused happily on the pile of mail. "You're playing America's heartstrings again in C Major. And I don't mind telling you that I think it's great."

Aaronson shrugged. "After Suzanne died, I guess I lost track of the meaning of life. Maybe I caught a glimpse of it again . . ." His voice faded until it was almost inaudible. "... like a flicker of sunlight through dark clouds."

"Mick, I don't care if you're smoking opium in the basement of your house. Whatever you're doing, keep it up. The last few weeks you've been doing the best writing of your life. It's coming from the heart." He turned away from Aaronson and sauntered over to the journalist's wall of fame. His eyes settled on one of Aaronson with Ronald Reagan, both on horseback, tipping their cowboy hats. "You never played golf with them, did you?"

"Not while they were in office," Aaronson said. "It interfered with journalism."

"I wanted you to know something else. What you've been writing ... well, it's meant a lot to me personally. It's made me think a lot about what this country has done for me, which is something I'd almost forgotten. Maybe I'd read too many of the stories my own reporters have been writing. Maybe I just caught the American disease. For too long a time, we've had too much good fortune that we've done too little to earn. So we've come down with spoiled complacency. This country may be the pits, and there may be some things that are in dire need of fixing, but you know what? I'd rather live here than anywhere else in the world.

"You know what I did the other day, Mick? I visited the Lincoln Memorial. I haven't done that in over a decade. I walked up to Abe and looked up at him. I looked at that craggy face and into those deep, soulful eyes." Corey stopped for a moment and drew a deep breath. "This is going to sound crazy, but I wanted to apologize to him. I wanted to tell him that I was sorry for neglecting the country that he died trying to hold together. *Out loud.* There wasn't anyone around, I had a minute or two, just him and me alone. 'I'm sorry'— that's all I wanted to say, and you know what? I got a lump in my throat. I couldn't talk, couldn't swallow. For a minute, I couldn't even breathe. So I looked up at him again, and the tightness . . . the sadness went away. Just like that. It was like those eyes, that face was saying that it was all right. That I might have blown it in the past, but I still had the future. Well, so does America, Mick. America's still got her future. You gave me my country back, Mick. And for doing that"—he stopped and drew another breath—"and for that I thank you."

Aaronson nodded. "Thank *you*, Corey."

Corey shrugged sheepishly. "Well, that's all I wanted to say."

Aaronson asked quietly, "Corey, do you mind if I use some of what you've just said in a column?"

Corey, enroute to the door, stopped in his tracks. "What? Column? Me?"

"I'll make you a confidential informant, if you like, but I think we all need a resurgence of patriotism. I might even recommend a personal pilgrimage to the monuments to renew your faith in the country."

Flattered, Corey nodded. "Yeah. That'd be all right. Sure. Go right ahead."

"Thanks."

"Thank *you*, Mick," he said, and walked quickly out of the office, blowing his nose.

Aaronson stared out the door for a moment, then dropped his eyes to the letter in his hand. *This is still a great country, and I owe it something.* He nodded in silent agreement. Victor was right. There were people out there who still had the capacity to revitalize America.

All they needed to know was that they were not alone.

It was beginning now, an awakening of feeling, the rekindling of the American spirit.

Victor's plan might work.

HARRY LAUTER

It had been decades since Harry had been in a place like this. It was dingy and stifling and reeking with stale tobacco smoke. A band on the stage played a loud approximation of what the crowd considered to be jazz. His eyes darted back and forth, scanning the room for suspicious faces. There was a look agents developed when they were in pursuit—studied nonchalance—that Harry had learned to recognize after years of being followed by the police of fifteen different countries.

Now the stakes were higher. Now he was playing against members of his own country.

He made his first pass through the bar and then started on a second. When he was satisfied the place was clean, he made a third pass, slowing as he approached the line of bar stools. He settled on one next to a barrel-chested man in a tweed jacket who was sipping a beer and chewing on a cigar.

"Hello, Arkady," Harry said cheerfully. "It's been a long time."

Arkady tapped ash from the cigar into the glass bowl before him. "Please," he said in a thick accent. "You must call me Andy. And yes, it has been a long time. Old friends like us should embrace, Harry Lauter. Unfortunately, I think this would not be the place to do it."

"Regrettable," Harry said. He turned his attention to the cigar. "Cuban?"

"Of course." Arkady tilted his head back and exhaled a large cloud. "From the Castro days. I had a large reserve."

"You haven't changed." Harry smiled. "So how's the espionage business?"

Arkady shrugged, blew smoke. "I can't complain. The French want NASA's new propellant formula. That should bring a fat fee. Several Japanese interests have expressed a desire for a prototype of the new Intel computer chip. I could retire if I deliver that one. But most of my clients pay modest fees for everyday, bread-and-butter espionage."

Harry nodded. "Arkady—Andy. You know if I had any money at all, I would pay you for this."

Arkady put down his cigar and waved his hand at the preacher. "And you, Harry? Are you still a man of God? And are you still on the trail of the words that he forgot to tell us?"

"He didn't forget," Harry said. "Satan had them buried."

Arkady laughed. "You and me, Harry. We're on opposite sides. You march with God. I skulk with Satan. But I keep my promises—even to Holies. I haven't forgotten my promise to you a long time ago. Besides . . . It wouldn't hurt me to open a small bank account in God's kingdom . . . as a hedge of course."

"I never meant to call in this favor, Andy, I swear. But things are happening . . ."

"Are you close to the scrolls?"

"That depends on what you tell me."

Arkady took a long, deep pull on his cigar. The bartender ambled over and took Harry's order for a Coke. Arkady blew smoke and squinted at the preacher.

"UFOs, Harry?"

"That's got to be the connection. Look, the scrolls describe travel by light. What does that sound like to you?"

"Angels." Arkady smiled.

"But," said Harry, "we've got a government that denies God. How are they going to explain it?"

Head enveloped in smoke, Arkady heaved an agnostic sigh.

"Who am I to deny God? Maybe they are angels, Andy. Maybe they're cherubim and seraphim. But maybe they're intelligent beings who've evolved farther and traveled farther than we've managed."

Arkady turned to Harry. "I envy you, my friend. You have this faith which cannot be denied."

"I believe," Harry said.

Arkady began a low and throaty laugh. But Harry cut him off.

"You know what else I believe, Andy? I believe that God delivered you into my hands. He selected you because your worldliness is merely the crust on a character of goodness and compassion. He had you assigned to the task of training insurgents to use the weapons you were smuggling. And He opened the eyes of the Turkish police so you would be caught and beaten and thrown into a cell with me—the only prisoner there who would bind your wounds and steal extra bread and broth to keep you from dying."

"You don't have to remind me of my debt to you."

"I'm just pointing out the hand of God in all that has happened to you and me. I've met a lot of people in prisons, Andy. Some of them taught me things that were useless. Others told me things I needed to know. But others now occupy positions which could prove very useful to me in my quest. Like you."

Arkady's stomach rumbled and he reached for his beer. "Why would God need a middleman, Harry Lauter? Particularly a sinner like me?"

"God raises up sinners to do His will just like He raises up saints, Andy. Look at Judas Iscariot. If he hadn't been so steeped in sin that he betrayed Christ, we would never have had the promise of salvation."

Arkady's shoulders heaved. He put a fist to his mouth to stifle a belch. "So Judas Iscariot burns in hell. That does not bode well for me."

"Judas hanged himself before he could be forgiven, Andy. Christ Himself would have welcomed him back into the fold if he had only asked. There's no sin too great."

"I owe you a debt, Harry. If it will also earn me some credit with God, I'm in no position to reject it."

Harry smiled. "I've learned never to underestimate His wisdom."

Arkady turned to face him. "How much do you know about things like Project Blue Book and other UFO-related investigations?"

Harry shook his head. "Almost nothing."

"Blue Book was supposedly the summary of an extensive investigation by your military. It contained enough threadbare material to placate the public. There were some inconvenient leaks. The incident at Roswell was the most notorious. Any insider can tell you that the bodies were supposed to have been moved to an air force base in Ohio. But the Pentagon prefers to suppress mysteries it cannot solve. So it swept the strange happenings under the secrecy stamp and discredited anyone who reported a UFO sighting. This campaign was supposed to be covert, but the bigger the secret, the harder some people work to uncover it."

"What have you uncovered?" Harry asked.

"In the years following the Second World War, strange things began to occur near nuclear test sites here and in my country. Each side thought the other was playing high-tech games. It was your side . . . the Americans . . . who discovered that the monitoring . . . the interventions . . . the unexplainable activity . . . originated elsewhere in the cosmos.

"So an investigation into the so-called UFO phenomena began in earnest. It was a disorganized squabble between the navy and the air force until President Kennedy organized an agency specifically assigned to investigate the problem. This agency doesn't officially exist, and it doesn't even have a name. We found it by tracing a narrow, barely visible money trail. If you were to follow it from the outside, your first stop would be the Internal Revenue Service."

"So secret it doesn't officially exist," mused Harry.

"Exactly. I think insiders call it the stealth agency. So when the military is bugged for information by UFO fanatics, they just say 'no comment.' "

"Why don't they just deny it?"

"Saying 'No comment' makes them appear guilty, attracts attention to the Pentagon and away from the stealth agency."

"So the military takes all the heat for this agency."

"Exactly. And the disinformation is all done through the military, which adds to their appearance of guilt."

Harry exhaled audibly and shook his head. "Incredible."

"No. Not incredible. Ingenious. And there is something more. Something else you wanted."

"A name?"

Arkady nodded. "An important name. The man at the end of the money trail. The man with his hand on the purse strings."

"Someone capable of hurting the agency? Cutting their funding or shutting them down, if need be?"

"Would a member of your own Congress be good enough?"

Harry's face flushed with triumph. "You're amazing."

"The money has to come from somewhere, my friend. This man is on the appropriate subcommittee that funds space-related projects. The space station, SETI, the shuttle program. This phantom agency is disguised as a piece of—what do you call it?—pork. This ... uh ... pork-barrel project exists merely to funnel the money to the IRS, which distributes the funds to the stealth agency."

"Who is it?" Harry demanded excitedly.

"Ty Cornell. Democrat. Representative from Massachusetts. The Boston area."

"I've heard the name," Harry said quickly. "What have you got on him?"

"He's conservative on defense, a fiscal moderate, a social liberal."

"Not that," Harry protested. "You know. What have you *got* on him?"

Arkady's lips split into a broad smile. "For terms of compromise, Harry?"

"God works in mysterious ways."

Arkady shifted in his seat. "Congressman Cornell is not what I would call easy to compromise. He drinks only socially, scorns mind-altering substances, and apart from some profound promiscuity during his college career, now seems devoted to one woman. His friends and contacts are all clean."

"So you can offer me no tools of persuasion."

Arkady raised a finger and waved it back and forth. "I never said that, Harry. What I said is that Congressman Cornell could not be compromised. But I think with the proper encouragement, he might reconsider whether to continue protecting the agency."

"What kind of encouragement?"

He shrugged. "You have told me of a raid. There have been disappearances. Strange rumors on the street. It sounds like the agency may be getting reckless. This could be an effective persuader for a man like Cornell."

"Specifics?"

"Harry, Harry." With one finger, Arkady tapped the side of the preacher's head. "You must use your American ingenuity."

Harry raised a hand in mock protest. "My American ingenuity tells me to invoke your Russian dirty tricks."

Arkady paused for a moment for beer, then wrapped a massive arm around Harry's shoulders. "This shall be like the old days. My expensive training against your government. One final time."

"With one difference," Harry said. "This time God is on your side."

Arkady erupted with laughter. Harry shifted uncomfortably on his stool, worrying whether his friend was laughing in the face of God.

SUSAN HILL

Mick Aaronson called Susan into the kitchen, sat her down in front of a cup of freshly brewed tea, and told her the way things were going to be.

First, the socialite and her strange companion would stay with him until the danger could be properly assessed. This would give him the chance to conduct further interviews.

"So," Susan said. "You think he's really an alien, then?"

"I think he's someone with superior intelligence and good ideas who should be listened to. As for his native habitat, I'll concede only that he's weird enough to be from out of this world."

"At least you're listening to him."

"I'm going to give him a chance. But at the first sign he might be a phony, he's out of here. It would be embarrassing if it got out that someone had convinced me he was from another planet. They'd say that's where I belong."

Aaronson laid out the strategy. Before the morning got too old, Susan was to pick up the government car they had confiscated and park it conspicuously in the porno district.

"Inside of twenty-four hours," he predicted, "the local thugs will have it stripped down to nothing. They'll scatter the parts—and any possible fingerprints—across the country."

That didn't appeal to Susan, but she would do it. She was a team member; she was prepared to play the game. But when the third part of the game was revealed, she nearly mutinied.

"I want you to spike the hospital-walkaway story."

"Spike it?"

"For the time being. The last thing we need is to proclaim to the world that a reporter from the *Tribune* is looking into the incident."

"But Mr. Aaronson—"

"No buts, my dear. If I'm to get what I want out of this gentleman, and if he's to cooperate fully, we've got to do what we can to ensure his security. That means keeping as low a profile as we can manage."

"What about his girlfriend?" Susan said bitterly. "How're you going to shut her up? With coke to keep her happy? Have you seen her lately? She's curled up in a ball on your couch."

"I don't think that's a drug reaction."

"Well, what if she needs lithium or something? Are you going to call a doctor and have him deliver it here?"

"Hold it, Susan. You want to run with the story. I know how that feels. But you've got to learn that sometimes you give up a big story to get an even bigger one."

With reluctant obedience, Susan buried the hospital story. And when the cloak-and-dagger thrill of ditching the government car had worn off, she settled back into the routine of the internship. She was assigned to cover more meaty stories than fuzzy animals, has-been actors, or Easter egg hunts. Yet the assignments that landed on

her desk seemed lackluster compared to what she had
been doing.

You've become addicted to the chase, she realized.
*Nothing's ever going to satisfy you again unless you're
digging after the truth.*

The realization startled yet stimulated her. That was
what Mick Aaronson had hinted would happen if she
pursued truth instead of perception. It would mean leaving the journalistic pack, he had warned, to explore uncertain trails on her own.

Mick Aaronson's schedule had tightened up after
Victor's arrival, and she had found herself missing their
discussions. Well, they had been arguments, really,
punctuated by Aaronson's finger poking her in the forehead and challenging her to "Think, Susan! Always
think!"

Susan sat at her desk staring at an assignment that
stared back up at her. Two hundred words on an auto
mechanic who had hit it big with a Powerball lottery
ticket given to him by an old lady whose tire he had
changed. When she called, she made the mistake of asking him a question that he undoubtedly had been asked
a hundred times. His answer was, *Whad'ya think? I'm
gonna spend the money on sex and booze!*

Then a hand fell on her shoulder, startling her. It was
Julia Roman, asking if things were better for her now
that she had escaped from the life-style department, and
telling her that some of the younger crowd were heading for a notorious newspaper bar to drown their frustrations. Did she want to come along?

Of course she did; she had the necessary frustrations
to qualify. But she was running late. She'd meet them
there shortly.

When she finally showed up, the scene was just
about what she had expected. Lyle Lovett was blaring
from the speakers but was nearly drowned out by the

clientele. Susan joined the group as one of the reporters was finishing a story that was clearly a source of great amusement to all.

"And it all happened because the neighbors complained about the smell," someone was saying.

"Well," said Julia Roman, "good riddance."

"You're in a great mood," Susan said. "Some famous serial killer die?"

Julia shook her head. "Worse. A sycophant."

"He must have royally crossed somebody to leave town like that," said the storyteller.

"Knowing him, he wasn't the one who did that to the apartment. It was probably the landlord, trying to get rid of the smell *he* left behind."

Susan shook her head. "Why the long faces?" she asked her grinning colleagues.

"The world of journalism lost a great man today," said a man with a mug of beer in his hand.

"It was last week," amended a woman who was snuggling closer to his side.

"And he was a real snake," Julia said, taking a long sip of her margarita.

"Hear, hear!" said someone else.

"A toast, then," said the man with the beer. He rose from the table, sloshing liquid out of his mug. Raising it high in the air, he said, "To Tony Watkins, wherever you are. *As long as it's not here!*"

More gales of laughter were followed by more spilling of drinks. Julia smiled at Susan. "Watkins was a parasite."

"Aw, Julia, you're being too nice," said the snuggling woman.

"Fortunately, he worked at the *Post*."

"Amen," said the man with the beer.

"He was one of those guys who hangs around outside

of gatherings and pops off a flash in the faces of famous people."

"The Robin Leach of the black-and-white snapshot crowd," said the man with the beer.

"Hey, hey," blurted someone else. "What's the difference between paparazzi and catfish?"

"I dunno. What?" someone else asked.

"Some are scum-sucking bottom feeders, and the others are fish."

The group erupted in laughter.

"So he didn't show for work on Monday, but it wasn't until Wednesday before they decided someone should check out his place, make sure he hadn't died of bile and wasn't being eaten by jackals."

"Gross!" said the snuggling woman.

"They got there and the place was cleaned out, stem to stern."

"He musta left town in one big hurry," the woman slurred.

Someone else suggested, "He was probably slapped with a sexual harassment suit."

"Wait, wait," said the man with the beer. "You balled up the story. It wasn't his colleagues who noticed he was gone, it was the neighbors. They complained because the smell was making them sick."

Susan was perplexed. "I don't get it. I thought you said he left town. But if there was a smell—"

"No, no, no!" the man with the beer waved his hands impatiently. "That was the disinfectant. He'd like, *nuked* the place with disinfectant, and it was making the neighbors sick. It was, you know, irritating their noses and eyes, and some of them were getting asthma attacks—"

"What did you say?" Susan blurted.

"He'd used a real strong disinfectant before moving out," Julia explained. "Who knows why."

"To wash away all of the clap germs he left behind," the snuggling woman said.

A sudden memory overwhelmed Susan. Dr. George Underwood's apartment. Empty, except for the smell. A smell that had burned her eyes.

No. No, it couldn't be ...

"Susan," Julia said. "Are you all right?"

"What did this guy do again?"

The man with the beer pantomimed taking a picture.

"He was a photographer," said Julia. "A stringer for the *Post*."

"And he specialized in getting in the faces of famous people," said the man.

"He got punched once by Sean Penn," said the woman.

"It was Axl Rose," someone else corrected.

"People like Ty Cornell?" Susan asked quickly.

Julia shook her head. "Politicians are a dime a dozen in this town."

"But if he was throwing a fund-raiser—"

"It would depend on who was there."

Susan shrugged. "The upper crust of society?"

"Maybe," the man said.

"Possibly," said Julia.

"A socialite with a new man in her life," Susan said to no one in particular.

"Susan?" Julia asked. "What's wrong?"

"I have to go," she said.

She rushed back to the *Tribune*, whispering under her breath. *"Tony Watkins, George Underwood, Tony Watkins, Doctor Underwood ..."*

As soon as she reached her desk, she wrote the names on a pad. *The doctor—the story was there all along, and I missed it! What else have I missed?*

Think, Susan. Always think!

She sat down at her terminal and accessed the archive

directory, then began combing through back issues of the paper, day by day. After going through a week's worth of papers, she added two more names to her list.

Amos White—D.C. Cop
Patrice Jackson—Prostitute

Then it occurred to her that she could search by category instead. She smacked herself in the forehead— *think!*—and entered a data search covering the last six month's worth of the *Tribune*. The subject was MISSING PERSONS: UNSOLVED.

After a moment, a list of stories spilled down the screen. And Susan Hill shivered.

Between December 1998 and March 1999 there had been three unsolved disappearances.

But since April, there had been an even dozen.

It had started with Dr. George Underwood and a nurse from the George Washington University Hospital. It had been assumed that they had run off together.

But then two members of an ambulance crew had also vanished.

Along with a maintenance man from Serena's condo.

And a clerk from a convenience store two blocks away.

A doorman from a nighclub that Serena was known to frequent.

A high-school junior who was the known steady of Kit Washington.

A marine sergeant who was a guard at the gates of the White House.

A homeless man who had recently cleaned up his act and had been preaching the gospel on street corners.

The cop and the hooker.

With the photographer, that made thirteen people.

Thirteen souls gone without a trace. All since April, when the visitor had first appeared.

Of course, Susan couldn't make quick assumptions. Not while she was studying under the great Mick Aaronson.

She spent the next few days making phone calls, interviewing families, bugging the police about leads or theories. The predatory animal within her had been loosed, and it felt great.

She had found her calling.

Mick Aaronson would be proud of her. If she ever got to speak to him again.

The information began to spill over her desk, so she dropped by a grocery store, finagled two orange boxes that still smelled of citrus and carted the whole mess of papers home with her. Then she ordered two pizzas and two liters of soda, sprawled on the floor with a pad and pencil, and began studying the files one by one, making notes, building her case, sorting out facts.

Halfway into her chronology, a disturbing thought entered her mind. She dismissed it.

Three-quarters of the way through, it came back again, louder, stronger. She could no longer keep it out of her mind. So she relegated it to the back of her mind.

At last Susan finished. She sat in the middle of her living room, staring at the pages of information and photographs that littered the floor. It was a compendium of random, scattered lives, all interrupted, all mocked by the photographs.

I'll bet they never dreamed it would be an intern from the Washington Tribune, Susan thought. *And they never had a clue that the linchpin in all of this was Serena Blake.*

And then the voice returned, shouting urgently.

It said, *You are tied to Serena, too. They may not*

know about Victor and Mick. But you have been openly collecting information on all of these people.

And then the fear came, so overwhelming and delicious that for a moment she felt intoxicated by it.

Think, Susan! Always think!

Out loud, she said, *"Oh, no!"*

I'm next.

The fear flared into panic. She crawled across the floor, gathering up the files and throwing them back into the orange boxes.

And then the telephone rang.

The noise shocked her. Her skin became gooseflesh, and she cried out.

She glanced at the clock. It was 3:27 A.M.

The phone rang again. She stared at it. Who would it be at this hour?

You know who it is, Susan.

It rang a third time. She picked up the phone and tried to sound as if she'd been asleep.

"Hello?" she rasped.

Click.

That was a worse jolt than the ringing. She slammed the handset back into the cradle, not able to get it out of her hand fast enough. Then she leaped to her feet and searched the room with her eyes, determining what remained to be packed.

No! There's no time for that! Get out! GET OUT NOW!

Susan was hyperventilating now. She bolted to the closet and threw on her windbreaker, fishing the car keys out of her pocket. With trembling fingers she set the door to lock itself and then stepped out into the hall, slamming it shut behind her.

She looked up and down the hall. Nothing.

Then she tried to force herself to walk calmly to the stairs, but she took three steps and her nerve broke. She ran hard, and when she reached the stairs, she took them two at a time, leaning against the rail to keep from falling, grinding her teeth to keep the scream inside from escaping through her lips.

Susan hit the first landing, turned fast, and started down the next set of steps. Two, four, six. She took them quickly, and then suddenly she felt a fierce burning in her right calf. It sent spines of fire up her nervous system and plunged her stomach deep into nausea.

"Not now," she whispered. "Not now not now—"

She paused, just for a second, to massage the charley horse out of her leg. Her fingers touched something soft and warm, then cold and hard.

Susan reeled and stared at her leg in disbelief.

Sunk into her right calf was a small dart with red feathers angling from it in three places.

Her mouth fell open. *This happens only in the movies,* she thought.

From the corner of her eye, she could see something dark moving her way from behind her on the stairs.

She tried to move her right leg, but it wouldn't respond. It was numb now, and the fire was spreading up her belly and down her left leg. Her eyes were beginning to water, and the staircase steps—there could only have been eight or ten more—began to fade and blur.

And then her nose picked up something that transported her straight back to the apartment of Dr. George Underwood.

Disinfectant.

With a cry, Susan thrust out her left leg and tried to place it on the step beneath her. It went down, down, down, pulling her away from the rail as it went.

Before she lost control completely, she caught sight of another black-suited figure, a twin of the ones who had come into Serena's apartment, running toward her from the front door of the lobby, arms outstretched.

Don't you dare catch me.

It was her last thought before her eyes closed, her brain shut down, and she began to tumble.

MICK AARONSON

Serena looked dead.

Aaronson had just walked in the door and had started to remove his coat when he noticed her there, lying on the floor, in a sprawl instead of her usual fetal curl.

He let his coat fall to the floor and ran to her side, grabbing her wrist and feeling for a pulse. It was there, weak and thready, but her skin seemed cold.

He called for Victor.

Then he tried to pick her up. But his old bones creaked and his muscles protested. So he rolled up one end of the rug she lay on, wrapped his fingers around the tube it formed, and dragged her into the living room.

He called for Victor again, then grabbed a cushion off the couch and stuffed it under her feet.

Victor appeared in the archway that separated the living room from the dining room. The faraway look on his face told Mick Aaronson that he had been watching C-SPAN again.

"Please," Aaronson said urgently, "something's wrong with Serena."

The visitor ambled over to the scene and knelt by Serena's head.

"Ah, yes."

"That's it? That's your assessment?"

"It's obvious that she is ill."

"Susan said she's addicted to cocaine. Is that true?"

"Perhaps."

"Perhaps?" Aaronson rolled his eyes. "Victor, there are some things that are absolutes. Death. Pregnancy. Taxes."

Victor said, "Susan is a perceptive young woman. Her diagnosis of Serena was correct, but it is now dated."

"You've been sneaking her to a methadone clinic while I'm gone?"

The visitor faced Aaronson. "I know you still do not believe completely, Mick Aaronson. But you must accept what I am about to tell you."

"Try me," Aaronson challenged.

Reaching into the pocket of his trousers, the alien produced the hypnotic stone. "With this device, I am able to manipulate my environment or influence sapient beings whose brains create certain patterns of electro-chemical activity. I can also alter what you might call reality by using great amounts of my own personal energy."

Aaronson, noting the silvery texture of the stone, grunted "At least it isn't a crystal."

"This is a device I used to give myself a more familiar human appearance, although the results were less than perfect."

"I suppose I should ask to see your true form."

Victor shook his head. "I need my energies for something which will require your assistance."

"You need *my* energy?"

"I need your presence, Mick Aaronson. This is the device I used to cure Serena of her physical addiction to cocaine."

"Go on."

"Perhaps you will understand the situation better if I explain it in sequence. You see, a rather violent man who called himself Ghost relieved me of this device when I first arrived here, and he discovered that it made people open to his suggestions. For a time he entertained his own passions and lusts with it, but his greed drove him to seek me out. When he found me, he wanted more, and in an attempt to convince me to surrender more, he used this device on Serena. That seemed to cause the state she is in."

"You're saying this—this *rock*—did something to her?"

The visitor nodded. "You see, one must exercise care when using this device on any species. Yours in particular, as we have sadly learned. If an experience with the device is not concluded properly, it can lead to neurotic behavior in certain individuals."

Aaronson folded Serena's hands across her stomach. "This is a little more than neurotic, Victor."

"I believe she has lost the will to live."

"So we need to get her to a hospital at once."

"No. We need to restore her will to live. She has not lost it, but it has been suppressed. We must find out why, and then revive it."

Aaronson said nothing. He just stared, as if his inbred skepticism were beginning to crack.

"I have energy enough to do this on my own, but such resolutions are generally done by more than one. So it could require more than one sitting. There is danger that I might lose her. Are you with me, Mick Aaronson?"

Aaronson looked at Serena's face, her skin so pale it was almost translucent. "You'd better give me the easy part."

"That will be done," said the visitor. "I will be the expediter. You must be the preceptor, the guide. You are to lead her to a place in her mind where she will allow me to do my work."

"How do I do that?"

"You must react to the way in which she perceives

you. Listen to what she says. If you seem to be at a shopping mall, have her take you to her favorite store. If you are on an automobile trip, you must ask her to drive. We must set her subconscious into a mode that will make her receptive to what I must tell her to do. Can you do that?"

"I think so, but she's unconscious."

"That is where the greatest energy expenditure will take place," said the visitor. He held the rock in the palm of his hand and stared at it. "You may feel some disorientation. You may feel as though you are not in control of your voluntary muscles. That's because it will be true. But no harm will come to you."

"But—"

Before he had a chance to finish, Aaronson felt himself go numb. The air around him seemed to thicken, time ground to a halt. His eyes darted and he began to panic, but then the visitor spoke.

"You will be able to speak."

Before he realized it, the words, *What are you doing to me?* were out past his lips.

"Attend." The alien motioned toward Serena.

"I'm ... I'm ... nervous," Aaronson said.

"You are perfectly safe."

The alien's lips turned up slightly, and he nodded. "Now I must wake her. This will take a moment."

Aaronson was expecting a physical manifestation, but it never happened. The visitor didn't levitate; the stone did not begin to glow; nor did the color suddenly return to Serena's cheeks. The alien sat immobile, rock in his outstretched palm, staring at Serena. Aaronson could feel sweat beading up on his forehead. It increased his nervousness.

"When do—"

"Sh," the visitor said quickly. Aaronson could feel energy draining from his body until he thought he couldn't take the strange, immobile feeling any longer. Then the visitor said, "Serena. Serena, wake up."

Her eyes fluttered open and rolled around, darting and fixing on things that weren't there. "It's dark."

"You are in familiar surroundings."

"Yes. Yes, I am."

"And look." With his free hand, the visitor motioned toward Aaronson. "Look who's here."

Serena's eyes rotated until they locked onto him.

"Say something," the visitor said softly.

"Hello, Serena," said Aaronson.

Serena's face stiffened. Her mouth dropped open and her eyes went wide. Both hands jumped up and covered her mouth as her eyes started to fill with tears.

"Oh, no!" she cried. "Joey."

CHRIS GALLAGHER

"All right. So you know what you're supposed to do?"

"Yuh," said the husky voice at the end of the phone.

"So what's the plan?"

"I, uh . . ." There was a long pause. Chris Gallagher listened impatiently. Wouldn't this guy ever get the story straight and quote it back without sounding like he was having a bowel movement? Finally the voice cracked in Gallagher's handset. "I, uh, am gonna go to Gallup, New Mexico. An' I'm gonna go eat hamburgers."

"Cheeseburgers, Alan. Double cheeseburgers with—"

"Bacon and onion, heavy on the mayo. And when I get spotted—"

"Where, Alan?"

"Huh?"

"What kind of burger joint do you go to?"

"Oh. Uh, none of the chains. Just mom-and-pop places."

"Good."

"And when I get spotted, I'm supposed to say that I didn't die in the seventies. That a doctor had put me in, uh, cryal—"

"Cyrogenic hibernation. Don't try and say it, Alan. Just tell what happened to you."

"A doctor froze me and told the world I was dead."

"Good, Alan. Then what?"

"That I'm looking for the son I had with the Mississippi waitress. And I'm gonna make a big comeback concert at midnight of January first, 2000."

"No, 2001," Gallagher corrected. "Remember, Elvis always opened his shows with the theme from the movie *2001*. You know, *bwam, bwam, bwaaaaaah*—"

Alan was unimpressed by Gallagher's singing. "I never saw that show," he said.

"Unimportant. Just remember *2001*."

"I started to watch it once, on HBO. I thought it was supposed to be about spaceships. It was about gorillas hitting each other with sticks."

Gallagher rolled his eyes. "Your phenomenal comeback tour is *when*?"

"Midnight, January first, 2001."

"And how long do you hang around?"

"Only until some, uh, overweight housewife with her hair in curlers snaps my picture."

"Great. Now do you have any questions?"

"Yeah. Do I have to do this?"

"Alan, how much are we paying you?"

As Gallagher waited for the reply, a messenger stopped at his desk and pantomimed, pretending to hold a phone to her ear, then holding up seven fingers. Gallagher acknowledged the message.

"I'll tell you what we're paying you, Alan. Two-fifty

a day plus expenses. You'll be gone at least a week. That's almost two grand right there. How many transmissions would you have to repair in order to get that kind of money?"

"Uh—"

"Don't answer that. I just want you to do it, okay? Call me when you get there. And don't go near a McDonald's or a Burger King. We don't want to get involved with a chain. Now have a good trip, Alan, and send me a postcard."

Gallagher slammed the phone down, shook his head, then punched line seven and picked it up again. "Gallagher here."

"Chris, this is Harry in D.C."

The hairs rose on the back of Gallagher's neck, and he sat at attention. "Harry. My man. Good to hear from you."

"I got the check. Thanks."

"Anytime. Like I said, Harry, that lead you gave me was gold. Pure gold. You deserved it."

"I'm glad it worked out."

"Did you see the story?"

"Actually, no."

Gallagher laughed. "That's because it hasn't been published yet." He paused for a half-second, calculating how big a lie he should tell. "The editor's waiting for the right moment to use it."

Harry suggested, "You may want to run it soon, when you hear what I've got to tell you."

"Is this another Jesus sighting? If it's anything like the last one—"

"It's better. Much better."

"All right. I'm listening."

There was no sound.

"C'mon, Harry. Let's hear it."

"You're forgetting something."

"Let's hear it. *Please?*"

"I have expenses, Chris. I'm trying to get—"

"I know, I know. Back to the Holy Land. All right, let me check my budget—"

"No need," Harry said. "I want five grand."

Gallagher came out of his seat. *"Five grand—"*

"But the last story was gold Chris, this one is platinum. No, it's plutonium. Absolutely nuclear."

"Five grand? Harry, for that much it better be the Second Coming."

"That's exactly what it is."

Gallagher's throat closed off. He couldn't say a thing.

"Chris? You there?"

Gallagher reached across his desk, grabbed a warming bottle of ginger ale, and took a huge swig.

"Chris."

"I'm sorry," he squeaked.

Gallagher's mind raced. *Try to be coy about this.* "By 'Second Coming,' you're talking about—"

"Jesus," Harry said. "Not the Jesus that artists have conceived. I'm talking about the *real* Jesus—the Messiah whom Isaiah described as not desired for His physical beauty."

Turning in his chair, Gallagher ransacked the top of his desk until he located a pad and pencil. "Oh?" he said, trying to sound noncommittal.

"Don't play games with me, Chris. I can detect your excitement in the tone of your voice.

"Give me a break, Harry. Is this legitimate or not?"

"Legitimate? There are legitimate witnesses who believe this is Jesus. He has performed legitimate healings and miracles. . . . As God is my judge, Chris, it's possible this IS the resurrected Christ."

Gallagher didn't believe in much of anything. But he drew breath silently. "What are the details?"

"Ten grand, Chris. In advance."

"C'mon, Harry. I'm on a budget here."

"I'm talking about the story of the century, Chris. No, it's bigger than that. It's the ultimate story. The Second Coming. The Millennium. In language you will understand, Chris, I'm talking about a massive circulation increase. It's worth far more than ten measly grand."

"Harry, we'll have to send a crew up for this. Photographer, writer, researcher. That's going to cost us."

"The Second Coming," Harry said. "The Millennium."

"Five thousand," Gallagher said.

"Excuse me," Harry said. "I thought I heard you say 'five thousand.' We must have a bad connection."

"Seventy-five hundred."

"That's not acceptable."

"Take it or leave it."

"Twelve thousand," Harry said.

"Twelve?" Chris yelped.

"Fifteen."

"Eight thousand," Chris said quickly.

Total silence.

"Nine thousand," Chris said, "but it had better be good."

"Good? The adjective is inadequate. Twenty thousand."

"Ten thousand," Chris said.

Nothing.

"Harry? Harry, you there?"

"Did you say ten thousand dollars?"

Chris cringed. "Yes."

"Well . . . all right. But only because you're my friend."

"Deal," Chris said. "but if this doesn't develop into the story of my career, I'm going to have to flee to the Holy Lands with you."

"You won't be disappointed. In fact, you may be able to talk to him, perhaps even get his picture."

"So what's the story?"

"It started with John Drury. You remember, a minor miracle. Well the word spread. John himself shouted it from the street corners. Then he began taking other unfortunates to see this stranger for back-alley healings."

Chris laughed. "Why would he be paranoid about doing healings?" He scribbled on his pad. *Check w/Drury re: covert healings, contacts.*

"I don't know. Maybe he isn't ready to reveal himself yet. All I know is that he couldn't keep the lid on all those little miracles. Now a cult movement is growing up around this stranger—right under the noses of the Washington cognoscente. But—"

"But what?" Chris demanded.

"Well . . . his talk seems rather . . . forceful. He heals these people and then he says that he wants to bring people together to heal the nation. The healing power, he says, lies within the people. The people must heal the government; the government cannot heal the people."

"What's his game? Is he a religious guru? A political fanatic? Or an escapee from the booby hatch?"

"I can't honestly say. There's something disconcerting about him. He seems sincere, yet strangely detached. He's highly intelligent and informed. Yet he's unsophisticated, even naive. I can't figure him out. I've seen a couple of those he's healed. John for one. And some socialite who was a cocaine addict."

"Who's that, Harry? The socialite, I mean?"

"Her name is Blake. Serena Blake, I think. She ran into this guy in one of the parks, and he supposedly cast the cocaine demon right out of her."

Chris scribbled, *Blake connection verified!*

Harry kept talking. "She's lined up a few friends with

money, and they're going to have him lay his hands on them. . . . Maybe I should show up."

Chris's mind was spinning. He struggled mentally to fit the jigsaw pieces together. "No," he blurted. "Stay away." He scribbled, *Money, society, build following, financing—FOR WHAT?*

"Chris," Harry blurted, "I've got a funny feeling about this story. The stranger . . . he has a guileless quality. There's nothing suave or subtle about him. In an odd way, he projects simple, moral principles. He's ugly as sin, but I have this sense that he's without sin."

There was a moment of quiet. "Chris . . ." Harry said weakly, "what if the stranger IS Jesus?"

"Harry. You called me so you could sell this guy down the river for ten grand."

"Sell him down the river?" Harry cringed.

Gallagher quickly added, "The publicity will rip off his mask and expose the real person behind it. Once this guy's picture appears on the front page of the *Weekly*, every nickle-and-dime panhandler and hypochondriac in the country will come to him for help. He won't be able to soak them for money. So if he's some kind of psychic nuisance, then he'll have to flee the country, and go recharge at Lourdes or something."

"I don't know," Harry said.

"Harry," Gallagher said, "are you still living in that dump on D Street?"

"Yeah."

"Tell you what I'm going to do. I'm going to send that ten grand out to you right now, Western Union. You should have it in a few hours. I want you to pack your bags and get your plane ticket to Jerusalem or wherever it is you want to visit and forget about this guy. If he's genuine, we'll see that he has all the benevolent work he can handle. And if he is a false god—"

"Maybe," Harry said hopefully, "he's the Antichrist."

"Okay. The Antichrist, then. Don't worry. We'll take care of this guy, Harry. You need to go to the Holy Lands and rescue those precious scrolls."

"Well—"

"Come on, Harry! You've been waiting long enough."

"I still have this troubled feeling deep in my gut. But . . . well, all right."

"Deal. Now where is he going to exorcise the cellulite demons?"

Gallagher furiously scribbled down the details as Harry recited them. The place was in Georgetown—*This guy is going after some serious money and support,* Chris thought—and was taking place within twenty-four hours.

He thanked Harry, told him to keep his eyes and ears open for anything else, and then hung up politely by punching off the phone line. A split second later, he reactivated the line and dialed another number. Kiernan answered on the fourth ring.

"It's Gallagher," he told his boss. "I know where the alien is, but we've got to act fast."

MICK AARONSON

A sheen of sweat caused Serena's face to glow, but the light in her eyes was dim and rapidly fading. She blinked slowly and deliberately, and her head began to roll loosely from shoulder to shoulder.

"Serena," said the alien.

She straightened her head and looked Victor in the eye. "I love you," she said in a hoarse voice.

Victor shook his head. "You cannot. You must not."

"I do. I love you." She started to rise from the floor

for perhaps the dozenth time that evening. Prompted by the visitor, Aaronson extended his hand, gently pushed against her sweat-stained T-shirt, and eased her back down to the floor. The experience of the last few hours had left her weak and at the edge of unconsciousness.

"It is a mistake, Serena. You must understand that. You can have no real love for members of my species. You must put such feelings aside, and you must look to life ahead as a human being. It is a proud and fine species you belong to."

Serena looked hurt. "Why are you talking like that, my love?" She reached her hands toward him, beckoning.

The alien shook his head negatively. "Enough," he said. Then he reached out and placed his hand against her forehead, appearing to Aaronson like a televangelist about to cast out a demon.

"Come to me," she pleaded.

"Serena, sleep," he said. As if a switch had been thrown inside her brain, her eyes rolled to the back of her head. Her lids closed, and her head slumped to one side.

"Enough," he repeated, then dropped the rock into the palm of Aaronson's hand.

The journalist spasmed as it hit his skin. For the first time in hours, he was again in control of his body. With wide eyes, he looked at what had been dropped into his hand. Then he reached up and let it slide onto the surface of his coffee table as if it were the derringer that had shot Abraham Lincoln. His head ached, his stomach hurt, and he badly wanted a drink.

"I can do only so much for her in one session like this," the visitor said. "What remains may be beyond what I can repair."

"Clearly," said Aaronson, "she has problems."

The visitor nodded in agreement. "She is fixated on

me. She had managed to suppress it, but when Ghost used the device on her, it weakened her resolution and brought her fixation to the surface."

"Whoa. What are you saying?"

"I suspect I became the object of her fixation because I am pheromonally identical to others of my species. She may have subliminally recognized this similarity when we first met, which would explain why she believes she is in love."

Aaronson shook his head. "I have no idea what you're talking about ... What's wrong with the lady? Cocaine scramble her brain?"

The alien stood and stretched; Aaronson did the same. Then Victor took the journalist by the arm and led him out of the room, out the front door and onto a vast front lawn, cut off from the surrounding terrain by lines of vigilant pines. The stars formed a bright canopy over their heads.

"Serena is quite sane," he said. "She is as sane as you. As Susan Hill. As any other member of your species."

Aaronson, following the visitor's gaze into the heavens, wondered aloud, "but she seemed to be in a trance. Her rambling made no sense. She had to have been hallucinating."

"Mick Aaronson, do you believe in the reality of our standing here at this moment in time?"

"Victor, I've seen more that challenge my own beliefs in the last forty hours than I have in the last forty years. I could probably talk myself out of all I've seen and heard and felt. But heaven help me, I'm beginning to believe ... although I wish I wasn't."

The alien nodded. "You are wise. You believe in the reality of all your senses tell you. Now you must believe what I will tell you. Serena is part of an experiment that my species has been conducting here."

"What kind of—"

The visitor held up his hand. "I have told you how these planets are seeded. First with bacteria, then simple flora and fauna then more sophisticated vegetation and animal life. Then the sentients."

"Yes."

"But I have withheld from you our procedures which monitor—" He looked up, as if the words he needed had been written in the stars. "What you might call 'quality control.' The integrity and strength of the genetic coding as it is replicated over and over again. We have found from our monitoring that the material used to construct your genetic coding was particularly resilient.

"In my species, mutation is much more of a tragedy than it is with yours. That is because of the basic substance from which our coding is made. Our projects on other planets have been jeopardized because mere exposure to environmental conditions produced a breakdown in the genetic material, threatening entire races of beings with extinction. What we have been pursuing for millennia is a coding material with enough sentience to be self-preserving, yet enough resilience to endure billions of replications.

"Mick Aaronson. We found that material in *Homo sapiens*."

Aaronson frowned skeptically. "That doesn't make sense, Victor. We have the same problems. There are environmental factors which damage us genetically."

"But not on the scale that we have encountered. We have peopled whole worlds with races subject to defective, undesirable mutations. They can never attain our achievement level, but they have their right to exist. Imagine it, Mick Aaronson. Entire worlds, populations, civilizations. Rising and falling. Living and dying. All the while never knowing—not even suspecting—that mighty as they are, they are merely the mistake of a genetic legacy.

"But this problem does not have to end in tragedy. Over time, traits manifest themselves which are desirable in other sentient forms which will be seeded on other worlds. So rather than take the mutagenic risks of synthesizing the materials to produce what is needed, we go straight to the source material of the desirable trait."

The alien's matter-of-fact discourse staggered Aaronson, who gulped air. "You're saying that if you want a basic trait such as our resilient DNA structure, rather than risk botching it in your own labs, you come and take it out of us?"

The visitor did not return Aaronson's gaze. "That is correct."

"Then Serena is"—Aaronson swallowed—"a donor. No, she kept rambling on about babies. What you're telling me is that Serena is a . . . *breeder*?"

"Crudely put, but essentially correct. The love she expressed for me was probably felt for the technician who took the genetic material selected for sentience on another world and fused it with hers. For a time she was pregnant, and may even have been subconsciously aware of it. Then the embryo was removed for more controlled incubation."

Aaronson stared querulously at the alien. "But I thought you said this planet was quarantined. And I thought you stayed away from the sentients while they were 'maturing.' Those were your words, Victor; *It's a struggle, but they must do it on their own*." Then the explanation struck him. "You were disobeying, weren't you? By gathering genetic material from us, you were disobeying your own rules. You were taking a shortcut . . . an unauthorized procedure . . . right?"

The visitor nodded sheepishly.

"Victor, there must be some method of enforcement ... some punishment for those who violate interplanetary restrictions."

"Mick Aaronson, I would not expect you to bear the burdens of your ancestors who promoted slavery. So you cannot hold against me a poor judgment that was made decades ago by my forebearers."

Aaronson interrupted him, demanding, "And what happens to the products of your little experiments, Victor? Are they going to get shuttled off to a backwater world like your other genetic rejects?"

The alien shook his head. "These are matters which I cannot begin to explain."

"No. Of course not. That's because you're too absorbed with the cosmic significance of whatever you're doing to be worried about what happens to a few insignificant individuals. Isn't that right? Who cares if you happen to use up some poor hapless *Homo sapiens* like Serena?"

"I care. I care about Serena. I care about the people of this planet."

"Well, Victor, nobody else from your world seems to care a damn. All they care about are their hybrids. Let me ask you something about that. It's now apparent that Serena's ramblings were real ... that she really saw and held a deformed baby. Why did they show her that deformed child? Why did they have her hold it? You want to explain that one to me?"

The alien slowly lifted his eyes and met Aaronson's glare. "Very well. The truth is that we try to work within very strict parameters, and with every regard for the subjects of our experiments."

"I'm waiting," said Aaronson.

"In the early years of the hybrid program, the carriers were *not* presented with a child. Thus they were left with subconscious memories of an actual pregnancy which went unresolved and created active psychosis. There were frequent breakdowns, suicides, and other mental aberrations.

"You witnessed the effects of my devise upon you and Serena. It was technologically designed to leave your species highly susceptible to suggestion. Initially we also thought that these same suggestions could counteract the subconscious memories of what the subjects had been through.

"But, we underestimated the power of the human heart. As it turned out, not even our strongest suggestions could prevent maternal bonding between mother and child. It defied anything we had seen previously. Suggestion could not resolve it. There was only one way we could deal with the problem.

"That was the presentation of the hybrid child to the mother. Presentation resolved those feelings. Presentation on a physical level was necessary to satisfy the human subconscious in its struggle to explain the phantom pregnancy. So they were allowed to hold a strange and unearthly child in their hands and were told it was theirs, and then it was taken away. But we have found that the sense of loss of the children they saw was resolved more easily through subconscious grief. And this process happened all the more quickly when the mother understood the true strangeness of the child she was holding. She understood that she could not give it the care that we could."

Aaronson drew a sharp breath and muttered, "It's still not humane."

"Perhaps you are right, Mick Aaronson. By your standards, what we do may not be humane."

The visitor tilted his head back up to face the stars. "I understand your feelings. And I now know the sting of the loss that the mothers feel."

"You understand? What have you lost?" Aaronson asked.

"Serena," the alien said quietly.

"Is she dying?"

"No. She is in no physical danger. And I believe the psychic danger can be repaired. Even your primitive methods would be able to do that much for her."

"Then what's wrong?"

"Serena believes she loves me, but she cannot possibly be in love with me. She is merely responding to my pheromones, the basest part of me. That is what has triggered her submerged memories and has caused her to mistake me for her 'lover.' Her entire relationship with me is based on her subconscious acceptance of me as the father of her child. But those feelings are based on a falsehood."

"Will you tell her the truth when she awakens?"

"Awakens or recovers? There is a world of difference. She will surely waken, but she may never recover."

"I thought you said—"

"She's likely to recover, it's true," the alien said. "But I don't really know. All I know right now is that for the first time I understand the pain that such uncertainty brings you. It is terrible."

Aaronson's tone mellowed. "In the last few years of Suzanne's life—she was my wife—when she was fading, I was torn between wanting her to live and wanting her suffering to end. It's love, Victor."

"But I love your race," the alien replied. "That is what brought me here. How could one person mean something so special to me?"

"There are many different kinds of love, Victor. I would think someone with your profound knowledge of our world . . . of our ways . . . would be aware of that." Aaronson looking up at the stars, caught himself wondering which one the alien was from. "Love ..." he said. "Apparently you have been infected with the most painful human affliction."

VINCENT BRICKELL

There was a lot that Vincent Brickell loved about his job.

He loved the money.

He loved his official ID card that had gotten him out of jail, no questions asked, on a couple of occasions.

He loved telling women that he had a mysterious, shadowy government job that he couldn't talk about.

But, most of all, Vincent Brickell loved the hunt.

He and Kiernan had twenty hours to plan this one. They drank strong coffee over a detailed map of Georgetown as they plotted the approaches the Team would make. They collected sophisticated, high-tech paraphernalia, including earplugs which interfered with certain frequencies to which the human brain was ultrasensitive—in case the alien's power of persuasion worked at that level—a pair for every member of the Team. Each would also carry a spray gun that spewed out sticky foam which dried heavy and hard in a matter of seconds. Late last year this gun had proven itself at the San Diego Zoo. It stopped a grizzly bear that had gotten fed up with its living conditions and had gone on a rampage.

They cataloged and assigned equipment. Those who had been affected by the alien's psychic attack were assigned less-important jobs like driving vehicles and diverting traffic from the area of operations.

On the way out the door, Kiernan made phone calls

to the CIA and FBI to let them know that there would be a raid in a Washington suburb within the hour.

At event-minus-30, they cruised past the house in Georgetown which would be their target. Kiernan jotted down license-plate numbers, and Brickell noted coldly that some of the vehicles had government plates.

"I'll give that preacher credit," Kiernan said.

"Still, I'm going to enjoy sending him out west," Brickell replied.

"Perhaps we'll keep him on the hook a while longer. He may be useful."

When it was event-minus-15, the other vehicles began to show up—three vans and two diesel trucks. The latter looked like refrigerator trucks for Bird's Eye frozen food, but were actually designed to transport human cargo. The pair of trucks waited innocuously in the parking lot of a fast-food joint a mile from the house while a black humvee patrolled the neighborhood. The vans paused long enough for black-clad men to jump out and disperse into the neighborhood's shadows.

Event-minus-5. A series of clicks and squeaks crackled over the radio in Kiernan's sedan. He strained his ears, carefully counting them all. When he was satisfied that everyone was in position, he directed Brickell to drive back to the neighborhood and park a half block from the target.

Event-minus-1. Kiernan keyed a tone burst into the radio and checked off the responses. "Everyone's in place."

Event-minus-15 seconds. Brickell said, "Jesus is coming."

Kiernan laughed. "No, tell Jesus *we're* coming." He peered out the windshield at the house, then climbed out of the car, eyes on his watch. "Send it."

Brickell mashed down the key on the microphone. He said, "Visit the garden."

There was no reply from the radio. But as Kiernan watched, at event-plus-15 seconds, the lights shut off at the house. He could hear voices inside rising in protest, which were drowned out by the movement of men bursting out from the shadows. Kiernan watched Brickell racing toward the house, then he followed.

At event-plus-30 seconds, Brickell mounted the steps and knocked on the door. After a moment the door opened and an older man with a flashlight in one hand and a tray of canapés in the other glared out at them. After one look at the dark helmets and grotesque breathers they wore over their faces, he started to slam the door. Brickell shot out his foot, kicking in the door as a dart thudded into the old man's chest. The tray and flashlight hit the floor, and the man fell backward into a staircase.

Brickell cocked his rifle, activated the laser sight, and waved in the foam guns. Teams of three went up the stairs, to the left, and to the right. There were screams from his left and the sound of goo being sprayed. More screams. Cursing.

"Now!" Brickell shouted as he bolted into the living room. The red dot from the laser played across paintings and sculptures and a pair of angry faces foamed to the wall. Immediately in front of him was an arch that led to the dining room. He heard more commotion from the kitchen. Beeps pierced through the plug in his ear.

He grabbed the mike that was Velcroed against his shoulder. "Emperor, this is Judas."

Kiernan's voice crackled from the plug. "This is Emperor."

"The rear guard is in place. Gethsemane is secure."

"Ten seconds," said Kiernan.

Brickell stuck the mike against his shoulder and then pulled a flashlight from his hip and swept the room with a powerful beam. It illuminated a scene of utter chaos. The Teams were rounding up groups of well-dressed men and women and herding them into corners. A few had been darted and were sprawled out on the thick carpet.

A squad leader emerged from the kitchen, head shaking. "Number One," he said. "The back part is secure. There's two guys foamed to the pool table in the basement."

"What about Jesus?"

The squad leader shrugged. "Negative. Just a lot of red-hot angry people."

A muffled voice said, "Brickell." It was Kiernan, holding a breather up to his face. "Any gas?"

Brickell reached up and pulled off his own mask. "Wasn't needed."

Kiernan lowered his hand and dropped his breather into the hand of the squad leader. "Target?"

"Haven't found him."

"Let's take an inventory," he said. "Find out just what these people know."

"You want to know what we know?" shouted an angry voice.

Kiernan swung around.

"If I were you, I'd be more concerned about your own future."

Kiernan grabbed Brickell's flashlight and walked over to one of the figures foamed to the wall. He grabbed it by the hair and pushed its head against the wall, then shone the light into its eyes.

He was looking into the face of Ty Cornell.

HARRY LAUTER

Through his binoculars, Harry could see that the secret was out. Police cars were arriving now, their lights strobing blue and red off the aluminum-siding canyons of the residential area. A tow truck pulled up and started to hoist one of the vans. The sidewalks filled up with neighbors who poured out of their houses to gawk.

It was a magnificent sight, just as Arkady had predicted. As Harry watched through the glasses, he felt a twinge of regret. Chris had been good to him. They had met in a Manhattan jail cell. Harry had been arrested for distributing religious tracts on the grounds of a public school, Chris for refusing to reveal the source of an inflammatory article he had written for *Mother Jones*. Chris's career had gone into a slide after that, and somehow he'd ended up at the *Weekly World News*.

Harry focused the binoculars on a tall figure who was shouting at a high-ranking police official. Harry was certain it was one of the people who had heckled him during a street sermon.

Clearly, Chris was connected with this man. As Harry watched the evolving chaos, he found himself marveling at God's efficiency, and whispered a prayer of thanksgiving.

When I was in that jail cell, I cried out. "Why me? Why am I jailed in America for spreading your word?" Now you have shown me your infinite wisdom and grace. For while I was in that cell, I met Chris Gallagher, who has been my earthly provider, my betrayer, and now the instrument of your revenge. And through your revenge, I am now free to pursue your truth, your light. The scrolls.

Ah, yes. The scrolls. Perhaps if Gallagher hadn't been so greedy, things might have turned out differently. But he had wanted to keep Harry around as a source for wild stories. In doing so, he had sealed his own fate. Gallagher had mentioned Harry's quest for the scrolls. But Harry had never confided in Gallagher, who obviously had learned about the scrolls from another source.

It was a timely slip on Gallagher's part. *Thank you, God!*

Harry collapsed the binoculars and slipped them into their case, then wriggled out from under the bush he had been using as his vantage point. He dusted the dirt off his jogging suit, slung the case around his neck, and trotted casually away from the scene of the crime.

Half a mile away, he stopped at an all-night drugstore and strolled inside, picking up a can of shaving cream and a couple of candy bars. He paused at the magazine stand and eased next to a man who had his nose buried inside the *Tribune*.

After a moment, the man spoke in Arkady's familiar accent, "How did it go?"

Harry picked up a *Computer Shopper* and opened it to a random page. "Andy, it was the most beautiful thing I've ever seen in my life."

"Typical of such a bloated government," Arkady said. "I learned how to cope with such a bureaucracy back home. Before."

"It was a government operation, all right."

"Be sure to watch yourself, my friend. You've wounded the bear now. They'll come after you."

"They won't find me," Harry said. "As of noon today, I'm officially homeless."

"I would take you in, but my own position is precarious. I hope you understand."

Harry turned to face him. "I more than understand, Andy. And some day I hope you come to realize that God raised you up for this very moment. Your whole life was a rehearsal for what you've just done for me." He took Arkady's hand and shook it.

Arkady smiled. "So. If that is my whole life, what do I do now that my purpose has been served?"

"Find Jesus."

"Perhaps I will." Arkady sighed. "It may be time."

Harry caught himself looking at Arkady in an open-mouthed stare. "You're serious."

"I *am* serious. I'm becoming old and mellow."

"You won't have to find him; he has already found you."

Arkady rattled the newspaper. "His way of getting one's attention can be most interesting."

Harry stepped back. "Are you trying to tell me something?"

Arkady laughed. "As a matter of fact, I have a secret that I should share with you before we part company. It is a secret that only you would appreciate."

"Yes?"

"I think you may be wrong about one thing." He twisted his hands around the newspaper and formed a roll. "I now perform the last act that God has placed on my agenda. I give you what you have been seeking all along." He pressed the paper into the preacher's hands. "Harry Lauter, I give you the scrolls." He stretched his hand out and gave Harry a solid handshake. "Thank you for introducing me to God." And he walked away.

Confused, Harry mumbled. "Thank you, Arkady . . . Andy."

Arkady paused at the cash register. He handed the clerk a bill and pointed at Harry; then, with a final nod, he exited.

Harry stared quizzically at the rolled-up paper in his hand, wondering what to do with it, when his eyes caught a jagged line of blue. Harry blinked.

It was ink.

Fresh ink, from a ballpoint pen.

Excitedly, he unrolled the paper. Arkady had left it

open at the editorial page, and had drawn a sloppy box around one of the articles. The headline proclaimed: YOU DON'T NEED ANCIENT SCROLLS TO MAKE YOU WISE. Underneath was a smaller heading, *The View from Here by Mick Aaronson*, nested next to a small picture of the columnist.

Harry shivered and started to read.

These days, trying to get your life straightened out has attracted a multitude of charlatans and thieves who a century ago would have been hawking snake oil from the back of a horse-drawn wagon. There are a million self-help gurus out there, each one willing to sell you their secret of success. The way they straightened out their own screwed-up lives, they will assure you, is *the* way to deal with all your personal ills and feelings.

In fact, the road to mental self-sufficiency is paved with broken glass. There's nothing that will make the trip easier. And along the side of the road are the carcasses of vehicles that were designed to make the trip go fast: EST, Scientology, Transcendental Meditation, New Age Crystal Therapy. Those who travel in these jalopies think they have completed their journey, but in fact they are merely stranded.

Others among us look for artificial aids to make the trip. Perhaps it's drugs. Or maybe it's the wisdom of the ages, scribed on the skin of some centuries-dead animal, complete with fanciful insights of creatures beyond our comprehension, who move from place to place on the beams of cosmic flashlights . . .

Harry cried out. The paper rattled in his hand. The clerk looked up from his perch behind the cash register and stared for a moment. Harry shrugged apologetically and looked back down at the column.

Well, drugs normally come in childproof bottles. They're even hard for a thinking adult to open.

The scrolls of ancient wisdom are buried under the floor of the high desert and are guarded by the harsh elements.

I think it's time we made a simple observation: *Maybe it worked out this way for a reason.*

That's right. Perhaps it's time we quit looking for the quick fix, the instant balm to make us wise, and look to ourselves for answers.

I'd bet money that's what those musty old scrolls would tell us to do . . .

He knows! Harry thought. *He knows about the scrolls!*

Then he told himself that it couldn't be right. The man was spouting off.

But no. The reference to the scrolls was all too clear. The beings that rode on veils of light. And the description of their location was too accurate.

The mysterious stranger in the park.

Now Mick Aaronson, the newspaper columnist.

Connected?

They had to be. The message of spiritual renewal that made up the rest of the column was in keeping with what was only hinted at in the fragments of the scrolls he had seen. It was almost as if Aaronson was saying *We don't have the scrolls, but we don't need them.* Or, as he put it bluntly in one of the last paragraphs, *It's time we got off of our collective butts and sought the answers for ourselves.*

He had to find this Mick Aaronson and talk to him.

Maybe Aaronson knew something about the scrolls that could be of help in his quest.

He had to act quickly.

MICK AARONSON

"Phil," Corey said, slapping down a phone-message slip. Then he tossed down another one. "Sally." Then he began dealing them out like cards at a poker game. "Montel. Trisha. Oprah. Leeza. Vicki. Ricki." He stopped. "This sounds like the Seven Dwarves." He began to deal again. "Bertice. Rolonda. Jerry. Charlie. Charles. Chuck." He paused for an audible breath. "Geraldo. Jane. Maryann. Jenny. Desdemona. Maury. And Bob."

Aaronson contemplated the pile of slips that now littered his desktop noting that the handwriting had become more and more illegible as the day had worn on.

"And those are just the talk shows." Corey reached into his breast pocket for another wad of papers and continued to litter the desktop. "These are the tabloid news shows. That takes care of television." He plunged his hand into the left pocket of his sport coat. "Magazines." The right pocket. "Eight book publishers and one movie producer. Trudy will be bringing up the requests for speaking engagements later."

Aaronson screwed up his face. "A movie producer?"

Corey plucked out a message and studied it. "This producer says, 'Tell him to write his own ticket. Any subject he wants.' He claims to have DeNiro interested."

Aaronson shook his head in bewilderment. "A movie?"

"Now," Corey said sternly, "if you're not going to

get an agent, will you please let Trudy weed through some of this stuff? Some of these people have already called two, three times in the last few days. You need to get back to them—even if the answer is no."

"I can't tell them all no."

"Then tell them all yes. Just get your column written twice a week."

"But I can't tell them all yes."

Corey threw up his hands. "Mick, you have to do something. To be perfectly cold and clinical about it, this is *your* problem. But until you start dealing with it, it's *my* problem. That makes me unhappy."

"Corey, you know I can't function until we find out what happened to Susan."

"The PD is on it—"

"The PD is on a million cases, Corey." Aaronson slapped his hands on his desk. "I feel I'm responsible for her. She was good, you know that? She has more talent than any intern who's come through these doors in a decade. Let me ask you, Corey. If it was someone close to you, would you let it go?"

"Close?"

Aaronson thought about it. "Yyess . . ." The word squeezed out, hesitantly at first, then gaining conviction. "It's been a long time since I had someone to worry about. It's kind of nice to know that I can still do it."

Corey tried to hide his smile. "To tell you the truth, Mick, I'm glad to know that, too. But at the risk of sounding mercenary, I hope it won't immobilize you. Things will work out. I'll pull strings. But I need you here." He indicated the phone messages that littered the desk. "You're doing something right, Mick. And good for you, but it's also great for us. I've got papers from all over the country falling all over themselves to get your column."

"All right," Aaronson grunted. "For you, Corey."

"Thank you. Now, would you please find it in your heart to call some of these people and let them know that you'll at least get back to them?"

"Okay." He started to gather up the slips. "Who should I start with? Vicki, Ricki, or Leeza?"

Corey laughed. As he turned to leave, he bumped into Trudy, who was looking down at her yellow legal pad.

"Who now?" Corey asked, rolling his eyes. "Leno? Letterman?"

"The Washington police," she said thinly. "They called about Susan . . ."

Aaronson leaped to his feet.

"They said it looks like she left town."

"What?" Aaronson shouted. "That's ridiculous!"

"You never know," Corey said.

"They called at her apartment. The place had been cleaned out. She apparently cleared the place out and even scrubbed it with disinfectant. Didn't leave behind so much as a speck of dust." Trudy tore the sheet from the pad and laid it on Aaronson's desk. "There's the name of the investigating officer and his number if you want to call. He said she probably got fed up with life in Washington and went back to Iowa or wherever she was from."

"Thank you, Trudy. If you'll excuse us . . ."

She ducked out the door. Aaronson nodded at Corey, who closed the door behind her.

"So what do you think?"

Corey spread his hands. "People do get fed up with life in the big city. Maybe she didn't want to disappoint you."

Aaronson crumpled the paper in one hand. "This just isn't true."

"You don't know that, Mick."

"Susan grew up in Philadelphia. You're going to tell me that she couldn't hack big, bad Washington, D.C.?"

"I don't know what to tell you, Mick."

"Then how about this? Susan was working on a story about missing persons in the Washington metro area."

"She got too close to a conspiracy, and they bagged her? And cleaned out her apartment? Is that what you're saying?"

"Exactly."

"Come on, Mick."

"No, Corey. *You* come on. You know what most of these disappearances had in common? Residences that were stripped of everything inside and sprayed with some kind of strong disinfectant."

"Mick, your emotions are distorting your judgment."

Aaronson picked up his telephone. "Do me a favor. Make a phone call for me."

"Mick—"

"Call Susan's landlord. Ask if she picked up her deposit refund."

"Come on, get real—"

Aaronson shouted. "Corey, I'll bet you all the money I get from the movie with Robert DeNiro that she didn't stop by to collect it. Now what can you tell me about an intern on your measly payroll who can leave five hundred bucks behind without worrying about it?"

"I don't know—"

"Of course you don't. So make the call, Corey."

He shook his head. "No. I won't. I can't. I'm not a reporter . . ."

"Then I'll do it. You'll still get the columns twice a week." Aaronson began muttering to himself. "I'll pull some of my strings. I've got favors out all over town. I'll get to the bottom of this in a hurry."

"All right," Corey said. "Do it. But if there's any abandoned warehouses to be checked out, you get one of the young turks downstairs to do it. I don't want you stepping into the line of fire while you're holding the million-dollar pen. Understand? You get yourself dead, I'm gonna have 'Headstrong Fool' put on your headstone."

" 'Investigative Journalist,' " Aaronson corrected.

"Fine," Corey strode to the door and opened it. "You have my blessing, Mick," Corey called back. "You need anything, you call me. You get yourself in trouble with the CIA or FBI or Hillary Clinton, I don't know you."

"Pray that I *do* get in trouble with the CIA. It'll make a better story."

"Don't push your luck, Mick." Corey walked out of the office, slamming the door behind him.

MAX KIERNAN

The office was small and grimy. The rent was too high, and it had no furnishings. The windows overlooking the rail yards were cracked and needed putty. The sink and the toilet were ancient and stained with rust. There was no guard. No night watchman. So the odds were high that anything of value would vanish. The neighborhood was also a haven for junkies.

Kiernan dropped the box on the floor, and it raised moldy-smelling dust from the carpet. Brickell barged in right behind him, lugging another box. Kiernan pointed, and Brickell dropped it.

"That's it, then?" Brickell stopped to wipe his forehead with his sleeve.

"No."

"We'll never get back into the office."

"This is the vital stuff," Kiernan said. "I'll sell it to

the Chinese before I let Cornell get his hands on it. He'll turn it all over to the ACLU."

Brickell laughed. "I think I could arrange for a fire to gut your office."

Kiernan shook his head. "We need to keep Cornell busy while we nab the alien. That'll buy us all the vindication we need."

"Let this be a lesson," Brickell said. "Never cross the man who's in charge of your funding."

Kiernan exploded. He grabbed Brickell by the front of his jacket and pushed him back into the wall. *"We were set up!"* he thundered. "That preacher caught on to us, and he fed Gallagher a line and lured us into a trap."

Brickell waited until Kiernan released his grip, then straightened out the lines of his jacket. "Why?"

Kiernan shook his head. "Maybe he thinks our ugly alien is tied in with the scrolls somehow. Maybe he thinks the alien can help him get to them. All I know is that I want that preacher out of the way."

"New Mexico?"

"No," Kiernan said icily. "Fish food."

"I'll handle it." Brickell interlocked his fingers and cracked his knuckles.

"No, you won't. Not yet. Let's let him outlive his usefulness first.

"He's outwitted the Turks. He's played cat-and-mouse with the Mossad. He caught onto us somehow and managed to use what he knew to take us for a ride. We've got to use that against him."

Brickell grinned. "You think he's going to lead us to the alien?"

"That's exactly what he's going to do."

"You think he doesn't anticipate that? He's going to be looking over his shoulder for us, everywhere he goes."

"Maybe, but the story of our recent fiasco is in the papers. He's going to expect us to lay low for a long time." Kiernan smiled, showing all of his teeth. "But we're not."

"I'd lay twenty to your ten that he's checked out of that rat trap he was living in."

"Doesn't matter," Kiernan said. "He's a creature of habit. He'll make a mistake. We'll find him."

"Excuse me, boss, but there's only two of us, one of him, and a lot of city to cover. If he's gone into hiding until he finds the alien, not even his old friends will know where he is."

"It won't be just us," Kiernan said quietly.

"Who, then? The Salvation Army?"

"Use your head," said Kiernan. "I want you to round up as many Team members as you can contact."

Brickell shook his head and sank down on one of the boxes. "I'm going to say something to you, Max, and I hope you'll take it in the spirit in which it's intended. You've finally lost it."

"Oh?"

"We don't exist anymore."

"We never existed."

"We had to turn in our credentials, our weapons."

Kiernan gave him a skeptical look. "You turned in your weapon?"

Brickell reached inside his jacket and pulled out his .45.

"You think some of the others managed to hang on to some of their souvenirs as well?"

"We've got no equipment, no vehicles."

"Our people have their own cars. We can improvise the rest. I think I can borrow a semi for transport. Maybe even a helicopter."

"Boss, you think the guys are going to do this gratis? How're we going to pay them?"

"If they're part of the team that's the first in human history to capture an extraterrestrial visitor, they should be paying us. When it's all over, they'll be able to write their own ticket." He stared out the window. "And they know it."

"How am I going to get in touch with them?"

"I have a personnel list. Start with that."

"What about surveillance, boss? Cornell's probably got the FBI watching us, tapping the phones."

Kiernan smiled. "You'll think of something."

"That alien also has an annoying habit of getting away from us. We seem to become incredibly open to suggestion when he's around."

"I've thought that out, too. I think I might even have a solution."

"Oh. You *might*?"

"Consider for a moment that I am the head of this organization for a good reason—I actually know what I'm doing."

"I was beginning to wonder."

Kiernan smiled sardonically. "Meanwhile, get in touch with as many Team members as you can. Make arrangements for them to stay in touch because the minute we get a line on where the visitor is, we're going after him. And if I'm wrong about any of this, Vince, then you can visit me in Antarctica."

"Sure," Brickell mumbled.

Kiernan opened his jacket and pointed to the small box holstered on his belt. "Got your cellular?"

"Aren't you afraid they'll turn the dishes on them to monitor us?"

"We can still be vague. Now I suggest you get a couple rolls of quarters and get to a pay phone and start finding out who's with us and who isn't."

Brickell shuffled out the door. Kiernan stacked the packing boxes until he heard Brickell's car pull out.

Then he checked his watch, locked the door, and hurried to his own car.

Twenty minutes later he sauntered into a strip bar on the District line between D.C. and Silver Spring. He slumped over a beer, idly watching an uninspired redhead grind to a rendition by the Rolling Stones.

"I don't know why you insist on coming to places like this," said a voice from behind.

Kiernan turned. It was Kemper from the FBI.

"Me," Kemper said, "I don't believe in buying beer you've already got at home."

Kiernan chuckled. "So tell me. What's new at the Bureau?"

"You can't begin to comprehend the trouble you're in, Max."

"That had occurred to me."

"This time it's serious. You've bitten the hand that feeds you. That violates the First Commandment."

"Petty," said Kiernan. "Petty bureaucrats. Petty politicians. All I have to do is keep my head above water until their thoughts turn to getting reelected."

"I don't think it's going to be that easy."

"You forget, I hold the keys to a few congressional closets. All I have to do is threaten to open the door."

"I don't think that Cornell will fold that easily."

"Look, all I really have to do is threaten to go public. The threat of exposing a fifty-year government program of cover-ups, harassment, and intimidation is enough to make any politician break out in a cold sweat."

"You're playing fast and loose this time, Max. Watch it."

"Let me tell you a story," Kiernan said, sipping on his beer. "This concerns Cornell's daddy, Alvin." Kiernan savored a mouthful of beer. "You remember that incident with Jimmy Carter out on the lake, and this rabbit comes swimming toward his boat, and he's there with his oar, trying to beat the sucker off?"

Kemper nodded. "Carter saw UFOs," he said.

"My point exactly," Kiernan said. "One of his pet projects was the declassification of everything on UFOs. He didn't know our agency existed.

"So anyway, Carter starts making the push to get this stuff declassified. Then along about the time of the rabbit incident, he gets more adamant about it. So Alvin Cornell tells him, 'Look, Mr. President, if you want to declassify all of this stuff, that's fine, but you're really going to be shooting yourself in the foot.' 'What do you mean?' Carter says, and Alvin gives him a list of influential lawmakers, Democrats all, whose help he's going to need to pass some of his bills into law. 'If you make me do this,' Alvin says, 'these guys are going to do everything they can to defeat everything you propose—even if you try to glorify Mother's Day.' See, they were going to look like incredible fools for funding a secret agency hunting little green men.

"So now his son, the hotshot, is one of those fools. He's full of bluster right now. But if we go down, he goes down with us. So let him be righteously indignant for a while. He might close down the office and grab up our records. He might try to handcuff us and threaten to pull the plug on all we've accomplished. But remember that first and foremost, he's a politician. He's going to wet his finger and hold it in the air. Then he'll bend in the direction that the wind is blowing."

"You sound sure of yourself."

Kiernan took a long sip from his beer. "I've been there before."

"With Cornell?"

"Not necessarily."

"But you can handle him."

"Without a doubt."

"What about someone with no political axe to grind?"

"What do you mean?"

"How would you handle a non-politician who was trying to blow you open?"

"Depends on who it is."

"A reporter."

Kiernan burped out a skeptical laugh.

"Not just any reporter."

"This is the real reason you wanted to meet me, isn't it?"

Kemper nodded.

"So, spill it."

"Mick Aaronson is on your case."

"What did I do?" Kiernan's gaze focused on the distracted redhead.

"He's asking a lot of questions," said Kemper, "about a certain reporter who is no longer in the D.C. area."

"Anyone I know?"

"Susan Hill."

Kiernan didn't react. He was suddenly absorbed with his beer.

"She was an intern working under Aaronson, and she was investigating a rash of disappearances in the D.C. area."

"So? She's a young kid—an intern, you said—who got homesick and went back to Nebraska or wherever."

Kemper shook his head. "He obviously doesn't think so. He's relentless."

Kiernan said nothing. Kemper grabbed him by the shoulder and whirled him around. "Listen to me, Max. Word came down right from the top of the agency to give Mick Aaronson whatever he wants. Now, that puts me in an uncomfortable position, since I happen to know more about this case than most people."

"What?" Kiernan demanded. "Have you forgotten the retainer I've been paying for your services?"

Kemper closed in on Kiernan. "Look," he hissed through clenched teeth. "You're not the only one in this town who can play hardball politics. There are others, and some are good at it. Mick Aaronson is one of them."

Kiernan sneered. "Mick Aaronson doesn't scare me."

"Listen," Kemper said. "Aaronson got the director to issue that directive. And he has big connections on both sides of the beltway. If he doesn't get what he wants, start shaking the tree. Then you and your James Bond boys and toys are going to fall out of it, bareassed."

"Aaronson's a dinosaur," Kiernan said. "He hasn't been able to get it up since Watergate. Source for source, favor for favor, I can match him."

"I'm warning you, Max. Back off. This guy has a core following. Talk of the town is that he's in the middle of a huge comeback. Even the New Age wackos are paying attention."

"Really?" Kiernan turned toward Kemper now, eyebrows up and eyes wide. "What's his pitch?"

Kemper shrugged. "He's been whining for years about how bad off America was. Now he's dispensing advice on how to save the world."

"He's preaching New Age philosophy?"

"He's not into the hard-core metaphysics. Most of it's just common sense. But some of what he's saying has that New Age lilt. You know. Spiritual renewal. Wisdom of the Ages—"

"Buried under the floor of the high desert," Kiernan said.

"Yeah."

"Scrolls of ancient wisdom."

"Yeah. He said that a couple of days ago."

"And how long has he been pontificating like this?"

A shrug. "A couple of weeks, I guess. Maybe a month."

Kiernan nodded. "And tell me, did Mr. Aaronson mention any details . . . about the scrolls I mean?"

"Not much."

Kiernan banged down his mug and stood up. "Now we have something better than scrolls of ancient wisdom."

Kemper watched Kiernan's performance with alarm. "Max, have you heard a word I've said?"

"Every word, my friend. You have helped me immeasurably."

He strode out of the bar, fingering the pouch on his belt. New Age. Ancient scriptures. Healing crystals. Alien technology. Old journalist. Young assistant. They were all pieces of the puzzle, and now they were almost all in place.

Susan Hill. The mystery woman with Serena Blake.

The witness to one of the greatest events in human history.

Just a scared little girl from Arkansas or Alaska or Arizona.

So when the water got deep, where did she go?

To the man who was her mentor. Mick Aaronson.

And what would Mick Aaronson do with the socialite and the alien?

He certainly hid them somewhere safe, Kiernan thought.

If they weren't with Aaronson, the old fox would know right where they were.

It all made perfect sense.

Kiernan flipped open the cellular phone and punched in a number. He put it to his ear. After three rings, Brickell answered with a noncommittal "Hello."

"What does the inventory look like so far?"

"Five out of twelve."

Thirteen to go, he thought. Maybe they could get another five. A dozen, counting himself and Brickell. They could make it happen. It depended on where Aaronson lived.

"Keep at it," Kiernan barked.

"I've got two who want to see a preacher," Brickell said.

"Forget it," Kiernan said. "Their souls can wait. We're going directly to Jesus."

"Are we?" Brickell asked skeptically.

"We are. Finish your calls and meet me at the new location."

"What about the evasion factor?"

"I have it handled," Kiernan said. "Just be there."

"Talk to you later." Brickell cut the connection.

Kiernan closed the phone and slipped it back into his pouch. It wouldn't be long, he thought. Then he would have them pick up the preacher and let him know what he missed—before he vanished from the planet.

Because, in the next few hours, they would have something better than the scrolls.

They would have their author.

SUSAN HILL

"Welcome to the club."

Just the effort of stirring hurt Susan. So much so that she wouldn't open her eyes. The moment she regained consciousness enough to feel pain, the voice had come to her.

"What they give you, it settle in your joints. Make them sore. You gonna hurt for a while, but you get over it."

Susan slowly, painfully opened her eyes. It felt as if sand were trapped under the lids. The light stung.

"Go slow. I got the lights off."

The speaker slowly came into focus—a short black girl with her hair pulled back high on her head. She wore a bright green jumpsuit, a color that did nothing for her. As Susan lifted her hand to her aching head, she realized that she was wearing an identical outfit.

"The answer to your question . . . before you ask it . . . is, 'I don't know.' I think we're out west someplace. Texas. Arizona. Wherever we is, it ain't like back home."

Susan blinked rapidly as her eyes adjusted. She watched the girl approach a set of blinds and peek out the window. Bright sunlight slipped in through the cracks, making Susan's eyes water.

"Lotsa sunshine. No trees. Warm out. But they give us air conditioning."

Susan tried to speak, but all that came out was a rasp.

"Oops," said the girl. "Forgot. Don't try to speak for a while." She walked over to a sink and took a glass from the shelf. It was wrapped in clear plastic. The girl tore the wrapper off, filled the glass with water, and offered it to Susan. "The answer to your second question is Heidi Wilson." She said the name with a certain amount of pride. "After the Cab Calloway song."

"Susan Hill," replied Susan. Her voice was low and gravelly, but it was the best she could do. She took another sip of water. "What about this building? Is it a school for wayward girls?"

Heidi laughed. "I'm not sure. Amos calls it 'the wrong place at the wrong time.' "

Susan jerked her head up. It hurt. "Amos. Amos White?"

The girl looked startled and took a step back. "You know him?"

"I know the name."

"This is weird," Heidi said. "This is too weird. But then, I should've known that—" She stopped, as if she didn't want to say.

Susan motioned to her. *Go on.*

Heidi shook her head.

"Then I'll say it for you."

She shook her head again.

"We're all from Washington, D.C."

Heidi yelped. "They tole us we been exposed to some kind of strange disease. They said they had to bring us out here, you know, quarantine us, and the dry air out here be good for us."

"They told you to say that to newcomers?"

Heidi looked afraid, but she nodded.

"You've been interrogated, haven't you? Questioned by someone?"

"Yes."

"And you know what this is all about, don't you?"

"It's weird," Heidi whispered.

"No, it's not," said Susan. "It's the truth."

The girl shivered.

"Something wrong?"

Heidi shook her head.

"You don't like thinking about it, is that it? You don't want to believe that—"

Heidi rushed forward and clamped her hand over Susan's mouth. "We ain't s'posed to talk about it. We can talk about anything we want, except that. Dr. George got in trouble for sayin' it was true."

Susan pulled the hand away. "Underwood?" she stammered.

"How you know everybody?"

Another sip of water. "I was checking on them. I'm a reporter with the *Tribune*."

Reporter?

"That's right, Heidi. My boss is Mick Aaronson." She waited for a reaction. "Do you know who Mick Aaronson is?"

Heidi shook her head.

"He's an investigative journalist. The best in the business. Nothing gets in his way."

Heidi smiled. "You mean like that brother on *60 Minutes*?"

"Something like that. When Mick Aaronson discovers I'm missing, he'll figure out that I've been grabbed. He won't stand for *that*. I can tell you that he won't rest until he's found me." She took another sip of water. "It's only a matter of time, now."

"Unless they grab him."

"No," Susan blurted. "Don't even think that, Heidi."

"Cain't help it."

"That's all right." Susan set the glass down. "So. What else can you tell me about this place?"

A shrug. "Dunno. They bring people in. We could always tell because one of us would get moved into a cell with someone else so's they could have an empty one for the new one. Then after a while, we'd see 'em in the lunchroom, or walkin' around outside."

"So what am I doing here with you?"

"They runnin' out of room," Heidi said. "They got so many of us, the man with the crazy eyes don't even come around now."

"Who's that?"

"Max something-or-other. He's the guy that questioned most of us. At first, anyway. He's a psycho. He's the one be askin' 'bout . . ." She looked around the room suspiciously.

"What you're not supposed to talk about?"

"Yeah. Kelly, he says—"

Susan held up her hand to interrupt. "Kelly Bradford?"

"Yeah."

One of the paramedics. "Go on."

"He says this Max be obsessed. He read a lot of that sci-fi stuff, be askin' the guards to bring him more in from town, buggin' them to death about it. He's got one with baby elephants on the cover, shootin' guns and takin' over the world. Weird. Anyway, he say Max is on a bug hunt. That's what he calls it. A bug hunt."

"So that's what you call this forbidden subject? A bug hunt?"

"Yeah. I think he got it from one of those goofy movies he be talking about all the time."

"Charming." Susan managed to sit up in spite of the pain. "Why don't you open the blinds? I want to take a look outside."

"Cover your eyes first," said Heidi. "Trust me."

Susan put her hands over both eyes and heard the rustle as the blinds were opened. Even though her eyes were shielded, the brightness still stung.

"You want me to close them?"

"I want you to tell me about yourself."

"I thought you knew about everybody here."

"All I have are names and possible connections with . . . with the bug hunt. So I know your name. I know you're sixteen. You're here because of Kit Washington."

"You know Kit?" The voice sounded hopeful.

Susan drew a long breath. "I had a run-in with him. To be honest, I found him unpleasant."

"Yeah," Heidi said sullenly.

"If I can ask you, what did you see in him?"

Nothing.

"Forget it. I'm sorry."

"No," Heidi blurted. "I want to talk about it—I think."

Susan said nothing.

"I mean . . . I don't know. What I saw in him, I mean. He wasn't great looking, but he was okay. Always had money. Wasn't great in bed, but he bought me stuff."

"You know where he was getting the money?"

A long silence, and then, "I did, but I didn't want to, you know? I mean, I wanted out of there, the neighborhood. And I thought, I stick with Kit, I give him some when he want it, he gonna make some major money and get out and take me with him. And maybe when we got out, I thought maybe we could take some of that money of his and buy into something straight. I want to have my own dress shop, where I design stuff and sew it. And maybe he'd go back and finish school and we could go straight."

The pain in Susan's eyes subsided, so she removed her hand. Even with her eyes still closed, it was so bright that she had to turn her head away from the window.

"Guess I was wrong," Heidi continued. "And Kit, you know, the money just made him crazy. I decided it was time to get away from him. But I couldn't."

"What do you mean, *couldn't?*"

Susan couldn't see, but she could hear Heidi's throat starting to close as her emotions started to rise.

"I mean I *couldn't.* I mean that he told me I was going to stay in his old apartment twenty-four hours a day and there was nothing I could do but do what he said."

"What did he do, lock you in?"

"No. I don't know why I stayed. It was like I had no other choice. I guess I been living with the sin for so long that it had become a part of me, and I let myself get stuck in it. I tried, I really tried. But every time I got near that door, I'd start to hurt deep inside. Physical, like."

Uncomfortable, Susan shifted. "Like you had no control over your own body sometimes? When he told you to do something?"

"Yeah. You know something about that?"

Think, Susan. Always think. Did she really want to be the one to tell her about Kit Washington's death? No. Nor did she want to explain the strange power that had come from the rock the alien had retrieved.

"I've heard of the phenomenon," she said. "Especially in women who are abused."

"You got that right," Heidi muttered.

"But if you couldn't go out of the house, how did you end up here?"

"Same way you did, girl. Some men in ugly black uniforms come into the apartment one day and shot me full of something. And when I wake up . . ." Susan heard her rattle the blinds.

"Everyone's had that experience, then."

"All the guests," Heidi said. "That what Max called us."

"And who are we the guests *of*?"

Nothing.

"The government?"

Heidi sniffed. "Who else you think got the money to do something like this to us? I mean, we're *citizens*. We got *rights*."

"Except renegade agencies," Susan murmured.

"What's that?"

"Nothing." Slowly, Susan pulled to her feet. "All right, Heidi. This is it. I'm going to open my eyes."

Her eyes hurt as they adjusted to the brightness, and even then it took a moment for them to focus. Finally, when she could fix on the contrast between the slats of the blinds and the outside light, she stepped over to the window and squinted out.

The window was thick bulletproof glass that gave everything on the other side a bluish tint. Throughout the glass was a grid of thin metal wires. Susan couldn't decide whether the wires provided reinforcement or were part of an alarm system.

Her gaze drifted out to the horizon. Heidi was right. It was nothing like back home. Trees were sparse, and a range of brown hills lay beyond a tight cluster of buildings. The sky was a bold, rich blue, and a squadron of dark, cumulus clouds tumbled across one edge, threatening a cloudburst. She recognized the starkness of the West from Clint Eastwood westerns.

The complex itself was military looking. The buildings were short, squat, painted white. A high chain-link fence topped with lethal-looking coils of razor wire enclosed the building she was in. Inside the fence, she could identify a large gazebo that shaded two picnic tables on a plot of green grass. At one of the tables sat a man dressed in a green jumpsuit, his nose in a paperback book. Beyond the fence, vehicles rumbled back and forth on an access road. Military vehicles. An occasional American car. No markings or license plates.

"So," said Susan. "What do you do for entertainment around here?"

"Wait." Heidi shrugged. "Sit around and talk. About what we did before and what we'll do if we get outta here. Kelly says it depends on how the bug hunt goes."

Susan slapped at the blinds and turned away from the window. "Guess I'd better learn to twiddle my thumbs."

"It ain't that bad once you get past all the questions," Heidi said. "They treat us nice here, like a big hotel that you can't leave. There's books and videos. But no TV from the outside. I sure miss my soaps."

"Lovely! I don't suppose they'd let me finish my story about you missing persons."

Heidi had a suggestion. "Want to finish your story? Maybe you want to talk with some of them in person."

"Right now?"

Heidi nodded.

"Let's go."

The girl walked to the door and opened it, just like that. She peered down the hall, then motioned for Susan to follow.

The hallway was off white, coated with tile. It occurred to Susan that the building might have been an infirmary on some military base. But the complex seemed too small. Maybe it had once been an infirmary and now was a brig or a holding center.

Think, Susan . . .

What did that tell her about this place? Small population . . . *Secret?*

What kind of secrets? Wartime secrets? Hidden in the American West?

The bomb, of course.

That made sense. Now, where would that put her? They tested those things—where? New Mexico. Nevada. And that town in Utah where John Wayne made Westerns. St. George, wasn't it? To protect the population centers in Las Vegas and Los Angeles, the bombs were always exploded when the wind was blowing eastward toward St. George. That town got a heavy dose of radioactive fallout. The memory of it made her head ache. She wished she'd paid more attention to the lectures on the atomic bomb in History 101.

Where are they?

She was still uncertain.

But what difference would it make if she knew her exact location? Whom would she tell? How would she get the word out?

The more Susan thought about it, the worse her predicament seemed. She missed the wisdom that Mick Aaronson had yet to impart. She wondered whether she would ever be able to write the missing-persons story that would win her a desk at any paper in the country—now that she was one of them.

But most of all, she thought about missing the end of the world. If Victor was right and it had to happen, she would rather see it from the nation's capital.

At the end of the hall, they came to what had once been a nurse's station, but was now a desk for an armed guard. Heidi waved to him and called him Frank, and told him that she was going to take the new fish out to meet the others. Frank waved them on, picked up a clipboard, and made note of that fact. When they came to the double doors that led outside, Susan glanced back.

"They run it kind of casual here, don't they?"

"They don't need to work real hard to keep us in."

Susan murmured, "I know what you mean."

Heidi pushed through the doors and led Susan out onto the lawn. The yard was bigger than Susan had first thought. The picnic tables were actually at the far end. That meant her room was also at the far end of the building.

The rest of the yard was scattered with people, all wearing green jumpsuits. Some were playing horseshoes, others were congregated around a keg of beer. A familiar scent directed her attention to another handful of people scrutinizing the smoke rising from a gas barbecue.

"This is the country club from hell," Susan said.

"You got it!" Then, in a general announcement, Heidi said, "Yo, listen up. This here's our new arrival. Her name is Susan Hill, and she's a reporter from the *Tribune*."

There were oohs and ahhs of approval.

A tall, handsome man approached and handed Susan a plate piled high with coleslaw, potato salad, and heavily sauced ribs. "Welcome, Susan." He smiled.

"Dr. Underwood," she said, amazed. "I've been researching you—" She raised her hand to point. "Veronica Summer. The nurse who was on duty with you the night—"

Underwood interrupted by putting a finger to his lips.

Susan acknowledged the warning.

"How about me?" asked the man pumping beer from the keg. "I'm missing from D.C."

"Amos White."

Susan looked around. It was as if all her photographs of missing persons had suddenly come alive.

As the faces began to gravitate toward her, Susan decided that Amos White was wrong. This was not the wrong place at the wrong time.

It was more like a nation of lost souls.

For the moment, she was their queen.

HARRY LAUTER

For a time, Harry regretted having said good-bye to Arkady so soon. He could have used the man's talents in stalking Mick Aaronson.

Trying to track him through the *Tribune* had reached nothing but dead ends, with a traffic jam at each. Since Aaronson had called for spiritual renewal, he had been inundated with spontaneous visitors. Harry couldn't get near The Great Journalist at the newspaper. Nor was his home address available from any of the normal channels.

But a former inmate, who had shared jail space with Harry in Denver, gave him the number of someone to call and told him what to say. Harry got Aaronson's address before dinnertime, figured the location on his worn Washington area map, and was on his way in a taxi as the sun was beginning to set.

Aaronson's house was located in the outskirts of Potomac, Maryland. The taxi driver dropped him off at a small gate, which Harry lost no time in clambering over.

A narrow driveway wound through trees to a small meadow in which the house sat, hidden from the prying eyes of the outside world. That was the supreme irony, Harry thought. The reporter had made a triumphant career of being the prying eyes of the *Washington Tribune*. And now, here he was, secluded and hidden away from the world he had spent a lifetime exposing.

Harry walked up the winding road to the house. *Trafficking in words has sure been good to this guy,* he thought, stopping to admire the house. It was big, solid brick. The lawn had greened nicely with the early spring and the trees were all fleshed out in green.

You're going to knock on this guy's door and tell him that a nameless, shadowy government agency is after him and his extraterrestrial visitor.

Harry considered it for a moment. Well, if he didn't tell the truth, he'd surely be dismissed as another crackpot. He'd probably be chased off by dogs.

But Harry, in this case, the truth sounds less rational than a crackpot story.

There was a sick sensation in the pit of his stomach. No, this adventure might not go well at all.

The whole objective is to reach the strange man and ask him about the scrolls, right?

Harry's grand dream now pivoted on this stranger who might be an alien. Or an angel. Or a cherubim. A seraphim. Maybe the Christ, Himself. When all was said and done, maybe.

But you're not going to find out anything unless you get inside that house.

The corners of his lips turned up. After all he'd gone through, the worst that could happen to him would be no martyrdom. He might get thrown in jail. Again.

That won't happen, Harry. God will give you the words to say.

He stepped onto the sidewalk and strode boldly to the door, between thickets of budding rosebushes. His finger sought a button and mashed it. From the other side of the door, he could hear a faint chime.

Harry waited, Nothing.

What if the others got here ahead of him and grabbed them?

He nervously surveyed his surroundings. The sun was behind the horizon now, and the light that had washed everything in hues of red was fading fast.

"Come on!" he said, and he mashed the button again.

There was still nothing.

Harry pressed his ear to the door. He thought he heard someone muttering or mumbling, and then muted footsteps. He straightened up and pasted a smile on his face as the doorknob rattled.

A woman with a thin, pale face peered out at him. "May I help you?" she asked in a whisper.

Harry's heart leapt. "Serena," he blurted. "Serena Blake!"

She jumped back.

"I recognized your picture from the paper! Praise God!"

Serena's hand flew to the door and began to slam it, but Harry was faster. He shoved his foot forward and the door bounced off it and flew open.

"Who are you?" Serena shrieked.

Idiot! You're scaring her!

Harry held up his hands to try and calm her. "Don't worry, Miss Blake. I'm here to help you—"

She tried to slam the door again, but Harry kept his foot in place. *"Who are you?"* she shrieked again, then turned and called out, "Victor! Mick! Help me!"

Serena moved backward, away from the door. After a

quick silent prayer to ask that the man of the house not be armed, Harry seized the initiative and stepped inside the house, closing the door behind him.

"Get away from me!" Serena cried.

"I'm not going to hurt you. I won't come any farther," Harry said, and he sat down on the floor, reasoning that if it worked for Mahatma Gandhi and Martin Luther King, it should work for him.

Quick, thudding shuffles from deep inside the house told him that people were approaching.

Please let this work please please please—

"What's going on here?"

Harry looked up. It was Mick Aaronson. His face was a bit more gaunt than his picture in the paper, but there was no mistaking those steely eyes, the prominent cheekbones, and stubborn chin. He was dealing with a presence.

"You must forgive me," Harry said. He noticed that Serena was fading away from them. She put her back against the wall and slid down into a sitting position. *Strange,* he thought. "I, uh, it's imperative that I—"

He stopped short.

Following Aaronson was the man he had seen in the park. The ugly little man who seemed to know so much. Here he was, in the flesh.

Harry stood, face beaming, and said, "It's you. It's really you."

Aaronson stepped forward and blocked Harry's path to the man. "Look," he said in a threatening tone, "I don't know what your problem is, but this woman is ill, and you've got no right to frighten her—"

"The scrolls," Harry said, speaking past Aaronson, hoping to establish contact with the strange, little man. "The scrolls of ancient writing. I know about them. I know where they are. You know where they are, too."

"So does everyone who reads a newspaper, by now,"

Aaronson growled. "Now, are you going to leave, or am I going to have to throw you out?"

"I don't think you could throw me out," Harry said. "Personally, I don't think the three of you combined could do it."

"Don't push your luck, pal."

"To get me out of here, you're going to have to call the police."

"Call the police," Serena said.

"I'm giving you ten seconds," Aaronson said.

"Nine," Harry said. "Eight. Seven. Six. Five. Four, three, two, one." He folded his arms. "Okay. What now?"

"You're an uninvited, unwelcome intruder."

"So pick up the telephone and call the police and I'll leave," Harry said. From the corner of his eye, he saw Serena cross her arms over her chest.

Aaronson turned to the alien. "Victor. Make him leave."

The visitor smiled at Harry Lauter. "No," he said. "We can trust him, Mick Aaronson."

"Hold it! We don't know this creep. Make him leave."

"Yes," said Serena. "Make him leave."

The visitor shook his head. "No. He is one of us. He is the proselytizer." Victor peered at Harry. "From the park?"

"Yes," Harry said. "Yes, yes."

"Yes," the visitor echoed. Then he said to Aaronson, "He is one of us."

Aaronson studied Harry's features. "He doesn't look like you."

"Not one of my kind. One of your kind. Like you and Serena. A believer."

He eyed Harry skeptically. "Who the hell are you?"

"A believer," Harry quickly confirmed. "And I've been through a lot for my belief."

"Victor," Aaronson said. "Remember what I told you

about people coming to the door and wanting to talk with me."

"He's a crazy," said Serena.

"You!" Harry cried, shaking his finger at the visitor. "You're helping him write his columns! Oh, praise God, I knew it! I just knew it!"

"This is one of those people," Aaronson continued. "He's got to leave. The sooner, the better."

"No," Harry said. "I can't leave. Not yet."

"I *will* call the police this time," Aaronson said. "In fact, this time, I'll do the counting. One, two, three—"

"No. *Please!*"

"—four, five, six—"

"I have an important message for you."

"—seven, eight, nine—"

"It's a matter of life and death."

"—ten. That does it. You're out of here, pal."

Aaronson started toward a telephone, but the visitor intervened, raising one hand and placing it on his chest to stop him.

"Mick Aaronson," the visitor said sternly. "Understand something. Once I came as a stranger to the door of someone important with a message of vital importance, and I was turned away." He looked at Harry. "The least we can do is hear this man out."

Aaronson looked from the visitor to Harry and back. With a sigh of resignation, he said, "You have two minutes to plead your case."

"Just make sure you hear all of what I have to say," Harry told them. "No matter what happens, I get two minutes."

"The clock is running," Aaronson warned.

"I've been kicked out of every nation in the Middle East because of my search for some ancient writings that have been long suppressed by certain governments. They've been buried even longer, hidden in caves, preserved by the dry desert air. I don't know all they contain but I do know a few of the details. They talk about great beings who travel in shafts of light from world to world."

Aaronson gave Victor a startled look.

You've got through to him, Harry told himself.

"They also tell of a celestial society of worlds without number, presided over by God and populated by his children—mortal worlds and immortal worlds, separated by veils of light. The scrolls offer fascinating details of this interplanetary society. That's why I was so excited when you mentioned the scrolls in your column, Mr. Aaronson."

"Hey," Aaronson said. "I only wrote about them once."

"Never mind." Harry rubbed his hands together. "Our government . . . They're not interested in these scrolls at all. They're interested in UFOs."

Aaronson exchanged a glance with Victor again. "Go on."

"Please don't ask me how I know this, but they have a special agency set up to deal with UFO-related phenomena. It's so secret that it doesn't even have a name."

"Yes?"

"All of a sudden the people who run this agency have been going crazy, turning this city upside down. One of their field agents wanted me to keep an eye out for anyone who was performing miraculous healings or unusual powers."

"So?" Mick Aaronson said, but the look on his face belied his casual tone.

"So suppose the scrolls described some kind of extraterrestrial intelligence that has mastered travel across the universe using light. I can't grasp it, myself. But there are people out there who can, who're clever at putting two and two together.

"So if you"—and he pointed at the visitor—"are

making a show that you know about these mysteries, then word is going to get back to these guys. Washington is no good at keeping secrets, as your revered host can attest."

"Your time is up." Aaronson moved forward.

The alien laid his hand on the reporter's arm. "He is welcome here. Let him stay."

"He hasn't convinced me, Victor, I'm sorry. After forty years in my profession, I know how easy it is for fanatics to convince you of what they believe in."

"You did not believe in me, either. His story has the ring of truth, Mick Aaronson."

"No," Aaronson said. "Not here, not now." He turned to face Harry. "I think it's time for you to leave."

Harry held his hands up defensively. "I'm leaving," he said, "but I warn you: you're in danger."

Aaronson leaned around Harry and opened the front door. "Life is full of risks."

"But not this kind of risk," Harry said. "People have been disappearing . . . people connected with *him*." He pointed straight at the alien.

"No!" Serena cried, her voice cracking. "Don't let them take Victor away!"

Aaronson froze. "Disappearances," he said tersely. "What do you know about them?"

"That government agency I was telling you about: I know they've got a guy that he healed."

Aaronson closed the door. He turned to the alien. "You didn't heal anyone, did you?"

"I helped his body reject what was foreign to it."

"His?" Aaronson said. "You mean you helped someone besides Serena?"

The visitor nodded affirmatively. "On my arrival here. I helped an intoxicated man. I needed some information from him, but he was too polluted to help. So I cured him."

"John Drury," Harry said. "He's missing now. And Mr. Aaronson, you could be next." He paused for a moment and looked the three of them in the eye. "Well, that's all I wanted to say. I'll leave now. Thank you for hearing me out."

He turned toward the door, but Aaronson caught him by the shoulder. "Wait a minute. What's your game?"

Harry shook his head. "I don't know what you mean."

"Why did you come here? Why did you tell us all of this?"

"I did it for the scrolls." He pointed at the alien again. "He knows about them, knows what's in them. I've been trying for years to rescue them and open them to the people." He hung his head. "Satan's put a lot of roadblocks in my way," he said sadly.

The alien spoke. "You have crossed a thousand miles through shifting, burning sands. You have traveled the outback of the desert on the back of a donkey. You have eaten the food of the infidels and ridden their camels. And nations have made you pay for your knowledge."

It was as if the stranger were reading his soul. "Yes," Harry acknowledged. "But I am only human. I'm flawed. I'm imperfect.

"You asked me what my game is, Mr. Aaronson. I'll tell you. I've got money, but not enough. My wits have been exhausted. I'm a weak vessel. And I thought that maybe God had raised up someone to take my place. To finish what I was called to do but have failed to accomplish."

Harry turned to the visitor. "I was wrong about one thing. God didn't raise you up. He sent you. All I wanted to know was that you were real. That you were really here. And now that I've done that, I can go."

Harry politely lifted Aaronson's hand from his shoulder. "I think I can buy you a little time," he said. "If they haven't disposed of my contact with the agency,

I'll give them some false leads. But they're clever, and they'll find you without me. So make use of the small edge I can give you."

His hand reached for the doorknob. Another hand fell on it. It was smooth and cool.

"You were not wrong," said the stranger. "Perhaps I was raised up for this. Just as you were raised up to bring this message to me."

Harry smiled. "Thank you. Now I can go."

"No," the alien said. "You must stay. We need someone with your instincts."

The alien started for the door.

"Wait a minute," protested Aaronson.

"Where are you going?" Serena asked.

"That is up to our new friend Harry Lauter."

Aaronson scowled.

"But I've got a column to put out. My function is to proclaim the truth—your message, Victor—to the world."

Victor held up a cautioning hand. "I sense that Harry Lauter is right. We must purchase for ourselves more time."

"You mean pack up and go?" Aaronson asked incredulously. "Where?"

"Anywhere."

Harry interrupted. "We'll need cash. Credit cards can be traced."

Victor nodded toward Serena. "She will be able to help us with that."

Serena managed a vacant laugh. "Money? That's one thing I have."

"How am I going to get my columns in?" Aaronson said.

No response.

"We need to pack," Serena said thinly.

"I *did* want to see more of this nation," Victor said.

Aaronson rolled his eyes. "I know I'm going to regret this. I'll get the car keys."

"No," Harry protested. "If they come here and find your car missing, they'll know we lit out. Leave it here. We can walk to the road, catch a bus, load up on cash."

"Excuse me," Aaronson said, "But this is your nation's Capital, and it's after dark."

"My device will protect us," said the alien.

"Yes, Victor will protect us," Serena said confidently.

"Two minutes," Harry said as the trio split and went their different ways. "We have to be out of this house in two minutes. No phone calls. We must simply disappear."

Aaronson opened a closet door and pulled out his London Fog. "We'll have to stop by the *Tribune*, so I can get a computer."

"No," Harry said. "Can't take the chance."

Pulling his coat on, Aaronson grumbled, then called up the stairs. "Serena, you'd better plan to empty your savings account!"

"Ready," Victor announced.

Harry couldn't suppress a laugh. The ugly little alien was struggling to pull an Atlanta Braves baseball jacket over a Smithsonian Institute sweatshirt. He crowned this wardrobe with a Washington Redskins cap pulled low on his head. Denims and high-top sneakers completed his costume.

"You look like a high school dropout," Harry said, and then showed him how to hold the shirtsleeve with his hand while pushing it through the arm of the coat.

Aaronson picked up a briefcase and a small leather pouch with the word SONY embossed on it. "Maybe this'll give me the chance to catch up on my Shakespeare," he growled.

Serena scuttled down the stairs with an overnight bag and a black raincoat draped over one arm.

Harry inspected them carefully. "This is never going to work," he groaned. Then with a helpless shrug, he said, "Let's go."

They trooped out the door and waited for Aaronson to lock it. Then they started down the driveway, single file, with Harry in the lead.

"The bus?" Aaronson snorted. "It's dark and we're taking the bus. I had a .38 back there. I should have brought it."

"I thought handguns were illegal in D.C.," Harry said.

"It was a gift from William Sessions. He was head of the FBI at the time."

Serena suddenly stopped, and Aaronson bumped into her.

"We're not going into the woods, are we?" she asked nervously.

Victor turned to her. "That was years ago, child. Come."

"We'll stay on the interstates," Aaronson said. "Big cities. Well lit."

"Don't make promises you won't be able to keep," Harry whispered. Then, to everyone. "Please, folks, we need to get moving."

He reached out and placed a hand on Serena's elbow to ease her along, but she twisted violently and broke away from them.

"No!" she cried. "I won't do it!"

"Serena," the alien said softly. "I am going. Do you wish to come with me?"

"My dear friends," Harry said. "We're supposed to be fleeing in terror, remember?"

"No!" she screamed, breaking away from the group. She bolted across the lawn, with Harry in pursuit.

"Victor," Aaronson gasped. "Use it! Use it!"

Harry pumped his legs hard and closed the distance. His first grab got him nothing but her empty raincoat. He pushed even harder and then launched himself at the panicked woman, hitting her in the small of the back and taking her down onto the cold grass. Her arms lashed out at him wildly and he caught them in his hands.

"You're not taking me!" she yelped.

"Serena," Harry panted. "Understand—"

"No." She suddenly went limp, her eyes devoid of any panic or fear. "They're here," she said.

"They are." He swallowed and tried to catch his breath. As he did, he realized she was right.

He could hear it deep in his ear.

Helicopter rotors.

"Aaronson! Victor!" he shouted as a beam of thin blue light pierced the darkness and began to play across the journalist's yard. "Scatter! Scatter!"

But it was too late. There was a new sound now, that of the grinding of gravel. As he watched, he could see a line of automobile headlights, turning off the main road and heading up the driveway.

And then they cut across the grass, aiming straight toward them.

DAY OF JUDGMENT

BETHESDA, MARYLAND / MAY 1999

THE VIEW FROM HERE
by Mick Aaronson

Column for 5/27/99—ROUGH DRAFT

Those of you who have followed this column faithfully know that after a detour into cynicism, I have been pondering what was still good about America—a country that I once loved.

I have found, to my surprise, that I am still in love with her. In spite of the crow's feet and wrinkles in her majestic face, she still inspires a profound passion.

There was a time when I was not faithful to her, or the ideals that raised her to greatness.

I disapproved of the company she had been keeping. She was growing in her way, and I was growing in mine. And I didn't like the way the years were dividing us.

Call it irreconcilable differences. I began to look for a more youthful mistress, one worthy of my ardor.

But even though I strayed and flirted, I have come home. And, to my great relief, the old girl has been forgiving.

Who else has allowed me to make a living by airing my grievances publicly? I daresay that each one of you has been accorded the same rights and privileges.

We have a unique relationship with this very special woman. She is still the best and the brightest the world has to offer. She welcomes all who seek her shelter. She gives opportunity to all who wish to work for the chance to better themselves.

Now she has come on hard times. She no longer has a line of suitors waiting to see her. She has made mistakes. She has faltered. She has stumbled.

Do we abandon this flower of our passionate youth? Or do we take her by the hand and help her to her feet, knowing in our hearts that the world can offer nothing finer than what we already have.

My friends, what I am about to tell you is the most important message I have ever written in all my years of Washington combat—of shooting and being shot at, of exposing villainies and being despised for it. Now the time has come for

AARONSON AND LAUTER

They should have scattered like rabbits.

That's what Harry Lauter was thinking as the lights closed in. Serena had ceased her struggling and he rolled off her, staying low on the ground, watching the approaching pandemonium.

The lights from the driveway had fanned out and were forming a circle around them on the lawn. The helicopter hovered overhead, playing its blue light in a circle, moving from Aaronson to the alien to Harry and Serena.

The whole drama was strange to Harry. Mick Aaronson was standing there, shaking his shaggy old head, perhaps wondering how his own government could perpetrate such an outrage. Well, he was too old to run from the vehicles that were tearing large divots out of the rain-soaked lawn. And then there was the strange little alien, who was watching the entire scene with great amusement. As the cars closed in, he smiled and raised his hands in surrender.

Harry looked up past the helicopter at the stars. "God," he said, "you've sent an idiot to save your creation."

The vehicles had completely surrounded them by now, and the helicopter had trained its beam on the alien. A large diesel engine gunned up the driveway. Harry could make out the silhouette of a semi truck pulling a reefer unit emblazoned with a picture of a smiling pig in a butcher's hat.

There was the sound of opening doors behind them, and men emerged from the vehicles, all in black, all carrying weapons, all wearing night-vision goggles. Some dragged what looked like fish nets and fire hoses.

"Stay where you are and nobody will get hurt," called a voice from under one of the black helmets.

Aaronson looked at the alien. "Aren't you going to nuke them?"

But the voice from the helmet warned, "If anything unusual happens to us, the personnel in the copter have orders to fire on all civilian targets."

"It would have no effect up there," the alien told Aaronson. "Perhaps this is best."

The commando who had spoken drew a flare from his jacket and struck it. It began to smoke, creating a pale blue light. He tossed it into the center of the lawn. The helicopter's beam followed it. After a moment, they could feel the breeze from the approaching whirlibird. They all looked up. A line was dropping from one side. Attached to it was a man in a sling. In a matter of seconds, the man touched down, shrugged off the sling, and motioned to the other soldiers. They grabbed Aaronson and Victor by the arms, hauled Harry and Serena to their feet, and lined them all up in a large pool of light.

Then the head commando approached. He was wearing a strange mask, which he pulled away to reveal solid, chiseled features and stone-cold eyes.

"Hello. You are now guests of the United States Government. My name is Max Kiernan, and I am your host." He studied the lineup for a moment. "Mick Aaronson," he said, pointing. "Serena Blake." He stopped at Harry. "You. You must be that preacher who scammed Gallagher." Kiernan smiled wryly. "Glad you could make the party. By the way, you owe me five thousand bucks."

Aaronson gave Harry a puzzled look.

"I'll explain later," Harry said.

"There will be no later," Kiernan barked. He took one step sideways until he came face to face with the alien. "And you," he said. "It'll be a pleasure to have you with us." He pointed to the waiting semi. "We're going to arrange a little reunion for you with some men you left behind in New Mexico. You might even meet some of the humans you've been screwing with."

Victor said nothing.

"I've got some really hard questions to ask you. See, you've created some incredible hardships for us." Kiernan waved his arms to indicate all of those who were present. "We've made a career out of hunting you down. Would you like to make a statement?"

The alien smiled and held his arms out, wrists parallel, ready for a pair of handcuffs. "Take me to your leader," he said.

Kiernan raised his hand to slap Victor across the face, but there was a wild cry from Serena. In a flash of teeth and nails, she jumped him. Kiernan stumbled backward, cursing violently, and both hit the ground hard. Harry took a step toward them; but the butt of a rifle slammed into his solar plexus, sending him to the ground, gasping for air. Aaronson tensed, but the sound of metallic clicking, *locking and loading*, deterred him. He remained still.

Kiernan squirmed under Serena's assault. He managed to grab her wrists with a gloved hand, but she slammed her forehead into his nose, with a crack that made the spectators gasp. As he rolled his head back in pain, she burrowed her head in his neck and started to bite.

"Shoot her!" he yelped. "Shoot her!"

For an instant, nothing happened. Serena's animal cries filled the air.

"Brickell, shoot the bitch!"

The soldier with the voice stepped forward. "Gladly," he said and raised his weapon.

"No!" Aaronson shouted.

"Shoot her!" Kiernan yelped.

But the air suddenly went dead. From up above, the

throbbing of the helicopter engine pitched into a loud whine which faded from hearing as the machine began to lose altitude and wobble away from the clearing. Then, as if all wired to the same switch, the vehicle engines all went dead and the yard plunged into darkness.

Serena stopped struggling.

Kiernan dropped one of her wrists, made a fist, and punched the side of her head. She grunted and rolled off him. He scrambled to his feet.

"Take them away!" he shouted. "Take them all away ... except the alien!" His eyes played across the scene, trying to make out what was happening. His men were dim shadows that remained motionless. Aaronson and the preacher stood frozen. Kiernan grabbed a flashlight from his belt and thumbed it, but nothing happened. He hurled it down and swore. "Brickell? Fenton? Jacobs?"

"They are all fine," said the visitor. "But they cannot respond."

Kiernan snarled. "Well," he said. "I *can* respond!" His fingers yanked the strap of his helmet from under his chin and tore it from his head. Except for his face, it was covered with shimmering metal. "Recognize this?" He tugged at the fabric at the side of his face.

The visitor nodded. "My suit."

"You guys should learn not to leave your technology behind." Now Kiernan cackled. "Not only is it impervious to damage, but it also protects my brain waves. And now I'd like to introduce you to one incredible piece of human technology." From under his jacket he pulled a large pistol. "It's called a Colt model 1911 .45 caliber semi-automatic. And I'm sure it'll blow a tiny little critter like you clean in half." His thumb clicked the safety. "Now turn off your technology."

The visitor shrugged. "Mr. Kiernan, I would oblige you if I could, but I am not the one who is doing this."

Kiernan's thumb clamped down on the hammer and

pulled it back. "You guys might be more advanced than we are, but you're lousy liars. Turn it off *now*."

"Instead of addressing me," said the alien, "I suggest you talk to"—and he pointed his finger straight up—"*Them*."

If Kiernan had looked up at that moment, he might have caught a glimpse of an object, flat and black, that was blotting out the stars in the night sky. But he was aiming down the barrel of the combat automatic, trying to line it on the shadow of his target.

Two bolts of light stabbed through the darkness. Kiernan felt two fiery bolts of pain pierce his eyes and hammer into his brain. He reeled backward, the gun bucking in his hand as his finger jerked the trigger. His other arm lashed out and covered his eyes. The next thing he knew, he was flat on his back.

Victor ran to Serena, pulling the stone from his pocket. He pressed it into the palm of her hand, and she sat up instantly.

"I told you they were here," she said cheerfully.

"Yes, they're here." Victor wrapped his hand around Serena's, then shouted, "All those who came with Max Kiernan must leave now. Go to your homes. Sleep well and forget all that has happened here."

One by one, like an army of zombies, the soldiers began to move away.

Serena watched Victor curiously. "What are you doing?"

He took the stone from her. "Serena Blake," he said. Then he turned to the others. "Mick Aaronson. Harry Lauter. By the force of my own will, I give to you your own free will. You must see and remember what is about to happen here."

Mick Aaronson gasped and staggered forward, then fell to his knees. Harry scrambled to his feet, then helped the old journalist up.

"Victor," Aaronson said. "What's happening?"

"Please witness," said the alien.

Now a strange sound filled the clearing. It started as a buzz, growing in volume until it was almost unbearable. Then a pinprick of light drilled through the center of a large maple tree. The tiny light beam split in two, one point moving up and the other down, drawing a thin film of liquid light between them.

The film began to wobble and distort, and static flared from the points. This produced a strange, dissonant music, and the film thickened, splashing blue white light across the front of Aaronson's yard. Pressurized air shot from inside the tree now. Both Aaronson and Harry raised their hands to shield themselves from the heat of the air and the metallic smell it carried. Their skin vibrated with a bass hum, and the light began to thicken.

Then, the shadows appeared. One followed the other, stepping out of the light's iris opening: small, delicate creatures with large heads and white skin and black, unblinking eyes.

"Angels!" Harry Lauter shouted joyfully.

"No," Victor shouted back. "God knows, we're no angels."

"What do they want?" Aaronson asked, blinking against the light.

"Me," the alien said flatly.

"They're coming to take you home?" asked Harry.

"This is the inspection team."

Harry scratched his head. "What are you talking about?"

Aaronson gave him a solemn look. "It's judgement day," he said.

There were a score of the small creatures on the lawn now, wandering in circles and examining the grass, walking up to the human beings, leaning in close, fascinated by them, and yet apprehensive about their proximity. One visitor tentatively reached out a finger and pressed it against Aaronson's forehead. He recoiled at the feel of it.

"Dear Lord," said Aaronson.

The tallest of the group was Victor's size and had assumed the position of leader, gesturing to the others, sending them scurrying across the lawn. Then the leader approached Victor, head bobbing up and down quizzically as if it could not comprehend this new humanoid form. They stared at one another for a moment, and then pictures began to fill the air, clear and distinct to the mind, yet not visible to the eye.

Harry yelped and rubbed his eyes, took one step backward, then sat down hard on the ground. "They won't go away!"

"They're talking," Serena said. "They talk in pictures."

The visions left distinct images on their minds, and yet their comprehension was blurred. Each impression was abstract and yet concrete, in vivid color that was limned in the purest shades of black and white. Information raced through their brains so quickly that it seemed to be slow motion—an experience of a lifetime that was over in a matter of seconds. And when it was done, they gasped in relief.

"What did it mean?" Harry cried. "What did all of that mean?"

Aaronson had lost his tongue. He could only blink in amazement.

Victor, his face devoid of emotion, approached Aaronson.

"I am leaving now," he said quietly.

"What's happening?" Aaronson demanded. "What will happen to us?"

Victor stood mute.

"Aaronson," Harry said. "What's wrong? Do you understand what all of this means?"

"I think they're making a final inspection. This could be the prelude to the destruction of the world. The whole human race."

Harry looked Victor in the eye. "Is it true?"

The alien turned away.

"Hey, only God can destroy this planet."

"I fear," Aaronson said softly, "We're the architects of our own destruction."

"What about the scrolls?" Harry shouted as Victor started to walk away. "Listen to me! There were promises made! They're on those scrolls! We've got it in writing!"

The alien kept moving.

"Hey, you!" Harry cried. "Victor! *You can't just leave like this!*"

"Leaving?" Serena cried. "Is he leaving? Victor!"

Victor, his arms stretched out appealingly, approached the leader. The air began to burn with images.

"NO! YOU CAN'T LEAVE!"

It was Kiernan on his feet again, waving the automatic.

Kiernan fired. The leader folded in half and then began to shrink, as if being sucked inside himself by the hole the weapon had made. By the time he stopped writhing, all that was left on the grass was a thin translucent skin.

Kiernan threw his head back and cackled. "What do you know? These critters aren't invulnerable!"

The other creatures panicked, flailing their limbs and running across the lawn like ants before a thunderstorm. Kiernan fired again, and another one collapsed and imploded, just as the first one had.

"God bless Samuel Colt!" he screamed, then lowered the pistol on another one.

"Kiernan!" Aaronson shouted. "Kiernan, stop it!"

Kiernan spun on the reporter. His face was caked with blood from the scratches Serena had inflicted. "What are *you* going to do to *me*?" He silhouetted the gun over Aaronson's heart. "Go ahead! Give me bad press in the *Tribune*! Nobody'll believe you! We spent a few million of the taxpayers' dollars to make sure of that!"

"Take it easy, Kiernan. You don't know what you're doing."

Kiernan's arm pivoted, fired, and then swung back to Aaronson. Another creature twitched on the ground. "Oh, yes I do. I've spent my life trying to catch up with these miserable little things." He swung the gun around to Victor. "And the last few weeks have been focused on him, in particular."

"Leave him alone!" Aaronson shouted.

"No." Kiernan shook his head. "I'm gonna put him on ice and charge Ty Cornell ten million bucks for a look."

With a look of sheer exasperation, Aaronson explained, "Kiernan, this planet is about to be scrubbed. All intelligent life is going to be wiped out. These creatures are here, I think, to make a final appraisal."

"So what have I got to lose?" Kiernan laughed bitterly.

Aaronson pointed to Victor. "He's trying to help us. He's the only one who can help us now. I'm asking—I'm begging you to lay off."

Kiernan shook his head. "Not until he tells me why he killed my mother."

"Your mother," Victor said softly.

"You took her away." Kiernan said accusingly. "I saw you. You came and got her and took her away. Then you brought her back and she wasn't the same. She never was the same after that."

"She destroyed herself."

"Yes," Kiernan choked.

"I shall explain. Over the course of our research, we found that we required certain genetic materials from human stock. The easiest way to obtain them was through your basic means of reproduction. We created a hybrid embryo within your mother using her egg cell and our engineered genetic materials. After a few weeks of development, we reclaimed the fetus and raised it in our own laboratories. Unfortunately, at the time this breeding program began—"

"Breeding?" Kiernan cried out and dropped his hands.

"—we were not experienced with the psychological impact that an unresolved pregnancy would have."

"You bred my mother like a barnyard animal?"

"She was not the only one. It happened to many. And for those inadequacies, I offer most supreme apologies on behalf of my species."

"You bred my mother and she killed herself, and now that your big experiment is over, you're going to blow us up. Just like that. Am I right?"

"I do not expect you to comprehend the reason."

Aaronson broke in. "No one is blowing us up. We're responsible for our own destruction."

"No," Kiernan said. "I don't want to hear it."

"I am truly sorry," said Victor.

"Yeah. You can afford to be sorry. You're catching the galactic bus out of here while the rest of us are supposed to get burned to ash." Kiernan still had a wild look in his eyes. "If I'm going to hell, I want you right there next to me."

He raised the gun. Victor closed his eyes. Kiernan's finger pulled back on the trigger. The hammer began to fall. But a flash of color blocked the way.

"Serena! No!"

Kiernan's arm was still flying up from the recoil when the creatures swarmed over him, their tiny hands pulling and pushing until he fell under their weight. He howled as they mobbed him, the Colt sliding across the damp grass to Aaronson's feet. Aaronson stared down in mute horror at the weapon. Then he saw one of the small white hands produce a control stone and press it into Kiernan's forehead.

"Oh no!"

The stone sank into Kiernan's skull. He convulsed violently, shaking some of them off. As his body lay twitching, they swarmed all over him again, their tiny hands tugging and pulling until they had removed the silver suit.

Aaronson grabbed the gun and fired it once into the ground. The startled creatures looked up at him, amazed that he hadn't obliterated any more of their number.

"That's enough!" he declared.

Serena lay on the ground, her head cradled in Victor's hands. Her own hands clasped her belly, trying to stop the red liquid that was seeping out.

"Serena."

"Victor?" she whispered.

"I'm here," he said.

She smiled.

Harry scrambled to her side. He pulled off his shirt, folded it, and knelt down to examine the wound.

Aaronson stepped back. The creatures abandoned Kiernan's prone form, and crowded around the scene of the alien and his fallen friend.

Harry placed the folded shirt over the wound, then placed Serena's hands back over it, telling her to press in. Then he stood, wiping his hands on his pants.

"She'll live," he announced. Then he whispered to Aaronson, "It's serious. She's gutshot. In a lot of pain.

If she goes into shock, we'll lose her. We've got to get her to a hospital. *Now.*"

Aaronson looked resigned. "What does it matter. It looks like we're all doomed." He turned to Victor. "Unless you want to save her life, Victor. But what would be the point?"

The alien laid Serena's head on the grass. One bloody hand came up to grab for him.

"Don't go," she begged.

"You must know the truth," Victor said. From the pocket of his jeans he produced the stone, which he clasped between his two hands. His body was convulsed. His mouth wrenched open in agony as his face began to sag and wither. At the moment when it looked as if collapse was inevitable, his body shimmered, and then filled out until he looked like the others.

Victor moved back to Serena and stared at her through dark, unblinking eyes. SERENA, he said soundlessly, I MUST LEAVE.

Aaronson and Harry stared in disbelief. Each realized that the words were not in their ears. They were behind their eyes, inside their brains, glowing brightly.

Serena's hand grabbed the fabric still draped on the visitor's form. "No."

The alien shook his head. As he did, words appeared inside Aaronson's head.

THIS IS FOR THE WOMAN'S BENEFIT.

"This is too much," Harry said. "This can't be real."

The other creatures had formed a tight knot around Serena now, their heads cocked, perfectly motionless, studying her and the movements of their colleague.

SERENA. I AM NOT THE INDIVIDUAL YOU THINK.

"I know who you are."

I AM NOT YOUR LOVER. I AM NOT THE SAME

BEING WHO TENDED YOU WHEN YOU WERE
YOUNG.

"It doesn't matter." Her grip tightened.

SERENA, I MUST LEAVE NOW. I VIOLATED
OUR RULES. I AM AN OUTCAST.

"Stay."

I MUST GO.

She pulled. Victor's head inched toward her bloody
face. "Then . . . take me."

YOU DO NOT KNOW WHAT YOU ASK, SE-
RENA.

"Yes I do. The baby." She coughed and spasmed.
"It's mine."

Victor looked up inquiringly at the other creatures.
They returned his gaze. Images streaked through the air.

VERY WELL, SERENA.

The visitor pressed the stone against Serena's forehead. Out of fear her eyes opened wide, then rolled violently to the back of her head. The visitor removed the
device and stood, letting her head slide to the ground.

WE GO.

"No!" protested Aaronson. "I can't let you take her."

Victor shook his strange new head. YOU DO NOT
UNDERSTAND, MICK AARONSON. IT IS ALL
RIGHT. SHE WILL BE SAFE. WE MUST RE-
TURN WITH THE OTHERS. I MUST ANSWER TO
CHARGES THAT I HAVE VIOLATED THE QUAR-
ANTINE, AND THAT I HAVE, AS YOU MIGHT
SAY, 'GONE NATIVE.'

"What will happen to you?"

IT DEPENDS UPON THE PERCEIVED SERIOUS-
NESS OF THE OFFENSE. I WILL LIKELY BE
STRIPPED OF MY POSITION AND STANDING.

"You'd better remember us."

I COULD NOT ALLOW MYSELF TO FORGET.
Victor beckoned to the other aliens. Slowly, they began

to gather the remains of their dead and move toward the funnel of light.

"Victor," Aaronson said.

The visitor stopped.

"What about the hybrids, Victor? According to what you have told me, our genetic material is spread all over the galaxy. I guess that means your quarantine was broken long before you came here."

TRUE.

"Then how can you be blamed for violating the quarantine?"

THE ENTIRE PROJECT WAS UNAUTHORIZED.

The other creatures followed Victor to the edge of the light where they gathered in a huddle, nodding and gesturing. The air around them filled with dark, runny smudges.

"He's really going to do it," Harry said. "He's really going to take off and leave us."

Aaronson's face fell, and his shoulders slumped.

Then, suddenly, the images around the light darkened, with flashes of kinetic lightning. Victor held up his hands in exasperation. And then the imagery became bright and opaque, in wide smears of color that obscured Aaronson's view. Some were pale and lifeless while others were bright and vivid.

"What's going on?" Harry asked.

"Trouble," said Aaronson. "I suspect."

With a look of fierce determination, Harry started toward the mulling creatures.

"Harry! No!"

Harry heard the journalist's call but kept going. His stomach tightened into a hard knot, pulling his testicles up into his body. He fought to control his breathing, mentally propositioning God.

I'm about to do the single bravest thing I've ever done in my life. I need you to quicken my mind and loosen my tongue and, if you please, to keep my legs going forward. At least promise me this, God. When you call me home, instead of Saint Peter, I'd like Job to meet me at the gates. I imagine we'd have a lot to talk about . . .

As Harry closed in, the images kept their distance from him.

Harry approached as close as he dared. He stopped, took his bearings and then shouted.

"Hey! I have an idea."

No reaction.

He called out again, this time louder. The images began to fade. But Victor and a couple others hesitated.

"I thought, uh, I thought that you might need the help of a man of God."

The remaining images perked up.

"I mean, uh, if it makes any difference, uh, I can vouch for this guy." He pointed to Victor. "He did some good things while he was here."

They were all staring at him now. Harry felt his knees start to buckle, so he locked them.

"Uh, he really tried . . ." Harry stopped. He was talking at the top of his voice, then remembered the added volume would not help them understand. He started again, pitching his voice lower. "He really tried to save us. Maybe he violated some lesser rule. But, sirs, it was for a greater good."

Harry looked at Victor.

"So I was thinking that maybe you would accept me in his place. He came here to save us. Can't I offer myself to save him?" Harry swallowed and closed his eyes.

God, if they take me up on this, I hope you'll be able to find me . . .

As one, they started advancing on him. Harry's first impulse was to retreat. But he remembered what he was there for and held his ground.

The periphery of his vision began turning into a whirlpool filled with colors and textures, swimming and swirling, mixing and separating, churning so rapidly that he had the sensation of flight. He shut his eyes and clapped his hands over them. The next thing he knew he was falling, really falling. The wet grass of Aaronson's yard cushioned his fall.

"I mean it," he said thinly.

Harry opened his eyes and started to sit up. But he couldn't. The aliens were standing around him, bent at the waist, staring down at him.

SACRIFICE.

Harry blinked in disbelief. The word was right there in front of him. "You talking to me?"

YES, HARRY LAUTER. WE SEE SOMETHING IN YOU THAT SERENA BLAKE DISPLAYED ALSO. IT CONFOUNDS US.

"What?"

WHAT IS THIS WILLINGNESS TO SACRIFICE YOURSELVES FOR OTHERS?

"We do it all of the time for those we love."

BUT YOU DO NOT LOVE ME, HARRY LAUTER. HOW DO YOU EXPLAIN THIS?

"Sacrifice? I mean, isn't that a basic precept?"

YOUR LITERATURE IS FULL OF ACCOUNTS OF SACRIFICE. THIS IS NOT MERE ENTERTAINMENT?

Harry replied thoughtfully, "Our fiction is a reflection of our reality. Sacrifice is not uncommon on our planet."

HOW IS THIS SACRIFICE ACCOMPLISHED?

"We have to learn it."

HOW IS THIS DONE?

Harry shook his head. "I don't know. Example. Concern. Love. Faith. Idealism. The same attitudes that motivated you to save Serena."

Victor turned to the other creatures and raised his hands. Images began to form and swim. For the first time, the earthlings could understand their discussion. IT WAS A MISTAKE FOR US TO EXPECT THEM TO ACHIEVE HOMOGENEITY. WE KNEW OF THEIR GENETIC DIVERSITY. BUT WE NEVER REALIZED, NEVER DREAMED THAT THIS DIVERSITY IS THEIR GREATEST STRENGTH. AND SOME OF THEM HAVE EVEN LEARNED THE SECRET OF ETERNAL PROGRESS—SACRIFICE.

The aliens began to nod their heads.

YES. YES. YES. YES. YES. YES. YES. YES. YES. YES. YES. YES. YES. YES. YES. YES. YES. YES. YES. YES. YES. YES. YES.

Then they began to scatter, returning to the tasks they had begun before Harry interrupted them. A few stepped into the light and vanished. Victor watched them go, and then walked toward it himself.

He turned abruptly.

THERE IS HOPE FOR YOUR WORLD, MICK AARONSON. THE SPIRIT OF SACRIFICE CAN DEFUSE THE FORCES OF DESTRUCTION. THE DARK FUNNELS ON YOUR HORIZONS CAN BE STOPPED FROM TWISTING CLOSER.

Aaronson lifted his hand to his forehead to shield his eyes.

GOOD-BYE, MICK AARONSON. I SHALL MISS OUR CONVERSATIONS.

"Me, too," he said.

And then there came another set of letters in a different set of hues.

GOOD-BYE, MICK. THANKS FOR HELPING US.

"Serena," he choked.

As Victor started toward the light, he called over his shoulder to Harry.

I GIVE YOU A CHARGE, HARRY LAUTER. YOU

MUST FIND SUSAN HILL AND THE OTHERS
WHO WERE SEIZED BECAUSE OF ME, AND YOU
MUST LIBERATE THEM. AND YOU MUST LIBER-
ATE THE SCROLLS.

"I accept."

A murky image drifted by. Two of the smaller creatures were escorting Kiernan toward the light.

WHAT SHALL WE DO WITH THIS ONE, they
asked.

Victor turned to Aaronson for the last time. HE HAS
BEEN CLEANSED. HE HAS NO MEMORIES OF
YOU. OR US. NOT EVEN OF HIS UNFORTUNATE
MOTHER. HE IS ... *MALLEABLE.*

Aaronson walked over and took Kiernan by the arm.
"What am I supposed to do with him?"

Victor smiled benignly.

TEACH HIM.

The last of the other small creatures were consumed
by the light. Victor took one last glance around him,
and then vanished. The odd music returned as the light
collapsed in on itself and became a dim glow on the
trunk of the tree. Eventually, it winked out.

Harry Lauter and Mick Aaronson looked at each
other.

The silence roared in their ears.

Then came the sounds of crickets.

After a moment, the night returned, and the stars appeared.

The dark was no longer frightening.